HEARTS of

A note from Simon Scarrow

How an idyllic Greek island inspired a powerful story of World War II resistance...

I had no intention of writing a Second World War novel about the Greek Resistance until I visited the beautiful island of Lefkas researching a different book altogether.

It was while I was on a boat trip to Ithaca that I came across a plaque close to the tiny port of Frikes that commemorated the heroic attack on a German patrol boat by members of the Greek Resistance. It was an unsettling feeling, as this was the most peaceful, serene setting you could imagine, and yet there was this shadow of the Second World War; one of the tiny ripples of this glob

Over the course of this research trip I came across other stories of what had happened on the island during the Second World War, and I began to put the pieces together. It's difficult not to be impressed by the Ionian Islands – they are a fabulous setting, and it is so hard to imagine them as a war zone; that is how my interest in the story began. It was simply that clash between the peaceful aspect of the present and what would have been pretty horrific events in the past.

We often wander through this world without much awareness about what happened before we were here. I wanted to write a novel that would bring life to those incredibly courageous men and women who were prepared to die to defend that beautiful place. If not for individuals who had been willing and ready to make a stand against the fascists, then perhaps I would have been making a very different trip – or no trip at all...

'Transports you back in time . . . I was able to feel like I was on the island . . . I loved the different views and personalities of the characters' Gillian Ashton, Goodreads.com

'An enthralling portrayal of a period in history where loyalty to one's country and those you love is called into question; it seizes a raw emotion from the sacrifices that people were prepared to make for the greater good' *Little Bookness Lane*, Goodreads.com

'An action-packed novel full of interest . . . Also contains a hushed stillness and encourages thought and reflection making for a captivating read' Liz Robinson, for Lovereading.co.uk

'A very powerful novel, shocking and heart-wrenching in parts but riveting throughout. Very well researched and written, this book will keep you guessing until the end. Highly recommended' Cathy Burman, for Lovereading.co.uk

'This is an excellent novel with powerful storytelling and well-crafted characters . . . I really enjoyed this evocative and emotional novel and found the detail compelling and interesting' Joan Hill, for Lovereading.co.uk

'Brilliant, exciting, moving story of Greek resistance during WWII. I loved this book' Ann Peet, for Lovereading.co.uk

'I write about what excites my imagination, about what I want to share with others – namely a passion for history.' Simon Scarrow

Simon's passion for history was sparked during his school years, when his teachers brought the subject to life by spinning a dramatic narrative or finishing lessons on a cliff-hanger. He went on to become a teacher himself but always wanted to write historical fiction, an ambition he has more than fulfilled with his growing list of *Sunday Times* bestsellers.

In HEARTS OF STONE, Simon saw the opportunity to transport readers to an era of which our parents or grandparents still have memories. His extensive research into the history of Greece and its islands during World War II unearthed aspects of history, such as the role of women in the Greek Resistance, that were completely new to him, and will be new to many readers. Powerful, authentic and unforgettable, HEARTS OF STONE shows one of our finest authors of historical fiction at the height of his powers.

To find out more about Simon Scarrow and his novels, visit www.scarrow.co.uk and Facebook OfficialSimonScarrow

SIMON SCARROW

HEARTS

of

STONE

headline

The right of Simon Scarrow to be identified as the Author of
the Work has been asserted by him in accordance with the
Copyright, Designs and Patents Act 1988.

First published in Great Britain in 2015
by HEADLINE PUBLISHING GROUP

First published in paperback in Great Britain in 2016
by HEADLINE PUBLISHING GROUP

2

Cataloguing in Publication Data is available from the British Library

Map © 2015 John Gilkes

ISBN 978 1 4722 1613 7 (A-format)
ISBN 978 0 7553 8024 4 (B-format)

Typeset in Bembo by Avon DataSet Ltd, Bidford-on-Avon, Warwickshire

Printed and bound in Great Britain by Clays Ltd, St Ives plc

Headline's policy is to use papers that are natural, renewable and recyclable
products and made from wood grown in well-managed forests and other
controlled sources. The logging and manufacturing processes are expected to
conform to the environmental regulations of the country of origin.

HEADLINE PUBLISHING GROUP
An Hachette UK Company
Carmelite House
50 Victoria Embankment
London EC4Y 0DZ

www.headline.co.uk
www.hachette.co.uk

For Nina
'A very wise owl indeed.'

CONTENTS

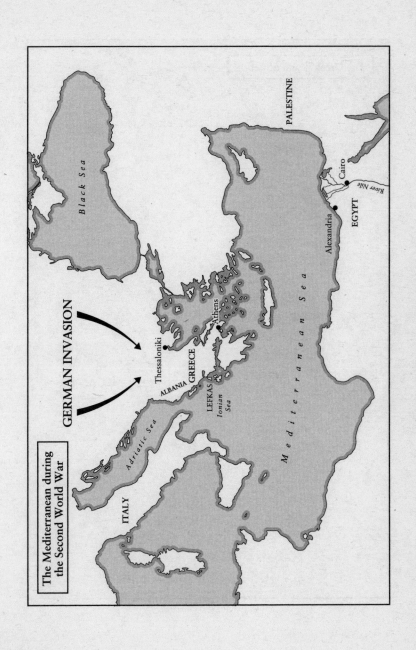

The Mediterranean during the Second World War

GERMAN INVASION

Black Sea

PALESTINE

Cairo

River Nile

EGYPT

Alexandria

Mediterranean Sea

Thessaloniki

Athens

GREECE

ALBANIA

LEFKAS

Ionian Sea

Adriatic Sea

ITALY

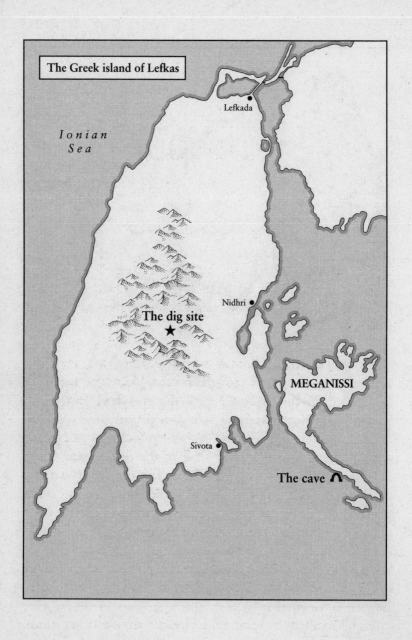

The Greek island of Lefkas

Ionian
Sea

Lefkada

Nidhri

The dig site

MEGANISSI

Sivota

The cave

PROLOGUE

Lefkas, September 1938

The shutter clicked and Karl Muller lowered the camera and smiled at the three teenagers, two boys and a girl, sitting on the bench. He coughed and spoke to them in Greek.

'That's it. All done.'

As he packed his Leica away in its leather case, the three teenagers stood up and crossed to the table where the latest findings from the archaeological dig had been placed. A student from Berlin was the only assistant still working with Muller; the rest had already packed up and returned home after the summons from the head of the department at the university. Not only this expedition, but the two others on the Ionian islands, and, as far as Muller knew, every other archaeology team around the Mediterranean, had been ordered to abandon their work and return home. All thanks to the deteriorating international situation. Muller had delayed for as long as possible, and had finally given in after the last telegram from Berlin ordering him to do as he was told, or face the consequences.

As he recalled the telegram he looked anxiously at his son.

Peter was tall for a boy of sixteen and could easily be mistaken for someone a few years older. He had yet to build muscle on his slender frame and as a result looked somewhat fragile. The glasses he wore only seemed to emphasise that. Muller sighed briefly. His son was all that he had in the world following the death of his wife several years earlier. He was afraid for the boy. Peter was staring in fascination at the latest discoveries uncovered on the site. In a better world he would be free to follow the dictates of his heart and his father's interests in archaeology. But the world was as it was, dominated by the hard-hearted credos of powerful rulers and their henchmen. They threatened war, and if they got their wish then Peter would be drawn into its perilous embrace. Muller had seen service on the Western Front in the first great struggle of the present century and could not forget its horrors. He prayed that his boy, and millions of others, would not have to share the same fate as the previous generation.

The girl had approached him shyly and was watching Muller as he packed his camera away. He turned to her with a warm smile. 'What can I do for you, Eleni?'

'Herr Doktor Muller,' she addressed him by his German title before continuing, haltingly, in the German taught to her by Peter. 'The picture you took. Is it possible . . . May I have a copy for myself?'

He nodded. 'Of course. I will see to it when I get back to Lefkada and develop the film.'

Eleni Thesskoudis smiled brilliantly, white teeth contrasting with the olive tone of her skin and the long dark hair that framed her oval face with its brown eyes. A pretty girl, he thought to himself. He could understand why Peter had developed feelings for her. It was obvious the boy was smitten, even if he refused to admit it to his father, denying

2

it in the adamant, embarrassed way that teenagers do.

'Thank you, Dr Muller. You are most kind.'

'And you know how to charm men to do your bidding, eh?' he teased and she gave a shy smile and shook her head before turning away to join her friends leaning over the nearest table. Peter was pointing at a shard of pottery, still carrying its delicately curved handle, and was explaining some detail to Andreas, the sun glinting off his glasses each time he looked up at the Greek boy. Muller turned his attention to the student sitting at the next table and cleared his throat.

'Heinrich!'

The student looked round, his brown hair neatly combed into place. Heinrich Steiner's shirt and shorts were stained with sweat and dust but Muller knew that he would discard them the moment he returned to Lefkada and change into his usual neat combination of flannel trousers and white shirt, with that wretched party pin fixed to the breast pocket. Muller approached him and stood on the opposite side of the table.

'Have you finished cataloguing the day's finds?'

'Almost, Herr Doktor. Two more entries and it is done.'

'Good. Then put them away and return to the villa. When you see the foreman tell him I want this all packed up first thing tomorrow. The finds are to go into storage in Lefkada. The same with our equipment.'

The student arched a brow. 'We are leaving it all behind?'

'What else can we do?' Muller shrugged. 'The university wants us to return at once. I'll have to try and arrange the shipment of our finds when I return to Berlin.'

The student nodded and turned back to his notebook and continued filling in the details of the last items in front of him. Muller turned back to the teenagers.

'You three can go with Heinrich. He'll drive you back into Lefkada. I'll follow in the car.'

'You're staying here?' asked Peter with a frown. 'But Andreas's father has invited us all to dinner tonight.'

'I'll be there. I would not want to disappoint Mr Katarides. But I have a few last things to deal with before I leave the site.' He pursed his lips and glanced round the small vale surrounded by steep hills. 'Before I leave it for the last time.'

'You'll come back, Father. Once the trouble has passed.'

Muller patted him on the back. 'Yes. Of course I will, and you. If you want to.'

Peter grinned. 'Try and stop me! Besides, I would miss my friends too much.' He gestured towards the other boy and girl and switched back to Greek. 'My father says we will be coming back. When the world has come to its senses.'

'Good!' Andreas flashed one of his rare smiles, then frowned briefly as the girl gave the German boy's arm an affectionate squeeze. 'We will be waiting for you.' He continued in a voice laced with irony, 'No doubt bored out of our wits with no one here to explain our own history to us in such fascinating and endless detail.'

Peter shook his head sadly. 'I am a civilised man amongst philistines . . .'

'Enough of your games, you young fools!' Muller interrupted as his assistant completed his work, snapped his notebook shut and rose from his bench. 'Go with Heinrich. Now.'

The impatience in his voice was obvious and Peter and his friends turned away from the tables and made for the path that led out of the vale in the direction of the camp where the members of the expedition lived when they were not at the house in Lefkada rented by the university. The tents, camp beds and stoves would all join the rest of the equipment to be stored in the warehouse to await the archaeologists' return. Muller watched them until they were out of sight and then waited another few minutes until he heard the rattle of the truck starting up. The gears ground, the engine note rose in pitch as Heinrich eased down the accelerator, and the vehicle clattered and jolted off along the rough track.

When at last the sound of the engine had died away and there was silence, Muller looked round the small valley. Nothing moved. No sign of life. Then he stirred, striding purposefully around the main excavation with its pegs and taut lengths of twine marking off each area. A section of the foundations of the large structure they had discovered lay half a metre below the surface of the ground, and had been painstakingly exposed over the last two years. Now it was to be abandoned, left to return to nature if the great powers of Europe decided to turn on each other again.

Muller left the main site and made his way through the shrubs and stunted Mediterranean oaks towards a nearby cliff. Emerging from the thin line of trees, he paused and glanced round, listening, to be sure that he was quite alone. Satisfied, he eased his way round a gorse bush and began to climb a narrow path that ran up the cliff. The ascent was not difficult, there were plenty of protrusions to use for foot- and handholds. Five metres up he came to the ledge that rose at a gentle gradient towards a finger of rock standing proud of the cliff face. Unless a person was close, the rock appeared to be part of the cliff. Indeed, it was only a week before that Muller had ventured up to the cliff, looking for a vantage point to take some photos of the whole site. It was then that he had noticed the geological peculiarity and climbed higher to investigate.

Breathing heavily from his exertions, Muller shuffled along

the ledge until he saw the dark opening, hidden from sight behind the rock. His heart quickened with excitement as he approached. At the mouth of the cave he felt the coolness of the space within, and shivered. Catching his breath, Muller crouched low and squeezed through the gap.

Inside, the light penetrated only a short distance, as no direct sunlight entered the cave. Muller pulled out the torch in his pocket and switched it on. Abruptly a shaft of light cut through the gloom towards the rear of the cool, clammy interior. The air was musty smelling and Muller's boots crunched on the small stones on the floor of the cave. He felt an excitement burning in his veins that he had hardly ever felt before. And then bitter frustration. Here was the great archaeological discovery of the age. And yet he could not take advantage of it. If only there had been more time. More time to explore the cave properly and discover all its secrets.

As he had done a handful of times before, Muller slowly approached the rear of the cave, where the hewn rock gave way to a flat surface. Two columns, cut out of the mountain, flanked a great slab of stone. It was featureless, save for a short phrase engraved into its surface, the work of a mason who had passed from this earth nearly three thousand years before, yet preserved so well it might have been the work of yesterday. Muller shone the torch at an angle so that the words would be clearly discernible. There was no mistaking the name, or the epitaph. One day, Muller vowed to himself, this discovery would make his reputation. The world would forever link his name to this place and the treasures that rested in the darkness beyond the wall of stone.

CHAPTER ONE

November 2013, Kent

'Why do I have to do this, miss?'

Anna had been walking back towards her desk, between the tables of the year nine class, and stopped to turn towards the voice. Jamie Gould stared at her with a questioning expression. She was aware that a number of other faces had looked up from their worksheets, waiting to see how she reacted. Anna knew the class well enough to identify those characters who were disruptive rather than simply clueless; Jamie was not one of the latter. Instantly her guard was up.

Anna cleared her throat softly. 'Do what exactly, Jamie?'

'This.' Jamie nodded at the worksheet, and his dark wavy hair shimmered momentarily. He was an undeniably handsome boy and Anna knew that many of the girls in the class were attracted to him. Including, regrettably, Amelia Lawrence, a studious girl who would be sure to get an A★ in history, provided she chose to study the subject for GCSE. Anna hoped very much that she would. She felt genuinely protective towards Amelia in that way that female teachers did about those female students they hoped would go on to achieve a decent future for themselves, unencumbered by children, and boyfriends or, God forbid, husbands and partners like Jamie Gould.

'The worksheet is part of the assessment process, Jamie,' Anna replied patiently. 'You need to complete the tasks so that I know how much you have learned about the topic.'

'But it's boring, miss.'

Anna smiled. 'There's no guarantee that everything you learn in school will be entertaining. Some of it is merely important. I'm sure you'd understand that if you gave your full attention to the subject, Jamie.'

There was a beat and she saw the hostile gleam in his eyes and instantly regretted her put-down. Anna despised those teachers who derived satisfaction from slapping down their students. As if there was the smallest kind of achievement in humiliating a younger, less educated and experienced human being. And yet she had just indulged in the same practice. Almost instinctively. There was no excuse for it, she admonished herself.

'Why should I pay attention, miss?' Jamie set his biro down with a sharp tap and leaned back in his seat, stretching out his legs. 'History's boring. There's no point to it. Why make us do it? It ain't like there's any use for it once I leave this dump.'

And that day can't come a moment too soon, my dear Jamie. Anna approached the table Jamie shared with five others, carefully selected to surround him with positive role models as if their work ethic might somehow be viral. She kept her expression neutral as she met his defiant gaze, hurriedly trying to decide how to deal with this latest assault on her authority.

'My, what a lot of issues you have raised. Where should I begin?'

'You should know, miss. You're the history teacher.' Jamie glanced round as some of the class laughed nervously and others regarded the confrontation with curiosity. Anna saw Amelia's lips flicker in a smile as she regarded Jamie. That smile, small, thoughtless gesture that it was, wounded Anna and she turned back to the boy with a cold expression.

'Yes, I'm the teacher, and it is my job to try and teach you. For your sake. What do want to be when you leave here, Jamie?'

'I want to do somethin' interesting. Something well paid. Not like being a teacher.' He paused. 'That's boring.'

'I see. Boring, is it?' There were so many responses desperate to find expression. The first, and most necessary to hold in check, was to tell the arrogant teenager that, on current form, he would leave the school with a clutch of poor qualifications that would be little more than attendance certificates and let him see how far he got with that during the present recession. Then there was the urge to explain what education was all about. How important it was, for Jamie, for everyone. How it underpinned everything that made civilised life possible. Anna decided it would be best to restrict herself to a more narrow argument.

'You say history is boring.'

'Boring.' He nodded. 'It's just stuff that's happened. Long ago. We can't change it. Means nothing to me. Nothing to anyone around now. We shouldn't have to waste time on this rubbish.' He stabbed a finger at his worksheet where Anna could see that his answers amounted to little more than a handful of words, begrudgingly scrawled in the spaces provided. A scribbled-out doodle extended down one margin.

Anna's gaze flicked up to fix on the boy's eyes and she saw there the peculiar hostility towards female teachers that she had seen in many boys in the five years she had been teaching. She tried to ignore it as she framed her reply.

'I find it impossible to share your opinion, Jamie. For me history is not boring at all. Far from it. History is like a great story, and it explains everything. It tells us why things are the way they are. That's why it's important. To all of us. Even you, Jamie. It's my job to try and make you see that.'

'You can't make me.' He clicked his tongue. 'You can't make me do what *you* want. And if I don't want to do history then you've no right to make me. Why can't I learn some proper stuff? Stuff that's going to help me find a real job?' There was a dangerous glint in his eye now and he leaned forward as his voice rose. 'What's all this about?' He picked up the worksheet and waved it in front of Anna. 'A load of crap questions about some bridge that fell down in Great Yarmouth over a hundred years ago. What's the point of it?'

Anna felt her heart beating faster and the familiar sick feeling swirling in the pit of her stomach as the boy challenged her. In truth she shared his dislike of the worksheets, with their tired old evaluations of primary and secondary evidence, but that was what the head of humanities at the school insisted on using. It was depressing to watch students working through coloured folders, differentiated by ability, year after year.

Anna tried to tailor her lessons to share some of her passion for history with her students but for a small proportion of them it was a challenge that would have exhausted even Sisyphus. She wanted to tell Jamie that she shared his opinion of the worksheets. She wanted to tell him about the great stories that filled the pages of history, about the characters, heroes and villains alike, who strove against each other or pursued daring courses of principle and enlightenment. To share with Jamie the powerful lessons of the past. A quote came to mind, a few lines on an index card she had pinned above her small workstation in the staffroom: 'Those who don't study history are doomed to repeat it. Yet those who do study history are doomed to stand by helplessly while everyone else repeats it . . .' She had put the card up to remind herself every day why she had chosen to become a teacher of the subject. One day, perhaps enough people would value history enough to break the cycle. Until then, she must contend with Jamie, and those like him.

A sudden movement caught her eye and she glanced aside quickly enough to see Lucy, a heavily made-up blonde girl, gesturing towards the clock above the whiteboard and making a winding motion with her hand. Jamie had seen it too, and then noticed that his teacher had shared it as well and gave a thin smile of defiance.

So that was it, Anna thought to herself. The familiar game of engaging the teacher to waste time until the bell rang at the end of the lesson. She felt cross at herself for falling for the ruse. She slowly drew a deep breath. It was all part of the give and take of the profession. It would balance out in the round, she told herself. There would be better lessons, where Jamie would simply content himself with being bored rather than disruptive, or better still, content himself with yet another unauthorised absence. She leaned forward and spoke in a calm voice.

'Jamie, there is no getting out of this. So you might as well make the most of it. Finish the worksheet, and don't disrupt the lesson any further, understand?'

Even as she spoke Anna mentally winced at the admission he had extracted from her. He had disrupted the lesson. That was his prize. His fruitless reward in his ongoing struggle against an authority that would grind him down in the end. And now the little idiot was grinning.

Turning away from his table, Anna made her way back to her desk at the front of the class and glanced at the clock.

'Ten minutes left. I don't want any more talking. Just

finish the worksheet. Those of you who complete it can hand it in at the end of the lesson. The rest will finish it for homework and let me have it first thing tomorrow. Get on with it.'

For a moment Jamie did nothing but stare defiantly back at her. Then he shrugged and picked up his biro and began to make small circular motions. Anna considered confronting him again and insisting that he do as he had been told but realised that it would only mean a renewed disruption to the lesson and even less work being done by the rest of the class.

It was with relief that she responded to the shrill ring of the school bell announcing lunch break. Before she could utter a word there was the customary shuffling as the students reached for their bags and began to put their stationery away.

'Finished sheets on my desk. I expect the rest first thing tomorrow, in my pigeonhole.' Anna had to raise her voice as chairs scraped across the worn vinyl floor and shoes and bags clattered against the metal legs of the tables. Jamie and most of the others made for the door. Only a handful headed for Anna's desk and hurriedly placed their work in a rough pile to one side of the class register. Amelia was the last to leave and she flashed a quick smile as she handed in her sheet, each answer box filled in neatly and fully. There was something about her smile that told of the embarrassment she felt for her teacher, and Anna nodded her head subtly to share the brief moment of understanding.

Then Amelia was gone and Anna was alone in the classroom. She wondered why so many schoolkids found it difficult to share her passion for history. It was hard enough battling a system that seemed intent on marginalising the subject in favour of 'relevant skill sets'. It was even worse when politicians used history as an opportunity to ram home some patriotic ideology, or to raise awareness of whatever contemporary social issue vexed the more pro-gressive members of parliament. Sometimes it seemed that there was no love of history for its own sake.

Anna opened her eyes and stood up, sweeping together the thin sheath of completed worksheets, and paused. There was a sheet of paper still on the table where Jamie had been sitting. With a sigh she crossed the classroom and picked it up. A series of ink swirls surrounded two lines written diag-onally across the sheet. 'History should be fucking history.'

Anna shook her head, then considered reporting this to the headteacher for him to take further action against Jamie.

'What's the point?' Anna asked herself quietly. She tucked the sheet under the others in her hand and turned to leave the classroom and make her way down the corridor to the staff-room. When she opened the door the scene was as familiar to Anna as the living room of the small terraced house she rented. More so, in many respects. The same people were sitting in the same chairs opening their plastic tubs and taking out their sandwiches, fruit and crisps. The sharp tang of filter coffee wafted from the short stretch of kitchen counter where the staff stacked their mugs. A few faces looked up and nodded a brief greeting.

Anna made for the doorway leading through to the narrow room lined with work cubicles. She had been allocated one as a newly qualified teacher when she first came to the school but no one had thought to re-allocate it and now Anna regarded it as her spot. She placed the worksheets on the shelf above the cluttered desk space and sat down. The school's IT technician had replaced the usual screen saver with a cosy animated fireplace surrounded by holly and Christmas stockings with a digital clock on the mantel counting down the seconds to the end of term.

The image vanished as Anna flicked the mouse, and then moved the cursor over to the login box and tapped in her email address and password, and the folder containing her applications appeared. She moved the cursor on to Facebook and double tapped. The familiar blue masthead appeared with the drop-down timeline and she quickly scrolled down the newsfeed. There was the usual round of personal updates, adverts and offers to join games or take part in a quiz. Anna read them without interest and then turned her attention to the three red icons at the top. Two friends of friends wanted to be accepted. She hit the not now button and moved on to the messages. There was one new item, from someone named Dieter Muller. Not a name she recognised and she opened it with a mild sense of curiosity.

> Is this the Facebook account of Anna Thesskoudis? Daughter of Marita Thesskoudis. Granddaughter of Eleni Carson (née Thesskoudis).

Anna was surprised. She did not know anyone called Dieter Muller, and she felt uneasy that he seemed to know something about her family. Her fingers hovered above the keyboard and and then tapped out a quick reply.

> Who wants to know, and why?

CHAPTER TWO

O nce the reply was sent, Anna switched to the BBC news website and glanced over the headlines before she went back into the main staffroom and made herself a coffee. Strong, black and sweet, just as her mother had always made it. The Greek way. Returning to her workspace, Anna set her cup down and went back to Facebook. There was another message from Dieter Muller.

> > I meant no offence. Just trying to track down a lead concerning a thesis I am preparing here in Munich. I should introduce myself. I am a German research student studying the expeditions to the Ionian islands that took place before the Second World War. I am looking for descendants of a Greek family who lived on Lefkas at the time. I came across the name of Eleni Thesskoudis who came to England shortly after the war as the wife of a British officer. Is Eleni your grandmother?

Anna read the message again, more slowly. She was innately suspicious of Facebook, having seen how it was routinely abused by students to play tricks on each other, and occasionally bully. Not even the staff were immune from such acts and she wondered if this was anything to do with Jamie. Better to be careful, she reflected as she composed a response.

> I don't know you and I am not in the habit of giving away personal details to strangers on Facebook. If you are for real then send me your email and proof that you are who you say you are.

She sat back and clicked her tongue. It was brusque to the point of rudeness. But despite wanting to know more about how this person, who claimed to be German, knew about her family, Anna was not going to be lured into some pathetic student prank or, worse, some kind of scam. She typed again.

> How did you find my name?

She saw a prompt indicating that the stranger was typing then one word came up in the message box.

> Google.

'Bloody Google,' she muttered. 'Is nothing private any more?' More words appeared in the box.

> Google led me to genealogy records and I guessed you might be on Facebook. Tried your name and so . . . Are you the person I am looking for? If not, my apologies. If so, then you might help me with some small details about your family's history in Lefkas.

That's all. You might find my research of interest . . .

Anna raised an eyebrow thoughtfully. Her grandmother's family owned a small supermarket in Nidhri. She had met them a handful of times when some distant cousins of her mother had visited England to see Eleni, and she had been there just the once, for a wedding, two years ago. They seemed to be a typical Greek family: loud, proud and warm-hearted. At least as far as any blood relative was concerned. Beyond the immediate family there seemed to be a number of ongoing feuds whose causes were so ancient that no one recalled what the original grievance was. Quite unremarkable, Anna decided.

So why were they of interest to Dieter Muller? He had found her through Google, and two could play at that game. She switched to the search engine and typed in his name, together with Munich University, and the list of references appeared. There were over three hundred hits but luckily only seven that combined the name and the institution. She clicked the first likely link and the page of the Archaeology Department came up, with the option to view the contents in English. Another click and a short delay and there was a page listing, alphabetically, the graduate students and their research project outlines. Anna scrolled down until she saw the name and opened the entry.

A fresh page appeared with a small portrait image of a young man who appeared to be her own age. His hair was short and dark and he wore rimless glasses above a neatly trimmed beard. There was an attempt at a smile to save himself from looking like a passport picture and Anna noticed a small red star stud in his ear. His expression was gentle enough, she decided. Certainly not threatening or unsettling. She turned her attention to his research statement and the translation was clear enough to get a grasp of his field of study. Sure enough, Muller was examining the programme of excavations carried out by German archaeologists on Ithaca and Lefkas in the years before the outbreak of the Second World War.

'All right, then, Dieter,' she said under her breath. 'You seem to check out.'

She typed a fresh message.

> What can I do for you?

> I would wish to interview Eleni Thesskoudis, if that is possible. Also, I would be interested to examine any photographs, diaries or other records of the era that I might be permitted to see.

Anna typed.

> You don't want much then! My grandmother is in her nineties.

> I understand. But, may I ask, is she sound of mind?

Anna had to smile. She had seen her grandmother only a month before on a visit to her mother's home in Norwich and Eleni's mind had been as pin sharp as ever, even if her body was stick thin and she only ventured to the post office once a week to claim her war widow's pension. Yes, she was of sound mind, and sharp-tongued too. Anna smiled as she recalled Eleni addressing her sternly, telling her that she should get on and marry someone. Life was too short, she

insisted, stabbing her bony finger as she spoke with a pronounced Greek accent. Eleni was compos mentis all right,
but that was not the true difficulty in any interview that the
German student might have in mind. Anna reached for the
keyboard again.

> My grandmother is sound of mind. But I doubt she
would be interested. From what she has told me of
her youth in Greece I suspect that she would not take
kindly to a German asking her to relive it. I don't think
I can help you.

> I am sorry to hear that. But think it over, please. If
Eleni is unwilling to grant an interview then perhaps I
could interview your mother or yourself concerning
what you, or she, may know? I am in London next
month. Could we meet and discuss this? I could
explain my project in more detail. I am sure it would
interest you.

Anna shook her head. Despite the politely formal tone of
his request she knew next to nothing about this Dieter Muller.
But something made her hesitate. It would be interesting to
know more about her grandmother's background . . . Then
she glanced up and saw the worksheets that needed marking.
There were twenty-five minutes of lunch break left. If she
worked quickly they could be dealt with and she would not
have to take work home. Her fingers tapped rapidly.

> Sorry, can't help you.

Then, feeling that such a brusque dismissal was a poor-spirited response to the German student, she added a few more words.

> I'm sure it is a very interesting project, but I have no time to spare to help you right now. Good luck with your research, Dieter.

There was a short pause and then the message 'Dieter is typing' appeared in the message box.

> I understand. If you change your mind then I give you my email: dietermuller3487@hotmail.com. Let me know. Best wishes, Dieter.

For a moment Anna felt tempted to continue the exchange and offer one last message, but then she glanced at the worksheets again and made herself close down the Facebook screen and log off from the computer. She pushed the keyboard back towards the flat-screen monitor, slid the paper in front of her and reached for a green pen to begin marking the first worksheet. As she worked through the student's responses Anna could not put aside the messages from the German and wondered precisely what it was about her grandmother that had provoked him to track her down. It had to be something significant. Something important. Something that Anna felt she needed to know for herself.

CHAPTER THREE

Anna woke early the next morning. She blinked her eyes open and automatically glanced at the clock on the bedside table. The dull yellow display told her that it was only six fifteen. Still half an hour before the alarm went off. The heating had not yet come on and there was a bite to the air in the room so she wriggled down a little further under the duvet. She recalled that there was still a new scheme of work for year seven that needed completing. Steeling herself, she slid out of the bed.

Pulling on a pair of tracksuit bottoms and her dressing gown, Anna slipped her feet into her slippers and padded across the landing to the small second bedroom that she used as a study and sat down at the desk. She had left her notes out in front of her computer keyboard the previous night so that they would not be overlooked and now reached for a pen. Then she paused, staring at the blank monitor as she rolled the pen slowly between her thumb and forefinger. She set it down and tapped the keyboard.

At once the computer stirred from its sleep mode as it whirred from beneath the desk and after a few moments the monitor flicked into life. Anna logged into Facebook and opened the exchange of messages between herself and Dieter

Muller. She read through them once again, and then reflected on the prospect of finding out something about her family's history. There were times when she felt that the subject she taught neglected the history of the vast majority of people. Untold numbers of remarkable experiences had been lost forever because ordinary people were overlooked and their memories went unrecorded. Perhaps she could do her bit to resist that process. She might discover something about the experiences of her grandmother during the Second World War. A story that would be worth recording and handing down to succeeding generations. Maybe it was even something she could use to inspire her students, to make them realise that everyone plays a part in the making of history.

Even though she had the German's email address Anna decided not to use it. She wasn't ready to establish that line of communication yet. Better to use Facebook messaging. So she leaned forward and typed.

> I apologise if I seemed rude yesterday. But your approach was a bit out of the blue, as we say here. Now that I've had a chance to think it over I would like to know more about your project. If you have any free time during your visit to London we could meet for a drink or a meal. I finish teaching on the 16th. So any time between then and the 23rd December would be good for me. Let me know if that suits you.

She sent the message and then stared at the screen for a few moments but there was no sign that any reply was being prepared. With a sigh Anna picked up her pen again and returned to her work, keeping half an eye on the screen. There was no response by the time she had finished the scheme of work.

In contrast to the swift exchange of messages on the first day that the German had got in touch, there was no reply from him that day, or the following week. Nor the week after that. She felt disappointed at first, then gradually it began to slip her mind as the term dragged on towards Christmas. Besides, she felt it beneath her dignity to send any follow-up message and decided that he must have given up on her, that it was just one of those brief flurries of communication that typified the social media.

Anna resolved to forget the matter entirely and concentrate on school life. Classes came and went. Jamie Gould was interviewed by the head of year about his poor attitude and the school's big musical production careered towards the grand opening night when the hall filled with dutiful parents and members of staff coerced into attending. After joining in the applause and then lingering to speak to some of the parents, Anna went to collect her belongings and head home.

The staffroom was empty, and she hurried through to the workroom to pick up her bag and the coat hanging over the back of the chair. The computer was still on and she went to close it down, hesitated, and logged into Facebook. There was a message waiting for her, from Dieter Muller. She quickly clicked on it.

> Apologies for the delay in replying to your message. I have been in Greece doing research. I am delighted to hear you will see me. Next week I am in London. Can meet you for lunch on Tuesday? I will pay of course. Shall we say one o'clock at Le Grand restaurant on Baker Street? Let me know if this is possible, soonest. Thank you. And best wishes.

Anna sat still for a moment, then reached for the keyboard and typed quickly.

> All right. I'll be there.

The streets of London were packed when Anna stepped out of Charing Cross station a few days later. To the left the usual crowd of sightseers visiting Trafalgar Square milled around street performers. The Christmas lights hung across the traffic like a latticework of stars glinting in the frosty air. The schools had broken up the previous Friday and hordes of children accompanied their parents as they bought the last of their presents.

Anna was genuinely curious to discover why Dieter had said she would be interested in his research project. If it could shed some light on her grandmother's past then it would be worthwhile. Eleni rarely spoke about her childhood to Anna, and mentioned little of what she had experienced during the war. Anna had asked her mother the reason for this reticence but she knew only the bare details from relatives from that side of the family.

The Greeks had suffered greatly from the German and Italian occupation of their country. In Athens alone over three hundred thousand people had starved to death. Conditions had not been much better in the countryside. Although there was more food to go around, the bitter conflict between the partisans, the *andartes*, and the fascists had led to reprisals in which tens of thousands of Greeks had been shot out of hand, and their villages razed to the ground. Eleni had been brought up on the Ionian island of Lefkas which, as far as Anna knew, had suffered least under the occupation. Perhaps Dieter Muller would be able to tell her something about that, as well as the period he was investigating, the years before the war when his countrymen had been more interested in digging up the past than crushing those who lived in the present.

As soon as the comparison had entered her mind, Anna felt a twinge of guilt. Remembering the war seemed to be something of a national obsession in Britain. The endless documentaries on television, and re-runs of *Dad's Army*, *'Allo, 'Allo* and *Goodnight Sweetheart*, and the shelves of Waterstones heaving with books about the war. Not to mention all the computer games she occasionally heard the boys talking about at school, and the childish headlines and images in the tabloid newspapers every time the England football team played Germany. It was over seventy years ago that the war had begun, yet it had lingered first as an open wound in the minds of those who had endured it, then an object of fascination for the following generations, and finally entertainment.

Anna knew that it was different in Germany. She had been to Berlin on a school trip and seen for herself the shrines to their national sense of guilt: the holocaust memorial and the museum detailing, with appalling frankness, the murderous barbarity of the Gestapo and the SS. Sometimes, the burden of the past weighed heavily on Anna and reminded her why she had become a history teacher. There was a duty to remember, to learn from the past, if only to better under-stand the present. And yet, in Britain there was an alarming tendency to trivialise the catastrophe that had ripped the heart out of the middle of the twentieth century and still scarred the dwindling numbers of those who had lived through it.

Her thoughts preoccupied her so much that she had already turned off Oxford Street and was heading north to

Baker Street before she was aware of it. Glancing at her watch she saw that it had just gone half past twelve and nodded with satisfaction. She would reach the restaurant first and try to identify Dieter before he saw her. She had the advantage of knowing what he looked like and would get a first impression before they introduced themselves. It was an old habit that went back to her first dates when she wanted to see the boys as they were before they put on the mask they hoped to impress her with. Mind you, she reflected, it was more than likely he would recognise her too; there was so little privacy these days, thanks to the internet. But this was hardly a date, she reminded herself. Just a quick meeting with someone who wanted to share some information that might shed a light on her family history. Something interesting. That was all there was to it.

She found the restaurant a short distance down the street. It had a small entrance with a large window to the side. A pair of printed linen curtains framed a display of baskets containing bread, onions, cheese and hams, with a large green jar of wine set to the side. Beyond the window Anna could see tables stretching back inside the restaurant, most of which had been taken by diners. That was good, she decided. Much less chance of standing out when Dieter arrived. Anna pushed open the door and entered. She was confronted by a bar at the end of a long counter. A dark-shirted woman with blond hair looked up from the till and smiled a greeting.

'Can I help?'

'Yes, I believe a table has been booked by a Mr Muller. I'm joining him for lunch.'

The waitress glanced down at the sheet beside the till and nodded. 'Please follow me.'

She led Anna towards the rear of the restaurant, between

two lines of tables, and her heart gave a little skip as she saw a man looking up from a table where he sat alone. Dieter had reached the restaurant first, and had been there some time, judging by the notebooks in front of him and a near empty glass of wine. Hurriedly closing his notebooks and shoving them in a small rucksack beside his chair, the German rose to his feet and offered his hand as Anna approached.

'Thank you for coming, Miss Thesskoudis.' He spoke her name slowly and carefully, in an accent that sounded vaguely American as much as German.

'That is right? Thesskoudis? I was not certain. Your mother is called Hardy-Thesskoudis, and your grandmother is Mrs Carson, I believe?'

'Yes,' Anna smiled. 'When my grandfather died she reverted to her Greek name, as did my mother. Until she married and took my father's name as well – at least until they divorced. I changed mine to Thesskoudis after he left us.'

The German blinked. 'I see . . .'

Anna laughed as she shook his hand, noting that it was warm to the touch and that he wore three ornate silver rings, the kind of jewellery she associated with art students.

'I think you'd better stick with Anna. Much easier to deal with.'

'Yes, I think so.' He grinned. 'And you call me Dieter, please.'

He gestured to the high-backed chair on the other side of the table and the waitress reached out. 'Can I take your coat?'

Anna nodded and slipped it off, and then sat down and made herself comfortable as Dieter resumed his seat. He raised an eyebrow enquiringly. 'A drink before we start?'

'A glass of dry white wine, thank you.'

'The same for me,' Dieter added.

The waitress turned away and there was a brief, awkward silence before Anna smiled. 'You look a little different to your photo on the university website.'

'Oh? How so?'

'Your hair is a little longer, and there was a stud.'

He self-consciously reached up to the yin-yang symbol hanging from his right lobe and then shrugged. 'The university prefers the graduate students to look professional for the public.'

Anna could not help a chuckle. 'Same with my school. You'd think from our handbook that every child came to school in a spotless new blazer and was permanently ecstatic at the prospect of another day's education.'

He considered this for a moment and pursed his lips. 'The ecstasy is optional in German educational institutions.' Then, realising what he had said, he laughed. 'I mean to say, the happiness, not the drug.'

'I guessed.' Anna felt herself warm to him and the initial strain of the introduction abated a little. She folded her hands on the table. 'So, you're studying for a doctorate in history?'

It was a clumsy attempt to steer him towards the purpose of his meeting and Anna winced inwardly as he replied.

'Archaeology. Rather than history.'

'A similar discipline, I would have thought.'

He looked surprised for a moment and tilted his head to one side. 'I suppose the link is close enough. There are many routes to understanding the past. You have an interest in history?'

'I teach it. At school. The Ashthorpe Victory Academy.'

'An academy? It sounds impressive.'

'Less so if you understood our education system. Basically it's a rebranded comprehensive school. No big deal. But I love teaching my subject. So, yes, I have a professional interest in history.'

'Good. Very good. Then we share an interest in the past. So, I'd better tell you why I have asked to meet you.'

Anna smiled encouragingly.

Dieter sat back and collected his thoughts. 'I am not the first archaeologist in my family. My great-grandfather was the first. A noted man in the field, back in the nineteen thirties. He was one of the best students of Professor Dörpfeld.' He spoke the name as if Anna should have heard of it. 'He in turn was an admirer of Schliemann, who discovered Troy. Like Schliemann, the professor was a passionate reader of Homer, and he wanted to continue Schliemann's work. No. He wanted to achieve something greater. He wanted to find the palace and tomb of Odysseus, the hero of Homer's second great work. You know the *Odyssey*?'

'I've read some of it, when I was at school.'

'Then you will know that after the war with Troy was over, Odysseus wandered for many years before he returned to his kingdom of Ithaca. At least that is the story that Homer tells. In truth, his return was probably without so much incident. He, and his men, came back from the war, their ships laden with spoils from Troy. Treasures that he would have kept in his palace. That was what Dörpfeld believed and he led an expedition to Ithaca to search for the remains of the palace of Odysseus.

'He and his followers, my great-grandfather amongst them, searched Ithaca for years, finding few ancient remains, never anything large enough to be the palace of a king. So he considered the possibility that the ancient sources might not provide enough information. Ithaca is a small island. If it had a king then it is possible that his realm extended to other islands nearby. So, my great-grandfather, Karl Muller, was sent to carry out excavations on Lefkas, while another colleague searched on Kefalonia.' Dieter raised his hands. 'It was, as the phrase goes, a long shot, but Karl accepted the challenge. I think, maybe, he hoped he would find something that would make his own reputation. I have his diaries of those years. His diaries, his notebooks and his photographs.'

'And did he discover anything?'

Dieter hesitated an instant. 'Not really. No. Just the remains of a large building. There was never enough evidence to identify it as the palace of Odysseus.'

'Oh.' Anna could not hide her disappointment. 'What a shame. So what's your interest? Do you hope to continue where he left off?'

The German smiled. 'Nothing like that. No. There's barely any trace left of the excavations. Just fragments. My interest is more, ah, ethnographic. I want to provide an account of the relationship between my great-grandfather's team and the local people at the time. My research is a comparative study between invasive and sympathetic archaeological methodology with respect to indigenous populations.'

Anna nodded slowly and Dieter caught her expression and laughed. 'It is really much less complicated than it sounds.'

'I should hope so.'

The waitress brought their wine on a tray and set the glasses down. They waited until she had walked away before Dieter resumed.

'So, I have my great-grandfather's records, and what I need is the other side of the story. The memories of those Greeks who worked alongside him at the excavations on Lefkas. That's where your grandmother enters the story.'

'Eleni? How? She was only a young girl at the time. I've

never heard anything about her being involved in any excavation.'

'But she was there. She is mentioned in the diaries. Eleni Thesskoudis. There are several references to her being present. She was a friend of my grandfather, Peter, who was also there on the island, accompanying his father.'

'What proof do you have that it was her, my grandmother?'

'I have checked the records in Lefkada. I have traced her to England. That is how I found your mother's name also. And yours.' He reached down into his rucksack and pulled out an iPad. 'Look. I will show you.'

He swept his fingers over the glass surface and then turned the device towards her to reveal a black and white image. Anna leaned closer and saw that it was a scan of an old photograph. Three teenagers, two boys and a girl, arms on each other's shoulders, sitting on a bench in front of several long tables piled with fragments of pottery and pieces of stone, some of which looked to have been sculpted. Beyond lay a patch of open ground dotted with shrubs and trees before the slope of a hill rose up in the distance. The boy on the left of the picture was darkly featured with wavy hair, a solid build and wearing long trousers and boots. To his side was a girl, also dark-haired, with similar Greek features, and to her right sat a taller boy, blond-haired and wearing glasses. All three were smiling and were clearly friends. She looked more closely at the girl and gave a slight start.

'That's her! That's Eleni.' She raised her eyes and saw that Dieter was smiling at her.

'Your grandmother. You see, I was right about her.'

Anna tentatively touched the screen with her fingertips and spread the tips apart to enlarge the image for a closer look at her grandmother. The grain of the image increased but it was still clear enough to identify Eleni from the similarity to a handful of pictures that Anna had seen when she had visited the house Eleni had lived in before she moved in with Anna's mother. In fact, she had a vague feeling that she had seen this particular picture before and strained her memory to try and place it. Questions tumbled through her mind.

'Who are the others? Where is this, and who took the picture?'

'One at a time, please!' Dieter edged back from her intent gaze. Anna took a breath to calm herself and let him continue. Dieter pointed to the taller boy.

'That is my grandfather. Peter Muller. He was sixteen at the time. Your grandmother was a year younger. The other boy. Andreas Katarides, was the oldest, seventeen. They were friends of Peter, from Lefkada. That's where the expedition rented a house while they conducted the search for the palace of Odysseus. Your grandmother was the daughter of the town's police inspector, and Andreas the son of a poet who had come to live on the island. Spyridon Katarides. He came from a wealthy family in Athens, but eloped with one of the servants. They had a child, Andreas, but his mother died giving birth to him. The family were angry and disowned Katarides. All except an uncle who sent him a comfortable allowance to live on, and raise his son. As to who took the picture, that was my great-grandfather. He took it at the site of the main excavation on the island. Here, I'll show you some more.'

Dieter flicked his finger across the screen and Anna saw more black and white images, some of which showed the landscape of the island, some the inhabitants, roughly dressed peasants, townspeople, fishermen, some images of ruins and then a handful of pictures of German soldiers wearing mountain caps, with a white flower pinned to the side. One picture caught her eye.

'Wait!' Anna intervened. 'Isn't that him? Your grandfather. Go back one. There.'

He stood, one boot braced on a rock, striking a pose, hands on hips. His jacket was unbuttoned, revealing a white collarless shirt beneath. At his feet was a backpack and a belt, attached to which was a leather pistol holster. Behind his glasses he was squinting into bright sunlight. But his face was largely unaltered, slightly more filled out perhaps, Anna mused.

'Is this during the war?'

Dieter nodded. 'After he joined the army. His father was forced to leave the island when the German authorities ordered him to return home and abandon the excavation. That was in nineteen thirty-eight. He had hoped the crisis would pass and that he could resume his work. He never did. He was killed during an air raid in nineteen forty-three.'

Anna felt uncomfortable and muttered, 'I'm sorry.'

'Don't be. It was nothing to do with you. It was the war. Anyway, my grandfather, like nearly all young men, was conscripted. He was selected for officer training and served with an artillery regiment. That picture was taken in Greece – Lefkas actually. He was posted there for a while, to act as an interpreter.'

Anna's eyes widened. 'He returned to the island? Did he meet Eleni and,' she thought back a moment, 'and Andreas again?'

Dieter seemed to wince, then smiled sadly and gave a single nod.

'That must have been difficult, for all of them.'

'They had become enemies, though they did not wish it.'

Dieter stared at the image of his grandfather. 'It was a terrible time, for Greek and German alike. My grandfather's diaries do not make for easy reading. He never spoke about the war to me or my father. I knew nothing of his record until after he died and I went through his papers and the Wehrmacht archives.' He flicked back through the images to the first one. 'This is how I prefer to remember him. And, in his diary, he says it was when he was happiest. I would like to find out more about that time. Even though, strictly speaking, my research is more concerned with the earlier period. And that is why I would like to interview your grandmother. To see what she remembers of the excavations. Particularly, where this picture was taken. I have tried to locate it when I explored the island, but so far, no luck.' He turned the iPad off and returned it to his bag before he addressed Anna again.

'I would ask you to talk to your grandmother and see if she will let me speak with her.'

Anna pursed her lips. 'I'll ask. But I must tell you that she still looks back on the war in a very unforgiving way.'

'I understand. But I am not my grandfather. My generation looks back on that time in horror. And shame for the stain it left on the reputation of Germany. Please explain that to her. My great-grandfather was the same. He despised the National Socialists. And he loved Lefkas and the people, and most of all the history of Greece. If anything, it is his reputation that I wish to restore when I finish my thesis. He could have become one of the greatest archaeologists of his age, or any other time. I believe he was on the verge of great discoveries. If he had only lived long enough to return to his work on the island . . .' Dieter suddenly gave a shame-faced smile. 'I am sorry. It is a burden for me. I should not impose it on you. I have asked enough of you already. Now!' He sat back and picked up the menu. 'We shall eat. You are my guest. Our business is over. We shall talk of other things over the meal, unless you wish to ask me more?'

Anna laughed, touched by his sweet politeness. 'Perhaps. Let us see.' She raised her wine glass. 'How about a toast?'

Dieter smiled and raised his glass. 'To what?'

She thought a moment. 'To healing old wounds. And uncovering the past!'

CHAPTER FOUR

The following weekend Anna took the train up to Norwich to see her mother and grandmother. The heavy leaden skies of the day before had cleared and the morning was bright and clear, with a chilly bite that presaged the arrival of winter. She felt a certain lightness to her spirit with the fine weather and the prospect of seeing her family again. As the train raced through the East Anglian countryside Anna put on her headphones to listen to her iPod. She smiled as she came across the Johnny Cash playlist. Her mother was a big fan and by default that made Anna familiar with the most popular tracks. She listened with delight as the deep, gravelly voice rekindled memories of her childhood spent in the kitchen as her mother cheerfully accompanied her hero while she prepared the evening meal. Like so many families where Greek traditions stuck hard, there was a pride in preparing food rather than reheating ready meals and Anna could almost smell the rich aromas of the family kitchen. Often Eleni had been there too, gossiping with her daughter in a mixture of accented English and native Greek, some of which Anna could follow.

As she listened to the music, her thoughts returned to the meeting with Dieter and his revelations, which had thrown a small light on her grandmother's past and inspired Anna to want to know more. It would have to be handled sensitively, she told herself. Eleni was an old woman, a frail woman, though her spirit was strong. Anna did not want to upset her. There was little chance of Eleni agreeing to be interviewed by Dieter, but Anna was keen to discover her story herself. She would decide later how much of it she was prepared to share with the German research student.

It was nearly midday when she reached Norwich and took a taxi from the station to the road where her mother lived, an avenue lined with semi-detached houses dating back to the nineteen thirties. It was close to the university and many of the houses were owned by academics, or rented by students, who had always made interesting neighbours when Anna had been a teenager going out at night for the first time. Now she felt a warm sense of remembered belonging as the taxi pulled up outside her mother's house. She sat for a moment looking up the short path to the front door with its leaded glass panel, small coloured panes arranged in a floral pattern, and smiled. Home. That's how it felt. Even now, eight years after she had left for university.

The doorbell still didn't work and she instinctively reached for the brass knocker and rapped twice. A figure appeared beyond the glass, misshapen, moving quickly. With a metallic rattle the door opened and her mother beamed, then embraced her tightly, kissing her on both cheeks.

'Anna! My dear. So good to see you again.'

'And you, Mum.' She could only lift one arm to return the embrace as the other hand was holding her overnight bag and, in any case, her arm was pinned to her side.

'Come in, come in out of the cold. I'll put the kettle on.'

Anna followed her inside and the door clicked shut behind

them. The house had a long entrance hall with a staircase rising to the left. On the other side was a lounge, dining room, and a large kitchen at the rear. The dining room had been given over to Eleni and was her bedroom, on the same floor as the small bathroom beyond the hall and back door at the rear of the kitchen. Anna nodded down the hall and spoke in an undertone.

'How is she?'

'The same as ever.'

They shared a smile before Anna's mother took her bag and made for the stairs. 'Go and say hello. I'll put this in your room. It's rented to a student, but she's away until after the New Year.'

Although the room had been rented out when Anna had got her teaching job, she still affected a pained expression. 'It's only been eight years and already you have replaced me with a stranger. That hurts.'

'Hah! It's a bedroom, not a shrine, my girl. And I need the income, teachers' pay being what it is. Now go and see your grandmother.'

As her mother climbed the stairs, Anna stared after her, noticing there were more grey streaks in the hair tied up in a bun, but her figure was still as slim as ever, something she took care over with regular visits to the gym at the university's sports centre. She had taken early retirement from teaching the year before and commenced a part-time Masters degree to give a focus to her life. Then as her mother passed out of sight on the landing, Anna approached the dining-room door and knocked lightly on the dark stained wood.

A reedy voice called out, 'Come in, girl! Come in.'

Anna turned the handle and entered. The room had been sparsely furnished when it had been a dining room. That had been her mother's taste in decor. But now Eleni's stamp was on every aspect. A bed sat in one corner with a crocheted coverlet spread neatly over the top blanket. There was a small walnut table beside the bed with a pink fabric lampshade atop a carved wooden stand. There was a bookshelf filled with books, mostly in Greek, a sewing box, long since abandoned as age took its toll on her joints, but kept all the same. Two armchairs were either side of a side table by the window which overlooked the small garden at the rear of the house, and was framed by long velvet curtains. A large patterned carpet covered most of the wooden floor and a mock wood-burner fan heater sat in the fireplace, beneath a mantel laden with framed family pictures. There was a stale smell in the room, a reminder of the days when she had smoked before her daughter had told her to stop and refused to buy any more cigarettes for her.

Eleni was standing in the middle of the room, one hand clutched about the handle of her walking stick while the other was extended towards Anna. Her hair, once long and jet-black, was now a dirty-looking grey and shoulder-length, tied back to reveal the heavily lined skin stretched over her skull. She wore a navy cardigan over a white blouse and a long dark skirt and thick stockings that disappeared into a fluffy pair of slippers. Her thin lips parted in a smile.

'Anna . . .' There was a breathless coarseness to her voice that came from many years of smoking. 'My dear Anna.'

Anna crossed the room and took the old lady's hand, feeling the tremor in the stick-like fingers. Eleni gave a quick squeeze and presented her cheek for a kiss, which Anna gave willingly before she stood back half a pace to look over her grandmother.

'How are you feeling?'

'Feeling? I am feeling as an old woman should. Stiff and delicate. What do you think someone of my age feels, hah?'

Anna smiled. 'As up for it as ever. Good for you, Yiayia.'

'Up? What? Never mind. Come, we go to the kitchen. Your mother prepares coffee for us.' She released Anna's hand and tapped her ear. 'Still good.'

She paced slowly across to the door with the aid of her stick. Anna went to help her, supporting her arm, but the old lady shook her off at once with a brisk jolt of her shoulder and Anna raised her hands in mock resignation. They made their way through to the kitchen where a long counter extended against one wall, with a gas cooker dominating the centre. On the other side of the room was a large wooden table surrounded by chairs with leather backs. It was a warm room, and light flooded in through the tall sash window beside the table. Anna's mother rejoined them as Eleni eased herself on to the chair at the head of the table. She rested her stick against the wall and settled down, straight-backed and imperious as her dark eyes looked over her granddaughter.

'Are you eating well, Anna? You look thin.'

'I'm eating properly, Yiayia.'

'Pshhh!' Eleni turned to her daughter. 'Look at her, Marita. Thin as a rake. You need to find a good man and settle down and eat properly.'

'There's a few things I want to do before I do that,' said Anna. 'Quite a few things actually.'

'We all say that, my dear.' Eleni leaned forward a fraction. 'You should get married.'

Anna had become used to such comments, and had endured them with regard to the two previous serious boyfriends she had brought to the house. She returned her grandmother's smile indulgently. 'I will marry when I am ready to marry. If I decide to marry at all, that is.'

The old woman wafted a hand dismissively. 'Young people think they will live forever. That is their tragedy.'

'And old people think that they have lived forever,' Anna replied. 'That is theirs.'

Eleni stared at her for a moment and then her face creased as she cackled. 'You have your mother's spirit. And mine. That's the Greek in you.'

'Speaking of which,' Marita nodded towards the cafetière, 'the usual? Or are you still drinking that instant crap you started buying at university?'

'The usual, please.'

Marita poured a generous amount of dark grains into the filter, topped up the reservoir and flicked the switch on. Soon the powerful aroma of coffee filled the kitchen, adding to Anna's sense of well-being.

'So, what's the reason for the unexpected visit?' Marita asked.

Anna thought quickly. She was wary of telling her about Dieter Muller and his research in front of Eleni. It might be better not to mention him. Not straight away at least. 'I wanted a chance to see you both before Christmas.'

'That's nice. So will you be spending it with us?'

'Of course.' There was a beat, then Anna cleared her throat. 'Also, I want to talk to Yiayia. About a history project I'm involved with.'

Eleni raised her thin eyebrows. 'Talk to me? About what?'

'When you were growing up. On Lefkas.'

'That was a long time ago.'

'But you remember it?'

'Of course.' Eleni wagged a finger. 'I am old. Not stupid.'

'I didn't think that for a moment. I wouldn't dare, Yiayia. Would you be happy to talk to me about it?'

'Happy? I think, yes. For the most part.'

'Good. Then let's have coffee, and we can talk.' Anna turned to her mother. 'If that's OK with you?'

'No problem. I need to go out to buy a few things for dinner.'

'Thanks.' Anna took her hand and her grandmother's. 'I can't tell you how good it feels to be home again.'

Anna closed the door behind her mother and returned to the dining room where Eleni was already settled in her armchair beside the window. Even though it was the middle of the afternoon, the sun had already dipped below the roofline of the houses backing on to their garden and the room was bisected horizontally by the glow of the sun high up on the walls, while the rest was in shadow. The room felt cool and Anna gestured towards the fan heater.

'Would you like that on?'

Eleni nodded. 'I feel the cold more and more.'

The heater hummed in the background as they faced each other each side of the low table. Anna was not certain how to begin the conversation. There was a short silence before Eleni spoke.

'You want to know about my childhood? You have not asked me about it before. Why now?'

'I never felt comfortable about it. Mother said that times were difficult and that it would only upset you.'

'Marita worries too much. I am old. All I have is memories. If I do not use them then what is left to me? It is true that the old times were . . . difficult. But it was not always so. Before the fascists came, life was good. We did not live as comfortably as you do, but we had enough to make us happy.'

'Your father was a police inspector, I think.'

Eleni nodded. 'A fine man. Strong and respected by all. But you know this.'

'Mother told me. But not much else. For example, I never knew if you had any friends.'

'I played with the other children in my school. I counted some as friends.'

'And were there any others? After you left school?'

Eleni hesitated. 'A few. Why do you ask me this?'

Anna chewed her lip and then took out her mobile phone. 'I think it's simpler if I show you something.'

She tapped the screen and then, warily, rose from her chair and knelt down beside her grandmother, offering her the device.

'I can't see this,' the old woman complained. 'I need my glasses. Over there, by the bed.'

Anna fetched them and her grandmother fumbled to get them on, balancing the middle over the bridge of her long nose. She picked up the phone again and stared at the screen, and gave a sharp gasp.

'Where did you get this?'

'It's a picture someone sent me. An historian. He said it would be of interest. That's you, isn't it, Yiayia?'

She watched the rigid expression on the old woman's face and then saw the corners of her mouth begin to tremble.

'How is this possible?' Eleni demanded quietly. 'How? Tell me.'

'As I said. It was sent to me.'

Eleni stared at the image and then thrust the phone back towards her granddaughter. 'No. It's a trick. Who would do a thing like this?'

She was shaking now and Anna felt alarmed by her reaction. 'It's just a picture of you with two friends. That's what I was told.'

Eleni closed her eyes tightly for a moment and her wrinkled hands balled into fists.

'Yiayia? . . . Yiayia, are you all right?'

Tears pricked out at the corners of the old woman's eyes and Anna felt a stab of fear and compassion. 'What is it? Tell me. What's the matter?'

Eleni wept in silence and Anna took one of her hands and eased her thumb into the palm and rubbed soothingly.

'I'm sorry. So sorry. I shouldn't have shown you that.' She was angry with herself. Angry with Dieter Muller for sharing the picture with her and bringing this all about in the first place. 'Yiayia, I'm sorry . . .'

At length Eleni swallowed and raised her spare hand to dab away the tears before she opened her eyes, and Anna could clearly see the pain there. Eleni pointed to the bookcase.

'Over there. Top shelf. You see the large brown book? There, at the back.'

Anna glanced round and nodded.

'Bring it to me, girl.'

Anna straightened up and did as she was told, easing the dusty volume from the bookcase. The leather cover was cracked and flaking away in places and Anna held it carefully as she carried it back to her grandmother and set it down on the table. Eleni leaned forward and tentatively stretched out her hands to touch the cover, and stroke her fingertips over it. Then, with a little nod to herself, she eased the cover open and began to carefully leaf through the thin card pages. There were letters, photos and a few pressed flowers. At one time they had been stuck down but over the years many items had come loose and she had to take care to prevent any slipping free of the book. At length she turned another page and there lay the same picture that Dieter had shown Anna two days before. It was an original photograph, not a scanned image.

'I've seen this album before,' said Anna. 'I remember some of the other things, as well as this picture.'

Eleni nodded. 'You picked it up once, in my house, many years before. You were four, no, five, at the time. Too young to know what it means to me, but young enough to be interested. So I did not mind, then.' She tapped a finger on the picture. 'I did not know there was a copy of this picture.'

She fixed her granddaughter with a piercing stare. 'There is only one way there could be another. Karl Muller took this. But he is long dead. So, his son?'

'Peter?' Anna saw her grandmother shudder at the mention of his name. 'No, not him. His grandson, Dieter, sent me the copy on my phone.'

'You know him?' Eleni hissed. 'He is here, in England?'

'No. No. At least I don't think he is in London at the moment. He said that he had to return to Germany to continue his research,' Anna explained hurriedly. 'He wants to know about the island, before the fascists came. Back when the Germans were digging for ancient ruins. It has nothing to do with the war, Yiayia. I promise.'

'He is a German. His promises mean nothing.' Eleni grasped her hand tightly. 'You will not see him again. You will not speak to him. Understand?' The intensity of her expression and sudden strength of her grip frightened Anna.

'But why? Tell me why.'

Eleni released her hand and sagged back into the armchair. She was silent a moment and Anna could see the pulse in her throat flickering like a candle in a draught. Then she sighed and spoke again in a calm voice.

'The Greek boy at my side in the picture is Andreas Katarides.'

'A close friend?'

She smiled thinly. 'Then, yes. But more, much more, later on. The other boy was also . . . a friend. Peter Muller.' She paused, and her voice hardened. 'That was before he came back to the island to murder us. Became our enemy. How can these things be?' She closed her eyes as she remembered. 'I try to remember that it was not always so. There was a time before . . . Before the great evil came to our little island.'

CHAPTER FIVE

Lefkas, September 1938

The camera shutter clicked and the three teenagers relaxed from the pose they had struck and held while Peter's father set the exposure and adjusted the focus. Karl Muller looked up and smiled at them.

'That's it. All done.'

As he lowered his Leica and reached for the camera case, Peter glanced at his friends and raised an eyebrow. 'Sorry. My father's something of a photography addict.'

Eleni laughed, parting her thin lips to reveal white teeth and a smile that Peter considered faultless, even though there was a noticeable gap in the top incisors. She shook her head.

'Don't apologise. That's all you seem to do about your father. He's a nice man.'

'Even for a German?'

'Especially for a German.' She nodded discreetly towards the young man sitting at the end of a long table laden with bits of pottery, small stones and other fragments that might hold some archaeological value. 'Unlike our friend over there.'

Peter glanced round. 'Heinrich?'

He watched his father's assistant carefully entering an item into the log. 'He knows his job and works hard.'

Eleni sighed. 'He's a cold one. I don't trust him.'

Andreas stirred at her side, his dark brows knitting together. 'He has offended you?'

'No. Not like that. I just don't like him much.'

'He had better not upset you when I'm around.'

She touched his arm briefly. 'You are not my brother. Nor my cousin.'

'No.' He relaxed his expression. 'Just a friend.'

'Exactly. And I can look after myself.'

Andreas smiled. 'Of course you can, little Eleni. You're fifteen. Almost a woman.'

She glared at him in jest and Andreas laughed. Peter joined in, a little pinprick of pain in his heart when her eyes lingered on Andreas just a moment longer than was necessary.

'Come on,' he said. 'Let's see what they've found today.'

He stepped out towards the table and the others followed. Peter visited the site most days but his friends came less frequently. They had become friends after Andreas's father had invited the German archaeologists to a dinner at his villa. Shyly at first, but quickly becoming close as youngsters will on a small island. The Germans had been digging in the valley for over eighteen months and interest in their painstaking methods had soon palled and the local people turned back to their routines. The most recent finds were at the end of the table where Heinrich sat on a camp stool. He delicately held up a fragment of fine pottery and closely scrutinised it for a moment before lowering it and entering several words in the comments section of the log.

Peter waited until he had set his pen down again. 'Anything interesting?'

Heinrich shrugged and gestured towards the scattered shards before him. 'One of the men unearthed this,' he responded in German. 'He broke it with the first stroke of his trowel. The times I've warned them to go in gently. So now we have a little reconstruction work to do. Or would have, if we hadn't been recalled. Have to wait until we return.'

Peter was conscious that his friends could not easily follow the exchange, despite his teaching them some German over the last few months, and switched back into Greek. 'How old do you think it is?'

Heinrich grinned at him, and the others. 'Late Mycenaean. Three thousand years old. And it's a fine piece. Look here.' He picked up one of the larger pieces and held it up for them to see. A row of delicately painted warriors, hoplites, ranged along the curve of the shard. 'I'd bet that this came from a wealthy household. Perhaps these are the remains of a nobleman's house. Or maybe that of a king. Either way, it's more evidence that your father is on the right track.'

Eleni edged forward and examined the small figures, marvelling at the brightness of the colours. 'Three thousand years old . . .'

'That's right. Back in an age when Greek civilisation was about to dominate the known world. A far cry from what it has become today, no?'

Andreas was silent for a moment before he responded. 'Every civilisation has its day. Perhaps Greece may rise again. As Germany has.'

Heinrich laughed. 'Ah, there's the difference. History does not repeat itself. The greatness of Greece lies behind it. The greatness of Germany is just beginning. Even so, there's much we can learn from the great nations of the past.'

Andreas arched an eyebrow. 'You think so?'

'I know it.'

There was a pause, and the heat trapped in the valley

seemed to add to the tension. Eleni tore her gaze away from the figures on the pottery and turned to Peter.

'There's something I need to ask your father.'

'Oh?'

'That photograph he just took, of the three of us. I would like a copy to keep. For when you leave, so I can remember. Do you think he would give me a print?'

Peter glanced towards another table where his father had finished fastening the buckles of his camera case and removed his wide-brimmed straw hat to dab the sweat from his brow. He stared round the valley before fixing his gaze on a nearby cliff which rose steeply up to the mixed line of stunted oaks and cypress trees that grew above and covered the hillside.

'Ask him. I'm sure he'll agree.'

Eleni flashed him a smile and turned away to approach Peter's father. Andreas moved further down the table, away from Heinrich, and looked over the other finds. Peter followed him, feeling awkward over the hubris of his compatriot. It was unfortunate, since he admired his father's assistant. Heinrich Steiner was robustly cheerful and had been an avid sportsman back in his native Bavaria. Moreover, he had won the respect of Peter's father, which was why he had been chosen from many applicants to join him on the site. In truth, Peter sought the same seal of approval and hoped to be like Heinrich one day. Nonetheless, he was sensitive enough to discern the friction between his father's assistant and some of the islanders, particularly his friends.

Peter cleared his throat. 'Are you all right, Andreas?'

The older boy did not look up as he replied. 'All right? Why shouldn't I be?'

'Heinrich didn't mean to offend. Sometimes he is, well, a bit too proud of being German.'

'Perhaps he has cause to be,' Andreas mused. 'Greece is only a small country, of little consequence. Germany has become a force to be reckoned with. It must warm your heart to be part of that, my friend.'

'I suppose,' Peter admitted. In the years since the National Socialists had come to power they had not ceased to proclaim that the nation had been reborn and a fine future lay ahead. It had been easy to be swept along with the euphoria and believe in it. But that was back in Germany. Since Peter had been with his father here on Lefkas, the affairs of their homeland had become remote and there was a lyrical serenity about the islands of the Ionian Sea, and its people, that diminished the grip of patriotism on Peter's soul. In truth, being here felt like a release. A different pace of history, as his father put it. Both of them were saddened by the need to leave the island, and friends, behind, until the diplomatic crisis had passed.

Anxious to change the subject out of deference to his friend's pride, Peter pointed out a fragment of stone, sculpted into a small, open-palmed hand. 'Look at this! Superb . . .'

Without thinking, Andreas picked it up and examined it closely.

At once Heinrich turned and said, 'Please put that back.'

Andreas did as he was told. His pride was pricked by having to obey a young man only a few years older than himself. He felt a momentary urge to defy Heinrich after the event, before sense returned and he mumbled, 'Sorry.'

The student flashed a brief smile. 'It's just that it's a valuable piece. The professor would have my hide if anything happened to it.'

Andreas stared back, until the German returned his attention to his logbook. Peter was embarrassed by the brief exchange, and blamed himself for pointing out the sculpture fragment to his friend. He began to move along the table, looking over the finds that had already been labelled, and Andreas followed him a short distance until they were out of earshot and whispered, 'What was that about?'

'There is a procedure. Nothing is to be touched until it is logged and labelled,' Peter explained.

His Greek friend sighed. 'I see. That man is a foreigner in my land, and he tells me not to touch what he has dug out of our soil.'

'He did not mean to offend you, Andreas.'

'Did he not?' Andreas sniffed and gestured at the finds spread out along the table in front of him. 'I wonder . . . Is this all not an offence in itself?'

'What do you mean?'

'This is not the ancient Greece of your schoolbooks. It is a different age. Yet men like your father – and I mean him no disrespect, he is a good man – feel free to come here and treat this land, and these objects he has dug up, with no regard for our feelings. These are the relics of my people's past. What will become of them? They will be boxed up and taken to Germany and put on display in a museum. If I should ever want to see the heritage of my people then I will be forced to travel to your country and pay for the privilege.'

Peter shook his head. 'It's not like that. These relics need to be cared for properly, so that they can be enjoyed by everyone, regardless of where they happened to be found. Besides, he has the permission of the Greek government.'

Andreas snorted. 'The permission of some corrupt official, you mean.'

Peter forced a smile. 'My friend, all Europe owes a great debt to your ancestors. We are all the inheritors of the great works of the ancients. It is a bond we share.'

'That's easy for you to say. And you may even mean it. But it does not change the fact that you are mining our past and taking it away.'

'We are preserving it,' Peter protested. 'That's all.'

'And is it not preserved here, in this ground?'

'Then who would ever see it? It has to be put in front of the world.'

'Maybe, but why not here, in Greece?'

The response was obvious but Peter managed to moderate his reply. 'I understand your pride, but if the past is to survive, it has to be looked after. When the museums are built here, all these relics will be returned.'

'I see. Just like the Acropolis frieze then?'

Peter gritted his teeth. 'We are not like the British. Germany understands the value of civilisation.'

'Really?' Andreas arched on eyebrow. 'We shall see, eh?'

Before Peter could respond they were interrupted by a shout from Professor Muller.

'Heinrich! Have you finished cataloguing the day's finds?'

They passed his father's car and made for the truck, an ageing Fiat, spotted with rust and coated with a layer of grime that made the already sun-bleached blue seem that much more faded. It had been an early purchase of the archaeological expedition when the flow of funds from the university had been more forthcoming. A thinly padded bench served as the seat for the driver and passenger, and sacking lay in the bed of the truck to cushion the loads carried back to Lefkada. Andreas handed Eleni into the back while Peter, as usual, went round to the front and slotted the starting handle into position. He took the grip in both hands and looked over the top of the radiator grille. Heinrich gave a nod and then Peter swung the handle round. It took three attempts before the engine choked into life. Heinrich gently revved it for a moment and then called out above the shrill rattle, 'That's it! In you get.'

After he stowed the handle, Peter walked past the driver's door.

'Not sitting in here where there's more shade? Gentler on the arse too.'

Peter hesitated, wanting to travel with his friends.

'Go on,' said Eleni. 'We can talk through the cab window.'

'Yes,' Andreas added. 'Sit, in there.'

Peter did as he was bid and walked round the front of the truck to take his place beside Heinrich in the tiny vibrating cab that smelt of petrol fumes and grease. As soon as the door was closed, Heinrich released the handbrake and thrust the stick into first gear. With a lurch the truck ground forward over the gravel track. Peter stuck his head out of the window to take one last look at the small valley where he had spent so much time over the last eighteen months, and then pine trees closed in on the track and cut off the view of the archaeological dig. Behind him he heard Andreas make a comment and Eleni laughed and the rest of the exchange was lost as Heinrich changed gear and accelerated up the slope. The still air of the valley was replaced with the warm rush through the open windows of the cab. Peter breathed in the familiar tang of pine and felt a brief moment of sorrow that he would not see the valley again for a long time. At least until the powers of Europe came to an understanding that allowed normal life to resume. It frustrated him that ordinary people like himself could get on well enough with those of other nations without rancour but those who held the reins of power found it so difficult to do the same.

'What will you do when you get back to Berlin?' Heinrich asked, breaking into his thoughts.

Peter pushed the frames of his glasses up the bridge of his nose to fix them in place as the truck jolted along the track. He cleared his throat and spoke loudly.

'Father has arranged a place for me at a gymnasium to finish my schooling.'

'And afterwards?'

'University. To study archaeology.'

Heinrich laughed. 'Follow in the old man's footsteps, eh?'

Peter winced at the disrespectful description of his father. 'I suppose so.'

Heinrich kept his eyes on the difficult route ahead of them, trying to steer carefully over the worst holes and bumps in the uneven track. 'Do you like the idea?'

Peter glanced at him. 'What do you mean?'

'You don't have to study archaeology if you don't want to. You could choose any subject. Or not. There are plenty of other things a man can do in Germany. Now that there's a new government, a new future.'

'Maybe, but I know what I want to study.' There was a brief pause before he continued. 'What about you? What will you do while the dig is delayed?'

Heinrich shrugged. 'I don't know. I've got a thesis to finish. But I'm not sure if I'll bother.'

'Oh?'

'I've had my fun here. But I've had enough of sweating under a hot sun, surrounded by rocks, dirt and scraps of pottery. At least for a while. I fancy some cool fresh air. I'll be going to my family's home in the mountains for a while. Do some skiing when winter comes. You like skiing?'

'Never tried it.'

'A shame. There's no experience like it. Give it a try some time.'

'Maybe . . .'

The conversation died as the truck made its way up the slope leading out of the valley. At length the gradient eased and the track joined a more established dirt road running along the side of a hill. To the left the trees gave way to stunted growths amid the parched rock. To the right the slope fell away towards the sea and the islands of the Ionian. Far off lay the mountains of the mainland, stretching along the horizon, stark in the absence of any haze. Peter's spirits rose, as they did every time they reached this point in the drive back to Lefkada. And he made a sudden resolution that he would return to the island, to this very place, whatever his future held in store for him.

'I shall miss this . . .'

'Really?' Heinrich shrugged. 'It's a all a bit too primitive for my taste. Take this road, for example. Typical of Greece. Probably hasn't changed much since the days of Odysseus. You've seen what they're doing back home. Fine new roads that cross the land from border to border. Quite a sight.'

Peter smiled at the competing views of what constituted a spectacle. For him there was a timeless beauty to these islands rising from the sparkling Ionian Sea. A feeling that was given an added warmth by the proximity of his friends in the rear of the truck. By his closeness to Eleni. He turned and looked through the narrow window at the rear of the cab. He could see the worn wooden rail immediately behind and the dark curls of Andreas's head. To the side were the longer tendrils of Eleni's dark hair, flicking about in the hot air swirling round the vehicle.

'All right back there?'

Andreas shifted round and sat up, clutching the edge of the rail. A moment later Eleni joined him, grinning happily through the window. For a moment all three exchanged a glance and then Andreas laughed spontaneously.

'What is it?' asked Peter.

'Nothing.' Andreas reached forward and shook his shoulder. 'Nothing at all! Just this. Just us being together now.'

CHAPTER SIX

Peter had washed and changed by the time his father returned from the excavation site. He was sitting on the balcony of the hired villa, a single-storey structure next to the sea, on the edge of the small town of Lefkada. There were four private rooms as well as a large formal room, used as the expedition's office, and a kitchen where a local woman prepared meals for the Germans. A handful of outbuildings stood a short distance from the villa. The largest and most secure was where the tools and finds were stored.

The sound of singing came from within as Heinrich prepared himself for the dinner appointment with Andreas's father. Karl Muller climbed the short staircase to the balcony and paused to take his hat off and mop his brow as he admired the view. The villa was in the shadow of the hill the local people called Vouno. The peaks on the mainland were bathed in the red glow of the setting sun and heat was just starting to fade from the air as insects buzzed and whined through the dusk. He glanced at his son and turned to stare out across the sea, both sharing the moment in contemplative silence. Then, with a sigh, he paced along the balcony and sat on the wicker chair beside Peter. His son poured him a glass of water from the jug and handed it to him.

'Thank you.' Dr Muller smiled gratefully and raised the glass and steadily drained it before setting it down on the small table between them. 'I needed that.'

He settled into the chair before he continued. 'I went into town before I came back. I had to send a last report to the university. There was a telegram waiting for me. All the travel arrangements are confirmed. There's a train from Rimini to Vienna, and another from there to Munich. We'll be leaving on the ferry from here the day after tomorrow.'

Peter's stomach lurched. 'So soon?'

'I'm afraid so.'

'There's not much time then.'

Karl stroked his jaw wearily. 'There always is too little time, my boy. You will come to appreciate that later in life. For now, enjoy the pace that is granted to youth. Later the years will rush past. As they have for me ever since you were born.'

He glanced at his son and smiled fondly to himself.

Peter brushed the words aside. In two days he would have left the island where he had begun to feel at home. This villa with its extraordinary views, the islanders and most of all his two friends. He could already picture himself on the deck of the ferry, gazing forlornly over its creamy wake at the receding outline of Lefkas. It would all go too fast, leaving him only memories. It already felt like a bereavement.

'Will we be coming back?'

'I hope so.'

'When?'

His father shook his head sadly. 'That is out of my hands, Peter. It will be decided by wiser heads than mine. I'm sure Herr Hitler and his ministers will find a peaceful way out of the crisis. He's proved himself adept at handling these things before now.'

Peter did not reply. He had only the vaguest grasp of politics and diplomacy. He was not really interested in such affairs. They did not yet impinge on him, and there were more pressing things to consider.

His father fished his watch out of the fob of his linen waist-coat and arched an eyebrow before easing himself up on to his feet. 'I'd better get ready. Katarides is expecting us by seven.'

He stretched his back and then walked into the villa, leaving his son alone with his regrets.

The poet's house was on a steep hill overlooking the town and the sea beyond. During the winter a stream flowed close by, filling the cisterns beneath the house, thereby providing a ready supply of water when the stream dried out in the summer months. Dr Muller drove through the gate and down the small drive to the house with headlights on as the last of the light faded from the sky. Even though Spyridon Katarides had been ostracised by his family, the stipend they had deigned to pay him provided him with enough to live comfortably compared to the majority of the islanders. The house was a neat two-storey building, painted white and blue. It sat in a large garden that had once been carefully cultivated but had been left to grow wild in the main. A wizened old retainer struggled to keep nature at bay when he was not catering to the needs of his master and Andreas. His wife, equally antique, served as cook and maid to the Katarides household.

At the sound of the car the front door opened and Katarides appeared, framed by the light from within. The poet was a slender man with dark features and a finely trimmed beard that lined his jaw. He came out to greet them with a warm smile as they climbed out.

'Herr Doktor. Good to see you and your son, as always.'

He paused very briefly and nodded to Heinrich. 'And you of course, Herr Steiner. Andreas says you are abandoning your dig on the island.'

'For a while, yes.' Muller sighed. 'I hope to be able to return before too long.'

'Good, good. Please come inside.' Katarides waved them ahead of him. The door led into a hall with a tiled floor, furnished with a number of cabinets, one of which contained a selection of shotguns and a rifle. A door at the back gave out on to a large terrace that seemed to hang above the town below, now a sprawl of lights in the darkness. The loud voice of Eleni's father, the island's chief of police, came to their ears. Demetrius Thesskoudis was a short, corpulent man with thinning hair, oiled and carefully combed across his scalp. He was standing with his back to the stone balustrade, facing the table where his wife, daughter and Andreas were sitting. A single electric light provided the illumination. Already it was surrounded by a halo of insects. The policeman was regaling them with a tale about an incompetent pickpocket who had been arrested. He turned as his host and the last of the guests emerged from the house.

'Ah, there're our German friends!' He strode clumsily across the terrace and grasped Dr Muller's hand and shook it effusively, before doing the same to Heinrich. He gave Peter a cheery pat on the cheek.

'I hear you'll be leaving us in a few days.'

Peter exchanged a glance with his father as he replied. 'The day after tomorrow.'

'That's too soon. We shall miss you, eh?'

Dr Muller smiled and then he reached inside his jacket and took out a small envelope and handed it Eleni. 'You wanted this.'

Eleni opened the envelope and took out the photograph. She stared at it for a moment before showing it to her parents and then replacing it in the envelope. 'Thank you, Herr Doktor. I shall treasure it. It will be good to be reminded of my friend.' She flashed a smile at Peter. 'He has taught me so much.'

Katarides gently steered his guests towards the table that had been set on the terrace. The three Germans sat opposite those already seated while Katarides took his place at the head of the table and Thesskoudis sat at the other end. As they settled, the cicadas began to shrill in the surrounding garden.

'It seems that this has turned out to be a farewell feast.' Katarides smiled ruefully. 'A pity. Especially as I have arranged a treat for you all. But more of that later. I shall miss you, Herr Doktor. There are too few learned people on this island, and this table holds those that are,' he added smoothly for the benefit of Thesskoudis. The policeman's wife, sitting between Eleni and Andreas, smiled discreetly for an instant.

'We'll be sorry to leave. Peter and I have become very fond of the island. And young Heinrich too, I expect.'

His assistant made a show of seeming to agree with the sentiment. 'Of course. Although I am looking forward to returning to Germany.'

Their host folded his hands together. 'May we expect to see you again, Herr Steiner? Once Europe's statesmen have returned to their senses.'

'Hard to say, sir. I have learned much from my time here. Perhaps I need new experiences. New horizons. Germany offers many opportunities to young men with ambitions.'

'That is what we have been led to believe. I am sure you are right to pursue a future in your homeland. There is little that Lefkas can offer a man like yourself, once you have exhausted your curiosity in the fragments of past ages. Young men should revel in more spiritual delights. They are creatures of flesh and blood after all.'

'Aren't we all?' Thesskoudis intervened with a wink. 'It's just that we lose the urge to act on it as we grow old, fat and content.'

'I've often wondered about that . . .' his wife said quietly.

Peter had met her on several occasions and found her to be a dour, firmly built woman of few words. He was surprised at her flash of humour.

Beside her Andreas met Peter's gaze and both struggled to hide their smiles. The policeman could not help picking up on his wife's comment and he frowned at her for a moment before his irrepressible good humour caused the severe expression to crumble and he laughed. Husband and wife exchanged a brief smile before Thesskoudis turned his attention to Heinrich.

'A word of advice, young man. Never marry for love. That is the swiftest road to living under a tyranny. That was my mistake, and now I am enslaved.'

His wife glared at him. 'Enslaved! Hah!'

This time everyone around the table chuckled and the atmosphere lightened. The poet's servant appeared, dressed in plain black trousers and a white shirt, and placed two decanters of wine on the table before pouring glasses for the adults. Then he looked questioningly at his master. Katarides gave a nod and the servant half filled the glasses of the younger guests before disappearing back into the house. The host raised his glass and proposed the toast.

'To friendship. To happy marriage. To knowledge. To beauty and art. I think that defines us all.'

The others raised their glasses and then drank.

It was late in the evening before the last of the dessert dishes had been cleared away by the servant and his wife. A bottle of raki had been left on the table and Thesskoudis reached for it and turned the label towards the light as he read.

'Ah, the good stuff. From Crete. Where the best raki comes from.'

The poet smiled at the compliment. 'You have family there, I believe.'

'Indeed. My father was born there, before he was sent to school in Athens.' Thesskoudis arched his eyebrows briefly. 'As a result of a village feud, you understand.'

There were nods around the table. Peter had lived among the Greeks long enough to know that feuds were common, and that no one discussed them in polite company, unless invited to.

'And in Athens he joined the police and was posted to Lefkada, where I was born, grew up, and married the most beautiful woman on the island, until the birth of our daughter of course.' He gazed at Eleni with unabashed pride and affection. 'So I am Greek, but in my heart I am Cretan. And, as such, I know that the best raki in the whole country comes from Crete. May I?' He nodded at the bottle.

'Be my guest,' said Katarides.

The policeman went round the table and filled the small glasses and then everyone drank. Peter had tried the fiery drink on a few occasions and did his best not to wince as it seared his throat.

'Ah!' Heinrich exclaimed. 'This, I shall miss. How about you, Herr Doktor?'

Peter's father coughed lightly. 'Yes. Quite unlike schnapps . . . Yet another reminder that the world is richer for the variety that different nations bring to it.'

'There is variety, and there is quality. It is not the same thing. Some nations are destined to greatness.'

'Like Germany?' asked Andreas.

Heinrich looked at him briefly and nodded. 'Exactly.'

'And other nations are destined to decline, no doubt.'

'Of course. It is the way of things. And some nations, some races, have passed beyond decline into utter decadence.'

Andreas's eyes narrowed. 'Like Greece?'

Heinrich shook his head. 'Not Greece. I was referring to the Jews, of course. They are so decadent that they no longer even have a country of their own, and have chosen to invest themselves in the nations of others, like parasites . . .'

'Parasites, you say?' mused Katarides. 'Surely your Jews are merely one detail in a long history of migration? The peoples of the world are in a perpetual state of moving and mingling. Who is to say that my Greek blood does not descend from that of Persians, Phoenicians, Romans, and yes, even Jews? Who is to say that the same is not true of your German blood, my young friend?'

'I am an Aryan, sir. I concede that my race is the consequence of mixed breeding in the past. But we have reached a state of primacy, if not perfection, amongst the peoples of the world. Having attained that, we dare not contaminate our bloodline with that of inferior races, least of all the Jews. And that is a view shared by every nation in Europe, and any other where the Jews have left their stain. We would be better off without them. Is it not so?'

The poet was still for a moment before he nodded slightly. 'Some might agree that it is so. Though I cannot help but find that a cause for regret.'

'Regret? Why should we regret the exigencies of history? We should embrace them.'

'And where will these . . . exigencies . . . lead us? What would you do with the Jews, the children of Israel?'

Heinrich hesitated and looked round the table to gauge the feelings of the others before he continued. 'If it was my decision, I would make them live apart from the rest of us.'

'Apart? Where?'

'I do not know. A homeland of their own where they can live in peace and leave the rest of us be.'

Katarides smiled. 'It's a bit too late for that. It was the Jews who gave us the Old Testament. It was the Jews who furnished us with the Son of God. And great treasures of art and knowledge besides. But you would know this better than I. Both you, and Dr Muller.'

Muller nodded. 'It is true. We owe a debt to the Jews. Both historically and in our own time. I served alongside them in the war. They shed as much blood for Germany as anyone else.'

'Some did, I am sure,' his assistant conceded. 'But most skulked far from the front line, undermining the real men at the front. In any case, this is all academic. The truth about the Jews is known now, and the weak must give way to the strong. It is the natural order.'

Karl Muller cleared his throat. 'We have talked about this, my dear Heinrich. All great nations rise and fall in their time. Even ours.'

'That was before, Herr Doktor. Now a new Germany is rising. One that shall last a thousand years.'

A flicker of irritation crossed Muller's face before he replied. 'I'm sure that all nations on the cusp of greatness made similar claims. History decrees otherwise. How can you doubt that, given the work that we do? Our profession furnishes the proof of the ephemerality of such ambitions. That much you have learned, surely?'

His assistant shrugged. 'We live in a new age . . .'

'No we do not. Every age is beset by the same delusions. Every leader is deluded by the sense of their own eternity, and the justice of their actions. From Xerxes to Caesar and down through the ages to Napoleon, Kaiser Wilhelm and now Adolf . . .' He paused and took a deep breath. 'No one is immune.'

His assistant stared at him coldly. Before he could speak further their host leaned forward and cleared his throat. 'It's all very interesting but let's not let the Jews spoil our meal, my friends. Besides, we have heard Herr Steiner's plans for the future and I would like to hear what our other young people wish to do with their lives. What about you, Peter?'

'Me?' He started self-consciously, his mind still on the awkward exchange between his father and his assistant. 'My future?'

Katarides smiled encouragingly. 'Yes.'

Peter struggled to organise his thoughts. 'I am not sure. I would like to become an archaeologist, like my father, I suppose.'

Karl Muller shook his head. 'You don't have to say that.'

'I know. But I would like it. You have taught me to understand the value of history. That it defines us all. Tells us where we came from, why we have become as we are, and that if we learn anything from it then we can perhaps improve things. Like you told me, Papi, those who do not understand history are condemned to repeat the mistakes of the past.'

Karl Muller chuckled. 'And those who do understand history are condemned to sit, unheard, and watch it happen.'

Peter felt hurt by his father's words and his pain was

evident and at once Karl relented and raised a hand to squeeze his shoulder affectionately. 'I am sorry. I have become cynical. Anyway, I would be proud to see you continue my work. Really. Now, what about you others?' He looked across the table. 'Eleni?'

The Greek girl glanced at her father before she spoke. 'I should like to travel. I want to see more of the world. I want to see America. I want to see Hollywood.'

'And how do you propose to do that, my girl?' Thesskoudis scoffed. 'You are as pretty as a peach, but not like the great beauties seen in Old Mikalos's picture theatre. You will never be a film star. You will make some man a proud husband one day. A good man, with prospects. And you'll make a fine mother, I'm sure.'

'Hush!' his wife hissed. 'Enough from you. Let the girl speak.'

'But what more is there to say, Rosa?' he protested.

'Whatever she wants to say. Speak, girl.'

Eleni coughed and continued in a quiet voice. 'I want to be married one day. And have children. But not until I have seen things for myself, and not just in magazines or on film. I want to find a good man. With prospects, yes. But one who will love and respect me.'

'As your father does me,' her mother said gently. 'He surely does. But there is no race to find such a man, my girl. He will come, in time. Until then, do as your heart bids.'

'Your mother is right,' said Katarides. 'While you are still young, see as much of the world as you can, read as many books as you can find. Don't be satisfied with the United States. Go to the Far East. Go south to Africa. Stand in the shadow of the pyramids and on the shores of Madagascar. Fall in love, Eleni. Not just once, but many times, before you marry. And then tell your children tales of all you have seen, and all you have known. Then you will have lived . . .'

'Thus speaks the poet!' Thesskoudis laughed and poured himself another raki. 'And have you done all these things?'

'Not as many as I would like,' his host admitted. 'But I will. Or die in the attempt.'

His guests laughed. The poet's gaze turned to his son. 'And you, Andreas. How would you answer the question? What are your plans? Since you seldom speak of them to me.'

Andreas's mirth quickly faded and he looked down at his hands. 'I know one thing. I will not become a poet. I lack the necessary feeling for words.'

'Yes you do. For now. But I am no less proud of you.'

'I do not ask you to be proud of me,' his son responded with quiet defiance. 'There are other paths a man can follow.'

'Of course there are. The choice is yours.'

'Then I have chosen.'

Katarides could not hide his surprise. 'Oh? Perhaps you should explain youself.'

Andreas ran his tongue along his lips and nodded, his dark eyes making his expression intent and determined. 'I have decided to join the navy, Father.'

The poet frowned. 'The navy? Why?'

'For the very reasons you gave. To travel and see the world.'

'There are other means.'

'I know. But I also love my country and want to serve Greece. And defend her.'

'From who? That blustering fool Mussolini? He will never amount to much. And when you serve Greece you also serve that scoundrel General Metaxas, and that milksop king of ours whose strings Metaxas is pleased to pull.' For the first time that evening, Katarides's composure failed him and a raw expression of anger and pain creased his features as he continued to address his son. 'Think again. If you serve men like Metaxas, then you serve those who would stamp down on democracy and even the expression of views that run counter to theirs. Andreas, you would be holding the gun that is pointed at those people of Greece who even dare to question their government. Would you point it at me? Your father?'

Andreas sighed. 'You tell us to choose our own paths in this life, and now it seems that you hold true to that principle only as long as I agree with your politics. I am not a leftist. I have read about what the communists have done in Russia. I do not want that inflicted on Greece. I have made my decision. I will join the navy. In fact . . . I have already sent my application to the naval academy.'

'Then pray God they turn you down.'

Andreas stared back directly, with a thin smile of satisfaction. 'I have already been accepted. I am leaving Lefkas to begin training at the end of October.'

'Oh, no . . .' Eleni muttered as she stared at Andreas with a pained expression.

Katarides was silent for a moment, and there was a tense stillness around the table. Then he sat back in his chair, picked up his raki and flipped it down his throat before he spoke again. 'I see. Now I know your mind. I hope it is what you want.'

'It is.'

'Then you will appreciate the treat I have arranged for tomorrow,' Katarides responded with a touch of bitterness. 'To say goodbye to our German friends.'

Peter exchanged a brief enquiring glance with his father but Karl Muller shook his head.

'A treat?' Thesskoudis grinned. 'And what would that be, my friend?'

Katarides folded his hands together again. 'I have hired Yannis Stavakis and his fishing boat. He will take us out to the islands tomorrow. I thought a final excursion would leave a favourable impression on Dr Muller, Herr Steiner and young Peter. Sufficient to tempt them back to Lefkas in due course. The cook has prepared food for the trip. It was my intention to make a day of it. And now, thanks to my dear Andreas, we will have one more crew member than I anticipated.'

Andreas stirred uncomfortably at the barbed remark and there was a brief silence before the policeman clapped his hands together.

'Capital idea! A boating trip. Why not?'

'I thought you would approve,' Katarides responded with a quick smile, then stood up and faced his guests. 'It is late. Given that we shall be starting early, an early night is called for. I hope you will join me tomorrow on the quay at seven in the morning. Now, I am afraid, it is time to bid you all a good night.'

CHAPTER SEVEN

Yannis Stavakis was sitting stroking his white beard while sitting on a mooring post and smoking a cigarette when his passengers arrived in two cars and parked them on the side of the street opposite the quay. His boat, *Athena*, was tied up alongside. She was one of the largest fishing boats in the harbour, over twelve metres from bow strake to stern post. A small pilot house rose from the weathered timbers of the deck and a large covered hold for the catch and nets took up most of the main deck ahead of the mast. Usually Stavakis sailed with a teenage boy to help, but this day he was intending to use the engine. His was one of a handful of powered craft amongst the fishing fleet and Stavakis maintained and spoiled his engine as if it was a delicate child. Even though he begrudged paying for fuel when he could get wind for nothing he delighted in the steady vibration of the engine and was content to charge Katarides more than sufficient to cover the cost of the diesel as well as the hire of his boat.

As it was early in the day the air was still and the sea glassy and smooth and the dawn haze almost obscured the shore of the mainland. The rest of the fleet had departed hours earlier, at the first sign of light, to reach their fishing grounds. Stavakis drew heavily on his cigarette, making it flare with a soft hiss, then flicked the butt into the harbour. He stood up and bowed as Katarides approached with his party.

'A fine morning, your honour.'

It was universally known amongst the islanders that the poet from Athens came from a wealthy family, and more importantly, his writing had won widespread acclaim. Not that many on Lefkas had read his work. And so he was spoken to with a measure of sentimental respect by those who knew him slightly, even if he preferred to be called Mr Katarides.

'That it is, Stavakis. Is your craft ready?'

'Aye, your honour. Welcome aboard.' He waved them towards the edge of the quay where the deck of the boat was a short step down. Peter quickly went first and reached out a hand to help Eleni. She smiled gratefully and went to sit on the small foredeck. The others climbed down, with Andreas carrying the hamper that held the day's supply of food and drink. Stavakis indicated a small cupboard at the stern.

'You can put it in there, sir.'

Besides the poet, his son, Dr Muller and Peter, there was Eleni and her father. His wife had refused to come, having no liking at all for boats.

'It is a shame that Herr Steiner could not join us,' said Katarides.

'Yes, quite,' Karl Muller replied. 'There were some final details that needed attending to. Paperwork, that sort of thing. I thought it best to ask Heinrich to deal with it rather than rush at the last moment.'

'That is a pity. I dare say he would rather be with us than stuck in the house dealing with such details.'

'I dare say,' Muller acknowledged, then quickly looked round at the boat, noting the clean paintwork and orderly appearance of the craft and its equipment. 'This looks splendid.'

Stavakis climbed aboard and made his way to the controls in the small pilot house. A moment later the engine coughed and turned over and, after the application of a little choke, settled into a steady rhythm. Water spat from the exhaust pipe. Satisfied that it was running smoothly the fisherman emerged to untie the mooring ropes and ease his boat away from the dock. As it drifted out he returned to the wheel, slipped the engine into gear and eased the throttle open. With a gentle shudder *Athena* moved away from the quay and cut a wide easy arc across the calm water of the harbour before passing the weathered mole first built by the Venetians centuries before.

Peter, Andreas and Eleni sat on the foredeck, legs hanging over the side, revelling in the air washing over their skin and through their hair. Their fathers sat amidship, holding the stays to steady themselves. The German had brought his hat but the brim lifted and threatened to carry it away and he had to hurriedly remove it and tuck it under his spare arm. The fisherman, who knew no other life than the sea, regarded his passengers with amusement as they grinned with unalloyed delight. Glancing up at the peaks on the mainland he saw that there was no sign of the thin clouds that usually heralded a stiff breeze later in the day. The Ionian rarely experienced any storms in the summer months, but sudden, powerful winds often sprang from nowhere, and passed just as quickly, leaving the sea flat and airless.

They passed through the narrow stretch of the channel at Kariotes and the sea opened out in front of them, the mainland to their left and the coast of Lefkas to their right, and ahead in the distance the islands of Sparti, Skorpios and the larger

Meganissi, the main feature of the day's trip. Here and there were the bright triangles of distant sails, clearly visible against the startling blue of the sea. Thin trails of smoke from powered vessels were the only marks against a flawless turquoise sky.

Muller turned and shaded his eyes as he stared towards Lefkas, picking out the hill beyond which lay the small valley he had devoted years of his life to exploring. It seemed to diminish in significance before his eyes, yet he, and only he, knew of the great secret it contained. One which he would reveal to the world when he was good and ready. And then he would bask in the astonishment and admiration of his peers and share the same legendary reputation of the great Schliemann himself.

'It is a beautiful sight,' Thesskoudis broke into his thoughts. The policeman had discarded his cravat for the day and wore a light jacket over an open white shirt. He smiled warmly at the German. 'Truly I am blessed to call the island my home.'

'Indeed. It is something of an oasis in a troubled world.'

Thesskoudis gave a dismissive wave. 'Forget all that. Such things come and go.'

'I hope you are right. But my superiors in Munich are sufficiently concerned to call us back.'

'Bah, a gang of nervous old women. Pay them no mind. After all, your Chancellor, Mr Hitler, is hardly likely to want another conflict unleashed upon the world. He served in the Great War and knows the face of battle. He will not let your people endure that again.'

'I suppose not.' Muller made himself smile. 'I should not worry.'

'There! We'll make a Greek of you yet!'

Katarides had been listening as he sat, face raised towards the sun, eyes closed, drinking in its warmth. 'Perhaps this is how diplomacy should be settled. A few men sharing a boat trip. Who would not find cause to agree on terms in such a paradise? Our leaders have forgotten the simple pleasures. Those are all that matter. The rest is detail but they mistake it for the truly important aspects of life. They have lost their souls.'

'And you seem to have been drinking, my friend!' Thesskoudis laughed loudly, his fat stomach shaking. 'I have the secret of your muse . . . raki! Eh?'

'Raki? Sometimes. It could also be a beautiful woman, or a child. Or a view such as this, or even a sensation.'

'But mostly raki.'

Katarides turned to him. 'Yes, she has the easiest virtue of any muse I know.'

The other men burst into laughter and were joined a moment later by Katarides, despite himself.

The sound caused the three at the bow to look round.

'They're having fun,' said Eleni. 'And why not? How can anyone not have fun on a day like this?'

Her lips parted in a wide grin as she raised her chin and breathed deeply. Peter saw her breasts lift sharply under the cream linen cloth of her blouse and he felt his heart quicken before he remembered that this was his last day. Tomorrow he would leave Lefkas and Eleni, and he felt a sharp sorrow at the prospect. He must do something, he told himself. He must confess his feelings for her before it was too late. After all, he fully intended to return to Lefkas as soon as possible. If she knew how he really felt, maybe she would return his affection in kind. As he thought, he was aware of the contact between their bodies, thigh to thigh, and every so often the movement of the boat caused her to sway slightly against him, and then against Andreas. The proximity of her, the warmth through the cloth between them, wreathed around Peter like a heady perfume as the sea glimmered and glittered close by. And through it all the chunk-chunk-chunk of the engine.

'It would be different if Heinrich was with us,' said Andreas. 'The swine . . .'

Peter turned to him, the sun glinting off his glasses. 'Swine?'

Andreas nodded. 'You heard him last night. All arrogance and ignorance. I pity you, Peter, if there are many like him back in Germany. I've heard that National Socialism has become like a religion to your people.'

Peter could not deny it. Even before he had left to join his father he had seen the changes in his country. The removal of certain teachers at the gymnasium he had attended. The disappearance of selected books, music and even newspapers. And everywhere the relentless optimism of the converted. It did indeed have the appearance of religious fervour and he was half in awe of it, and half afraid. But there had still been plenty of relatives and friends of the family who had regarded the new regime with bemusement and quietly mocked their pompous salutes and fancy dress. It could not endure, they said. Yet Adolf Hitler and his followers seemed to be the darlings of fate. Success after success had fallen into their laps and nearly all Germany loved them for it. Maybe Heinrich Steiner was no different. Had it not been for his father's devotion to his academic discipline, and insistence on sharing that with Peter, then perhaps he too would have been seduced by the promise of the thousand-year Reich.

'Heinrich's not so bad, when you get to know him,' said Peter. 'He works hard.'

'So does our servant's mule, but that alone is not enough

in the company of others. He is a dullard. I can just see him pulling on one of those brown shirts and shining his boots the moment he returns to Germany.'

'But you are the one who wants to put on a uniform and join the navy,' Peter replied pointedly.

'Ha!' Eleni laughed. 'He has you there, Andreas!' Her laughter died away and she stared at him seriously. 'Did you really mean it?'

'Of course.'

'But I thought you were teasing your father. I was certain of it.'

'Then you were wrong.'

'But why? Why do it?'

'For the reasons I gave.'

'But there are other ways to travel and see the world, Andreas.'

He shrugged. 'But I love my country. We live in uncertain times, Eleni. I want to protect my country. My family . . . My friends. You.'

She gazed back at him for a moment, and then struck him lightly on the chest. 'You're teasing me!'

'No.'

She shook her head in wonder and turned abruptly to Peter. 'He's mad. Tell him so.'

He wanted to agree, to spare him from any dangers that might befall Greece. It was a small country, on the fringes of diplomacy. Peter knew that well enough from the news he read from home. Yet if Andreas was to attend the academy of the Royal Hellenic Navy then he would be far removed from Eleni. Far enough and for long enough for Peter not to have to share her attentions should he one day return to Lefkas.

'Andreas is right. It is the duty of everyone to protect their country. I would do the same if I were him.'

'See?' Andreas nudged her. 'Peter understands.'

'You're both boys. What is there to understand? You all like uniforms and weapons and the idea of being brave. That's all you think about . . . No. Not quite all.' she concluded with a shy expression, then shot her hand out. 'Look!'

Fifty metres ahead the sea churned and turned white and flashes of silver darted above the surface as a school of sardines was forced to the surface as they were hunted by larger, stronger fish. The three watched transfixed as the prey tried to escape amid the spray of violently disturbed water. *Athena* passed close by and Stavakis spared the spectacle a cursory glance as he steered with the tiller between his knees and opened his tobacco tin to roll another cigarette. Ahead, the long silhouette of Meganissi opened up before them. The sun had risen well above the mountains on the mainland and spread its warmth over the Ionian Sea. Stavakis eased the tiller to starboard a fraction as he altered course towards the channel between Meganissi and Lefkas. As he had anticipated, from the clearness of the sky, the air remained still and the water flat. The poet and his guests would have a fine day of it, the fisherman thought contentedly.

In front of the pilot house the three men had taken off their jackets to be more comfortable, and were sitting on the hold cover. They had finished their small talk and were enjoying the pleasure of being out at sea on such a fine day. At length Thesskoudis stirred and nodded towards their children.

'It does a man's heart good to see the youngsters so happy. It is truly a golden age to be. With everything to look forward to for the first time. Before experience begins to spoil the pleasure of it all.'

Katarides looked at him with a surprised expression. 'My dear Inspector, I had no idea you had the melancholic soul of a poet.'

The other man shrugged. 'We are no different, my friend. We feel the same about life, joy, sadness, beauty. Like all Greeks. The difference is you possess the skill to set it down in words. That is a gift I shall never have. While you write poetry, I write reports. I suppose both serve their purpose. Besides that, I have all that I could wish for in life. And I pray to God that my Eleni has the same.'

'She's a fine girl,' said Katarides. 'No. A fine young woman. I am sure you are proud of her.'

The policeman smiled self-indulgently and then, as Greeks do, he returned the compliment. 'As you must be about Andreas. A handsome lad. I know Eleni likes him, though she does not say so. But then, I am sure she is not the only girl in Lefkada who feels the same about him.'

Katarides stared at his son. The broad shoulders were hunched forward slightly as he sat wedged up against the girl, the fringe of his hair stirring in the air. 'He reminds me of his mother. I see her in his face. Now he is all that is left of her, besides memories. If I lose him, I lose everything.'

'Come now! There is no danger of that. He is strong and healthy.'

'He is that. Just the kind of young man required by governments for their wars. And that makes me fearful.'

'That is the kind of fear shared by all parents, in every age. That is life, my friend.'

'But this age worries me.'

'Why this more than any other?'

'Dr Muller knows why.'

The German had been only half listening and now started

and turned towards his companions. 'What's that? What do I know?'

Katarides smiled sadly. 'I follow wider events as best I can. After all, I am invested in mankind. And what I see in your country concerns me, Herr Doktor. Your assistant is not untypical of those who support the new regime, is he?'

Muller thought briefly before he admitted, 'No, he is not.'

'As I thought. And it disturbs you. That is why you bury yourself down here in these islands. To escape what is happening in Germany.'

'I am here because this is my work.'

'That's part of the reason.'

'It is the only reason, I assure you.'

'I am not convinced. Why else would you bring your son with you to live here? Are you trying to protect him, I wonder?'

Muller remained silent and eventually he looked down at his clasped hands. 'It is true that I would rather not be party to what is happening at home. I do not want to be involved. Here, at least, I can do something useful and worthwhile. And remove Peter from the influence of those I disagree with.'

'Like Heinrich?'

The German nodded. 'Yes.'

'And yet you allow a Nazi sympathiser to work alongside you?'

Muller pulled a face. 'I did not know about his politics when I chose him.'

'I see.' Katarides nodded. 'Where does this all lead, my friend? Tell me, what do you really think of your country's leader, and his followers?'

Muller breathed deeply and emptied his lungs in a sigh of

resignation. 'I fear they will lead Germany to a calamity which will destroy our nation, and more besides. I am convinced Hitler wants war. Everything points to it. Every mark spent on weapons, our children raised to behave like soldiers, every dissenting voice drowned out, or silenced. And everywhere, absolute insistence on blind obedience to the will of one man.' He closed his eyes. 'It is a nightmare that my people have embraced and made flesh in the light of day. There will be war . . . Again. There is an appetite for it amongst those who determine the fate of nations.' He stopped, opened his eyes and looked up with a forced smile. 'I am sorry, my friends. I did not mean to be so morose.'

'There is no need to apologise.' Katarides patted his hand. 'I thank you for your honesty.'

'Well, I hope you are wrong,' said Thesskoudis. 'I have more faith in our leaders. They will not let there be another war. I can't believe that they would allow that. Besides, what can we do about it, eh? Let it not cloud our minds. Let us enjoy the day, and enjoy being with our children. They are too young to be troubled by the world they will inherit. So banish all thought of it, at least for today.'

The poet glanced at the German and arched an eyebrow.

'For today then,' Muller agreed and looked at the three young people sitting on the foredeck. 'That much we can do for them.'

'There.' Stavakis pointed towards the limestone cliffs running along the south of Meganissi. His passengers turned to follow the direction the fisherman indicated and a moment later Peter glimpsed the dark opening in the grey rocks and grinned.

'I see it!'

As the boat neared the cave they saw the wide limestone arch and the turquoise water stretching into the shadowed interior. Stavakis eased back on the throttle and chose a spot twenty metres from the mouth of the cave. Throwing the engine into neutral he came forward and ushered the youngsters off the foredeck so that he could open the lazarette and take out the anchor. He eased the anchor over the side and let the chain run through the steel guard posts. Then he released his grip and there was a splash and a roaring clatter as the anchor plunged down through the clear water into the depths. The fisherman let the chain run out and then a length of rope before cleating it tightly and stretching up and rubbing the small of his back. He returned to the rear of the boat and a moment later the engine died away and then the only sounds were the gentle lap of the sea against the base of the cliffs and the coarse cries of a pair of seagulls wheeling through the hot air above the island.

'Is this as close as we can get?' asked Muller. 'Could we anchor inside the cave?'

Stavakis shook his head. 'Too risky. There are some big rocks just below the surface. This is close enough. You can swim into the cave, if you like.'

'Swim? I don't think so.'

'Why not?' asked Katarides, running a finger under his collar. 'I need to cool off. Who else is coming? Thesskoudis?'

The policeman laughed and shook his head. 'Not me. I can barely swim a stroke.'

Katarides looked forward. 'And you three?'

'I'll go!' said Eleni.

Thesskoudis turned to her. 'I'm not sure that's a good idea, my girl. Hardly appropriate. Besides, you have no costume.'

'I have brought costumes for us all,' Katarides announced. 'Eleni can wear one of those.'

'I'm not sure I can allow her—'

'Tshh! Nonsense. Why deprive the girl of the chance?'

'What about the others?' Thesskoudis asked, hoping that they would demur and discourage Eleni from entering the water.

'I'll go,' Andreas announced and then Peter took up the challenge as well.

Katarides smiled. 'It's settled then.'

He stripped off his shirt, picked up the bag containing the costumes and towels and moved round behind the pilot house to change. The boys joined him and then moved forward to allow Eleni the necessary privacy for her to put on her borrowed costume. She emerged in a blue and white striped bathing suit that Andreas had last worn a few years earlier, her hair tightly tied back with a thin ribbon. She stood before the others self-consciously as they looked at her.

'It's a bit big,' she said, plucking at the loose cloth over her breasts. Peter glanced aside with embarrassment before he removed his glasses and carefully placed them on top of his small bundle of clothes.

Andreas cocked his head to one side. 'You look good in that. Really.'

Katarides clapped his hands together. 'So what are we waiting for? Let's have a race. First one to that rock there, just inside the cave. Come.'

He clambered over the side and dropped clumsily into the sea with a big splash. He emerged an instant later flicking the water from his face as he reached up and clasped the side of the boat. Andreas climbed on to the foredeck and dived in, creating a neat circle of spray. Eleni and Peter followed the example of the poet and then all four were lined up against the hull, holding on.

'Ready?' Katarides asked, leaning out to look along the line. 'Go!'

The four swimmers surged forward in a flurry of limbs and spray as they struck out for the wide opening of the cave. Both Katarides and his son swam regularly in the sea off Lefkada and soon took the lead. Peter did his best to keep up, kicking out furiously as his arms stroked through the water. As was to be expected in a culture that looked on the idea of women swimming with disdain, Eleni's lack of experience caused her to lag behind, but she made a characteristically determined effort to do her best as she attempted to chase the others. On the boat the other men looked on with bemused expressions until Stavakis cleared his throat loudly and spat over the side.

Halfway to the rock Peter saw that he was closing on Andreas and his father and he drove himself on, desperate to prove himself in front of the others, and Eleni in particular. Ahead, Katarides was starting to fall behind his son and as they came within the last ten metres of the rock, Peter overtook the poet, with Andreas only a length in front. His Greek friend slowed and looked back, and then kicked hard, cutting across Peter in a final rush to the rock. He slapped the hard surface and gave an incoherent shout of triumph.

Peter reached out to the rock beside him, gasping for breath. Andreas's father joined them.

'You swim like fish, both of you.'

Andreas shook his head with a rueful expression. 'You let me win . . . Like you always do.'

'No, my son. Not any more . . . And where is Eleni?'

All three turned to see her splashing steadily towards them.

Katarides spoke quietly over their laboured breathing. 'She's got great heart, that one. She has the making of a fine woman.'

With a final few strokes she joined them and clung to the rock as she caught her breath. 'Who . . . won?'

'Andreas,' Peter replied. 'Of course.'

He gestured beyond the rock. 'Why, this cave is huge!'

The roof of the cave curved high above them and beyond the opening to the sea it stretched to the right, in a dog-leg. There was a small strip of sand at the far end, where the roof was at its lowest. Due to the gloom it was hard to judge the distance to the tiny beach.

'Let's swim over there.' Peter suggested, then turned to Eleni who was still breathing heavily. 'If you can manage it.'

She splashed some water in his face and immediately began to swim into the dim recess of the cave. Peter set off after her. The others watched them briefly before Andreas turned to his father.

'Are you coming?'

'No . . .'

There was something pained in his manner that caused Andreas to pause. 'What's the matter, Father?'

'It's nothing, really. I came here once before, with your mother. When I was only a few years older than you are.'

'Oh.'

Katarides reached out and squeezed his son's shoulder affectionately. 'You go. I'll wait here a moment and return to the boat.'

His son nodded and then eased himself away from the rock and swam after his friends. Katarides's gaze followed him for a while and he felt the warm glow of paternal pride in his heart. There was an ache too. The very presence of Andreas always reminded him of the wife he had lost. He should not have agreed to return here, he decided. The memory was too painful. He took a deep breath and headed back towards the boat, rocking very gently on the calm sea. Behind him the echoes of the splashes made by the youngsters echoed off the rock face.

As Peter neared the thin crescent of the beach he lowered his feet and found that he could easily touch the sandy bottom. He waded in until his chest rose from the surface and waited for Eleni to find her footing. Andreas was still some distance off.

'I wonder how long this cave has been here,' Peter mused. His thoughts flitted to the tales of ancient mythology he had been raised on. If the cave had existed in the age of Odysseus then maybe the king himself had known of it, or even come inside and stood in the same place where Peter was now. The thought thrilled him.

Eleni cupped a hand to her mouth and called out, 'Cooieee!'

The cry came back to her, shrill and distorted, before it quickly died away. She grinned with pleasure. Peter smiled back and then attempted a yodel, laughing at the cacophony returned to him from the rocks. They experimented with some more noises while waiting for Andreas to join them and then all three waded through the shallows and slumped down on to the cool sand and gazed back down the length of the cave to where the sun shone in at a steep angle, turning the surface of the water into a glittering, shimmering spectacle whose reflections danced across the cave's interior.

'Quite beautiful,' said Eleni.

'Yes,' Peter repeated, looking at her sidelong. 'Very.'

She was aware that she was being watched and turned to him, a slight frown on her brow. 'What is it?'

'Nothing. Just thinking about this place. The people who have been here before us, all the way back to antiquity. I don't know, it's almost like there's something of them still in the air.'

Andreas shrugged. 'That's the sort of thing my father would say. I like it well enough, but . . .'

'But?' Eleni nudged him.

'It is just a cave.'

'Just a cave. Have you no soul, Andreas Katarides?' Eleni scolded him. 'There is a magic here, if you would let yourself feel it. As Peter does.'

'If I were younger, then maybe I would feel it. But I can't afford to think like that when I enter the naval academy. I will have little time for sentiment.'

'But that is later. Now you are one of us. You can still share your feelings with your friends. Can't you?' she concluded with a slight pleading tone. 'Surely this moment in this place means something to you?'

'I shouldn't bother with him,' Peter interrupted in a light tone. 'He thinks he is too grown up for us, Eleni.'

'If that's so, then he is a fool. We are friends. Firm friends. That's something that lasts longer than childhood, if it means anything. Will you forget us when you join the navy, Andreas?'

'Of course not.'

'Then why distance yourself from us now?'

He thought briefly. 'You are right, Eleni. I am sorry. It's just that—'

She quickly pressed the tips of her fingers against his lips. 'Shh! Say nothing else. In fact, let's be quiet for a moment. And make a wish.'

They did as she bid them, and sat on the cool sand and

gazed towards the flickering display of light and colour at the opening of the cave. At length Eleni drew a deep breath. 'There. It's done. I have made my wish.'

'And?'

She hesitated a moment. 'I wished that we three would be together again one day. When we are all grown up, and still good friends. I can think of nothing I want more at this moment. What about you, Peter?'

He smiled warmly at her, and felt a small stab of guilt and pain as he lied. 'I wished the same.'

'And you, Andreas?'

The older boy pursed his lips. 'Why not?'

'Is that what you wished for?'

'It is now.'

Eleni grinned. 'Very well then. Let's promise that it will be so. Let's make a vow that we will do this again. Whatever we choose to do, wherever we go, whoever we meet, we swear that we will never lose touch with each other and that we will come back here, as friends, and share this again. Swear it.'

'I swear it, Eleni,' Peter agreed at once.

Andreas looked at them both indulgently and then shrugged. 'Why not? Together again one day. I swear it.'

CHAPTER EIGHT

Norwich, 2013

'And did it happen?' asked Anna.

Eleni glanced at her. 'Did what happen?'

'Did you ever go back to the cave?'

'No. Not that cave at least. Nor did I end up seeing much of the world. We did meet again, but not in the way that I had hoped we would, my dear.' She smiled thinly. 'It was foolish of me to even suggest it. But you will know how impulsive young girls can be.'

An image of her year nine class flashed through her mind, with Amelia casting a forlorn look at Jamie. 'Oh yes. I know that well enough.'

They shared a smile across the generations before Anna spoke again. 'It sounds like you had both of those boys eating out of your hand.'

Eleni nodded. 'I knew that Peter had feelings for me. But as good a friend as he was – *then* – I never felt the same about him. I did not wish to tell him, and hurt him. It was Andreas who had won my heart. Tall, handsome and perhaps a little too serious, but the first man I ever loved.' Eleni gave a dry cough. 'I'm thirsty, my girl. Could you make us some more coffee?'

'Of course, Yiayia.' Anna rose from her chair.

'And there's some biscuits there too.'

'Yes, Yiayia,' Anna paused at the door. 'Anything else?'

Eleni shook her head. She waited for her granddaughter to leave the room and the door to close before she gazed down at the faded photograph album in her lap and began to leaf slowly through the early pages again, pausing to stroke one of the pictures with a trembling finger.

Out in the kitchen Anna filled the cafetière, turned the kettle on and then pulled out a stool and sat at the counter. She began to think over what her grandmother had told her about her early life in Lefkada. Anna already knew a little about her childhood, but very little of the war years, nor the years immediately before and after the catastrophe that befell Greece. It had been fascinating to hear Eleni's recollections, and to get some sense of the characters of Dieter's forebears, as well as some further description of Andreas. Clearly there had been a tension between the three of them all those years ago. Had that been the catalyst for whatever had followed? Anna wondered.

The urge to know more was tempered by a little guilt. Eleni was old and frail, despite the strength of her spirit and the sharpness of her mind. Anna would need to be careful not to distress her.

When the coffee was ready Anna took down a plain china mug from the shelf beside the cooker and poured the dark liquid. Eleni drank coffee strong and black, with two heaped spoonfuls of sugar – 'as dark as the devil and as sweet as an angel's kiss', as she used to say to the young Anna when she used to make her grandmother's coffee. It had always made Anna think she was brewing something special, something magical.

Taking down the sugar pot she dropped in two spoons before giving the mug a good stir. The biscuits, as ever, were in an old Quality Street tin and Anna placed a selection of custard creams and chocolate digestives on a side plate before returning to her grandmother's room.

Eleni hurriedly closed the photograph album and set it down beside her chair, leaning it up against a dark varnished leg.

'Thank you, my dear.' She smiled as Anna set the mug and plate down on the table beside her. 'You're not having any?'

'Not today. Only when I am teaching and need to have all my wits about me. That's when I hit the caffeine.'

Eleni tutted. 'Is it so hard to be a teacher? In my day, we feared them. If we could not answer a question or, worse, answered back, then . . .' she made a quick slapping gesture with her hand.

'Yes, well, that sort of discipline is a thing of the past.'

'A pity.' Eleni nodded, missing the point. 'The world always changes, and not often for the better.'

Anna saw the chance to further her line of enquiry and cleared her throat lightly. 'Speaking of change, what happened after Peter and his father left the island? Did they manage to return, before the war began?'

'No. It was the last time I saw Dr Muller. A pity. I always thought he was a good man, for a German.'

'And Peter?' Anna already knew the answer but wanted to glean as much additional information as she could.

Eleni was still briefly before she nodded. 'He came back to the island. But he was not the same Peter by then. That is a lesson life needs to teach us. Some people, even those you consider friends, are never what you think they are. Or at least they become something you no longer recognise. Anyway, my dear, I'd rather not think about him.'

'All right. What about Andreas? Did he go and join the navy?'

'He did. Early the next year. That was nineteen thirty-nine. I didn't see him for several months. There were letters. But he seemed distant, and just told me the details of his training, never anything more.'

'More?'

'About how he felt. I missed that. Before, he had talked to me, looking me in the eyes, and he made me feel . . . good.'

Anna chuckled. 'You had a crush on him.'

'Crush?' Eleni's expression hardened. 'Yes, I understand the term. No, it was not a crush. That's too light a word for what I felt.' She paused and smiled at the unintended pun. 'You youngsters lack the quality of feeling my generation once knew.'

'Do you really think so?' Anna challenged her.

'Of course. I see the newspapers. And some of the programmes on television! Like your mother watches sometimes. *Big Brother*, I think.' Eleni's features wrinkled with distaste. 'Bare bodies and stupid, shameless fools.'

'Oh, it's not that bad. Just a little harmless entertainment.'

'Really? Your generation seems to surround itself with such rubbish. Not just on television. All those magazines in the supermarkets. Those small computers and telephones that you carry around like tiny shrines. Always twittering and such.' She raised her hands in exasperation. 'You no longer know what is important in life. You no longer know what it is to care enough for the big things that really matter.'

'Such as?' Anna was no longer smiling. She felt irritated by her grandmother's dismissal of the world that had left the old woman behind. It was such a trite response to change that she almost felt embarrassed by Eleni. 'What are the big things that matter then, Yiayia?'

'Your family, marriage, children and respect for the

traditions in which they live. That's what matters, Anna.'

'And you think I don't care about that? And neither does anyone else my age?'

'Not enough. Not any more. Look around you, Anna. How many of your friends are married? How many have divorced? How far would they really go to protect their loved ones? Do they have any respect for their country? What sacrifice would they make for anything that did not involve their selfish interests? Eh? Answer me that honestly.'

'We still care for the things that matter. If we ever had to face danger, like your generation did, then I am sure we would do our best to overcome it.'

'How do you know that, unless you are put to the test? You have life so easy. You have never known hunger. Never been in fear of your life. Never seen your loved ones killed before your eyes . . .'

'I can't deny that. But there is plenty of suffering elsewhere in the world. And many young people do what they can to help.'

'Oh?' Eleni eased herself forward. 'What is it that you do then? What sacrifice do you make?'

Anna took a calming breath. 'I support charities . . . I am a member of the Green Party.'

Eleni cackled and clapped her thin bony hands. 'Such a noble creature! Do you really think those are sacrifices worthy of the name, my girl?'

'They're all I have time for. Life is busy these days. But I like to think that I would do what was right if I ever had to be tested, as you were. In any case,' Anna continued in a lighter tone, 'your generation had few distractions. You had more time than my generation does.'

'Did we though?' Eleni sat back and seemed to sink into

her chair so that she almost seemed to be little more than a crumpled throw hastily slung on to the piece of furniture. She reached for her mug and her hand trembled as she raised it to her lips and took a cautious sip. She held the mug in both hands for a moment to savour its warmth, then returned it to the side table. Fixing her gaze on her granddaughter, she spoke again in a strained tone. 'When I was young every minute of life was precious. Every morning I woke I felt like it would be my last. I never expected to live to this age. To have children, or grandchildren. Every breath I took was a gift, Anna. That's how I regarded time.'

She fell silent and after a moment reached for her mug again and began to blow gently across the surface. As Anna watched her the only sound in the room was the intrusive rhythmic ticking of a clock on the mantelpiece. At length Anna steeled herself and spoke again.

'You are talking about the war.'

Eleni's brow knitted. 'Of course I am. Those who lived through it are cursed to never forget. Even now, I can close my eyes and see it all. Sometimes I go back there in my dreams. I live it again . . .'

'Would you tell me more about it?'

'Why?'

Anna leaned forward and took her grandmother's hand and spoke with real feeling. 'Because I am interested. I want to know you better.'

'Before it is too late, and all my memories are gone?'

Anna hesitated. 'Yes. So much is lost if it is not shared. I am a history teacher. I appreciate the value of the past. You know things that are important to pass on to younger generations. Some things should not be forgotten.'

'They should not,' Eleni agreed emphatically.

'I want to teach my students about what you experienced. I want them to understand what you went through so that they don't take things for granted, like you said. Will you talk to me about it, Yiayia?'

'Yes, of course. What do you want to know?'

Anna rested her elbows on her knees and leaned closer. 'Tell me what you can remember of the war. You were describing what happened after Andreas left for the naval academy.'

'Yes, that's right . . .' Eleni collected her thoughts. 'That was in nineteen thirty-nine. A terrible year. At the time we were largely unaware of it. We carried on living as we always did. I finished school. There was little point in a girl continuing to get an education in those days when all that we were supposed to do was get married and bear children. So I helped my mother about the house and she in turn began to look for a suitable husband. Not that she told me. I didn't need to be told. I knew. I also knew that I wanted Andreas, and that the longer he stayed away, the less he would remember the girl waiting for him back in Lefkada.'

'Did he tell you that he had feelings for you?'

'He never said it, but I was sure that I saw it in his eyes, the day he left. Which made it all the more painful for me when I imagined that Andreas would soon forget about me once he reached the academy in Piraeus.' She paused for a moment, staring out of the window, then suddenly looked round.

'Sorry, my dear. I forgot where I was . . . Ah, yes. Nineteen thirty-nine. You're a teacher, I'm sure you know the history of that year better than me. There was a radio in a coffee house by the harbour. We heard all about it there. The Germans had already humbled the Czechs and turned on Poland. As the months passed, war came to be seen as inevitable. We Greeks hoped to be spared any part in it. Even though General Metaxas had oppressed his people in the same way the fascists had in Italy and Germany, he had no desire to join their alliance. Perhaps he was shrewd enough to see what lay ahead for Hitler and that fat *kerata*, Mussolini, and wanted to spare himself and his people. I don't know. Either way, Greece was not ready for war. We heard that Poland had been crushed between the Germans and the Russians and then it seemed that nothing happened over the winter into the next year. I remember praying in the church that the fighting was done and that there would be peace, just so that there was no prospect of Andreas being drawn into the conflict.'

'What about Peter? Did you think about him?'

'Of course . . . He was too young to be a soldier that year. All the same I worried about him and his father. I wrote them a letter but there was no reply. My father told me that it was because the postal service between Germany and the outside world was already tightly controlled by the Nazis. War made it impossible to communicate with Peter. Then, in spring, the Germans attacked France. Andreas was due to have leave them, but it was cancelled at the last moment and he was assigned to a submarine crew. The Greek government could see the way things were going and King Georgios gave orders to prepare for war.' Eleni puffed her cheeks. 'It is so different now. There's no monarchy in Greece these days, of course. Some say that might be a good thing, but look at the state of Greece now!' She frowned. 'Where was I? Ah, yes. King Georgios. He was a weak man, and we Greeks knew it and despised him for it. Too weak to deal with the fascists. Mussolini wanted to win some glory for himself. Germany had conquered France, so he turned to Greece, determined to have a war with someone Italy could defeat easily.'

A defiant glint shone in her eyes as she continued. 'At least that's what he thought, no doubt. The Italians had occupied Albania and started to stage attacks on their own outposts, claiming our forces were responsible and that Metaxas was attempting to provoke a conflict. He stayed his hand, but began to mobilise our forces in readiness. Even the naval cadets. Then we heard the news that a Greek warship, the *Elli*, had been torpedoed in the harbour at Tinos. The ship sank, hundreds died, and even though everyone in Greece suspected the Italians, Mussolini claimed that it was a British submarine that had carried out the attack. And still Metaxas refused to take the bait. That was in August. Two months later, having tried everything, Mussolini told the Greeks that they must let his armies cross Greek territory to reinforce Albania. If we did not let him trample over our land, then he would declare war on us.' Eleni shrugged wearily. 'What could Metaxas do? He may have been a dictator but he was enough of a Greek to stand up to Mussolini and tell him "No!"'

Eleni took another sip of coffee and closed her eyes for a moment. Silence returned to the room and Anna sat still, waiting for her to continue. At length Eleni coughed lightly and looked up.

'So we were at war. The very thing I had come to fear most. You know Lefkas. You know that it faces the coast of Italy across the Adriatic Sea. There was nothing between our island and the fascists and we were afraid. Not so afraid that we were prepared to let them take our country without a fight. It was just the fear that comes when facing great uncertainty. And, at that time, I wondered if I would ever see Andreas alive again . . .'

CHAPTER NINE

Sivota, Lefkas, December 1940

The Royal Hellenic Navy submarine *Papanikolis* lay along-side the wooden pontoon that extended from the quay. Camouflage netting had been rigged over the vessel, the pontoon and the short stretch of open water between them and the shore in order to give some semblance of consistency to the shape of the bay to any enemy aircraft flying over the island. There had been many in the early days of the war, but the Greek fighters at the airfield at Preveza had shot down several and now the Italians gave the area a wide berth, save for the occasional reconnaissance aircraft, flying at high altitude with an escort. Too high to make out sufficient detail on the ground.

Which was as well, Sub-Lieutenant Andreas Katarides decided as he disembarked from the caique that had conveyed him and a handful of replacements from the mainland. Despite the camouflage netting there was plenty of evidence of activity that would reveal a military presence to any discerning photo reconnaissance officer. Three trucks were parked at the end of the quay and several crates of shells for the deck gun, as well as a row of torpedoes lying on their chocks in the open. The tents of the artificers and other maintenance teams lay in neat lines at the edge of the nearest terrace of olive trees. Worse still were the rainbow hues of a fuel spill that covered a broad expanse of the bay close to the hidden submarine.

Stepping off the gangway Andreas lowered his kit bag and stared across at the boat he had been assigned to, fresh from the academy. The graduation of his class had been brought forward to cope with the demand for men to fill out the ranks of the rapidly expanding navy. Andreas had been fortunate to secure a posting to a regular crew. Many of his comrades had been sent to serve on hastily converted vessels, or the handful of recommissioned ships dating back to the turn of the century. They would be deathtraps if ever they were unfortunate enough to come up against any of the more powerful warships of the Italian navy.

By contrast, *Papanikolis* was a modern vessel, bought from the French some years earlier. Her captain was equally formidable, Andreas had learned. Lieutenant Commander Iatridis was one of the most experienced submariners in the Hellenic navy. He had addressed the cadets at the academy shortly before the war between the great powers had broken out. Even though he was a thin, short man, Iatridis had a a deep, booming voice and he had had a dramatic effect on the aspiring young men with his fiery patriotism and fierce devotion to the service. Here was a man that Andreas felt he could willingly follow into battle and he had been delighted when he had been told he was to serve under Iatridis.

The submarine itself lay low in the water, painted dark grey, with sleek lines. The narrow deck was crowded with sailors passing supplies down through the hatches. Forward, several men manned a hoist as they strained to guide a torpedo into the angled chute leading down into the racks behind the tubes. A small Greek flag hung limply from the post at the rear of the conning tower. Andreas looked round the bay towards the cluster of whitewashed houses that lay behind the fishing boats drawn up on the beach. A handful of men were busy mending nets, chatting loudly as they smoked pipes. Beyond, some women busied themselves with laundry at a shallow stone trough, kneading the bundled cloth roughly before taking the clothes out to dry. Children chased each other in between the buildings while infants sat close to their mothers, playing in the dust. A narrow track, barely wide enough for the lorries, wound up through the olive terraces and then into the oak trees and gorse where the incline became steeper. And so the track continued, zigzagging up the side of the hill until it joined a wider road linking Sivota to the rest of the island.

It had been over two years since Andreas had last visited the quiet fishing village and he felt a tinge of sadness that the war had intruded on its solitude and disfigured the placid scenery. At the same time, from a professional perspective, the submarine's base was well-chosen. The entrance to the bay was invisible from the open sea, due to the dog-leg in the channel. There was enough deep water for the submarine to turn easily and the steep sides of the surrounding hills sheltered the vessel and her crew from attack by air. Now that he considered the prospect, Andreas looked along the ridge line and saw a sandbagged machine-gun post, the fat barrel of a Hotchkiss gun pointing up at the sky with a sentry lounging beside it, leaning on the sandbags as he stared out to sea. A quick glance round the bay revealed the presence of two more posts covering the base. Hardly sufficient to defend it from a serious attack, but more than enough to give the sailors warning of the approach of the enemy by sea or sky.

The other replacements had already started off on the short

walk along the shore to the pontoon and Andreas hefted his kitbag on to his shoulder and followed them. A sailor armed with a rifle was standing guard at the end of the pontoon and the new arrivals presented their papers to him. From the brief manner with which the sailor glanced at the official forms Andreas guessed that like many of his countrymen the sailor was barely literate. He waved the ratings through and then stood stiffly to attention and exchanged a salute with the young officer.

'Sub-Lieutenant Katarides, appointed to *Papanikolis*,' Andreas announced formally. 'Where can I find the captain?'

The sentry turned and indicated a small cluster of tents erected in the shade of the nearest trees. 'Over there, sir. Seated at the table.'

Andreas nodded in acknowledgement and put down his kitbag. 'See to it that this is taken aboard for me.' Then he strode towards his new commanding officer. Iatridis sat in his whites with a panama hat shading his eyes from the glare as he attended to paperwork. He looked up as soon as he became aware of the young officer approaching his desk, but kept his pen poised above the form he had been completing. He did not speak for a moment after Andreas had made his introduction, but ran his eyes over the new arrival and ended by staring hard at him. Andreas forced himself to meet his commander's gaze unflinchingly. Iatridis had a broad, worn-looking face, heavily weathered and lined, with a small, neatly trimmed moustache that merged with the dark stubble on his heavy jowls. His dark eyes were sharp and glinted with intelligence. His body, however, seemed to belong to another man with its slender, wiry frame from which his clothes hung loosely. There was a pause before Iatridis nodded slightly, with apparent satisfaction, and lowered his pen and stretched his back.

'I asked for you by name, Katarides. Do you know why?'

'I assume it had something to do with my knowledge of these waters, sir.'

'That, and the commendation of your instructors at the naval academy. They seem to respect your ability well enough, and I need good men on my boat.'

'Thank you, sir.'

Iatridis's lips lifted in a brief smile. 'Don't thank me so readily. I'll be taking the *Papanikolis* to sea the day after tomorrow. That won't give you much time to familiarise yourself with the boat and the crew but that can't be helped. You'll serve as my navigator. The previous incumbent failed to meet the standard I require from my officers and has been reassigned to shore duties. If you fail me the same will happen to you. Understand?'

'Yes, sir.' Andreas felt a passing instant of anxiety before his resolve hardened. 'You can rely on me, sir.'

'I'm going to have to, Lieutenant.' Iatridis removed his hat and ran a hand through his thick dark hair. 'We're at war. This is what we have trained for. We did not want to fight, but it has been forced on us and now we must defend Greece, and our people, with our lives. So far, our brothers in the army are holding off the enemy. From the latest reports it even appears that we are driving those Italian dogs back. Now it's our turn, Katarides. But I must warn you, our navy is badly outnumbered and outgunned and when we sail to war there's a good chance we will not be coming back. My orders are to patrol the Adriatic and attack Italian shipping wherever it is encountered. Priority targets are supply and troopships. Naturally they are likely to be protected, which will make our task hazardous. But, as I said, we are at war. It is our duty to make sacrifices for our country. Even these boys.' He gestured towards the sailors toiling on and around the sub-marine. 'Many of them have been in uniform for a matter of months and hardly any of my men have ever seen a shot fired in anger. Come to that, nor have I.' He shared a quick smile with Andreas before his expression became serious again. 'So, the time has come for us all to be tested, Lieutenant, and I am determined that we shall not be found wanting.'

'I am confident we will all do our duty, sir.'

'Of course you are,' Iatridis responded briskly. 'You'd better stow your kit and find the first officer. Lieutenant Pilotis is on board. He'll show you your station, and assign you a berth. Dismissed.'

He saluted casually as Andreas stood to attention and snapped his hand to the brim of his cap, as he had been taught at the academy. Then he turned and relaxed his posture as he strode towards the pontoon and made for the gangway. Crossing the narrow wooden board he stepped on to the steel hull of the submarine. A thrill of excitement coursed through his veins at the sensation of setting foot on *Papanikolis*. This was the moment his training had led up to. This was the moment when he stopped being a cadet and became a leader of men.

Andreas was aware that some of the men were casting glances his way, already judging him. He straightened his back and took a long appraising look up and down the length of the boat, trying to appear as professional as possible. Steeling himself, he ducked through the hatch into the attack bridge and stood over the hatchway leading down into the heart of the submarine.

'Coming down!'

The metal rungs of the ladder rang dully under his boots and a moment later he stood on the plated deck of the main bridge. The sounds of voices from other compartments carried on the still, humid air and Andreas felt hemmed in by the pipes, valves and dials of the vessel's controls. In the middle of the cramped space stood the gleaming columns of the submarine's two periscopes and ahead the seats for the men who controlled the steering planes. The air stank of diesel oil and sweat. A short, thickset man in a stained boiler suit, unbuttoned to his breast, leaned over the navigation table, concentrating on a slide rule. Wisps of his light brown hair lifted under the influence of an electric fan slowly sweeping the centre of the bridge.

Andreas cleared his throat. 'Where's the first lieutenant?'

The man looked up with a weary smile. 'You found him.'

Andreas was surprised by the first officer's scruffy appearance but he quickly stiffened and saluted. 'Sub-Lieutenant Katarides, sir. Just arrived from Athens with orders to report to *Papanikolis*.'

'So I understand. You, and those other green recruits I saw stumble off the caique.'

Andreas had experienced prejudice towards newcomers at every stage of his short naval career, but it still piqued his sense of pride. He knew better than to let it show and kept still and quiet while his superior watched him with an amused expression.

'Relax, Katarides. I'm sure you'll do fine. You're to be the new navigator, right?'

'Yes, sir.'

'Then this is your station.' He stood up from the small table and waved Andreas over. 'Don't suppose the navy equipped you with any new charts or equipment?'

'I have my own set of instruments, but no charts, sir.'

'That's a damn shame. Ours are years out of date. I sent a

request for fresh charts months ago.' He shrugged. 'But you know what the ministry is like. I swear to Holy God that if we lose this war it will be because of the bureaucrats on our side rather than the soldiers, sailors and airmen of Mussolini.'

Andreas could not help smiling and the two shared a brief laugh that eased the tension.

'Mind you,' said Pilotis, 'from what I've heard the bureaucrats in Italy are working hard for our side in return. That's the only explanation for the poor show the Italians are putting on. They have more men and more guns but somehow don't manage to put the latter into the hands of the former. Which is as well, otherwise Metaxas would be out on his arse and King Georgios would be running into exile.'

The frank expression of his disdain for the leaders of Greece might have shocked Andreas more if he had not grown up hearing the same refrain from his father.

'So, you are good at maths?' Pilotis cocked an eyebrow.

'I passed fifth in my class, sir. That's why I was chosen to specialise in navigation.'

'Good, then you'll know what to do with this.' Pilotis tossed the slide rule to Andreas who nearly fumbled the catch. 'What did your father do? Banker? Accountant? Teacher?'

Andreas shook his head. 'A poet.'

Pilotis looked surprised and froze for an instant. 'A poet? Holy God, what is the son of a poet doing in the navy?'

'The same as any other Greek, sir. Defending his country.'

Pilotis chuckled. 'Good answer. I'm sure they loved you at the academy . . . Wait, a poet you say? Not any relation of Spyridon Katarides? He's supposed to live in these islands, I think.'

'He does. Right here on Lefkas.' Andreas hesitated. 'He's my father.'

A smile slowly stole across the other man's face and he nodded gently. 'Well, well . . . I've read your old man's work. Good stuff. Even when he was trying too hard to be great. I preferred his early poems, where he describes the pleasures of wine and women. Went off his work when he turned his attention to our geography and ancient heritage. Still, I expect you must be proud of him.'

'Of course. I am proud of all my family.'

'And what does he make of his little boy now, I wonder?' Pilotis cocked his head to one side. 'Katarides was a bit of a radical, I recall. Denounced both the King and Metaxas in his time and had no love of the military. And yet, here you are.'

'My father's politics are his own, sir. I have chosen a different path.'

'Evidently . . . And from the strained note in your voice I conclude that the radical poet disapproves of his conventional son.'

There was a beat as Pilotis waited for a response, but Andreas stared back stolidly, his lips pressed together in a thin line. The other man shrugged.

'Never mind. Art's loss is the navy's gain. Serve the captain well and you'll do fine aboard *Papanikolis*. You've already met him, I take it?'

'Yes, sir.'

'And what do you make of Iatridis?'

'Sir?'

'You cannot be unaware of his reputation.'

Andreas did not like this line of questioning and resolved to be cautious about passing any measure of judgement on his commanding officer. 'I saw Lieutenant Commander Iatridis speak at the academy. He is a respected officer, sir.'

'Not respected by all, though.' Pilotis raised a grimy hand and ran it through his hair. 'His superiors took a dim view of his call for the navy to take the offensive at the Italians at the outbreak of hostilities. And even before then. The captain was all set to torpedo the first Italian ship he came across following the sinking of the *Elli*. He said that the sooner we bloodied Mussolini's nose, the sooner the Italians would back down and leave Greece alone. Metaxas and his friends in the navy ministry took the opposite line and hoped that if they did not react to the provocation then peace could be maintained. Some hope of that.' Pilotis sniffed. 'You know how it is with bullies. If you don't give them a reason to respect you then you only invite further aggression. For what it's worth, I agreed with Iatridis . . .'

He looked questioningly at the newly arrived officer. Andreas felt increasingly uncomfortable but he grasped that he was being tested by Pilotis.

'It was my impression that we should have taught the Italians a sharp lesson at the time as well,' he said.

Pilotis nodded. 'Good. That's the kind of view that our captain, and the rest of us, approves of. So, welcome aboard, Katarides.' He stretched his back, automatically tilting his head just enough to avoid the valve above him in the cramped space. He offered his hand and Andreas took it and they shook. 'Now that those spaghetti-lovers have given the captain the excuse he needs, they're going to pay for their treachery with blood,' he concluded with a cold, ruthless edge to his voice.

For a moment there was a stillness in the confines of the submarine, then the breeze of the fan washed over the two men and Pilotis stirred. 'Did the boat bring you here directly from Athens?'

'Yes.'

'Then you haven't had time to visit your home. A pity. I doubt that you'll get the chance before we go to sea. Perhaps there may be time when we return.'

Andreas noted the hope offered in the first officer's last words and responded with a smile. 'I hope so. I haven't been home in over two years.'

'Your father will be pleased to see you. Perhaps he'll even write you a poem about it, eh? And there'll be friends glad to see you. A woman perhaps?'

Andreas tried to ignore the fishing and coughed. 'Can I see my quarters, sir?'

'Quarters?' Pilotis smiled. 'Your bunk is in the next compartment, with the rest of the officers. Only the captain gets his own cabin on the *Papanikolis*. Come, follow me.'

The first officer turned and led the way through the bridge and ducked through the hatchway into the next section of the submarine. A narrow corridor led between a handful of openings on either side. Beyond the range of the fan the air was uncomfortably foetid.

'Radio room to the right.' Pilotis gestured towards a cell with a single seat in front of a large wireless set that left just enough space for the operator to use as a desk for his code book and notepads. 'Toilet to the left. There's just the one on this boat. Apparently the designers added it as an afterthought, given that there's seventy in the crew. Just pray that it doesn't break . . . Next one's sound detection and the cook is opposite. Then there's the captain's cabin, officers' wardroom,' he indicated a narrow table and padded bench with storage cupboards behind, 'and here's the officers' bunks.'

Andreas glanced round his companion and saw three bunks on either side. Just wide enough to lie down on and too low to allow the occupant to sit up. There was a shelf on the inside of each bunk and upright lockers at the end, one for each man. Andreas saw that his kitbag had been leant against the lockers.

'The top bunks are for me and the chief engineer. Then the second officer and you. The lower bunks are for the warrant officers. Make yourself at home, Katarides.'

Andreas looked ruefully at the private space allotted to him, about the same size as a coffin. He frowned at the comparison and a brief, haunting vision of himself trapped in his bunk as the submarine sank passed through his mind. He forced the thought aside as he glanced back to Pilotis and made himself smile. 'Home . . .'

They were interrupted by the clatter of boots on the steel rungs in the bridge and a moment later the captain hunched down to look through the hatch.

'Pilotis, I need you to run an errand for me.'

'Yes, sir.'

'Sparks just told me some damned fool in supplies has sent us the wrong crystals for the radio set. We'll need replacements. There's an army detachment up in Lefkada. We can try them. I'd send someone else, but I think it had better be an officer if we're to get anywhere.'

'Yes, sir.'

'Besides, you're due a break. Get yourself a drink while you're there.'

'Thank you, sir.' Pilotis grinned. 'I could use one.'

He turned and exchanged a look with Andreas and then his smile faded. He coughed as he turned back to his captain. 'Actually, sir, I've still got a few tasks that need my attention. Why not send Katarides instead? He'll not be missed.'

Iatridis pursed his lips in surprise and cast a quick look at the new arrival before he clicked his tongue. 'That's fine by me, Number One. Katarides?'

'Sir!'

'Sparks is ashore in the radio tent. He'll tell you what you need. Take one of the lorries and a driver. And while you're in Lefkada, see if you can bring back some cases of beer and a few bottles of raki.'

'Yes, sir.'

The captain disappeared and a moment later they heard his boots on the bridge ladder again. Andreas turned to Pilotis.

'Are you sure about this?'

The first lieutenant clapped him on the shoulder. 'Of course. Take the opportunity to see your old man. Might be the last you get for a while.'

Andreas smiled gratefully at him. 'Thanks.'

'I shall want something in return,' said Pilotis.

Andreas eyed him warily. 'Oh?'

'Nothing you can't afford.' Pilotis looked vaguely embarrassed. 'Just a signed copy of one his collections, if he doesn't mind, eh?'

CHAPTER TEN

The door opened as the truck rattled to a halt in front of the villa and Andreas saw the familiar face of his father's cook peering cautiously out from the dim interior. It was late in the afternoon and the sun had already slipped behind the mountain that loomed behind the house, and the dark ridge stood starkly against a bright orange sky. As the sound of the engine died away, he told the driver to remain with the vehicle. Andreas climbed out and approached the house, surprised at the feeling of melancholy that settled on his heart. This had been his home from birth. He knew its every corner, every crack in the walls and yet it somehow felt like a different place now. As if it was a distant memory. There had been changes, he noted. The garden was less well tended than before and paint had begun to peel from the wall beside the front door.

The cook squinted and then offered him a relieved smile and eased the door open to admit him.

'Master Andreas, you're home at last.' She stood back to look him up and down. 'You seem taller since you left to join the navy. But now you're home.'

He stopped just inside the threshold and embraced the familiar musty odour of the house. 'Not today, I'm afraid,

Anastasia. I only have a brief time.'

- She frowned. 'I don't understand . . .'

'I have to return to my ship tonight.'

'Oh . . .' Her smile faded.

'How are you faring? And Alexis?'

She lowered her gaze. 'My husband died two months ago . . . After the news that our son had been killed.'

Andreas dimly recalled the youth he had known when he was very young. Shortly before he left the island for the mainland. 'I'm sorry for your loss. The war?'

She nodded, not trusting herself to speak. 'Stelios was fighting in Albania. We did not find out how it happened. There was only a letter from the government. Your father read it to us. It broke my husband's heart . . .'

She closed her eyes tightly and Andreas saw that it was not only one heart that had been broken, and now only hers endured. He touched her shoulder gently. They stood still briefly before she sniffed and took a deep breath and raised her head again. 'You'll be wanting to see your father. He is on the terrace, Master Andreas. He has missed you. We all have. Come.'

She closed the door and led him through the hall to the rear of the house. Outside, the terrace lay unswept and dry leaves and small pine cones were heaped in corners where the wind had trapped them. His father sat in a chair beside the table looking out from the balcony towards the sea. His hair had not been cut for some time and now lay on his shoulders, the first streaks of grey showing against the darker curls. He wore a plain white shirt and black trousers. Beside him, on the table, was a bottle of raki and an empty glass. He did not stir at the sound of footsteps and merely commented, 'I'll take my meal here, I think.'

Andreas exchanged a quick smile with the cook and she stopped and waved him on. He continued, stepping as softly as he could across the weathered flagstones. At the last moment his father eased himself forward and looked round. His face bore a tired expression but it quickly faded and he smiled with delight as he rose to his feet and opened his arms.

'My boy!'

Andreas stepped into his embrace and they exchanged a kiss on each cheek before his father held him at arm's length and scrutinised him. 'I cannot deny that you have become a grown man now. An officer in the navy. Quite a transformation from the boy who used to sit on my knee while I told him tales of our past. Do you remember?'

'I shall never forget, Father.'

'Nor should you. Some memories are the most precious possessions of all . . . While others are a curse.'

Andreas smiled. 'I know that line. The last poem from the collection you published while I was at the academy.'

Katarides laughed. 'So you found time to read that during your training. I am honoured.'

The irony of his words was not lost on Andreas and he felt the familiar ache at his father's mocking disapproval. But before the feeling could take root his father ushered him into a spare chair and turned towards his cook. 'Another glass here!'

She nodded and disappeared into the house. Andreas sat and stared out from the balcony at the hazy hummocks of the islands and islets of the Ionian Sea. 'I never grow tired of this view.'

'I know. It is a fine thing. I find it something of an inspiration, particularly in these trying times. Men fight their wars, but the world continues, more timeless than the exploits of any hero that ever lived.' He looked steadily at his son. 'So? Are you here on leave? Finally. I had feared you had forgotten about me. I haven't had a letter from you for nearly two months.'

Andreas turned his eyes from the view. 'I've had so little spare time since the war began. My class was commissioned early and sent to the fleet. I was kept on to train as a navigator before my first posting. I would have written to you to explain but there was no chance to do so.'

'And yet they have allowed you to come home?' Katarides's brow creased anxiously. 'Is anything the matter, son?'

'No. Nothing.'

'Then why are you here?'

'It's just a brief visit. My boat is at Sivota. The captain sent me to Lefkada for supplies. I'll have to leave within the hour.'

'It will be dark soon. You know how bad the road is. It would be better if you stayed the night and left for Sivota in the morning.'

'I can't. My captain is expecting me to return tonight.'

His father stroked his hair. 'A pity. I wish there was more time . . . There are things I wish to say to you.'

A soft scuffle of slippers heralded the approach of Anastasia and she set another glass down on the table before returning to the house. The poet poured his son a glass of raki and held it out for him. Andreas nodded his thanks and sipped the fiery liquid.

'Good?'

He nodded to his father. 'Better than the stuff I am used to.'

'Pah, that's Athens for you. Nothing decent to drink there, unless you are one of Metaxas's wealthy cronies. They'll be pleased with themselves, I imagine. Now that the war is going in their favour. It seems their fears about Mussolini and his fascist legions were misplaced. I always thought they were blustering buffoons. They'll run back to Italy, tails between their legs, and Metaxas will claim all the credit for "his" great victory. You can be sure of that. And then we'll be stuck with the little despot for many years to come. Sad times, my son. The good die in battle, while the perfidious politicians reap the rewards. With luck it will all be over before you have to play your part in it.'

'I shall do my duty,' Andreas responded firmly. 'My boat is sailing to war in the next few days.'

'Boat? I had hoped our navy had a few ships at least.'

'It is a submarine, Father. We call them boats, not ships.'

'A submarine? Infernal contraptions. What sane man goes to sea in a machine designed to sink?'

'It is perfectly safe. Besides, I had no choice in the matter . . . I tell you, it is the Italians who are in danger, once we get amongst them.'

His father stared at him, then emptied his glass and poured some more raki. 'You are determined to become the hero, aren't you?'

'I am just serving our country, Father. As every Greek should.'

'That's what you think, is it? As simple as that. My country, right or wrong, putting yourself at the service of vile scoundrels like Metaxas? What is war, Andreas, but the pitting of one worker against another, at the whim of their masters and for the profits of their backers? War is little more than a crime, thinly veiled in bogus notions of duty and honour. You talk of serving your country. If you meant that then you would take off that uniform and refuse to fight. That is what all young men should do and put an end to this great evil once and for ever.'

Andreas listened to this with a growing sense of frustration as he slowly rolled his glass between his hands. 'You may be right. It would be good if all mankind turned its back on war. But as long as some young men refuse to take off their uniforms then the rest of us can never know peace. That is what I understand by my duty to serve my country. To protect it from those who seek to wage war against the rest of us.'

'But don't you see? The process must begin somewhere. If a handful of men say no, then others will follow. When enough follow, anything is possible. Why should you not be amongst the first to show their defiance to the warmongers?'

Andreas had noticed the faint slur beneath his father's words and knew better than to try to argue with him when raki had worked its influence on his mind. Besides, he had no wish to argue. He had come to the house to pay his respects to his father and in the hope that he might have changed his mind about his son's choice of career now that war had come to Greece. In truth, he was angry. His father's idealism might be a fine quality for a poet but in a world where the idealism of great nations had been perverted into the fanatical pursuit of power, there was no choice but to make a stand here in the present, for the sake of the future. Only then could people be free to talk of ideals. Until then he would fight to protect his country and his people. That was a simple enough duty, and one that served a clear moral purpose: defending liberty. There was no higher purpose anyone could aspire to, Andreas felt. There were no arguments, no philosophies, that could topple that essential truth. Good conscience demanded that tyrants like Mussolini and Hitler must be opposed.

He suddenly thought of Peter and his father, and felt sadness weigh down his heart. What had become of them? Andreas had known them as friends. He could not easily believe that they would support the Nazis. Soon Peter would be old enough to don a uniform. Would he choose to do so and serve Hitler? Or would he strive to oppose the leader of his nation? Perhaps he would fight for his country, in spite of Hitler. Just as Andreas was determined to defend Greece in spite of Metaxas.

As he recalled his friend so the chain of his thoughts inevitably moved on to Eleni. It had been his intention to visit her as well as seeing his father and yet he had chosen to put it off until after visiting his home. It was almost as if he was giving himself an excuse not to, Andreas realised. He felt a surge of blood in his veins as he thought of her. He pictured Eleni in his head the last time he had seen her. Still young and untouched. He had not felt confident enough to ask if her affections for him ran beyond friendship, and had often tormented himself over his timidity in the long months he had been at the naval academy. It would be better to live in doubt than to know for certain that she did not feel for him as he had come to realise he felt for her.

'Well?'

Andreas broke off from his thoughts. He fixed his gaze on his father and saw the challenge in his expression, as if daring his son to defy him. Andreas was too tired for a confrontation. He took a last sip from his glass and set it down on the table before standing and looking down at his father, no longer the authoritative, celebrated figure that had dominated his childhood.

'I did not want this war. But what I want is immaterial. I have to go now.'

He nodded a curt farewell and made to turn towards the house.

'Andreas . . . Please.'

The plea was impossible to resist. He turned his gaze back towards his father and saw that all the anger and arrogance had crumbled away. All that remained was an open expression of anxiety. The poet's mouth struggled to frame the words his heart yearned to say to his son.

'Be careful, Andreas. You are all I have left. All that is of any value to me in this world. Come back to me.'

Andreas felt his throat constricting. He breathed deeply. 'I will come back. As soon as I can.'

'One last thing, my son.' Katarides reached under his shirt and took out the small locket he kept close and slipped the chain over his head. He pursed his lips and then eased the catch open to reveal two black and white portraits. One of a slender young woman with piercing eyes and the other of an infant. He held it out for his son to see. 'Do you recognise her?'

'Yes, from pictures only . . . my mother.'

'And my wife. The person I loved most in this world. The baby is you, a few months after you were born. I lost her, and now you are the one I love most in the world, Andreas. I could not live if I lost you too. So, take that and look after it. One day you can return it to me. Meanwhile, it may bring you luck. Take it.'

'Father, I—'

'I said, take it.'

Andreas held out his hand. His fingers closed round the locket and he turned and strode back through the house. Anastasia emerged from the kitchen as he reached the door and Andreas nodded a brief farewell. He closed the door behind him and crossed the drive to the truck. The driver had been dozing and now hastened to sit up straight as Andreas climbed into the cab.

'Back to Sivota, sir?' he asked as he started the vehicle and eased the choke until it was running smoothly.

'No. Not quite yet. Take me back into the town.'

The driver shot him a surprised look and then shrugged. 'Yes, sir.'

The home of Inspector Thesskoudis and his family was a plain building in the heart of the town, close to the main square dominated by the prefecture and the Church of St Spyridon. There was a small garden to the front, separated from the narrow street by a low whitewashed wall. Brightly coloured blooms rose from pots lining the short path from the gate to the front door and Andreas lifted his nose to appreciate their scent as he paused in front of the house. The evening air was cold and the sweetness of the flowers was more muted than on summer nights. Even so, the smell instantly evoked memories of previous visits and he felt his pulse quicken as he took a deep breath and rapped the heavy iron door knocker. The muted conversation that emanated from within died away at the sound. A moment later the inside latch was lifted and the door opened to reveal Eleni's mother. At first she did not recognise him, and Andreas hurriedly swept the cap from his head and smiled.

'Andreas!' Her lips parted in a warm smile. 'Sweet God . . . Come in, come in.'

He stepped inside and she closed the door behind him. They stood in the main room of the ground floor. Andreas recalled that the door to the rear led to a yard at the back surrounded by storerooms. To the side, stairs rose steeply to the first floor. There was one other door, leading to the large kitchen and family room which was dominated by a large table. Light shone through the opening.

'Who is it?' Inspector Thesskoudis demanded.

Andreas made to answer but the woman raised a finger to her lips to silence him and beckoned him towards the door. She entered first. Looking past her, Andreas saw her husband hunched over a newspaper as he read by the light of the single electric bulb hanging above the table. Beyond, Eleni was standing by the stove cutting a loaf of bread into thick slices, preparing their evening meal. The inspector looked up. 'Well?'

'We have a guest.' She could not help a soft laugh. 'Look.'

Mr Thesskoudis raised his head and muttered an oath before heaving his ponderous body up and hurrying over to take Andreas's hand.

'Young Katarides! No, no longer young. A man now. It's good to see you again, my boy!' he gushed.

Andreas beamed back but his eyes shifted to the far side of the room where Eleni had half turned, knife poised in her hand, a look of shock on her face. She lowered the blade quickly and dusted her hands on a frayed cloth before touching her hair into place and joining the others.

'You look quite the military man!' Mr Thesskoudis enthused, stepping back a pace from his guest. 'So what brings you here?'

Andreas gave his explanation as briefly as he could.

'I heard there was a submarine at Sivota.' Mr Thesskoudis nodded. 'Thanks to my position I was informed about that. It has been my job to keep things running smoothly to help our boys at the front.'

'Pfftt!' His wife shook her head. 'Don't listen to him. His job is the same as it ever was: trying to manage the villagers' feuds and stopping the communists from making trouble.'

'I am entrusted with keeping the peace,' Thesskoudis responded indignantly.

'Keeping the peace? A bit late for that in this world . . .'

Andreas smiled at the exchange, fully aware of Eleni hanging back behind her parents.

'So, have you fought the Italians yet?' Thesskoudis demanded. 'Shown them a bit of Greek spirit, eh? Those greasy bastards deserve to be whipped back across the sea, and we Greeks are the men to do it!'

'Language!' his wife scolded. 'And what kind of a host are you? Andreas, come, sit at the table.'

He did as he was told and sat with her husband and daughter around one end of the table while Mrs Thesskoudis fetched a bottle of raki and some glasses. The young man was conscious of the effects of his earlier drink with his father. It would not do to return to Sivota and present himself to his commanding officer the worse for wear. But there was no question of refusing the hospitality of his hosts and he raised his glass along with them and joined in the chorus.

'*Eviva!*'

'I'm afraid I cannot stay for long,' Andreas told them. 'My driver is waiting in the square to drive me back to Sivota.'

Mrs Thesskoudis pursed her lips. 'A shame.'

'Yes,' Eleni added. 'A shame. I am sure you have so much to tell me, tell us.'

The last words were spoken quickly and Andreas looked at her searchingly, hoping that he knew the reason for her moment of awkwardness. 'There will be plenty of time for that, once the war is over, Eleni. And, yes, there is much I would like to say to you.'

There was a brief quiet before Mr Thesskoudis leaned forward and stared intently at the naval officer. 'And how long do you think it will take to kick the arses of those Italians? The newspapers say we are forcing them back into Albania and that victory will come any day. But they would say that. They'll say whatever the government tells them to say. So what's the truth? You must know.'

'I am only a junior officer. I have heard that our soldiers are having the best of it in the mountains. Our airmen are enjoying some success too, and the navy does what it can. But our surface fleet is no match for theirs. Only our submarines, like the *Papanikolis*, can take the war to the Italians.'

'As I am sure you will.' Mr Thesskoudis slapped his hand down. 'Make sure they suffer. Sink me a battleship, young Katarides. Make your father proud and give him something to write a poem about. Not that dull old stuff he's been writing lately, but a real poem. An epic. It'll make a modern Homer of him.'

'I'll do my best.' Andreas smiled.

'Or course you will!'

Eleni was not smiling, but staring at him intently. 'Be careful, Andreas. Don't take any chances.'

'Pah!' her father snorted. 'He's an officer, girl. He must take chances if we are to win the war and he is to prove himself a hero worthy of his country. Isn't that right?'

Suddenly the room seemed too hot, his hosts too close to him and Eleni's expression strained. He wished that her parents would leave them alone. Just long enough for him to speak with Eleni, to confess that he had missed her in Athens, that he would be grateful if she waited for him to return from the war so that he might seek her parents' permission to court her. Beneath consideration of the required formalities his heart burned with longing. He was surprised at the intensity of it now that he sat opposite Eleni. All that he craved was a sign from her that she felt the same. Then he would be content to return to his submarine and sail to war.

But no one moved around the table. There was no sign that Eleni's parents perceived his need and he a felt frustration simmering in his veins. He glanced down at his wristwatch. It would be midnight before the truck returned to Sivota after a long drive along the rough tracks that passed for roads on the island.

'I must go.' He looked up apologetically. 'I just wanted to make sure that you are all well.'

Mr Thesskoudis smiled. 'All the better for seeing you. Isn't that right, Eleni?'

'Yes, Father,' she said flatly.

Andreas stood up and the others followed suit. Before her father could intervene, Eleni spoke quickly. 'I will see Andreas out, Papa. You still have to finish reading your newspaper.'

He stared at her in surprise and his mouth began to frame a reply before his wife patted him on the hand. 'Quite right. Sit there, I'll finish preparing the meal. Take care, Andreas. We'll remember you in our prayers.'

He nodded his thanks and followed Eleni out of the room towards the door, his fingers working nervously in the stiff material of his naval cap. She reached for the latch and hesitated an instant before lifting it and easing the door open. Andreas stepped past her and then turned, his pulse quickening as he spoke softly.

'Eleni . . .'

She stared up at him in the gloom of the twilight settling over the island.

'Holy God and the Blessed Virgin look after you,' she whispered and rose on her toes to kiss him on the lips. He just had time to close his eyes and feel the warmth of her breath on his cheek and then she pulled back, staring into his eyes intently.

'Do your duty, then come back to me, Andreas Katarides.'

He tried to lean forward to kiss her back but Eleni backed away into the house.

'Go now,' she said.

Andreas was still for a moment, too surprised to react. Then he heard footsteps in the street and the spell was broken as he turned instinctively. Two old ladies swathed in black passed the house without regarding him. He heard a click behind him and turned back to see the door closed. He stared at the painted wood, his heart pained, but elated. After a moment's stillness Andreas walked away, back to the square and the waiting truck.

CHAPTER ELEVEN

March 1941

Lieutenant Pilotis drew a deep breath, cupped his hand and bellowed, 'Cast off forward!'

Andreas watched as two shoremen on the pier eased the thick loop of cable up over the wooden bollard and tossed it towards the crewmen waiting at the bow of *Papanikolis*. The slack slapped into the water before the men drew it in and stowed the cable in the locker. On the submarine's conning tower Pilotis turned his attention to the aft deck and shouted another order to the men on the stern mooring. Untethered from the pier the vessel began to drift away very slowly. Beneath Andreas's feet the deck vibrated as the engine turned over easily, a plume of blue-grey smoke billowing from the exhaust port.

At the rear of the conning tower Iatridis took a last puff from his cigarette and then flicked the butt into the sea.

'Take the boat out to sea, Number One. Then steer off the end of Cape Kavos Kiras and then east. The navigator will give you a further course when I've briefed him.'

'Yes, sir.'

They exchanged a salute before the captain made for the hatch and called down a warning before he descended. When he was sure that their commander was out of earshot, Andreas muttered, 'Looks like the old man is in a foul mood.'

'Hardly surprising,' Pilotis replied discreetly. Then he turned his attention back to his duties and dipped his head towards the voice tube. 'Engines ahead slow.'

The order was repeated back to him and the note of the engine changed and the *Papanikolis* edged away from the pier as water swirled in its wake. The first lieutenant gave a few course corrections before the submarine entered the channel and headed out to sea. Andreas leaned on the coaming of the tower, gazing back towards the quiet village of Sivota receding behind them. This was the fourth patrol they had been sent on. The previous missions had taken them south-west to cover the approaches to the west coast of Greece and had proved utterly futile. Aside from the sighting of a distant Italian destroyer and the emergency dive that had followed, there had been no excitement, let alone any opportunity to deal a blow to the enemy. The captain had raged against the incompetence of his superiors, demanding that *Papanikolis* be sent north to interdict the enemy shipping supplying their armies in Albania. But each time he was told that the navy's duty was to guard against a possible surprise invasion of the homeland. So the submarine had been obliged to patrol an empty stretch of ocean, lookouts scanning the horizon for any sign of enemy vessels or aircraft hour after hour.

Each time the patrol ended, the submarine returned to Sivota to refuel and reprovision while the ammunition for the deck gun and spare torpedoes lay unused in her hull. The captain's frustration was shared by his crew, all the more so as the vessel had received strict orders to remain ready to leave the temporary base at a moment's notice. As a result there had been no leave granted to any man and Andreas had not been able to return to Lefkada. To know that his home and his love lay no more than half a day's drive away fed his longing to see both and starved his patience.

As the long grey shape slipped out of the bay into the open sea and the first waves burst over the bows, Pilotis spoke. 'What do you think it will be this time? South-west again?'

Andreas shrugged. 'We'll know soon enough.'

The captain had received a coded message the previous evening in two parts. The first had ordered him to ready his vessel for sea, the second was to be read and acted upon only after *Papanikolis* had left its base. Both officers directed their thoughts down through the conning tower towards the captain sitting in his cabin as he digested his new instructions and prepared to give his orders to the crew. The lookouts took up their positions and began to scan the horizon with binoculars as Pilotis ordered the helmsman to steer a course for the southernmost cape of Lefkas. As the vessel settled on the new course the voice pipe gave a short trill and Pilotis leaned forward to listen and then turned to Andreas.

'Captain wants you.'

Andreas raised an eyebrow. 'Did he say . . . ?'

Pilotis shook his head. 'Not giving anything away. Get going.'

'Coming down!' Andreas shouted through the hatch and then hurriedly clambered down the ladder into the humid stench of the bridge before picking his way through the crewmen to the captain's cabin. The thin sheet of wood that served as the door was latched open and Andreas knocked on the varnished surface.

'You sent for me, sir.'

Iatridis looked up, a sparkle in his eye. 'Come in, Katarides, and shut the door.'

The cabin was not much longer than the cot bed and just

a little wider, barely enough room for the captain to squeeze into the chair at his desk. Andreas had to shuffle round the door in order to close it and then stand against it as he faced his commander. The coded message lay beside the captain's decoded notes on a chart spread across his desk. Air from a small fan caused an unweighted corner of the chart to flutter, but that was not enough to prevent the sweat breaking out on the captain's brow and staining his shirt. Even so, his good spirits were at once evident to the navigation officer.

'The naval ministry has finally come to its senses!' He tapped the message. 'We've been ordered into the Adriatic to intercept Italian shipping. See here . . .' He cleared the sheets away from the chart and Andreas could make out the island of Corfu and the Albanian coast to the north.

'This is our patrol area. Naval intelligence has reported a marked increase in Italian activity. They suspect it's the build-up for a new offensive. We're to strike at any targets of opportunity in this area. Of course there's some danger from escort vessels and aircraft, but at last we'll have something to aim our torpedoes at. That'll please the lads. Meanwhile I want you to plot a course to the patrol area. From there I want a search pattern plotted. Nothing predictable, understand?'

'Yes, sir.'

'We're to remain in the area until we've exhausted our ammunition.'

Or we are sunk in turn, Andreas thought. That was the reality he and the rest of the crew faced now. Even so, he felt a sense of exhilaration at the prospect of making a contribution to the defence of his country and all those he knew and loved. For several months he had been an onlooker while his comrades in the other services had been tested in battle. Now it was his turn at last.

'What are you waiting for?' Iatridis frowned. 'Get to work.'

'Yes, sir.' Andreas saluted and shifted round the door and closed it behind him. As he retraced his steps to the bridge compartment he was aware of the expectant looks of the other men but forced himself to keep his expression neutral. At the navigator's table he selected the appropriate chart from the deep pigeonholes beneath. He spread it out and slipped the edges under the clips before he reached for his instruments in the locker above. Ignoring the inquisitive looks of his comrades, Andreas leaned over the chart and began to plot the course of the *Papanikolis*, his lips spread in a soft smile of contentment.

'Periscope up,' Iatridis ordered quietly.

A mechanical whine filled the bridge as the broad steel tube extended towards the surface five metres above the top of the conning tower. The only other noise was the whirring of the fans and the soft hum of the electric engines as the submarine ghosted along at four knots. The lookouts had sighted the leading ships of the convoy in the dying light, silhouetted against the setting sun. The Greek submarine was in the perfect position to attack, lying directly ahead of the Italian vessels and hidden by the darker sky to the east. As soon as the convoy had been spotted, Iatridis had given the order to submerge and the submarine descended to periscope level to await its prey. It had taken no more than two hours before the sound of engines carried through the water and hull to the ears of the crew, waiting in silence for the captain to give the orders to begin the attack.

The periscope motor stopped and Iatridis leaned his head towards the rubber-trimmed eyepiece. He slowly rotated the instrument and then eased it to a stop and was silent for a moment before he spoke to Andreas who stood by, pencil poised, ready to plot the position of the enemy vessels.

'Destroyer bearing eighty degrees off port bow, speed . . . fifteen knots, range . . . four thousand metres.' He rotated the periscope slowly, shuffling his feet to keep pace with it, then slowed to a stop again as he continued. 'Five, six cargo ships, line astern. Leading vessel bearing ten degrees to port, range six thousand metres. Speed, eight knots. Looks like a troopship.'

As Andreas made notes of the captain's observations, Iatridis continued rotating the periscope to sweep the horizon and then stepped away and gave the order for it to be lowered. They moved to the chart table and Andreas took up his grease pen and marked the positions of the Italian vessels as closely as he could calculate, anxious to make no mistakes under the watchful eye of his captain. When he had finished he straightened and Iatridis quickly considered the chart, his sharp mind calculating distances and timings. He nodded to himself and took a sharp breath.

'We'll close to two thousand metres and fire a spread at the leading ship. As soon as the fish are in the water we'll turn away from the escort destroyer and move in closer to the rest. With luck they'll panic and separate and give us the chance to sink some more before the destroyer bears down on us. Then we'll be forced to dive deep and make evasive manoeuvres. Our friends in the Italian navy couldn't hit a barn door if they were standing in front of it!'

The men at their stations in the bridge grinned at the comment and Iatridis indulged them briefly before he gave his first order.

'Increase speed to six knots. Stay on this course for ten

minutes then turn ninety degrees to port and stop.'

Lieutenant Pilotis nodded and repeated the order to the men at the steering controls as he started the timer. The noise from the electric motors increased in pitch as the *Papanikolis* eased through the depths like a shark closing on its prey. The distant rumble of the convoy carried clearly through the steel hull of the submarine and grew in intensity as the Italian ships drew nearer. Andreas fancied that he could even feel a small vibration in the deck beneath his boots, over and above that caused by the submarine's motor.

'Steer ninety to port!' Pilotis barked as the timer reached ten minutes. 'All stop!'

The submarine began to swing and the crew reached for handholds to steady themselves as the deck tilted beneath them. Slowly it levelled and the soft trickle of water running past the outside of the hull diminished. Andreas glanced round the compartment and saw the tense expressions of his comrades as they listened to the throb of the nearest enemy ship's propeller.

'Up periscope!' Iatridis commanded, impatiently clenching his fists as the eyepiece rose to meet him. He bent and met it, and swung the instrument to left and right before settling on a target several degrees off the starboard bow. 'Ahhh . . . there you are, my friend,' he said softly, before his tone hardened. 'Navigator, enemy destroyer bearing twenty degrees to port and moving away. Mark it up.'

'Yes, sir.'

'Number One, prepare bow tubes, one to four.'

Pilotis repeated the order then stepped to the voice tube to relay it to the weapons officer. Andreas heard the sound of voices, the clink of chain and the rumble of the torpedoes on their runners as the crew hauled them forward into the tubes.

Inner hatches clashed shut and then there was stillness before the first lieutenant broke the silence on the bridge. 'Weapons officer reports torpedoes ready, sir.'

'Very good, Number One.' Iatridis shifted the periscope. 'Target is troopship, ten degrees angle on the bow. Range eighteen hundred metres. Prepare to shoot.'

'Prepare to shoot!' Pilotis spoke loudly and clearly into the voice tube.

There was a pause and Andreas felt a slight pain in his hand and glanced down to the see the grease pencil clenched tightly in his fist. He made himself relax his fingers and saw the sweat gleaming on his skin.

'Torpedoes one to four, shoot!'

An instant after the order was repeated Andreas flinched at the shrill explosive hiss as the torpedoes were blown out of their tubes by a blast of compressed air. Then the whine of the torpedo propellers cut in as Pilotis turned to the captain.

'Torpedoes away, sir. Two minutes to impact. The clock is running.'

'Very good. Steer forty-five degrees to starboard, speed six knots. Reload the tubes.'

Andreas bent over the navigation table to plot the new course and update the enemy's positions. He could guess the captain's intention. While the escort attended the stricken troopship the others would scatter and the *Papanikolis* would move freely amongst them, picking off the easiest targets while keeping clear of the Italian destroyer for as long as possible.

When he looked up, the timer was running down towards the impact. The second hand had not reached the last ten seconds when there was dull rumble that resonated through the hull. The crewmen glanced at each other with excited expressions but before anyone could cheer there came the sound of another detonation.

'Two hits!' Pilotis clapped his hands together in delight. 'The *Elli* is avenged!'

This time his companions cheered and Andreas was about to join in when the captain rounded on his men with a furious expression.

'Silence! Silence, you fools!'

Every tongue stilled and the men turned back to their stations. Their captain glared round the compartment. 'We are at war! This is not a bloody game. You all have a duty to perform. Do it!'

He allowed a moment for his words to sink in before snapping an order for the periscope to be raised again. Despite the two fans and the cooling effect of the water on the hull, Andreas saw that every man's face was beaded with sweat.

'New target! Cargo ship bearing five degrees off port bow. Turning to cross our bow. Range seven hundred! Ready tube five. Shoot when ready!'

Andreas felt his heart beating furiously as he imagined the hapless Italian vessel swinging directly into the path of the submarine. The range was close and it would be almost impossible to miss. Another hiss of air sounded through the compartment and the crew stood still, struggling to restrain their excitement as they braced themselves for the detonation. The sound of the cargo ship's propeller seemed deafening to Andreas and he gritted his teeth as he waited for the shattering roar of the torpedo's explosion. But there was only a faint clang of metal on metal and the growing drone of the propeller.

'Holy fucking God!' Iatridis growled through clenched teeth. 'A dud torpedo. What have those French bastards been selling us?' He paused and composed himself and returned to the periscope eyepiece. 'Too close now. New target . . .'

He began to rotate, seeking out another enemy ship ploughing through the sea in the dusk. Then he rattled out fresh instructions. 'New target. Tanker. Thirty degrees off starboard bow—'

'High speed propeller, closing!' the hydrophone operator interrupted urgently. 'Bearing . . . one eighty. Right behind us, sir!'

Iatridis lurched round to face the stern and seemed to flinch before snapping upright. 'Dive! Periscope down!'

Pilotis did not need to repeat the order as the ratings on the dive-plane controls pressed them forward. The deck began to angle sharply and a pair of dividers slid across the chart. Andreas snatched them before they dropped off the table.

'Make depth one hundred metres!' said Iatridis. 'Steer hard to port!'

The angle of the deck became more disorientating in the cramped confines as the *Papanikolis* began to roll through the turn and Andreas felt the acrid bite of nausea in his throat and prayed that he would not be sick in front of his crewmates. The fabric of the submarine began to groan under the strain, then he heard it: the muffled rumble of the destroyer's propellers.

'Slow to four knots,' the captain ordered.

Pilotis glanced back at him anxiously, then nodded and repeated the order to the helmsman. Andreas felt the hairs on his scalp tingle as he heard the exchange. What was Iatridis doing? Why slow down? Then some calm place in his mind recalled the rudimentary introduction course to the world of the submariner that he had taken at the academy after he had been told of his first posting. Sound carried very efficiently through the medium of water. Higher speeds generated more noise; the captain was trying to make it harder for the enemy to trace their course.

Papanikolis settled on her new course, perpendicular to her old direction, and continued to dive.

'Passing fifty metres,' the first officer intoned. 'Fifty-five . . . sixty.'

Andreas became aware of a new sound, a protesting groan as the pressure outside the submarine's hull increased the deeper it went. Above them the sound of the destroyer's propellers increased.

'He's right on top of us . . .' a voice muttered.

Iatridis swung towards the man. 'Keep your mouth shut.'

Pilotis's eyes were fixed on the depth gauge. 'Eighty metres.'

'Sir!' The hydrophone operator looked up anxiously, his hands clasping his headphones to his ears so that he might hear the sounds in the water around the submarine more clearly. 'Depth charges!'

Fear gripped every man in the compartment at the words, even the captain, before he recovered and bellowed, 'Seal all compartments! Crew, brace!'

Andreas and a rating rushed to the heavy hatch heading forward and swung it into the frame and turned the locking handles until they were tight. Another man closed the stern-facing hatch. More clangs and clatter sounded from the other compartments before the crew found themselves handholds and grasped tightly as they waited. All trace of excitement had gone from Andreas's thoughts. The only thing that remained was naked terror as he imagined the heavy drums packed with high explosive sinking towards them.

He glanced round and saw a rating standing beside the air tank controls, eyes clenched shut and lips trembling as he muttered, 'Holy God, save us . . .'

'Ninety metres,' said Pilotis.

The captain nodded. 'Level off.'

'Level off, yes, sir.'

The dive plane controls were eased back and a moment later the angle of the deck became less acute.

That was when the first depth charge exploded.

It was like a titanic hammer blow struck against the hull of the submarine. Far more violent than anything Andreas had expected. The vessel shook and his ears filled with the roar of the detonation and the rattle of loose fittings around him. One of the men cried out in alarm and others swore oaths or called on God to preserve them. As the shockwave passed on, Andreas's chest heaved and he felt a surge of ecstatic relief that he was still alive. That was before he realised that it had only been the first depth charge in a pattern dropped by the destroyer. The rest went off in a rolling barrage that battered the submarine and shattered the wits of all those trapped within as the cold steel shell tossed from side to side in the dark depths of the sea.

CHAPTER TWELVE

Explosion after explosion ripped open the sea around the submarine with a shattering sequence of roars that rocked the craft from side to side. In the bridge compartment of the *Papanikolis* the crew clung desperately to whatever came to hand and tried to stay on their feet as the submarine was mercilessly battered by the depth charge patterns dropped by the Italian destroyer circling overhead on the surface. The concussion pierced Andreas's eardrums and pressed in on his eyeballs with a terrifying crushing sensation. All the time he was certain that the hull would split open under the tremendous forces it was being subjected to. A torrent of cold seawater would sweep the length of the boat, dragging it into the deep where the pressure would crumple the vessel and her helpless crew.

'Number One!' Iatridis yelled above the din. It took two attempts before Pilotis gathered his wits enough to respond.

'Take us down to one hundred and twenty metres. Turn to starboard and reduce speed. Slow ahead!'

'Slow ahead, yes, sir.'

The submarine's deck inclined again for a short while and it barely edged through the darkness. Now the sound of the steel ribs of the vessel under great strain was almost continuous, even if the explosions were further off and more infrequent as the Italians lost track of their submarine. Andreas began to sweat freely as he closed his eyes and began to pray for the first time in years.

A hand grasped his shoulder and shook him roughly. 'Eyes open, Katarides . . .'

Andreas forced himself to obey and saw his captain looking at him anxiously. He was speaking quietly and in a far gentler tone than before. 'You must help set an example. You're an officer. Return to your work. You need to plot that last turn.' He nodded towards the chart table. 'Control your fear. If the men cannot take their lead from you then we are lost, and cannot serve our country, and protect our families. Do you understand?'

'Yes, sir.'

'Good. Do your duty, then.'

Andreas snatched a deep breath and reached for his pencil and ruler and marked the course change as accurately as he could. The captain made his way round the compartment, calming his crew, before he returned to the navigating table and examined the chart and the last known positions of the enemy. There was a handful of distant explosions and then no more. Andreas could not shake the thought that this was only a lull in the enemy's attack. Soon they would detect the Greek submarine again and resume their depth-charging.

'Hydrophones, what can you make out?' Iatridis asked.

The crewman had taken his phones from his head the moment the explosions began, to save his ears, and now hurriedly put them back in place, adjusted them and began to sweep the instrument for the enemy. His comrades waited impatiently for his report.

'Well?' Iatridis demanded.

'Cargo ships are very faint, sir . . . I can hear the troopship breaking up.'

'What about the destroyer?'

The hydrophone operator turned his dial, stopped and turned it back and froze. He winced. 'High-speed propellers closing. Bearing . . . one sixty off port bow. Estimated range, three thousand five hundred metres, sir.'

Andreas felt his stomach tighten at the man's words. He glanced at his watch and noted the time and direction on the chart. Iatridis examined the plottings.

'He's going to pass over us in five minutes or so. We'll turn inside him, remain at this level, stop the motors and keep silent. He'll lose any chance of staying in contact. Then he'll face a choice. He can continue the hunt, or round up the other ships and continue towards the Albanian coast.' He glanced up at Andreas. 'A little test for you, Katarides. What would you do in his shoes?'

The question was unexpected and it took a moment before Andreas could collect his thoughts sufficiently to respond. 'Sir, I have not been counting the explosions, but the enemy must have used up a considerable number of charges already. If I was him I would need to use what's left sparingly. I'd wait for a positive contact before I tried anything. If we remain silent he will have to decide if we have made good our escape or if we are still here, waiting for him to leave the area.'

The captain nodded approvingly. 'Go on.'

'At the same time, he will be concerned about the other vessels in the convoy. They will have been terrified by the attack and looking out for themselves. The longer he leaves them to their own devices, the harder it will be to gather them up. The destroyer's captain has already lost one ship. If he loses any more he'll have to answer for it to his superiors.

On the other hand, he can save face by sinking us.' Andreas paused and marshalled the arguments to make his conclusion. 'If I was him, I would search for another few hours. No later than midnight. Then I'd give up, gather the convoy and put as much distance as possible between myself and the submarine under the cover of darkness to prevent us having any chance to renew the action. First light is just after five in the morning. He has to be out of sight by then.'

'Very good, Katarides. I think you have grasped the essential details. Let's hope our opponent does as well, eh?'

'Yes, sir.'

Iatridis straightened up. 'New course. Port ninety. Engines stop.'

The submarine glided round and the noise and vibrations of the electric motors ceased.

'Silent routine,' the captain ordered. 'No moving. No talking.'

'Yes, sir.' Pilotis nodded and repeated the order, informing the other compartments through the voice tube. After the turn was completed the *Papanikolis* lost way and slowed to a stop and lay suspended in the sea, one hundred and twenty metres below the surface. Andreas marked off the position and then set the pencil and instruments aside. Around him the other crewmen sat in their seats or stood at their stations. No one spoke and the silence and stillness seemed unreal after the frantic terror of the depth charge attack and the tense escape that followed. Soon afterwards he could hear the approaching destroyer, a muted thrashing sound that steadily increased in volume and pitch before it began to diminish. The captain crossed to the hydrophone operator's station and gripped the back of his chair as he spoke softly.

'What's he up to?'

'He's passed over us, sir, heading away. The bearing is not constant.'

Iatridis clicked his tongue. 'He's circling us. Carrying out a search pattern. Let me know if he starts moving off.'

'Yes, sir.'

Iatridis returned to the periscope and leaned his back against it as he cleared his throat. 'Relax, boys. If there's one thing in life you can count on it's the impatience of the Italians. They'll give up soon enough.'

Pilotis exhaled nervously and reached up to his breast pocket and took out a packet of cigarettes.

'No smoking,' Iatridis ordered. 'We've been down here four hours already. Going to be a while before we risk surfacing. The air will start getting stale soon. Best not make it any more uncomfortable, eh?' he concluded with a slight smile.

Pilotis nodded and returned the packet to his pocket. 'I'll tell the rest of the crew, sir.'

'Do that. But keep the noise down.'

Pilotis nodded and reached for the voice pipe. Following the casual manner of his captain, Andreas crossed his arms and sat against the corner of the chart table. The air already felt hot and humid, despite the weak breeze blowing from the fans. He could feel the sweat on his brow and trickling down from his armpits, and the cloying stink of diesel and his companions caught in his throat and made him feel slightly nauseous. The hands of the large clock on the instrument panel edged round slowly as they waited. From his basic training, Andreas knew that the submarine's underwater endurance was no more than ten hours as far as the air was concerned. The carbon dioxide would begin to build up, poisoning the crew. He estimated that the submarine's batteries must have used only half their charge. But while they were motionless, it was the air supply that was their main concern.

Several times they heard the sound of the destroyer coming and going and waited impatiently for the hydrophone operator to make his reports to the captain. Iatridis nodded each time and made no comment.

Midnight passed and Andreas felt his head begin to ache and each breath he took did not seem to satisfy his need for air and left him feeling ever more fatigued. The enemy destroyer carried out one more search pattern, passing directly overhead at one point and filling the hearts of the submarine's crew with fresh horror before it continued on its way without renewing the attack. The sound of the propellers faded away and then there was silence from outside the hull and only the laboured breathing of the men within. The captain waited a full hour from the last report of the hydrophone operator before he stirred, hands on hips, and addressed the men in the bridge compartment.

'Rise to periscope depth.'

'Yes, sir.' Pilotis turned to the men charged with controlling the air tanks. 'Blow main and transfer from forward to rear.'

Compressed air forced the water out of the buoyancy tanks and the submarine began to rise, slowly at first and then faster as it clawed its way up from the depths. As the pressure on the hull eased so did the metallic groaning from its fabric and the crewmen exchanged looks of relief and mumbled prayers of thanks. As the vessel slowed its ascent and stopped at periscope depth the captain took a final report from the hydrophone operator before ordering the periscope to be raised.

'The moment of truth.' Iatridis smiled wryly and then

swept the horizon. 'The troopship is still afloat. Capsized, but still there. No sign of the destroyer, or any of the other ships.' He stepped away from the periscope. 'Down scope. Surface the boat, Number One. Make ready to start diesel engines.'

Andreas lowered his head into his hands for a moment and rubbed his tired eyes, scarcely able to believe that the ordeal was over. He felt ashamed of his earlier fear and hoped that his captain was the only one who had detected his true feelings. He had never before imagined the depth of terror he had experienced and regarded his earlier passion to serve his country and fight the enemy with a sense of self-loathing. What fool would ever endure such a thing? Trapped and helpless in the confines of the *Papanikolis* had put him in mind of being buried alive. There had been moments when it took all his remaining self-control to stop himself scrambling up the ladder into the conning tower and seeking to escape through the deck hatch. And yet he was safe. He had survived, and his dark, morbid mood gave way to a feeling of exultation that he was alive.

He heard the water cascading down the hull as the submarine broke the surface. Iatridis led a small party of men up the ladder and through the hatch on to the conning tower. A blast of fresh air washed into the compartment and Andreas stood by the ladder, head tilted back to enjoy the salty scent. The diesel engine started and idled with a mechanical rattle that vibrated the whole boat.

'All clear!' the captain shouted down. 'Pilotis, open fore and aft hatches, and stand down from silent discipline. The men can smoke if they want. Add the time to the log, 03.40 hours.'

As the orders were relayed, Andreas cupped a hand to his mouth and called out, 'Permission to come up, sir?'

There was a short pause before the reply came. 'Yes, Lieutenant. Come on, you may find this interesting.'

A frown flickered over Andreas's features before he clambered up the rungs and emerged in to the cool night air. The lookouts were at their posts scanning the horizon. It was a dark night with no moon and the only illumination came from the stars. A thin band of differentiated shadow marked the boundary between the sea and the sky. Andreas breathed in deeply and smiled as the breeze lifted his hair and made his perspiration feel cool.

'Look there,' said Iatridis, pointing off the port beam.

Andreas rested his forearms on the coaming and squinted in the direction the captain had indicated. At first he thought it must be a distant island, then he recalled their position and knew that was impossible. Then it moved ever so slightly and he realised he was looking at the capsized hull of the troopship, just over a thousand metres away. He could just make out the rudder and propellers, and then he fancied he heard a voice cry out. But it might have been his imagination. He had enough experience of the sea at night to know how it could work on the senses, particularly if a man was exhausted.

'It'll be light soon,' said Iatridis. 'You'll be able to see more then.'

'Why is the ship still afloat, sir?'

It seemed wrong to Andreas. Two torpedoes should have sunk her, removed the ship from sight, and conscience. Now it served to remind him of the enormity of their deed. A ship, a huge complicated machine, had been destroyed by the crew of the *Papanikolis*. It had been a troopship. Many men must have died. He heard another cry from that direction and fancied he saw a dark mass in the water. A lifeboat most likely. There was a chance that a good number of those on board had survived. Where there was one lifeboat there were sure to be more. It helped to salve his conscience.

'We'll head north-east,' said Iatridis. 'Try to pick up that convoy again. See if we can improve on our score, eh?'

He smiled and Andreas tried to share his mood, telling himself that they had done their duty. This war had been forced on them. The men who had been on the troopship were on their way to fight Andreas's countrymen. They had brought this on themselves. If only they had remained in Italy. If only their leader had not attempted to force his will on other nations, this would never have happened.

'Slow ahead,' the captain called down the voice tube. 'Steer north-east.'

The engine note changed as the command was carried out and at once the deck shook beneath their boots. Not the usual rhythm, but a harsh, violent vibration. Iatridis exchanged a surprised look of alarm with Andreas and called down to the bridge compartment again. 'What the hell is that? Stop the engine. Pilotis, report!'

There was a short delay, and then the vibration stopped. Iatridis rapped his fingers on the coaming while he waited. The rungs of the ladder sounded and a moment later the chief engineer clambered on to the conning tower. He was a short, bald man, wearing stained overalls.

'What's happened, Markinis?' the captain demanded.

'Starboard prop shaft has been damaged, sir. Must have been one of the depth charges. Either that, or we've lost a blade from the propeller. We'll know when there's enough light to put a diver over to inspect the damage.'

'Can you repair it?'

The engineer shook his head. 'Not in the open sea, sir. It might require a dry dock to do the job.'

'Shit!' Iatridis balled his hands into fists. 'What speed can we get out of the starboard engine?'

'Speed, sir?' Markinis shook his head. 'Sir, we can't use the engine at all.'

'We have to. I must catch up with the convoy.'

'If we try to run it, we'll cause more damage.' The engineer shook his head. 'I'm sorry, sir.'

Iatridis sucked in a deep breath and patted the man on the shoulder. 'Not your fault. Very well then, shut the engine down. We'll remain here until first light and see what's happened. Get one of your men ready to dive over the side.'

Markinis saluted and climbed back down through the hatch.

The captain turned to Andreas with a rueful smile. 'Of all the luck.'

'Yes, sir.'

But Andreas was still reliving the hours of hellish torment and was achingly grateful just to be living. The loss of the use of an engine seemed a small price to pay for such good fortune. They could still return to base using the port engine. While he could understand the captain's frustration, in his heart he wanted nothing more than to return to the safety of Sivota and deal with the demons he had discovered in his heart so that next time he would be truly ready to go to war. He would leave behind his boyish enthusiasm, knowing full well the reality of the conflict he would face.

Half an hour passed and a thin blur of light smudged the eastern horizon and grew in strength, gradually banishing the darkness over the sea and revealing the consequences of the previous night's action. Andreas began to pick out the men floating in the swell. They had been left behind by the convoy, abandoned because it was too much of a risk for any ship to stop and make an easy target of itself as it attempted to pick them up. What Andreas had previously thought was a lifeboat turned out to be a collection of rafts, crowded with men, clinging to each other. But there were far more men still in the water, many with life vests but more clinging to wreckage or treading water. There were bodies too, small dark humps rising and falling in the gentle morning swell. Large patches of oil floated on the surface, smooth and unruffled like the surrounding sea. There were more men there, covered in black slime, flailing feebly as they struggled to reach open water. And behind them all, the ponderous bulk of the capsized hull. A handful of survivors had clambered on to the exposed steel plates and lay there waiting to be rescued.

'So many of them . . .' Andreas murmured.

'What do you expect? It's a troopship. They pack every man they possibly can on board for the short crossing from Italy.'

'What's going to happen to them, sir?'

Iatridis shrugged. 'That's not our problem. Their navy will come looking for them. Or they'll send search planes. But not before we've left the scene, if that's what's worrying you.'

'I was more concerned about them, sir.' Andreas gestured towards the hundreds of men in the sea and on the rafts. Some of the men nearest to the submarine were already striking out towards it, crying for help. 'We should do something for them.'

Iatridis smiled coldly. 'What do you suggest, Katarides? Give them all a ride back to the nearest Italian port?'

'No, sir.' Andreas flushed. 'But we can offer them some help for their wounded.'

'Forget it. They came to us looking for trouble and they

found it. I'll not lose any sleep over their suffering.' He glared at his navigation officer and then seemed to relent. 'I'll send an open signal to their navy once we're well clear of the area, and tell them where they can find their friends. But that's all I'm prepared to do.'

They were interrupted by the clang of a hatch opening against the hull and turned to see the engineer and one of his men in a mask and breather kit emerge on to the aft deck. The engineer issued his instructions and the man slithered down the side and splashed into the sea, disappearing from view.

Turning his attention back to the enemy, Andreas saw two men close by. One of the lookouts drew the captain's attention to them.

Iatridis stared at the swimmers for an instant before he snapped an order. 'Take a side arm and go down there. Tell them to stay clear of the boat. If they try to get aboard, shoot them.'

'Shoot them, sir?'

'Are you deaf, man? Do as I order!'

The lookout saluted and hurried down into the submarine. He emerged shortly afterwards from the forward hatch and began to shout at the Italians who had reached the dive plane and were holding on to it as they recovered their breath. Andreas could see that they were both young men, like himself. They shouted back, angrily at first, then pleading. The crewman shook his head and drew his pistol and pointed it towards them. There was another exchange and then the crewman fired and a spout of water burst into the air close by the Italians. They quickly released their grip and swam a short distance away and trod water, heads rising and falling on the swell.

'That bloody diver is taking his time,' the captain growled, turning his attention to the stern of the submarine. Andreas raised an eyebrow. The man had only been gone for a few minutes and just then his head broke the surface and he climbed back on board. There was a brief exchange before the engineer strode up to the conning tower and tilted his head back to report.

'It's the propeller, sir. We've lost a blade and one of the others is damaged.'

'Very well,' Iatridis said through gritted teeth. 'Back to Sivota it is. Katarides, return to your charts and plot a course.'

As Andreas made for the hatch the captain called down an order for the remaining engine to start turning and the helmsman to steer south-east, towards the Ionian islands. As his head drew level with the deck, Andreas cast one look back at the Italians in the water and felt a sick horror at the pitilessness of the war he had become a part of.

CHAPTER THIRTEEN

Sivota

'How can I be expected to defend my country if my own side refuses to let me!' Lieutenant Commander Iatridis raged as he tossed the message on to his desk in contempt. On the other side of the desk sat the other two officers of the crew. The sides of the tent had been rolled up to take advantage of what movement of air there was in the stifling bay. Around them there was little movement. It was just after midday and the submarine's crew and their shore-based comrades were resting in the shade of their own tents and the stubby trees that grew up the slopes around Sivota. Only two sentries were on duty, tasked with keeping the local fishermen and their families away from the navy's property. They stood on the shingle of the beach between the village and the camouflaged pier where the submarine was moored, rifles grounded as they sweated in the glare of the sun. It had been over a week since the *Papanikolis* had limped back to its base under the power of its remaining engine. The damaged propeller had been removed from its shaft and a request had been sent to Athens for a replacement.

The following day, 6 April, the Germans had begun their invasion of Greece, finally coming to the rescue of their beleaguered Italian allies. In the ensuing chaos the officials at the department of naval supplies seemed to have lost sight of the submarine's urgently needed replacement propeller blades. Despite several increasingly angry radio messages from Iatridis, there had been no satisfactory response.

'It's been five days since the Germans crossed the border from Yugoslavia and Romania,' said the captain. 'They're making a far better job of it than the Italians. Thessaloniki fell two days ago and now the latest signal from the naval ministry says that the enemy are marching on Athens. Naturally, they exhort all patriots to stand firm and fight the fascists. Which is all very well, but without two propeller blade replacements there is no propeller for the port engine, and without the port engine the boat is in no condition to go to war with any chance of making a difference. We'll be too slow to intercept enemy shipping, and too slow to evade the enemy if they spot us. All for the sake of a pair of fucking propeller blades, which some pen-pusher in his neat little office in Athens can't be arsed to sort out for us. A sorry state of affairs, gentlemen.'

Andreas and Pilotis had kept still and silent during the tirade and were now aware that their captain was expecting a response. They exchanged a brief glance and the first lieutenant gave a slight nod of encouragement. Andreas shifted on his chair as he spoke up.

'Indeed, sir. What will you do?'

Iatridis pursed his lips briefly before he decided. 'We'll have to make our own arrangements. We can't rely on Athens any more. They have too much on their plate to deal with and we'll be forgotten in the chaos that is unfolding. It'll all be over before the *Papanikolis* can have any effect on the outcome.'

'Do you think we can defeat the Germans, sir?' asked Andreas.

'No. Greece will fall.'

'Even with the help of the British? The radio reports say that they are sending tens of thousands of their men to support us. And their planes and warships. We have already beaten off the Italians. Why not the Germans as well, sir?'

'Because they know their business, Katarides. They have been preparing for this war ever since Hitler came to power. They are better trained, better equipped and better organised. And do not put too much faith in our British allies. They have sent too little to make much difference. Their equipment is inferior and from what I have heard from Athens, they reached the front just in time to join the retreat.' He smiled gently at his two young lieutenants. 'The war in Greece is lost, my friends. That much is already certain.'

Pilotis frowned. 'Then what shall we do, sir?'

'What can we do?' the captain answered. 'Nothing, until the propeller is repaired. Even then, we shall not affect the outcome. But there will be no surrender. I will not let any German set foot on my boat. I would sooner sink her myself first.'

Andreas nodded his agreement, determined not to give in to the Germans. The soil of Greece was sacred and so was her honour. As long as her people fought on then their honour at least would be saved from the invader. Then he thought of Peter, his friend. Old enough now to be a soldier and fight for his country. It was impossible to believe that he would wage war against the country he had come to know and the people he had counted as friends. But then Peter would have no choice, not if he was a soldier, or sailor or airman. He would be obliged to fight by those who commanded him. Andreas was suddenly sickened by the thought that he might one day confront his German friend in battle, however unlikely the event. Would Peter try to kill him? Would he, in turn, be prepared to kill the German?

'However,' Iatridis broke into his thoughts, 'I would rather not scuttle the *Papanikolis* unless I have to. If we can't get the navy to send us the spare parts we need then we'll have to improvise.'

He drew a chart across the table and spread it out, weighting the corners with stones. Pilotis and Andreas leaned forward as their captain pointed to a port on the mainland. 'There's a good boatyard at Preveza. I visited it once a few years ago. Used to be a ship-breaker and there's plenty of scraps and parts still around. Bound to be a few propellers. If we can't match anything to the damaged blade then we might be able to find something that can be altered to replace the entire propeller. If we can do that then we can still play our part in the war.'

'And what if Greece is defeated, sir?' asked Pilotis. 'What then?'

Iatridis folded his hands together. 'Our armed forces may be defeated, but never our country. The government, together with the king, will go into exile. Most likely seeking shelter with the British. I think they will make for Egypt. From there they will continue to lead our people against the enemy. They will need every man, every weapon that can be removed from the clutches of the Germans. That includes the *Papanikolis* and her crew. We shall do what damage we can to the enemy and then it is my intention to sail to Alexandria and serve the government in exile or offer our services to the British. We will continue the fight, just as our people will do all that they can to resist the Germans and Italians who occupy the mainland, and islands like this one.' Iatridis regarded them closely. 'It may be several years before Greece is free again.

The crew will have to leave their families behind. They won't like that but it can't be helped. We must continue to do our duty for as long as we can. Is that clear?'

'Yes, sir,' Andreas and Pilotis replied.

'Good. Then there's no time to waste. Katarides, I want you to have the damaged propeller loaded on to a truck. Drive to Preveza and get it repaired or replaced. Then get back here as soon as possible. We'll leave Sivota as soon as the propeller is fitted. We won't be returning. We'll destroy any supplies or equipment we can't take with us.'

'What about the shoremen?' asked Andreas.

'They will be coming with us. It'll mean the boat will be crowded but that can't be helped. I want to save any man who can be put back into action against the enemy later on.'

'Yes, sir.'

'Then get the lorry loaded and set off.'

Andreas stood up and made ready to go.

'One more thing, Katarides.'

'Sir?'

The captain smiled at him. 'While you are passing through Lefkada you might want to make your farewells to your family and friends. Chances are you won't be seeing them again for a long time. But don't take too long over it, eh? Just say what you have to and leave them behind.'

Andreas bowed his head gratefully. 'Thank you, sir. I'll be quick.'

'You'll have to be. I imagine it won't be long before the Germans make their appearance. We have to quit the island before then. Just get that propeller fixed so we can get the boat ready for action and get out of here before we get trapped in Sivota. Go.'

They exchanged a salute and Andreas turned to leave,

striding out of the shaded tent and into the bright sunlight. As he made for the crew tents his heart lifted at the thought of seeing Eleni again. It was a bitter-sweet prospect given that he would have to tell her that it would be the last time for many years. But it was better than having no chance to take his leave of her. This time he vowed that he would reveal his feelings for her, and if she felt the same about him, then he would swear to return when the war was over and ask for her hand in marriage. The thought filled him with anxiety and he wondered if he dared to go through with it. If she turned him down, it would wound his heart grievously.

His thoughts were interrupted by the faint drone of an engine. Andreas stopped to listen, thinking at first that it must be a boat passing by the entrance to the bay, or even entering it. He turned to look but saw nothing, no movement across the water that stretched between the headlands. There was a shout from the slopes above and he turned to see one of the lookouts on the hill waving to attract the attention of those down in the bay and then pointing up at the sky. A handful of sailors spilled out of the shadow to look up and Andreas shaded his eyes as he squinted into the bright light and scanned the azure heavens, dabbed with towering columns of dazzling white clouds. The sound was more distinct now and it took another few frustrating moments before Andreas finally saw the dark speck approaching from the west.

The captain and first officer hurried out to join him close to the nearest of the trucks and Andreas did his best to point the aircraft out to them.

'There, to the right of the cloud . . . See?'

'Yes,' Iatridis muttered. 'Got it.'

'What do you think, sir?'

Iatridis did not hesitate. 'The enemy. Italian most like.'

Pilotis lowered his hand and turned to his captain. 'What shall we do, sir?'

'Nothing we can do. Apart from praying that we do not attract his attention. With luck he's high enough not to see through our camouflage netting. Best get the men under cover and not make any unnecessary movement.'

Pilotis turned to the sailors emerging from the tents under the trees to join their comrades watching the approaching aircraft. 'Get back under the trees! Now!'

The men scrambled back into cover and continued to watch from between the branches while the three officers calmly made their way back to the captain's tent. They had almost reached it when a sharp rattle of machine-gun fire blasted across the bay.

Iatridis spun round. 'What the devil?'

All three officers turned to stare up at the lookout post nearest the entrance to the bay. They picked out the sailor standing behind the mounted machine gun. As they watched, a fresh arc of tracer reached up towards the approaching plane and the rattle of the gun followed an instant later.

'Cease firing!' Iatridis bellowed, then drew another breath and cupped his hands to his mouth and repeated the order. Andreas saw a pile of small-arms ammunition crates at the end of the pier, and the speaking trumpet resting on top of it. The captain strode swiftly in the direction of the lookout, still shouting towards the man as a fresh burst of tracer leaped up into the sky, falling well short of the plane. Andreas ran to the pier, snatched up the speaking trumpet and hurried after Iatridis, shouting through the mouthpiece, echoing the order to cease fire. There was a final burst before the sailor paused, then looked down towards them. He froze for a moment and then released his grip on the weapon and stepped away, letting the barrel point directly up.

'Who is that fool?' Iatridis demanded.

The distance was too great to identify the man but Andreas had been responsible for the lookout rosta that day and hurriedly recalled the names and positions of the men assigned to the afternoon watch.

'It's Appellios, sir.'

'One of the new recruits?'

'Yes, sir.'

Iatridis swore bitterly. 'Be a bloody miracle if the young fool hasn't given away our position.'

'Want me to place him on a charge, sir?'

'What's the point? The damage is done . . . All we can do is hope the pilot of that plane is just as inexperienced as young Appellios.'

The officers stood and watched as the plane seemed to crawl across the sky until it was directly above the bay. For a moment Andreas was sure that it would continue on its leisurely course, but then it began to circle.

'Damn,' Iatridis muttered. 'He must have seen the tracer.'

'Should we try to shoot him down, sir? Concentrate the fire of the other lookout posts?'

The captain considered his options quickly and shook his head. 'No more shooting unless I give the order. Have the anti-aircraft gun crew go to their station and then we'll wait and see what our friend up there does.'

While the captain stood and watched the plane, Andreas ran to the crew tents and called out the gun crew and then ran with them back to the submarine. They climbed on to the wide platform at the aft of the conning tower and began to load the heavy ammunition cartridges on to the Oerlikon.

The gunner pressed himself into the padded shoulder braces and swung the heavy weapon on its mounting as he took aim at the aircraft. Although it was beyond the range of the machine guns it was within reach of the Oerlikon and Andreas addressed the man quickly.

'Do not open fire unless the captain gives the order.'

'Yes, sir.'

Andreas crossed to the nearest locker and took out a pair of binoculars and rejoined the others as they stood, straining their eyes to keep track of the plane through the netting. He looked up through the gap in the netting directly above the anti-aircraft cannon, adjusted the diopter on the binoculars and tracked on to the aircraft, controlling his breathing as he tried to steady the image.

'Italian markings . . .'

'And now they've seen us,' a voice muttered. 'Thanks to that fucking green fool on the hill. I'll knock his teeth out the moment I get the chance.'

'Quiet there!' Andreas snapped.

The bay was still and the only movement came from the fishing village where several figures had emerged to gaze up at the aircraft flying overhead. Andreas briefly considered ordering them to take cover but decided there was little risk from an enemy reconnaissance plane. The tension began to build as they waited and sweated. The Italian pilot continued his inspection of the bay from a high altitude for nearly a quarter of an hour before he returned to his old course and continued to the east, slowly losing altitude until he had passed out of sight over the hills surrounding the bay.

Andreas lowered the binoculars and breathed with relief. 'Gun crew, stand down.'

He leaned on the coaming as the gun crew left their

stations by the weapon and sat down around it, in the shade. The captain came striding down the pier and called out, 'Did you see the markings?'

'Yes, sir. Italian.'

'As I thought. They'll be reporting that they were fired on. With luck they did not see anything else and that's why they continued on course. It's time we left Sivota. Get on the road to Preveza as soon as you can, Lieutenant.'

'Yes, sir.'

'The engineer's over by the crew tents. Get him and his boys to heave the prop on to the truck then you can be on your way.'

Andreas nodded, returned the binoculars to the locker and swung himself under the railing and climbed down the rungs on to the main deck. He had just joined the captain on the jetty when the latter froze and cocked his head to one side.

'Sir?'

'Shhh! Listen . . .'

At first Andreas could discern nothing out of the ordinary, then there was a brief snatch of noise, the unmistakable sound of an aircraft engine. It faded in and out, muffled, and it was impossible to decide which direction it came from. Both officers were gazing around as the gun crew rose to their feet and looked up. It came again, louder this time, and seemed to echo on the slopes of the hill closest to the jetty.

'Gun crew, action stations!' Andreas yelled, an instant before the sound of the aircraft swelled and it flashed into view round the headland, flying low up the bay towards them, no more than fifty feet from the surface of the water. It was a twin-engined light bomber and as it banked to line up with the jetty, Andreas saw the muzzle of the forward machine gun flash. Spouts of water leaped up from the surface of the bay, racing towards the submarine. An instant later they struck the hull and conning tower with a deafening ringing clatter. The crewmen ducked down and the air filled with the throbbing roar of the bomber's engines. Andreas stood his ground, more through surprise than courage, and saw the plane racing towards him. He could see the pilot staring grimly through his cockpit windshield and then the machine swept overhead in a gigantic blur of motion as the pilot opened the throttle and clawed for altitude as he climbed out of the bay. There was a shrill whistle and flash of flame and an instant cloud of smoke and dust a moment before the concussion struck those on the conning tower and sent them reeling. At once Andreas staggered back to his feet, shaking his head to try and clear the ringing in his ears. The bomber had already climbed out of the bay and was banking away. In its wake small stones and earth were still pattering down amid the swirling dust above the craters where the two bombs had struck.

It had happened so fast that not one shot had been fired back at the enemy. One bomb had landed close to the sailors' tents, the shockwave flattening the nearest and leaving several men sitting on the ground stunned and unable to move. The second had hit one of the trucks which was now on fire, fierce red flames roaring about the wreckage. Andreas saw the captain lying face down on the jetty and felt a surge of panic before Iatridis began to move, drawing himself up and struggling to his feet unsteadily. He shook his head and looked round quickly as Andreas came running up to him.

'Sir, are you all right?'

There was blood dripping from the captain's nose and he cuffed it away on the back of his hand and nodded. 'Yes. Yes. All right. I'm fine.'

Iatridis took in the scene and quickly issued his orders. 'Get the wounded seen to. I'll deal with the fire . . . Where's Pilotis?'

Andreas looked and could not see him anywhere. He recalled that the last he had seen of him was shortly after the plane had been sighted. Close to the truck . . . He felt a cold fist clench around his stomach. He looked round the tented area quickly but there was no sign of the other officer. The captain recalled the position at the same time and also stared towards the blazing vehicle. Both watched in silence for a moment before Iatridis cleared his throat.

'Too bad for Pilotis . . .'

Andreas nodded mutely.

'He's gone, Katarides,' the captain said flatly. 'That makes you the new first officer. I need you, the crew needs you now. We'll grieve later. Understand?'

'He might have been somewhere . . .'

'He was there. I saw him a moment before the bombs fell. He's dead. Now carry on, Lieutenant!' The captain pushed him towards the men lying and stumbling amid the flattened tents. Andreas ran across the open ground towards the crew tents, calling on the nearest men to assist him. One man lay still on the ground, his head close to a rock, a pool of blood spreading out around his shattered skull. The rest had lesser injuries or were just dazed. By the time Andreas had seen to them all, the captain and some of the other men had extinguished the flames that had engulfed the truck and were standing close to the charred remains of a torso. If it had ever been the man once known as Pilotis then Andreas could see no resemblance to him any more.

'Cover that up,' the captain ordered one of his men. 'And see if you can find any more pieces. Before the other men see anything.'

'Yes, sir.'

Iatridis turned to his surviving officer. 'Report.'

Andreas cleared his throat. 'One dead. One with a broken arm. Otherwise minor flesh wounds and some of the men are suffering concussion, sir.'

Iatridis nodded slowly. 'We were fortunate. It could have been much worse . . .' He glanced across the bay, then up the steep slope the bomber had had to negotiate to get clear of Sivota. He shook his head in wonder. 'Who would have thought an Italian would have the balls to do that?'

Andreas said nothing. He was looking around at the aftermath of the sudden attack. The plane had come and gone so quickly. It was hard to believe that moments before, the bay had been a peaceful haven. Now a thick pall of black smoke hung in the air and an acrid stench of burned rubber filled his nostrils.

'Sir, I'll have to use another of the trucks to get to Preveza. With your permission?'

The captain shook his head. 'There's no time for that. Even now I expect our presence is being reported. We have to leave, before they send more planes to bomb Sivota. We have to get out of here as soon as we can. Not just for our sakes.' He gestured across the bay to the small cluster of houses and fishing boats on the far side. 'If they see that the *Papanikolis* is still here then they'll hit the village as well.'

For a moment the decision weighed heavily on Andreas as it meant that there would no longer be any chance of seeing Eleni before he was forced to leave Lefkas. Then he pushed the thought aside. He was a naval officer. He had greater responsibilities to take care of. Neither he nor his country could afford the luxury of personal indulgences at this moment.

'We must leave,' the captain repeated. 'Start getting the men on board, then all the supplies of food we can carry. The same goes for the fuel. Everything else must be destroyed.'

'What are your plans then, sir?' asked Andreas. 'If we have only one propeller we won't be able to go into action.'

If he was surprised or angered by the effrontery of his subordinate then Iatridis did not show it. Instead his expression hardened into a look of determination before he replied.

'If we can't fight, then so be it. I will not surrender the boat. We'll make for Crete. If we're lucky we'll reach a shipyard where the propeller can be repaired, and I will take us back to war to fight the Germans. And if we are cornered by the enemy then I will not hesitate to scuttle her.' He stared into the young officer's eyes. 'If anything should happen to me, it will be your duty to see my wishes are carried out. Is that clear, Katarides?'

'Yes, sir.'

'In the meantime I shall want good, reliable men manning the lookout positions. I do not want a repeat of what happened earlier.'

'I'll see to it, sir,' Andreas said mildly. He could see that Iatridis seemed shaken by the near miss, and blood was still seeping from his nose. It began to drip down the front of his white shirt.

'Carry on, Number One . . . That is your position for the present. Better get used to it.'

'Yes, sir. You can rely on me, sir.'

The clop of hoofs interrupted their exchange and both officers turned to see an elderly man approaching on a donkey. He wore a suit and the long trousers of those more used to living in towns, or at least affecting urban pretensions. He had emerged from the trees where the track began its climb up and out of the bay. He glanced anxiously at the smouldering ruin of the truck and the flattened tents before he clicked his tongue and steered his small mount towards Andreas and his captain. He addressed Iatridis.

'Are you the captain of the submarine?'

'I am. Who wishes to know?'

The man eased his leg over the saddle and stood beside his donkey. Standing as stiffly as he could in front of the captain of the *Papanikolis*, he bowed his head and explained his presence.

'I am Stephanos Mercudios, mayor of Nidhri. I have been asked to bring the captain a message from Inspector Thesskoudis of Lefkada. The inspector called me before noon to give you a warning.'

'Warning?' Iatridis frowned. 'What warning? What for? Speak up, fellow.'

'If it please you, sir, the inspector wishes to inform you that German troops were seen advancing along the causeway that links the island to the mainland this morning. There were hundreds of them, supported by armoured cars and artillery. The inspector suggests that you quit Sivota as soon as possible while you are still able to save your vessel.'

'The Germans are on the island already?' Iatridis shot an anxious glance at Andreas. 'How long ago was this?'

The old man stroked his jaw as he recollected. 'I was called in my office at ten this morning and immediately set out to warn you, sir.'

'Ten! That was nearly three hours ago. Lefkada is, what, thirty kilometres from here by road? Holy mother of God, they could be here by the end of the day. Assuming they know about this base. Let's hope they're content to take Lefkada and stop there before they spread out across the island.'

A tight ball of fear clenched in the pit of Andreas's stomach. 'The plane! The Italians will report our presence to them. If they haven't already.'

'You're right. Even if we allow for the delay while the Italians inform their allies through the usual channels, it won't be long before the Germans know about us. And being Germans, they'll come for us at once. We have to get ready to leave as soon as possible.' Iatridis thought quickly. 'That will take some time, and if the Germans are near it would be best to leave under cover of darkness anyway . . . All right then,' he concluded steadily. 'I'll take charge here. But if the Germans come then we'll need to delay them. That'll be your job, Katarides.'

'Sir?'

'I want you to take the last two trucks and ten men and guard the approaches to the bay. You can have the machine guns from the lookout posts, and some grenades. There are plenty of choke points on the road to Nidhri. Set up your defences and wait. I'll send word when it's time for you to pull back to Sivota. With luck we'll abandon the base and be far out to sea before the first of the enemy arrive.'

'Yes, sir.'

'One thing more.' Iatridis turned to the old man standing by his donkey. 'I want you to go back to Nidhri at once. One of the lieutenant's trucks will drive you there. Stay in touch with Thesskoudis. The moment he reports the Germans are heading this way, you let us know. Have a signal fire ready. Something that makes plenty of smoke. Light it the moment you see the first Germans approaching. Is that clear?'

The old man nodded and then looked anxious. 'And what about my donkey?'

'What?'

'Who will take care of him?'

'That doesn't matter! There's a war on,' the captain said angrily.

But Andreas knew the islanders well enough to know the value placed on a good animal – unlike his mainlander captain, who had been born and raised in Athens. Andreas cleared his throat and intervened.

'Your donkey will be taken care of. I'll have one of the fishermen look after it until you return. All right, sir?'

The islander narrowed his eyes as he stared across the water to the village. 'I don't know . . . Some of those men are rogues. We've had trouble with them for many years.'

'We are all Greeks,' the captain fumed. 'This is no time for petty feuds. Put your country first and deal with the real enemy. Now tie your bloody beast up and get on that truck.'

The local man scowled, then replied, 'I'll do as you say. For Greece. But be warned, this matter will be settled between us when the invaders have gone. You'll see.' He jutted out his stubbly chin in a gesture of defiance and then flicked the reins of his donkey and led it across to the nearest clump of trees.

Iatridis glared after him in frustration before he turned back to his subordinate. 'You have your orders, Lieutenant. Now pick your men, collect your weapons and go.' He paused and then grasped Andreas's hand. 'And Holy God watch over and protect you.'

CHAPTER FOURTEEN

Andreas was satisfied with the position he had chosen: just beyond the junction with the track leading down to the village of Poros in the next bay. In the other direction the road led down a long bare slope towards Nidhri, providing scant cover for anyone advancing up towards the waiting Greeks. Andreas had sited one of the Hotchkiss machine guns amid the rocks above the road to the left and the other light machine gun was hidden on the edge of the treeline on the other side of the road. Both positions would be able to sweep the road as well as cover each other from any attack. The rest of the men, six in all, were hidden amongst the rocks over-looking the road, armed with the Mannlicher-Schönauer rifles that dated back to before the previous war. Old weapons but accurate and deadly enough for the task in hand. There was one other man with the party, Appellios. He deserved another chance after the incident with the enemy aircraft, Andreas had decided, and was now posted on top of the hill with a clear view of the road before it rounded the bend and approached his waiting comrades.

All was in order. The men were in place and had been instructed not to open fire until Andreas fired the first shot. He had gone to each man in turn to make sure that they were ready and knew what he had planned. They were to defend the road until they received word from the captain to pull back to the submarine. If the enemy had not appeared by that point, they would return to the trucks which had been parked before the junction, facing downhill, and drive back to Sivota. If the Germans did reach them then they would hold them off until ordered to withdraw, or until their position became untenable. In that event Andreas had instructed that one section would fall back while the others covered their retreat to the next bend in the road where they in turn would set up and allow their comrades to fall back. And so on, leapfrogging along the road to Sivota, thereby buying the rest of the crew enough time to complete preparing the submarine for sea and to destroy those supplies that they could not carry away with them. It was a desperate plan, and Andreas knew that there was a good chance that neither he nor his men were likely to live more than a few more hours.

From their elevated position they had a clear view across the sea towards the headland and half an hour after they had settled down to wait, Andreas's attention was called to distant movement over the mountains on the mainland. High above the peaks white lines curved and spiralled and it took a moment before Andreas realised he was looking at the contrails of aircraft. As he watched he wondered if there were aircraft locked in combat amid the slowly etched white lines which looked so graceful from such a distance. Then there was a tiny flash and a thin dark trail dropped from the sky behind the crest of the hill and all was still again.

Andreas eased himself down beneath the scented boughs of a pine tree and settled on a bed of brown needles. He was a short distance from the two men manning the second Hotchkiss machine gun, a youngster named Papadakis whose

169

face had been heavily scarred by acne, and Stakiserou, a seasoned petty officer, with a fine black moustache and muscular arms, one of which carried a tattoo with the legend '*Papanikolis* – danger from the deep'. Around them the only movement was the flickering flight of swallows sweeping over the hillside as they snatched insects out of the afternoon air. Andreas glanced at his wristwatch: fifteen hundred, two hours since they had left the frantic activity in Sivota bay. There were still four good hours of daylight remaining, and, as yet, no sign of the Germans. He glanced towards the top of the hill where the lookout was positioned. There was little shelter from the sun up there and Andreas hoped that Appellios was not taking the opportunity to rest the way that some of his countrymen were inclined to do when they found themselves not required to be active. Perhaps he should have posted a more seasoned man up there, Andreas reflected. But even if Appellios failed in his duty for any reason, there would be ample warning from the direction of Nidhri when the mayor gave the word to light the signal fire.

Andreas had heard the stories about German brutality in Poland and France and if there was any truth to them, he feared for his fellow Greeks. He feared for Eleni and her family. Already they would be hearing the tramp of German boots through the streets of Lefkada. Andreas felt a cold fury at the thought of any harm befalling her or her family. To prevent that he was prepared to fight and die if need be. This would be a very different kind of conflict to the one he had experienced aboard the submarine. This time the enemy would be close enough to see their faces. It would be his finger on the trigger and his responsibility for pulling it. This would be his fight. He was in command and the sudden realisation of his responsibility for the men around him frightened him. He must not let them down.

And yet Iatridis had said that the war was already lost. If that was true then what was the point of fighting on? If the result was in no doubt then the reasonable thing to do would be to put an end to the fighting and save lives. What difference did it make if he and these men stood their ground here on some remote island and defied the German invaders? They might kill a handful of the enemy but they would be over-whelmed in the end. Andreas had few illusions that they would be able to survive the retreat to the submarine. They were sailors, used to serving at sea. Not soldiers trained for this kind of warfare and bolstered by a string of unbroken success across the battlefields of Europe. Even if they did reach the *Papanikolis*, what then? A perilous voyage across the Mediterranean to exile in Egypt. With the war going the way it was, the Germans would defeat the British and all that would have been achieved was a delay to the surrender of the submarine and her crew and needless loss of life.

This train of thought was undermining his will to fight and Andreas frowned at himself before turning towards his comrades on the machine gun.

'Stakiserou,' he said quietly.

'Sir?'

'That tattoo on your arm. Have you always served on the *Papanikolis*?'

The petty officer shook his head. 'Started out on the *Elli*, sir. Served on her until the navy bought a couple of submarines from a French shipyard. Fancied a change and applied for a posting. I'm a plank-holder, sir.'

'What's a plank-holder?' Papadakis asked.

'It's what we call a man who has served in a boat since its commissioning.'

'Why a plank-holder?'

The petty officer shrugged. 'Don't know, lad. Just is.'

Andreas propped himself up on his elbows. 'The term dates back to the old days when warships were made of wood. At least, that's what I heard at the academy.'

'But the submarine's made out of steel,' said Papadakis.

The petty officer glanced at Andreas and raised an eyebrow wearily before he responded. 'It's a tradition, you idiot. Like these.' He tapped the insignia on his arm, two yellow stripes with two crossed cannon barrels under the lowest chevron. 'I'm a marksman, but doesn't mean I shoot with a bloody cannon, lad. Fuck me, where did they find you?'

'Eh?' Papadakis frowned.

'Never mind. Just do what I say, and keep feeding me the ammo belt when the time comes. That's all you have to worry about.'

The young recruit nodded and turned his attention back to the empty road. Andreas also turned his eyes towards the road and Nidhri in the distance, still and serene, and heedless of the war which had engulfed the mainland. Then he caught a flicker of movement and glanced down to see that a mosquito had landed on his forearm and begun to feed on his blood. With an impulsive gesture Andreas slapped his spare hand on the insect, leaving a tiny red smear and the crumpled black remains of the creature. He stared at it for a moment and smiled to himself as a thought struck him. So that was it. He and his men were like the insect, inflicting a momentary and insignificant attack on a military leviathan. They too would be swatted as he had crushed the mosquito but they would have momentarily commanded the attention of the giant to their existence and their will to inflict the tiniest inconvenience on their enemy, a mere pinprick. But they would have made their mark all the same and, like the insect, they would be remembered if only as an irritant that had drawn a single drop of blood.

It was a fanciful idea, and it put him in mind of the kind of metaphors his father so liked to use in his poetry to make points about the universality of experience. What would the great Katarides make of this current situation? Andreas wondered with a smile. It had poetic potential, as did all heroic stands against great odds.

'Go tell the Spartans . . .' he muttered to himself and smiled at the conceit.

'What is it, sir?'

He looked up and saw the petty officer staring at him. 'Nothing . . . Tell me, Stakiserou, what were you planning on doing if you had been posted to another vessel?'

'What do you mean, sir?'

'Your tattoo. As far as I am aware there is only one *Papanikolis* in the navy. What was your plan in the event that you were sent to another vessel?'

The petty officer sniffed. 'Never gave it any thought, sir. It's the submarine or nothing for me. I'm a plank-holder, and I'm not going to give her up for anyone else, or to anyone else, let alone some fascist who can't even grow a decent moustache.'

Andreas laughed and shook his head, pleased to have such a man at his side. Then his laughter died in his throat as his gaze shifted back towards Nidhri. A column of dark smoke was rising up from the boatyard on the edge of Vlicho bay. It was too dark for wood and billowed in a thick, oily stain against the background of the sparkling sea.

'Is that it?' Papadakis asked. 'Is that the signal?'

'What does it look like, you fucking idiot?' the petty

officer growled. 'It's time to earn our pay.'

Andreas reached for his binoculars to view the distant scene, nearly three kilometres away. He followed the snaking road towards Nidhri and then he saw them – a line of vehicles emerging from between the whitewashed buildings. A small vehicle led the way, a car. Then came a column of trucks, eight, he counted. At the rear was an armoured car. The column halted and four of the trucks turned off the road and stopped, soldiers disgorging from the rear and spreading out around the vehicles. A moment later the remainder of the small force continued along the road before disappearing from view behind the side of the hill that sloped down towards Vlicho bay.

Andreas lowered his binoculars. 'They're coming.'

He recalled the layout of the road and the way it climbed up from sea level into the hills and made a quick calculation. 'They'll be on us within half an hour.'

The petty officer spat. 'How many of the bastards, sir?'

Andreas paused briefly to estimate the enemy strength. 'At least fifty men, and they have an armoured car.'

'Fifty!' Papadakis shook his head. 'We don't stand a chance.'

Andreas stood up and turned to the youth. Papadakis was little more than a year younger than him, and already there was a gulf of authority between them.

'Seaman Papadakis,' he said in a calm voice. 'We have the advantage. We hold the high ground, we will be firing from concealment and the Germans will be forced to come at us up a narrow road. Save your pity for them. We must kill as many of the enemy as we can, as quickly as we can. Think on that. If we don't, then they will kill us. And if we don't hold them back then our comrades are also lost, and the *Papanikolis*. The captain and the others are counting on you, Papadakis. Are you going to let them down?'

The young sailor stiffened. 'No, sir. Not me.'

Stakiserou laughed and slapped him on the back. 'There's a man! We'll show them.'

Brushing the pine needles from his uniform, Andreas stepped into the open. 'I'll tell the others what to expect and be back in a moment.'

'Yes, sir.'

He trotted through the rocks and stunted bushes on to the road. Even though it was early April the air was hot and still and his voice echoed off the rocks as he moved down the narrow dirt track and called out to his men. At the bottom of the two-hundred-metre stretch of road that he had chosen for the ambush site, just before it curved round the side of the hill and began to zigzag down towards Nidhri, he shouted up to the lookout.

'Appellios! . . . Seaman Appellios!'

A figure rose cautiously, head and shoulders clearly silhouetted against the sky. 'Sir?'

'You see 'em?'

'Yes, sir.'

'When they get within half a kilometre, you give me the signal. Hold your rifle up. I will wave to show you I've seen you. Clear?'

'Yes, sir.'

'When I give the order to open fire I want you to concentrate only on their officers and NCOs. Only them. You'll be in the best position to pick them off and I don't want you drawing attention to yourself. But you must watch for the signal to withdraw, and when you see it, get back to the trucks. Don't stop for anything.'

'Yes, sir.'

'Then Holy God and the Virgin Mary look after you, Appellios.'

'And you, sir.'

Andreas turned and strode back to his position beside the machine gun and eased himself down behind the boulder he had chosen for cover. Taking up his rifle he checked the bolt mechanism again and then loaded a magazine box, chambered the first round and settled into a good shooting position, legs splayed and body lying at an angle to the long barrel of the Mannlicher. He was conscious of his heart racing and his hands felt cold and clammy. He eased the rifle down and rubbed them on his chest before forcing himself to breathe calmly while he waited.

Time seemed to stretch out as his ears strained to catch the first sound of the enemy's approach. Then he heard the faint whine of a motor as it shifted down a gear and was revved to cope with the increasing incline of the slope beyond the hill where Appellios was stationed. The noise grew as the other vehicles followed suit and a moment later a figure rose on the hillside and held his rifle aloft in both hands. Andreas raised an arm and waved steadily from side to side until the lookout dropped out of sight.

'Make ready!' Andreas called to the machine-gun crew and Stakiserou pulled back the cocking lever and it snapped back with a metal clatter. Beside him knelt Papadakis, feeding the ammunition belt from its case and offering it up to the weapon. Then all three waited, still and tense, as the growl of the approaching vehicles steadily swelled in volume. As the noise grew, it seemed to take an eternity before the first vehicle appeared round the corner of the hill and entered the stretch of road Andreas had chosen for the ambush. He felt his heart give a lurch as he saw it was the armoured car. It must have changed positions in the column.

'Shit . . .'

He had planned to open fire while the last truck was on the corner, blocking the armoured car. Now it would have to be dealt with. He turned and glanced at Stakiserou and muttered, 'Wait for me to shoot first.'

The petty officer grunted an acknowledgement, keeping his eyes fixed on the approaching enemy.

The armoured car's engine strained as it continued up the slope, dust rising in its wake. A man in a side cap stood in the low turret, hands gripping the steel rim as he scrutinised the way ahead. Behind came a small car with four men in it, two wearing officer's caps. Then the first of the lorries, open, with ten or twelve men sitting on the benches on either side of the bed. Few wore their helmets and Andreas could see that some were laughing as they shouted to their companions above the din of the vehicles. He raised his rifle and felt a nervous trembling in his limbs before he angrily forced himself to concentrate, to think of nothing but taking aim at his enemy and waiting until the right time to open fire. He sighted on the man standing in the armoured car, lining the German up with the pin on his muzzle and the notch at the rear, close to his eye. He breathed steadily, fighting the urge to pull the trigger. He must wait until the last truck was abreast of the men hiding amongst the rocks above the enemy column.

As the armoured car rumbled closer, to within fifty metres, Andreas could make out the details on the face of his target. A broad forehead above glasses that glinted as they caught the sun. He was reminded of Peter. For an instant he was seized by the sudden fear that it was his friend. That some horrifying trick of fate had placed Peter in front of him. He dismissed the thought, it was almost impossible that it could be so, and now the man was close enough for Andreas to be sure that it was not. He breathed in deeply, pulled the butt of the rifle into his shoulder and gently squeezed the trigger.

CHAPTER FIFTEEN

The violence of the recoil and the numbing blast of the shot shocked Andreas and he instinctively blinked. His eyes opened just in time to see the German in the turret lurch back, throwing his arms in the air before he slumped inside the vehicle. The Hotchkiss burst into life with a deafening rattle close to Andreas, drowning out the fusillade of shots ringing out from amongst the rocks. The other machine gun joined in, spraying bullets into the first of the trucks, striking men down as they began to scramble off the vehicle when the driver braked. Behind, the other lorries stopped abruptly and the men jumped off the rear, under fire from the rocks, and Andreas saw more of them fall.

There was a sudden flash and roar as the first of the grenades hurled by the ambushers exploded and then there were more blasts along the line of the road. Detonation after detonation, drowning out the rattle and crack of small-arms fire and sending clouds of dust swirling into the air. One landed close to the first truck and there was a bright flare and a loud thud as the petrol tank caught fire and exploded in a brilliant fire-ball of red, orange, gold and black. Two men close by were engulfed in the flames and then staggered off the road, human torches blazing before they fell and writhed. The armoured car swerved to the side of the road and ran on to the banked earth at an angle.

'Bastards!' Stakiserou shouted as he hunched low, squinting down the barrel of the Hotchkiss, traversing left and right as he fired. Brass cases leaped from the side of the weapon, tumbling to the ground. At his side Papadakis gritted his teeth against the deafening storm of sounds assaulting his ears and concentrated on feeding the ammunition belt as steadily as he could.

Andreas worked the bolt on his rifle, adjusted his aim and lined it up on the small car. The driver and the two officers had leaped out and were sheltering behind it as they looked for their opponents amongst the rocks above the road. Some of their men were firing back blindly and puffs of shattered stone were bursting off the boulders around the ambushers' positions. Shutting his left eye, Andreas aimed at the nearest of the officers and fired. The bullet caught him in the shoulder and the German spun round and fell on his back. At once his companions realised that they were caught in a crossfire and hastily pulled the wounded officer off the road and over the lip of the slope beyond. Andreas shot again and missed and then they were out of sight.

The clatter of the machine guns continued uninterrupted as they sprayed bullets along the line of the German convoy. Andreas lowered his rifle and saw that at least fifteen men were down while most of the others had taken cover. A handful had worked their way a short distance up the slope and were exchanging shots with the Greek sailors.

'Stakiserou!' Andreas shouted, waving his hand to draw the petty officer's attention. He carried on shooting, his face contorted into a snarl, until Papadakis punched him in the arm and pointed. The din of the Hotchkiss immediately ceased.

'Up there! The men on the slope. Keep their heads down! Don't let 'em get any closer to our lads.'

Stakiserou nodded and shifted his aim, then the Hotchkiss clattered again and Andreas saw clods of soil and shards of stone leap into the air around the Germans attempting to work their way up the slope. One man slumped down and his comrades dropped and pressed themselves to the ground. An instant later a second truck was engulfed in fire as the bullets of the other machine gun struck home, and flame and smoke billowed along the road, obscuring the view from Andreas's position. Stakiserou fired a few more shots and then paused, searching for fresh targets as the men on the slope kept up their attack. One by one the surviving Germans sprinted or crept for the cover of the lower slope, diving over the edge of the road and out of the line of fire.

The sound of shooting gradually died away, save for an occasional shot as a head was raised or there was a suspicious movement amid the undergrowth beside the road. Andreas looked down the line of the convoy and saw that the car was riddled with bullets, as were the two surviving lorries, while the others blazed. The straining note of an engine drew his attention back to the armoured car. The driver had succeded in freeing the vehicle from the earth bank and was reversing it back on to the road. Already the low turret was swinging towards Andreas and his companions and he could see the muzzle of the machine gun foreshortening.

'Get down!' he called out.

A moment later the German gunner opened fire and at once the branches of the trees above them were shredded by bullets, causing a deluge of twigs and pine cones. All three men flattened themselves as their position was raked by the machine gun. Then it stopped. Andreas stayed low, breathing hard, and then cautiously raised his head. He could see the armoured car, slowly reversing back towards the ruined convoy. The turret turned as the barrel of the machine gun angled up towards the rocks and it opened fire again in short bursts to force the ambushers to stay in cover.

While it was suppressing the Greeks, Andreas saw the uninjured German officer rise into a crouch and wave his men forward, along the edge of the road towards the front of the convoy. The intention was clear.

'They're going to try and outflank our men on the slopes. I don't think the officer has seen us.' Andreas pointed him out. 'Let 'em get up and get closer. The moment they are alongside the armoured car, open up.'

'Yes, sir.' Stakiserou nodded and turned to Papadakis. The latter was still lying face down, pressing himself into the ground, trembling. The petty officer gave him a shove. 'Get up, you! We've still got work to do. Feed me the ammo. Come on, Papadakis! Up!'

Andreas already knew what had to be done while his comrades kept the enemy occupied. The armoured car had to be dealt with to prevent it pinning his men down and giving the Germans a chance to mount a counter-attack. Crawling over to the Hotchkiss, he picked up the haversack containing the grenades.

'Keep their heads down. I'll deal with the armoured car.'

Stakiserou shot him an anxious look and then nodded. 'Be careful, sir. We'll do our best.'

'Good luck!' Andreas patted the petty officer on the thigh and turned to crawl away. Slinging his rifle across his back he stayed low, working his arms and legs as he made his way along the edge of the pine trees and then the lip of the road towards the armoured car, whose turret was constantly moving and occasionally firing short bursts. He could hear snatches of exchanges between the enemy as they gathered themselves to make a move. Then, not more than ten metres ahead, he saw a helmet rise above a rock and an instant later a pair of eyes widened as they saw the Greek officer making towards them. Andreas clawed at the strap of his rifle but it was caught tightly against his shoulder. At the same time the German rose into a crouch and brought up his Mauser to shoot. There was just time for Andreas to feel an ice-cold certainty that he was about to die when the Hotchkiss fired again and the German's helmet snapped back and he fell behind the rock. A stream of bullets followed to discourage any more of his comrades before Stakiserou ceased shooting. A moment later the armoured car returned fire, and the trees directly above the machine-gun position trembled and shattered under the impact. A large branch snapped and fell down on to the two sailors as Andreas watched. If they were pinned down then nothing would stop the enemy from working their way round the ambush position, climbing into the rocks and attacking the remaining Greeks from the flank and rear.

Andreas knew his men depended on him and he must do his duty, despite his fears. He muttered a brief prayer to calm his shaken nerves, and then continued crawling forwards. The sound of the armoured car's engine was close now and he fumbled with the buckle of the haversack before reaching inside for one of the grenades. The hard, milled surface felt cold in his hand. The time had come for him to act, yet still he hesitated, knowing the risk he faced. This was the great test and he felt his courage wavering at the prospect of death. Then his mind calmed at the thought. The certainty of death if he refused to move balanced against the probability of death if he rushed towards the armoured car. In the end it was a logical decision.

Snatching a deep breath, he rose into a crouch, and saw the front plate of the armoured car no more than fifteen paces away. The turret was swinging back towards the rocks. Through the driver's viewing slit he could see the man's head was turned away, towards one of his companions, and Andreas clamped his jaw tightly and ran forward in a crouch, his heart beating wildly inside his chest. His gaze was riveted to the armoured car, then he heard the shout of alarm from the side of the road. He was halfway there, boots pounding on the dry, rutted road, when the first shot was fired from his right.

The sound instantly alerted the driver and he turned back, seeing his foe running directly towards him. His mouth opened and he shouted. The turret began to swing faster, arcing round towards Andreas. He ran the last few paces at a desperate sprint and threw himself on to the front of the vehicle, his spare hand snatching at the straps holding the water cans to the side. He hauled himself up beside the barrel of the machine gun and felt it lurch as it opened fire. But it was too late to scare the Germans now.

He tore the pin out and balled his hand round the grenade as he swung up and looked down into the turret. It was no more than a second but he took in every detail of the interior. The terrified face of the gunner looking up at him. The body of the man he had shot at the start of the ambush slumped on the floor of the vehicle, hand clasped to his chest, his face contorted with pain. The back of the driver, hunched over his steering wheel. The brass cases of spent rounds littering the drab grey of the interior. Then the gunner snatched at the pistol holder on his belt and Andreas threw his fist down, hard, striking the man on the nose. He winced and opened his hand and the safety lever sprang out as the grenade fell into the armoured car with a loud clatter and rolled back under the gunner's seat. There was a cry of alarm as Andreas jumped clear, and stumbled, rolling over then half rising and running a few steps on before the grenade went off with a roar. Flame and smoke shot out of the turret and through the driver's slit and Andreas sprawled on the ground, gouging his cheek. The sharp pain concentrated his mind and he rolled on to his side and looked back.

The armoured car's engine was still running and it began to roll back steadily until it hit the car and stopped. Smoke rose from the turret and the barrel of the machine gun aimed at the sky. There was no sign of life from within, no sound, and then Andreas saw the spray of blood on the plate in front of the driver's viewing slit and felt a tremor of horror at what he had done, which quickly gave way to a sense of triumph.

The explosion had momentarily caused the shooting to stop as the combatants' eyes were drawn to the spectale of the knocked-out armoured car. There was a harsh cheer from the trees where Stakiserou and Papadakis were positioned, and the cry was taken up along the side of the hill. From the Germans there was only a brief, ominous silence, and then an angry shout and an uneven volley of rifle fire and the staccato crash of a machine pistol. Andreas heard the impact on the ground around him and lay as flat as he could in the hope that he might not be seen, or at least be taken for a corpse. His men returned fire, adding their shouts of triumph and defiance at the men who had invaded their country.

As the exchange of fire reached a crescendo, Andreas rose into a crouch and ran back up along the road and then dashed across and over the edge before making his way back to the machine-gun position. Stakiserou let out a delighted greeting at his reappearance and paused in his shooting.

'You have the heart of a Spartan, Lieutenant! Heart of a Spartan. Fuck me . . .'

He shook his head and opened up on the Germans again. Beside him, Papadakis regarded his officer with an awed expression, smiled awkwardly and then turned his attention back to feeding the belted ammunition into the Hotchkiss. Andreas slipped the rifle strap over his head and set the weapon down before he lay on his side breathing heavily, trying not to tremble.

'They're running!' Papadakis shouted. 'Look!'

Rolling on to his knees, Andreas risked a cautious look and saw that the Germans were indeed on the move, falling back towards the corner of the road and the safety of the far side of the hill. The Greeks fired a few shots after them and then the guns fell silent. A cheer sounded from high up and Andreas saw Appellios rise up, waving his rifle from side to side as he shouted with elation.

'What is that fool doing?' Stakiserou snarled. 'Get back under cover . . .'

Andreas jumped up and waved his hands frantically to attract the lookout's attention and motion him to get down.

A rifle cracked, the sound echoing up the slope. Andreas saw the young sailor freeze in motion, his rifle held over his head. Then he fell, out of view. A sick feeling swelled up inside Andreas. There was a dreadful stillness before the petty officer cleared his throat and spat. 'What are your orders now, sir?'

The ambush had succeeded far better than Andreas had anticipated. They set fire to the remaining German lorries and the armoured car and retreated in both of their own vehicles to the next position. Nearly two kilometres down the road was another natural choke point on the junction above Sivota bay. It would take the Germans a while to catch up with them, Andreas calculated. They would proceed far more cautiously along the road towards Sivota and there would be no element of surprise for the Greek rearguard. They had bought their comrades a little time, but now there would be a heavier price to pay when the Germans attacked again.

Besides the death of Appellios, another man had been killed and two wounded, one seriously. There was no time to waste on retrieving their comrades' bodies and they were left where they had fallen. Andreas sent the wounded back to the submarine in one of the lorries while the other was parked, ready for the final dash down the winding road that led into the bay. He had six men left. Once they had set up the two machine guns, he gathered them together by a roadside shrine for a last word before they faced the enemy once more. They regarded him calmly and he was impressed by their cool demeanour. Even Papadakis seemed to have got over his earlier nerves.

'We've given the fascists a beating they'll not forget,' Andreas began with a smile. 'I estimate that we've killed or wounded a third of their number, at least. That still gives them the advantage in terms of numbers and the next time they will be ready for us. It'll be a far harder fight, make no mistake about that.' He looked at each man in turn. 'Are you ready to do your duty?'

'To the end!' Stakiserou replied fiercely, bunching his fist. 'We'll show 'em, sir.'

The others chorused their agreement.

'Good. I expected nothing less.' Andreas nodded and then

turned his attention to more immediate issues. 'We have plenty of ammunition for the rifles, but we're down to less than five hundred rounds for the machine guns, so, Petty Officer Stakiserou, I would be grateful if you were to expend your ammunition in a more conscientious manner this time. If you continue spraying lead at the Germans the way you did, you threaten to bankrupt our country.'

The sailors laughed as Stakiserou affected a scowl. Andreas continued, 'We have used most of the grenades too, so use what is left sparingly. There are two for each of us. Make every one count, and every bullet.' His expression became more serious. 'I won't lie to you about our chances. Some of us, maybe all of us, will not live out the day. But I will not throw our lives away. We'll hold them off for as long as we can. If we run out of ammunition, or they look like getting round our position, I'll fire the flare. You fall back to the lorry as soon as you see it. Don't stop for anything. Or anyone. We'll have to leave our wounded behind and hope that the Germans honour their obligation to treat enemy casualties. That goes for me too. I don't want any heroes. Greece will need every man that she can save from the battlefield to take our country back. It is our duty to fight and survive to fight again. Don't forget that . . . Any man who gives his life in vain will be on fatigues for a month.'

Stakiserou roared with laughter and Papadakis looked confused for a moment before he got the joke and joined in cheerfully, his mirth making him look more foolish than ever, and Andreas felt a stab of pity that he was putting the youth in danger. He would rather send him back down to the submarine but now every man was needed to hold the Germans back and buy time for the boat to be made ready to sail. He glanced down the slope towards the bay and could see the tiny figures of men toiling away to load supplies and rolling the fuel drums on to the jetty to fill the *Papanikolis*'s tanks. A safe distance away the supplies that the captain had decided would have to be left behind were being heaped in a pile, ready to be set on fire. On the other side of the bay, in contrast, the people of the fishing village had come out to sit and watch and Andreas could not help a passing feeling of guilt at the prospect of abandoning them to the German invaders. But that could not be helped.

He turned back to his men. 'Go to your positions and watch for the enemy. There will be no signal this time. Open fire as soon as you see them. But make sure that is what you see. I do not want any man shooting at a rabbit by accident and giving our position away. Only shoot when you can see them clearly. Good luck.'

The small rearguard shook hands with each other and muttered a few words of encouragement before they made their way to their places. Andreas surveyed the ground again. It was not as favourable as the first ambush site in that the Greeks would not be able to exploit the high ground and have a crossfire. However, the cliff to their left and the steep ground to the right meant that the Germans would have to approach on a front of no more than fifty paces wide, through the scrub either side of the road. The Greeks were on a slight rise covered in olive trees with an old drystone wall running in front. The wall was adequate protection from small-arms fire and would serve to conceal their number. Once again Andreas was reminded of his ancient forebears at Thermopylae and could only hope that he and his men fared better than the Spartans.

He took his place in the centre of the line, between the two machine-gun crews, and the last two riflemen guarded the flanks. The lorry was parked fifty metres away, where the road curved behind the olive trees. The warm spring day was coming to an end as the late afternoon sun dipped towards the mountains at their backs. He had prepared a loophole in the wall that gave a clear view along the road and rise over which the Germans must advance, and settled down to wait. This time he found that his early fears had gone. In their place was a fatalistic determination to defy the enemy. He smiled wearily at the prospect of dying the same day as he had discovered he had what it took to be an officer and lead his men in battle. He wished there had been more time to prove himself, and to serve his country. But that was not likely to be the outcome, something he accepted with a calm deliberation that pleasantly surprised him.

The Germans were upon them sooner than Andreas had expected. Barely ten minutes after he had addressed his men a wizened shepherd with a dark cloth wrapped round his grey hair began to drive his flock of sheep across the road and towards a narrow track leading up the cliff to their left. He was halfway across the open ground when some of his sheep shied away from the road and ran in the direction of the wall, bleating nervously. The shepherd raised his staff and ran forward, then stopped and stared for an instant. He turned and broke into a stiff run towards the cliff. A short burst of automatic fire blasted across the open ground and one of the sheep leaped into the air and fell heavily, before several bullets slammed into the shepherd's back and he stumbled and fell face first and his charges scattered in all directions about him.

'What did they do that for?' Papadakis said loudly. 'Why shoot the old man?'

'Shhh!' Stakiserou hissed angrily. 'Just keep your mouth shut and be ready with the ammo.'

Andreas raised his binoculars and slowly swept the crest of the rise and then stopped breathing as he saw a helmet in the grass, then another, and a shot rang out to his left as the sailor on the flank fired. At once the shot was returned from several points and bullets cracked off the weathered stones of the wall around the sailor's position. A moment later there was a dull thump and a faint whistling in the air just before an explosion burst amongst the trees behind the Greek position.

'They've got a mortar!' the petty officer cried out to Andreas.

'Makes no difference,' he called back. 'We're in good cover and they can't see us. They'll just be wasting time and ammunition if they're counting on blasting us out.'

His words sounded hollow even as he spoke them and when he heard the whistle of the next mortar bomb, Andreas pressed himself down into the ground and felt his guts clench in terror before the explosion erupted in front of the wall, to the left of his loophole. The enemy were firing bracketing shots, he realised. One too far, the next adjustment falling short, but the third would land somewhere in between, close to where they lay. He was not the only one to realise the significance of the first two bombs.

'Keep your head down!' Stakiserou snapped at the young crewman, who was jeering at the enemy.

Papadakis regarded him with the haughty expression of one who had recently discovered his courage and falsely concluded that it made him invincible. He bit his thumb at the Germans and spat. A burst of fire rattled against the stones away to the right and so they missed the whistle of the next shot and the explosion caught them by surprise. There was a red burst just behind the wall and a deafening blast before they were showered with earth and shattered twigs and small branches. As the falling debris swiftly subsided, the petty officer shook his head. 'That was close.'

Papadakis lay flat beside him, refusing to move until he was given a booted prod and then he jerked into life and looked up at his comrades with a terrified expression.

'Still alive then?' Stakiserou grinned.

The next shot landed further along the wall, the blast blowing a small gap in the stonework. Those that followed ranged down the edge of the olive trees as the Germans tried to unsettle the nerves of their opponents while they prepared to attack. Andreas and the others readied themselves, staring hard towards the grass and rock outcrops lining the rise in front of them. There was one more explosion before the defenders heard a harsh shout. At once a party of four men jumped up and raced a short distance to the right of the German line, close to the base of the cliff, weaving as they went to put off the Greeks' aim. Andreas swung his rifle round but before he drew a bead on the rearmost man they dropped to the ground. An instant later another party scrambled up on the other flank and repeated the manoeuvre.

'We'll concentrate our fire on them.' Andreas pointed. 'The other machine gun can cover the cliff.'

Two more parties rushed forward across the ground in front of the wall and a burst of fire from the second Hotchkiss brought down one of the enemy, doubling the soldier up before he rolled to a stop and lay writhing. Each time some of the Germans moved, their comrades provided covering fire, aiming for the area where they had spotted muzzle flashes. Their leader knew his craft and his men were well-trained and confident, Andreas realised. He kept his attention focused on their right and then he saw the movement he had been waiting for. The Germans rose and began to run forward again. Andreas tracked one and fired, an instant before Stakiserou opened up and the ground around the Germans erupted in spouts of soil and shattered stone. Two were cut down, spinning under the impact of the bullets, while a third was struck in the leg and threw himself to the ground. The last man sprinted on a short distance, chased by a trail of bullets as the machine gun caught up with him and struck him. His arms flailed as his rifle spun through the air and then he fell.

'Hah!' the petty officer grinned. 'Got 'em all!'

His celebration was cut short by a spray of bullets smashing into the stones of the wall and the branches overhead. The enemy had brought one of their own machine guns forward, Andreas realised, and were laying down suppressing fire while their comrades made a succession of short dashes towards the Greek positions. He risked a quick glance through his loophole and saw the shiver of the grass that gave away the enemy machine-gun team. He took aim with his rifle and loosed the rest of his magazine in their direction and the enemy ceased firing. Long enough for Andreas to look over the ground and assess the situation.

The Germans had approached to within fifty metres of the wall and would soon be close enough to hurl grenades, before launching their final assault. It was almost time for Andreas to order his men to retreat. First they would shoot up the enemy positions and then make a withdrawal before the Germans reacted.

'Mortar!' Stakiserou yelled and Andreas flattened as he heard another whistle. The round struck in front of the wall, but instead of exploding, it detonated with a soft crump and smoke swirled around the impact point and began to disperse. Andreas saw the danger at once. The enemy was laying down a smokescreen to mask their attack. Andreas rolled on to his side, wrenched his flare pistol out of the haversack and opened the breech. He rammed a cartridge in, snapped the pistol shut and aimed into the air and fired. The flare whizzed into the sky and burst in a bright white glare.

'Let's go!' Andreas ordered his companions. 'Back to the truck, now! I'll cover you.'

He remained at his loophole as Stakiserou and Papadakis took the Hotchkiss off its tripod and fell back through the trees. Andreas saw further movement to his left as the other sailors withdrew, then he turned back to the enemy as another smoke round landed and added to the dense white veil spreading in front of the wall. He heard a voice call out to his left, not far off, and turned to fire twice in that direction, and then again to the right, and emptied the rest of the magazine to the flank. He reloaded and listened again. There were more voices and then he saw a figure approaching through the smoke. Snatching his rifle round, Andreas took aim and fired at once and was gratified by the sight of the man collapsing. He fired again in that direction and off to the left before scrambling to his feet and racing after his men, crouching low as he flitted beneath the olive trees.

There was a short pause before he heard the Germans shouting. The enemy's machine gun rattled out again and Andreas heard the cracking and splintering of wood behind and to his right, followed by the explosions of hand grenades. He saw the road ahead of him through the trees and ran on, out into the open. The truck was to his right and the petty officer and Papadakis were climbing on to the back while the rifleman jumped into the cab and made to start the engine.

Andreas raced towards them, looking for any sign of the others emerging from the trees.

'Set up the Hotchkiss!' he shouted.

Stakiserou nodded and bent to his work over the bed of the truck while his assistant opened the last ammunition tin and readied the belt. Andreas paused to reload his rifle, then clambered up beside them and raised his weapon. He heard an outburst of shots from the direction of the trees.

'Get ready!'

They waited, poised to spray the olive trees at the first sign of the enemy. There were more shots and then German voices calling out to each other. The lorry's engine coughed into life and the driver revved the engine in neutral to warm it up.

'There!' Papadakis pointed quickly.

The others looked and saw the figure stumbling out of the shadows beneath the trees. The late afternoon sun slanted through the canopy and trunks and dappled his sailor's uniform with splashes of orange light. He had been shot in the shoulder and blood soaked his shirt beneath the hand he clasped to the wound. He saw the truck and was turning towards it when Andreas saw more figures rushing out of the gloom.

'Stakiserou! They're coming. Shoot 'em!'

The petty officer swung the machine-gun barrel and fired a burst into the trees. The Germans scattered as they dived for cover. Andreas beckoned frantically to the injured sailor and the latter ran towards them, an instant before bullets struck the road where he had been standing. The bed of the lorry lurched under Andreas's boots and he turned and banged his fist on the driver's cab.

'Wait for my order! Wait, damn you!'

The vehicle stopped jarringly and Andreas's side struck the back of the cab painfully. Hissing a curse, he turned back as the wounded sailor reached the truck and tried to heave himself up into the back, grimacing with pain as the machine gun blasted out above his head. Andreas hurriedly set his rifle down and pulled the man up and in, his ears ringing with the clatter of the Hotchkiss. Even though the Germans had gone to ground they were now firing back in earnest and the wooden rail on the side of the truck splintered as a Mauser round tore through it.

'Go!' Andreas shouted at the driver. 'GO!'

Slamming the vehicle into first gear, the driver let the clutch up too quickly and it leaped forward, threatening to stall before he caught it with the clutch, adjusted the accelerator and the lorry shuddered down the track away from the olive trees. Through the rosy-hued dust thrown up in its wake, Andreas saw the flashes of gunfire and the field-grey uniforms of the soldiers emerging from the trees. Then they reached the junction of the track leading down to Sivota and the truck slowed for the turning. Stakiserou and Papadakis had to stop firing to hold on to the side of the vehicle to keep their footing while Andreas did his best to steady the wounded sailor with his spare hand. The gears ground as the driver wrenched the steering wheel towards the head of the track and Andreas felt the sailor jerk in his grip as a warm spray splattered his cheek. He glanced down and saw a gaping red hole in the side of the man's head. His eyes stared up, wide in death, and his jaw hung open.

'Shit.' Andreas gritted his teeth bitterly and let go of the man. The truck bounced along the track that zigzagged down towards the bay, and out of sight of the Germans. But the enemy had smelled blood and would continue the pursuit,

Andreas knew. They would not be far behind the truck, determined to wipe out the handful of Greeks who had inflicted such heavy losses amongst their comrades. Unlike the truck, they were not obliged to use the track and could descend directly down the slope at the end of the bay. Sunlight flickered through the trees as the driver took the pitted and rutted surface as fast as he dared while his passengers held on tightly.

Then there was a gap in the trees and Andreas snatched a brief glimpse of the bay and saw the exhaust smoke trailing up from the submarine's stern as the crewmen hurried aboard and climbed down through the deck hatches. Flames glittered at the base of the pyre of abandoned equipment and supplies. Andreas saw the captain standing on the conning tower beckoning to his men. The anti-aircraft gun swung towards the sound of the earlier shooting and the crew stood ready for action. Then the trees blocked the view again. Two more turns, Andreas recalled as he held on. The truck swerved into the penultimate straight for another hundred metres, turned again and then the trees opened out either side of the track. The track divided, the right branch heading towards the village while the left made for the jetty where the *Papanikolis* was ready to depart. Two men stood at the bows, another two at the stern, ready to slip the moorings, and the gangway was still in place.

The truck rattled into the open and steered directly for the jetty. Andreas and the others shared a nervous smile of relief at their escape. Then there was a shrill clatter and a line of dark holes stitched across the roof of the cab. The lorry began to turn as the stricken driver's foot came off the accelerator, and as it slowed it struck a pothole and turned on to its side, throwing its passengers and the machine gun out across the dirt and shingle. Andreas fell hard on his shoulder and felt the snap of a bone. He groaned as he sat up in agony. The engine was still running and a wheel spun. The machine gun lay close by, still attached to its stand and half on top of Papadakis, who lay sprawled in a daze. The driver was dead, the body trapped beneath the truck, leaving his torso and bloodied head exposed. The petty officer was already on his feet, seeming unhurt. He glanced round the end of the lorry and swore.

'Holy God, those fascist bastards are quick off the mark!'

Andreas struggled up, gritting his teeth at the sharp pain of his broken collar bone. Up the slope he could see the enemy. Some, fitter and more nimble than their comrades, had run directly down the slope and were only a hundred metres away from the truck.

Stakiserou reacted swiftly, straining as he picked up the Hotchkiss and set it up at the end of the truck. Papadakis snatched the last box of ammunition and staggered to his side. The petty officer nodded his thanks and fed the belt into the breech before pushing the younger man away.

'Get the lieutenant back to the boat!'

Andreas looked at him and shook his head. 'I'm injured. You and Papadakis go. I'll stay.'

Stakiserou ignored him as he crouched behind the weapon and took aim. 'Sorry, sir. I can't hear you.' He cocked the weapon and fired a quick burst before the officer could react. Then he glanced over his shoulder at Papadakis. 'What are you waiting for? Go! Get him out of here!'

The sailor nodded, thrusting Andreas towards the waiting submarine as the petty officer fired again. The deeper crack of the Oerlikon joined in, shooting its explosive shells in amongst the trees. Andreas thought about protesting but was steered away by the young sailor who put an arm round his back and pushed him on. Bullets zipped past as they reached the jetty and the crewmen on the mooring lines crouched low, waiting for the order to cast off. Some of the German rounds glanced off the hull with a shrill crash. Andreas could hear the short staccato bursts of the Hotchkiss and smelt the acrid stink of diesel fumes as he ran. Then they were at the end of the gangway and Papadakis helped him across on to the deck of the *Papanikolis*.

'Get him below!'

Andreas glanced up and saw the captain's face looking down over the coaming of the conning tower. Then Iatridis looked up and cupped his hands to his mouth.

'Cast off for'rd! Cast off aft!'

'Wait!' Andreas protested. 'Stakiserou is coming!'

Iatridis looked down again with a pained expression and shook his head. The submarine's starboard engine rumbled a deeper note and the gangway splashed into the water as the vessel got under way. Andreas looked back towards the truck and saw that the Hotchkiss was no longer firing. The petty officer's body lay slumped over the weapon. Some distance beyond him the Germans scattered and scrambled for cover as the Oerlikon blasted them again. A handful of shots flew after the *Papanikolis* as she slowly slipped out from under the camouflage netting and swung gently towards the entrance of the bay and the open sea beyond.

CHAPTER SIXTEEN

Norwich, 2013

Dusk was settling over the city and the room felt gloomy and cold as Eleni folded her spotted bony hands in her lap.

'That was how it was when the Germans invaded and Andreas fought them for the first time. He told me about it later, when we met again. How he had first gone to war . . . He remained there for the rest of his life. Poor Andreas, he never saw the world at peace ever again.' She closed her eyes for a moment and pressed her lined lips together before she blinked and forced a slight smile.

'I found this while you were making a drink earlier.' She reached down to her cardigan pocket and brought out a stained black and white photo with a decoratively cut edge and placed it on the table between them. 'It was with the loose photos in my drawer. It was amongst Andreas's effects when the British finally gave them to me years after the war. Such a little box to carry the mementoes of a lifetime . . . Anyway, there, see what a handsome man he was.'

Anna reached for the photo. She saw a man in an army uniform with a beret, standing smiling, arms clasped behind his back. Some distance behind him stood the pyramids of Giza. Anna recognised his features clearly enough. Not so different from the picture with Eleni and Peter, but his face had filled out and his build was more solid. It was true that he was handsome, but in that stiff, old-fashioned way that Anna could not quite take seriously.

'I thought he was in the navy.'

'He was. That was taken several months after his submarine escaped to Egypt, when he was working for the British.'

'Why Egypt?'

Eleni thought a moment. 'Where else was there to go? The enemy controlled most of the Mediterranean. Egypt was the closest territory still controlled by our allies. Besides, that was where King Georgios and what was left of his government had fled when Greece was invaded. While we starved, they lived in comfort in Cairo. Meanwhile, most of our people who had escaped the occupation went to Egypt in the hope that they would find a way to continue the struggle. As for Andreas, there was little for him to do when he came out of hospital, even though he was desperate to fight the fascists. Commander Iatridis wanted to take the *Papanikolis* out to attack enemy shipping but the Greek government in exile refused to risk the few warships they had saved from the Nazis. Eventually they got sick of his demands and replaced Iatridis with a captain more willing to obey their will. Meanwhile Andreas had been chosen for other duties. About the time this photo was taken.'

'Oh?' Anna leaned forward. 'What was that then?'

Eleni shook her head. 'I'll tell you in the morning, child.'

Anna watched her grandmother in silence, wondering at the account she had just been given. Eleni had seemed old all her life, always the same irascible and shrewd lady who moved with a brittle elegance. But now it was as if Anna was seeing her afresh, and as her grandmother had spoken it was almost as if she could see the young woman Eleni had once been. So full of life, and in love for the first time, only to have to endure the invasion of her peaceful island home by the Nazis.

As she considered Eleni's description of the early days of the German onslaught, the analytical side of Anna's brain cautioned her. This was Eleni's account of what Andreas had told her, many years ago. It was bound to be compromised by being told second hand, so many years after the events concerned. It might not be a reliable version of what had really taken place. Then again, what version of events ever was? As a lecturer had once pointed out to her at university, what people understood by 'history' was made up of what had actually happened, what historians said happened, what people thought had happened and, increasingly, what film, television, novels and the internet represented as having happened. Given that, anyone who sought an accurate historical 'truth' was doomed to frustration at best and complete misunderstanding at worst. And yet, Eleni's words carried the conviction of truth in them and she had depicted the characters, their feelings and the settings so vividly that it was hard not to accept the veracity of her recounted experience. Perhaps history belonged to whoever could tell the best story, Anna mused.

The sound of the front door opening interrupted Anna's thoughts and a moment later her mother entered the room.

'Anna, love, will you give me a hand with the shopping?'

'Of course. Do you mind, Yiayia?'

Eleni shook her head. 'You go and be a good girl. Besides, I am tired. I will rest a little before dinner.'

She gave a brief smile and nodded towards the door and Anna rose from her seat and followed her mother into the hall and out on to the path leading to the street. The sun had dipped below the roofline of the terraced houses opposite and the street was washed in blue-tinted shadow. Anna shivered at the cold and realised how hot her grandmother's room had become over the last few hours. Her mother's Vauxhall Astra was parked just outside the small gate and she lifted the tailgate to reveal several shopping bags stuffed with groceries. They took two bags each and turned back towards the house.

'Have you had a good chat?' asked Marita.

'Very interesting. We've been talking about her childhood all afternoon.'

'Oh?'

'Well, not really childhood, I suppose. It was more to do with the war years.'

'I see.'

Anna picked up on her mother's strained tone at once and glanced at her as they approached the front door.

'You first.' Marita stretched out a hand and held the door open. They placed the bags down in the hall and went back for the rest. As she closed the front door, Anna's mother raised her eyebrows and spoke softly.

'She's never really told me a great deal about what went on at that time, you know. It was never spoken about when I was a kid and it seemed too late to raise the subject again when I grew up. Seems she's been more forthcoming with you.'

'I guess.'

'I wonder why.' Marita frowned.

'Does it upset you, Mum?'

'What? No. Of course not. Just seems a bit strange that she should open up to you rather than her own daughter, that's all. Now, let's get these bags into the kitchen and put the shopping away. Then you can help me prepare dinner.'

A short time later Marita stood over the stove frying onion and garlic and browning some minced beef while her daughter chopped tomatoes and courgettes.

'How was she when you were talking?' asked Marita.

'What do you mean?'

'She's not been very well in recent months. Had a cold a while back that took her a long time to shake off. Mum isn't as strong as she was. It's funny, I knew the time would come, but it feels too soon, somehow. Like neither of us is quite ready for it. She seemed to be the same person for so long. But now she's very old. Oh, she's in great shape for her years. Or was. But now I'm worried about her.' She looked up from the large frying pan and smiled at her daughter. 'I expect you'll feel the same when my time comes.'

'That's a long way off yet!'

'You think so, and then . . . there you are. I never thought I'd be middle-aged and now I spend more and more time worrying about what I eat, dyeing my hair to hide grey roots and wondering if I'll ever find another man to be with. Now that I have Mum to look after I doubt that any man will be interested in me, beyond a quick pint and a one-night stand.'

'Mother!' Anna stopped cutting and stared at her wide-eyed. 'Where did that come from?'

'It's true enough. I'm getting to the age when men stop taking any interest. I'd better get used to it.'

'That's rubbish. You're still an attractive woman. And there are plenty of fish in the sea.'

'But I don't want a fish, I want a man.'

They both laughed and continued their preparations for the meal for a while before Anna spoke again.

'I'm envious of Yiayia. She's experienced so much in life.'

'That's because she is older.'

'No, it's more than that. She has lived through great changes. The war, the struggle afterwards. Things we'll never know. And I think it has given her an understanding of what really counts.'

'Maybe, but we all see great changes. Look at how much the internet has altered the world. My goodness, I'd never have imagined a fraction of the things that people would be able to do with computers in my lifetime.'

'But none of it feels very real,' Anna responded. 'I spend more time than I should on Facebook and Twitter, and before that playing *Angry Birds* and *The Sims*, but none of it feels real to me. I have never met most of my "friends" on Facebook and most of the time the only thing they have to talk about is who they are having a coffee with. That and posting dumb pictures of pets doing cute things. It's not life-enhancing stuff, is it?'

'And perhaps you should be thankful for that. Would you really prefer to go through what your grandmother had to endure?'

Anna considered this for a moment and tilted her head slightly to one side. 'Do you know, I think I might. After all, she lived through the greatest event of the last century. She found love when she was young. Real love. I'd trade that for the wave of trivia that makes up my life.'

Anna finished the last courgette, took the heaped board over to the cooker and carefully swept them into the pan. Her mother gave them a brisk stir to work them into the simmering ingredients already cooking.

Anna watched her for a moment, enjoying the aroma in the kitchen.

The door to Eleni's door clicked and she emerged from her darkened room and entered the kitchen, walking stiffly with the aid of her stick. She lifted her nose and sniffed.

'Moussaka? Or what passes for it in this house . . .'

'Thank you, Mother,' Marita responded with a shrug. 'It won't be ready for a while yet.' She glanced at the clock. 'We'll eat at about eight.'

'I can wait.' Eleni crossed to the kitchen table and pulled up a chair and eased herself down stiffly before hooking the handle of her walking stick over the corner of the table. 'A drink while we are waiting would be nice.'

Marita turned to her daughter. 'There's some white in the fridge. You remember where the glasses are.'

Anna nodded and a moment later set a glass down in front of Eleni, handed one to her mother and sat down with a glass of her own. Once the moussaka had been layered in a cooking dish and placed in the oven, Marita joined the others and raised her glass. '*Eviva.*'

Anna smiled as she joined in and took a sip. 'Nice . . . It's good to be home. Good to be sitting at this table with both of you again.'

Marita cleared her throat. 'I hear you've been talking about your memories of the war. Anna said it was fascinating.'

'I don't know about that. It was the truth. It is all I have left from those times.' Eleni took the glass in both hands and raised it to her mouth for a tentative sip and nodded approvingly. 'Good . . .'

There was a brief pause before Marita spoke again. 'You were talking about Andreas, the friend you had when you were young. I should like to hear some more about him myself. You've never said much before. Not to me at least,' she concluded in a reproachful tone.

'You never really asked, my girl. Besides, I was younger then, and the memories were still too fresh in my mind.'

Marita caught her daughter's eyes and mouthed, *I told you.* 'I don't think you should try to remember too much about that time if it distresses you.'

'Pshhh! I am strong enough for that. It is only when I speak of Andreas that my heart becomes heavy. But I will feel better in the morning. I can continue telling Anna about him then.'

'Of course,' Anna agreed, hiding her frustration. 'But what about the situation in Lefkada, Yiayia? After the Germans came. What happened then?'

Marita shot her daughter an irritated look but Anna pretended not to notice and smiled encouragingly at Eleni. The old lady took another sip of wine and set the glass down gently as she collected her thoughts.

'Even though it was the Germans who arrived first, they did not stay long. Within a month they had handed the island over to their Italian allies. It seemed that the Germans considered that policing duties were all that the Italians were good for. Besides, they needed every German soldier that could be spared for the invasion of Russia that began later in nineteen forty-one. So the Italians took over. I remember it well. Our people were summoned to the main square to witness the Italian flag being raised over the prefecture. I can remember my mother crying and my father saying that our freedom had been taken from us. All I knew then was that Andreas had gone, and that I had no idea what had become of him. So I cried too. For myself.'

She breathed deeply and then chuckled. 'Do you remember that film you showed me some years ago, Marita? The one about the Italian occupation of a Greek island? I cannot recall the title exactly. It made me laugh. You said you didn't think it was supposed to be a comedy, and I explained to you that

I was laughing at it, not with it, as the English say. I can tell you, there was nothing funny about the Italian occupiers. Nothing charming. They swaggered about the island as if they owned it. Taking the best of everything for themselves and beating up anyone who protested, and then throwing them in jail. My father was forced to work for them. He did his best to protect our people but was not thanked for it. As his daughter, I was insulted in the street and bullied by the local youths. The only place I felt comfortable, outside my own home, was when I visited Andreas's father. When the Italians came, he refused to leave his house. When they billeted some men there he shut himself up in a few of the rooms. I used to take him bread and milk from the town, and he continued my education. Taught me to read and write better, and gave me books from his library to help me improve myself. I think even then he saw that Andreas and I were meant for each other, and if his son survived the war then I would need to be more worthy of him. I did not resent him for that. I wanted to learn. To be more like Andreas.'

She looked at the other two. 'You have no idea how it was for girls then. You have so much more choice than I knew in those days.'

Anna smiled. 'We still have some way to go, Yiayia.'

Eleni waved a hand. 'Oh, I know all about that. Women's rights and things. Bra burning and that sort of nonsense . . . But it was different then. A girl had to fight for what she wanted. Really fight. As I found out soon enough. But I get ahead of myself, no? I was talking about life with the Italians. Bastards. We hated them, and they ruled over us with their fists, boots and guns. Even so, we had no idea that worse was to come when the Germans took over the island when Italy turned on their allies two years later. Some of us tried to fight back against the fascists, but what could we do without modern weapons? We needed help . . .' She paused, a strained expression on her lined face. 'I will talk more of this another time, after we have eaten and I have slept. In the morning.'

The meal was accompanied by the constant flow of light conversation that Anna had delighted in when she was a child growing up in the house. It all seemed so easy, so comfortable and familiar. After a moment she began to think about the handful of men she had had relationships with. Some she had loved. But none with the passion that it seemed Eleni and Andreas had found at a time when the world was in flames around them. Anna found herself almost envying her grandmother. Then she frowned. Perhaps she was projecting a romantic aura over the past and reading more into Eleni's experience than she should.

After dinner they made some coffee and moved to the living room to continue the conversation against the backdrop of a soap opera. Eleni appeared to grow weary of talk and her attention drifted to the television set. Once the programme was over she slowly rose to her feet and Anna helped her back to her room while Marita made her a cup of hot chocolate. With the old woman safely in bed, Anna said good night to her mother and took a glass of water up to her old bedroom. Once she had cleaned her teeth and put on her pyjamas, she took out her laptop and settled back against her pillows. She powered up and went on to Facebook.

As she had hoped, Dieter Muller was online and she messaged him a brief greeting.

> Hi Dieter. How's it going?

There was no immediate response and she scrolled through her news feed and saw that an old university acquaintance was celebrating her son's second birthday. Anna smiled slightly at the images of the boy's cake-smeared face, feeling an ache of longing for the day when she too would become a mother. Then a window popped up with Dieter's name.

> Hi Anna, I am fine, thanks. You?

> Good. I am visiting my mother. I have spoken to Eleni.

> And?

The German's response seemed abrupt and Anna felt a flicker of irritation as she typed in her reply.

> My grandmother's account of her early years was very interesting. She seemed to have liked Peter, before the war at least.

> The war changed people. Wars always do. Did she say anything about the work my grandfather was carrying out on the island?

> No more than you already told me.

> A pity. I had hoped to discover more. I have been uncovering some very interesting material here in Germany. My great-grandfather's personal notebooks give a very different account of his work to the logbooks of the excavation. I think he had made a discovery he

did not want to share with anyone else. That's why I need to speak with Eleni. Did you mention my request to her?

> Not yet. It did not seem like the right time.

> Why?

> Because her memories seem very painful to her. If I am going to mention you and your research then I'm going to need to do it carefully. Your work might seem very important to you, but she is my grandmother and I care about her. I won't upset her.

> I understand. I would not expect you to upset her. However, if I am right, then I am close to discovering something very important and Eleni can help me with that. Not just me, but everyone who shares an interest in the ancient world. It's important.

> So you say. What could be that important?

There was a lengthy delay before his answer appeared.

> I can't tell you. Not yet. I will as soon as I can. I give you my word. Until then I ask you to trust me.

Anna gave a frustrated hiss.

> Why? You are asking a lot of me, and more importantly my grandmother. You said you could tell me something of her story in return. So far I have had nothing.

> All right. I am in London again this week. Let's meet and I will tell you what I know. In confidence. You understand?

> Yes . . . Where shall we meet?

> Easiest for me is the British Museum. There is a restaurant up the stairs behind the old library. Do you know it?

> Yes.

> Then shall we say Tuesday at 1pm? Is that acceptable?

Anna thought a moment. That would be during the holiday. She nodded to herself and typed back.

> I can do that. I'll talk to her again tomorrow and see what else she can remember. But I will want something from you in return. Or I won't share any more with you. Sorry, but I have to look out for her.

> Look out for her?

> English expression. Means making sure you act in their best interest. Do you understand?

> I see. Tuesday then, agreed?

> Yes. See you then.

His message window closed and Anna lay staring at the

screen for a little longer. She felt as if she was misleading Dieter. When she had first decided to speak to Eleni it had been mostly to help him, but now she was doing this for herself. To discover more about her family's history. There was little chance of arranging any interview with her grandmother for Dieter, that much was clear. Some old wounds never healed. But perhaps there was something she could get from Dieter and his research. More information about her grandmother, from Peter's perspective. That would be worth knowing.

Closing down the computer she shut the lid and tucked it under her bed before lying back and staring up at the ceiling. There was a chink in the curtain and every so often a pale beam of light would sweep across the Artex as a car passed in the street.

Her thoughts drifted back to Eleni's tale and the picture that she had shown her before dinner. Anna sensed that Andreas's story was only just starting to get interesting, and she found that she was anxious for morning to come so that she could learn more.

CHAPTER SEVENTEEN

'The most difficult part of working for the *andartes* was that it was important that as few people as possible knew what I was doing,' Eleni explained as she brushed the crumbs off her lap into the palm of her other hand and flicked them on to her plate. Anna had gone out to the bakery early in the morning to bring back a selection of croissants to share over breakfast. Her mother had already gone off to work at the university library after a hurried breakfast of cereal.

Anna swallowed her mouthful of pain au chocolat and cleared her throat. '*Andartes*? What does that mean?'

'I thought I'd told you. That's what we called those who fought in the resistance. We were a mixed group.' She smiled fondly as she remembered. 'Most of the men came from the hill villages. Some were shepherds. But there were also a few from the towns. One was a teacher. Another man had owned a share in a cargo ship. But that was sunk by the Italians and it ruined him. And there was me. Because I used to visit the Katarides house I acted as a go-between for the resistance in the town and the hills. I also spied on the Italians. They had an eye for the island's womenfolk so it was easy to play them along and get them to reveal bits of information that might be of interest to the *andartes*.'

214

'Wasn't that dangerous?'

Eleni looked at her granddaughter as if she was a complete idiot. 'Of course! If they had discovered what I was doing I would have been thrown in jail. Or worse. And perhaps they would have punished my mother and father as well.'

'Did they know what you were doing?'

'Not at first. I did not want them to get involved. In any case, they would have tried to stop me. At least, that would have been true for the two years when the Italians were in charge. Then, in nineteen forty-three. Italy surrendered and joined the Allies. The Germans had been expecting it and had made their preparations. They crushed those Italian troops who tried to resist and took the rest prisoners. That's what happened on Lefkas. The Italians gave up their weapons and marched into captivity on the mainland, leaving us to the Germans. And then we discovered what true tyranny was.'

Her expression became strained for a moment. 'But I am getting ahead of myself . . . Let me tell you about the early days of the resistance. One of the first demands the Italians made of us was to hand over all our firearms. Some people did, but most did not. They chose to hide them. Most of the guns on the island were antiques. Blunderbusses, shotguns, a few old rifles dating back to the previous century. But our men were good shots, as the enemy began to learn to their cost. Of course, what we needed were good weapons, explosives and so on. And also radios. The few that were on the island were soon confiscated and we felt cut off from the rest of the world. What we craved above all was news of the war. To know if the fascists were telling us the truth about their progress, or whether they were lying and we could live in hope of their defeat.'

Eleni leaned forward to pat Anna's hand and chuckled.

'These days, you and your friends can look everything up on the internet, no? Press a few keys and find out everything. Just like that!' She gave a feeble snap of her fingers. 'But in our time, it was easy to cut people off and starve them of information. It is strange how much you miss the news when you cannot get it . . . Anyway, we felt left to ourselves. If no one else could help us then we'd fight the Italians on our own. It started with small acts of sabotage. Some of their lorries were set on fire. Then a supply depot. In retaliation they arrested the local prefect and seized all the private vehicles on the island. In compensation for the burned lorries, they said. We also noticed a change in their attitude. They had been arrogant at first, but nothing is more ridiculous than an arrogant, puffed-up Italian and we laughed at them behind their backs. After the first attacks they began to treat us more harshly. Early the following year they nearly beat to death a boy I knew who they caught painting anti-fascist slogans on the walls of the prefecture where they had chosen to establish their headquarters. It was the boy's father who took the next step. He lay in wait for a patrol marching through the hills above Lefkada and shot dead a sergeant. The colonel in command of the Italian garrison reacted at once. He rounded up ten men and had them bound and placed against the wall of the prefecture and announced that unless the man responsible for the death of his sergeant was handed over by the end of the day then all ten of his captives would be shot.'

Anna sucked in a breath. 'What happened?'

'The father gave himself up. He was a man of honour. At the time that counted for something. We had yet to learn how empty such gestures were in the kind of conflict that the island was caught up in. The colonel released his prisoners, and put the father up against the wall and gave the order for him to be shot.'

'Were you there when it happened?' Anna asked with a shiver of horror.

'Yes. Like most of the townspeople. We stood in silence as they tied his hands and tried to put a blindfold on him. He refused it, twisting his head violently from side to side, all the time shouting, "God save Greece!" Again and again. Someone in the crowd tried to take up the cry but was instantly clubbed to the ground by an Italian soldier. So we stood and watched as they raised their rifles and fired . . . I remember it felt as if the sound had hit me like a blow. I clenched my eyes shut and when I opened them the father lay on the ground. He was not moving but the Italian officer in charge of the firing squad still strode to the body and stood over it, drew his pistol and fired into the man's head. It filled my heart with hatred for the Italians and I resolved to fight them any way I could, until they were driven out or I was killed.'

Again, Anna stared at her grandmother in shock, finding it hard to reconcile the courage and determination of the younger Eleni with the frail old woman sitting in front of her. 'Were you not afraid, Yiayia?'

'I was. Only a fool would not be. But I knew I had to do what I could to put an end to the evil that had come to Lefkas. It was the same for many of us. In more peaceful times we would not have believed ourselves capable of standing up to tyranny at the risk of our own lives, or capable of doing what we did later on. War changes a person's heart, Anna, my dear. It changes a person. Sometimes so much it is hard to recognise them any more.'

She let the weight of her words sink into her granddaughter's mind before she continued. 'The execution hardened the hearts of those who had decided to resist and in the weeks and months that followed the *andartes* grew in number and they became more bold. More patrols were ambushed, more soldiers killed. They tried to set their own traps for us but the local people nearly always found a way to warn our fighters of the danger and only a few islanders were ever lost that way. It was at this time that the first British arrived on Lefkas. They had been sent from Cairo to assess the situation on the island and see what could be done to help the resistance.'

'How did they get to Lefkas?' asked Anna.

Eleni drained the dregs of her coffee and winced when she discovered that it had gone cold.

'By submarine. Not the *Papanikolis*, if that's what you're thinking.' Eleni smiled knowingly. 'That would be a little too much coincidence. Ha. No, it was a British submarine. They landed their agents by night in one of the bays on the south of the island. There were two of them. An officer and a radio operator. The officer spoke Greek with a terrible accent and the radioman spoke no Greek at all. Since no one was expecting them they were taking a terrible risk. Luckily they ran into a shepherd before they stumbled into any Italian patrols and he was able to guide them to his shelter in the hills before going to fetch the leader of the local band of *andartes*. At first our man was suspicious of the new arrivals.'

'Why?'

'It was possible that they might not be who they said they were. They might have been German agents for all we knew, trying to infiltrate the resistance. So they were blindfolded and taken to a cave in the mountains while their story was checked out. That's where Andreas's father comes back into my story. Katarides could speak some English and he was brought to the cave to interview them. I was visiting his house at the time so I went with him. He was convinced that they were who they claimed to be. Even so, the leader of the band, an olive grower named Michaelis, demanded more proof. He had one of his men dress in an Italian uniform that had been taken from a soldier who had been killed in an ambush. The man was brought into the cave and thrown down in front of the British. Then Michaelis put a pistol in the hand of the officer and told him to shoot the prisoner. He said if the officer was who he said he was then he would prove it beyond doubt by executing his enemy.'

Anna was shocked. 'What did he do?'

'He refused. The British officer made to hand the gun back but Michaelis told him that if he did not shoot the Italian, Michaelis would shoot him, then his radio operator, and then the prisoner. Again the officer refused and said something that made no sense to us.' Eleni paused and smiled at Anna. 'The officer said that it would not be cricket to shoot an unarmed prisoner in cold blood. He tried to explain himself and Michaelis burst into laughter and pointed the gun at the prisoner and pulled the trigger. Nothing happened. He had loaded it with blanks. He embraced the officer and told him that he must be who he said he was. A German spy would have shot the prisoner without hesitation. The officer laughed in relief and everyone else joined in. After that we all sat around a small fire and shared bread, cheese and raki while the officer explained his mission.'

'What was his name?' Anna interrupted. 'Did you find out?'

'I was getting to that,' Eleni responded with a trace of irritation in her tone. 'He was Lieutenant Julian Carson. I discovered that later. At the time he told us to call him Manoli.'

Anna frowned. 'Why would he do that?'

'My child, we were playing a very dangerous game. We all adopted false names which we used from time to time. We had to protect ourselves from being identified by the enemy however we could.'

'Then what were you called, Yiayia?'

'Me? I was Malia. That was what I was called the moment I left my home and family and worked for the resistance. So that is how I was known to Julian when we first met.'

'Wait a minute.' Anna frowned and then her eyes widened. 'Julian Carson? My grandfather?'

Eleni nodded. 'Of course.'

Anna shook her head and could not help smiling. 'I had no idea that's how you met him . . .'

'Why would you? This is the first time we have talked about this in any detail.'

'I just wish I had known some of this before.'

Eleni bowed her head apologetically. 'Anna, you must understand, this is all a bit painful for me. Remembering those days opens deep wounds in my heart . . .'

Anna stared at her in concern. 'Would you rather we stopped?'

'No. Not now. I have begun my story and will finish it.'

'You don't have to, Yiayia,' Anna said gently.

Eleni leaned forward and patted her hand. 'It will not kill me to continue. Don't worry. Now, where was I?'

'You were telling me about my grandfather.'

'Julian, yes.' Eleni settled back in her chair. 'To tell the truth, I did not care for him at first. He did not seem to take things seriously. He seemed to treat our situation as some kind of sport. His superiors in Cairo had sent him to Lefkas to see if there was any organised resistance and find out what we needed to help us in our fight against the Italians. Then report back. He talked to Michaelis and the other leaders who came to the cave. Michaelis told him how many Italians were on the island, and what kind of weapons they had and where their main forces were stationed. Once Julian had collected all the information he needed, he signalled Cairo that he was ready to return and the submarine came back for him. They picked him up from the same beach he landed on. The radio operator remained with us, and Katarides had to translate for him and try to teach him some Greek.'

'I don't understand. Why was he left behind?'

'To train some of the local people how to use the radio equipment and also to keep open a line of communication between the resistance and our British allies in Cairo. It was a lifeline to the outside world. Sometimes the operator, Markos we called him, was able to pick up news and Katarides would listen and tell us what the Allies were saying about the progress of the war. At the time we believed them as much as we disbelieved our enemies. Whatever the truth was, we just wanted to believe the opposite of what the fascists were telling us . . . When you are being force-fed, the food you choose to eat always tastes best.'

She looked out of the window for a moment, squinting into the bright daylight. Anna thought about the picture her grandmother had painted of the Italian occupation, and the implication that worse was to follow when she described the German occupation of Lefkas. Eleni seemed lost in thought; her eyes grew used to the glare of the clear sky and her face relaxed. Anna fancied she saw the glint of a tear, but then the old lady hurriedly dabbed her eye and turned back towards Anna and smiled self-consciously. 'Sorry, I forget sometimes how it was.'

Anna stroked the back of her hands affectionately. 'Like I said, we can stop if you like. Or change the subject. I mean it.'

'That's not necessary,' she replied huskily and then coughed to clear her throat. 'I'm fine now. What was I saying?'

'You said that Grandfather returned to Cairo. What happened then? Did the resistance get the weapons and equipment they needed?'

Eleni nodded. 'Yes. It was a month or so later. The submarine came back with a different officer and several cases of guns and ammunition and picked up Markos at the same time. There were also spare batteries for the radio and a charging machine, and even some mines and grenades. The new officer was much more serious. He had been sent to train the *andartes* and show us how to use the explosives. Though he spoke good Greek he did not respect us much and Michaelis soon grew to despise him. They argued frequently about the best way to fight the enemy and then, one day, it came to a head.

'Michaelis had set an ambush a short distance from Vafkeri. The British officer had set mines along the edge of the road where the Italians would race for cover once the first shots had been fired. But one of our fighters, not much more than a boy really, panicked and opened fire too soon, before the enemy even reached the mines. There was a short exchange of fire. A few of the enemy were shot down and one of our own men. The officer set the mines off to cover our retreat and the *andartes* hurried back to their cave. I was there and saw what happened next. The British officer was furious, he shouted insults and hit the boy, again and again, before Michaelis pulled him away. When the officer went to hit the boy again Michaelis drew his gun and shot him in the leg. He told the officer that if he opened his mouth again then he'd shoot him in the head.'

Anna swallowed. 'And did he shoot him? Did he kill him?'

'No. The man had finally come to his senses and kept his mouth shut. Katarides and I did the best we could to treat his wound and a message was sent to Cairo saying that he had been wounded and needed to be picked up. We got rid of him a few nights later.'

'Did he live?'

'I don't know. I never heard of him again. At least it showed the British that we would not just roll over and do what they told us to. After he was evacuated they obviously decided they needed to find someone else to help us. Someone who understood the people of Lefkas . . .'

CHAPTER EIGHTEEN

Cairo, April 1942

The noises of the street carried through the high windows of the anteroom where Andreas sat alone on one of the uncomfortable wooden chairs lining the wall. Above, an electric fan spun round on a low setting, barely stirring the air enough to offer him any comfort in the late morning heat which lay over the city like a stifling blanket. The walls were whitewashed and slightly stained where cupboards had once lined the room. The floor was wooden and smelled pleasantly of polish, a welcome hygienic odour after the pungent sour smell of the streets he had walked through to reach the former offices of the Oriental Wares Trading Company. The sign still hung outside the modest entrance, but the company had long since moved to Port Said. An Egyptian doorman stood outside in his galabeya, just as if the company was still in residence, but as soon as Andreas had entered the building it was clear that a very different kind of enterprise was being run from the premises.

A thickset man in khaki shorts and shirt was seated behind a desk in the entrance hall. He checked Andreas's name against a list and guided him up the stairs to the anteroom. On one side of the building was a busy street, thronged by traders, hawkers and off-duty servicemen seeking the sultry delights offered by the souks and the less salubrious bars and clubs the great city had to offer. The other side fronted on to the Nile, offering fine views of the steamers and feluccas that carried goods up and down the river.

Andreas wore a simple cotton suit over an open shirt. His naval uniform was back in his room at the Continental Hotel where it had hung for over two weeks since his arrival in Cairo. He had been summoned to the city on the orders of the Greek government in exile and simply been told to wait for instructions to be delivered to the hotel. He had spent the first few days enjoying the comforts of the Continental. The bar was popular and there were always plenty of British officers with whom to practise his basic grasp of the language. One in particular had taken Andreas under his wing and introduced him to the best restaurants and clubs of Cairo. Although Patrick Leigh Fermor, or Paddy as he had insisted on being called, had only just arrived in the city, his easy charm and good looks had already won him an opening in Cairo's glittering social world. There was also a pool and Turkish bath to delight those staying at the hotel after spending months campaigning in the baking desert.

For Andreas, it was a welcome relief from the fervid atmosphere of Alexandria where the *Papanikolis* had been berthed ever since escaping from Sivota bay. Her propeller had long since been repaired, but the only voyages she had undertaken since then had been to deliver agents and weapons to the resistance fighters in Crete. Andreas had missed the first mission while recovering from his broken collar bone and the infection that had set in during the submarine's transit to the safety of Alexandria. Since then he had begun to resign himself to the boredom of living ashore in the cramped quarters assigned to the remnants of the Royal Hellenic Navy.

Until he had been summoned to Cairo.

After the first week he had grown tired of waiting at the hotel and the only telephone call he had made to the offices of the exiled government had resulted in a curt explanation that he was to remain where he was and wait. So Andreas had decided to explore the city and the day before he had wandered into the Club de Chasse and approached the bar. He ordered a beer and took a seat close to the small fountain in the courtyard. There was an old copy of *The Times* and he picked it up to practise reading English. He had not been sitting long when he heard a discreet cough and looked up to see a dapper man in tennis flannels smiling at him.

'I say, do you mind if I sit here?'

Andreas glanced round at the other empty seats and tables meaningfully. The other man flicked a tendril of brown hair back as he waited for a reply.

'Of course, please do.'

'Thank you, old boy. Most kind.' The man slipped into a chair opposite and Andreas became aware that he was being scrutinised in a generally amiable manner. Still, he did not care for it and looked up from the newspaper with an arched eyebrow.

'Can I help you?'

'Your accent is Greek, if I'm not mistaken.'

'Yes.'

'Then you might be the chap I'm looking for. Lieutenant Katarides?'

Andreas nodded. 'That's right.'

The man leaned forward and held out his hand to shake. 'Then I'm terribly glad to make your aquaintance. I'm John Huntley. Johnny to my friends. Look here, do you mind if we talk in Greek? It's just that there's rather too many foreign fellows in Cairo these days. Yourself excepted!' He laughed briefly, then continued in fluent, if not quite mellifluous, Greek. 'I'm actually the reason you have been asked to come to Cairo.'

Andreas looked at him closely. A more English-looking individual it was hard to conceive. In addition to his attire he had the fair complexion and neatly cut hair so typical of the young officers seen everywhere in the city. There was also the air of earnest enthusiasm that Andreas had noticed in so many of the type. It was hard to decide on his age. The man might have been anything between twenty-five and forty. If it was a masquerade then it was certainly a fine performance. All the same, he decided to exercise caution.

'I'm not sure I understand you.'

'Oh, of course. Very sensible of you. Look here, Katarides, I would not dream of putting you on the spot like this, so I'll give you my card and you can clear things with your chaps in the Greek government in exile. They'll vouch for me. The reason you're here is that I have an interesting proposition for you. Something I think you'll quite like actually. If you decide you are interested then do call on me at the address on the card. Shall we say eleven tomorrow?' he asked and then shook Andreas's hand once again and rose to leave without waiting for confirmation. 'I'll see you on the morrow then!'

He turned to stroll back across the courtyard. Andreas looked down at the small business card that had been so neatly pressed into his palm. He read the name and the address, then finished his beer and went to find the nearest telephone.

That had been less than a day ago, and now Andreas heard footsteps approaching the anteroom and sat up expectantly as a thin man in glasses and wearing army shirt and shorts appeared from the end of the corridor and nodded a greeting.

'Colonel Huntley will see you now, sir.'

'Colonel Huntley?' This was the first that Andreas had heard of his rank, even after the telephone call to his superior in the optimistically titled Admiralty Office of the government in exile. He had just confirmed that the British had approached the Greek officials to ask if there were any officers who were familiar with the Ionian islands and who could be spared for special duties. In view of the fact that Andreas had been born and raised on Lefkas his name had been put forward.

'Yes, sir. Please follow me.'

They went down the corridor and passed a few open doors that led into empty offices. Some were sparsely furnished, with paperwork out on the desks, but there was little sign of any other life. They came to a closed door on the side of the building overlooking the Nile and Andreas's escort stopped and rapped the door frame.

'Come!'

He twisted the door handle and stood aside to usher Andreas in. It was a large office nearly ten metres long and half as wide, with huge windows taking full advantage of the view. The shutters had been swung back and light flooded in, washing the interior in a warm glow. There were three desks, two piled with papers and one bare desk behind which sat the man Andreas had met the day before. He stood up and offered the same smile as he held out his hand.

'Ah, Lieutenant Katarides, good of you to come,' he said as if welcoming an unexpected guest. 'Can I offer you some tea or coffee?'

'Coffee please, sir.'

Huntley looked up towards the man standing outside in the corridor. 'Watkins, two coffees, if you would be so kind.'

'Yes, sir.' The orderly saluted and turned to stride back down the corridor. The Englishman sat down and winced, then opened a drawer and took out a small bottle of tablets and unscrewed the cap before tapping two into a glass of water. At once the tablets fizzed into life and turned the water opaque. Huntley downed it quickly and began speaking in Greek.

'Perils of spending too much time drinking with the chaps from the brigade. Anyway, I thought we'd have a little chat. Find out a bit about each other before discussing any weightier matters.'

'I was told that I was being considered for some kind of special duties, sir.'

'Ah, yes, quite. We'll come to that in good time. First I need to find out a bit more about what kind of a man you are. I already know a little through official channels.' He paused and tapped a thin file lying in front of him. It bore the crest of the Royal Hellenic Navy. 'You have a good record, and your former commanding officer speaks highly of you. I was particularly taken by the account of your rearguard action in the hills above Sivota. Reads like a *Boys' Own* adventure novel. Terribly exciting!'

Andreas recalled the fear that had gripped him that day, as well as the loss of his comrades. But there had also been a fleeting moment of euphoria at the height of the action. He regarded the Englishman steadily.

'I did what was necessary, sir.'

'No doubt, but you displayed a certain dash, which is the kind of quality I am interested in. Aside from that you are commended for your navigating skills and professionalism. It's clear that you could go far in the service of your country. But not necessarily just through the navy. There are many ways in which a good man can further the cause against the Hun and his Italian tail-coaters.'

The orderly returned and set the steaming cups down on the desk before leaving and closing the door behind him.

Huntley slid the file to one side and rested his elbows on the table as he stared at Andreas. 'So much for the official account. Aside from that, I know that you can hold your drink, that you have a decent grasp of English, that you get on well with people and that you can be discreet about your beliefs and the things that you observe. Like that incident at the Kit Cat Club with Brigadier Sims and his lady friend.'

Andreas shifted uncomfortably as he recalled the night he and Paddy had spent at the garish club aboard a boat moored on the Nile. They had stumbled across the senior officer in question loudly fornicating up against a wall. After a brief exchange of pleasantries they had passed on and the noisy liaison had resumed. Paddy had explained that Sims had a senior staff post and that if any word of his loose morals and indiscreet behaviour in a city teeming with enemy agents slipped out then the man's career was finished. So Andreas had not repeated what he had witnessed. And at once his eyes widened in realisation.

'You've had someone watching me since the moment I reached Cairo . . .'

'Well, from the moment you checked into the Continental at least.'

'Lieutenant Leigh Fermor?'

'That's right. Only known him briefly but Paddy's a good man. I asked him to take you on and see what kind of a fellow you are. As it happens he also speaks very highly of you, so I wouldn't feel too chippy about him. Leigh Fermor is a fine judge of character and you wouldn't be here now if he had not vouched for your qualities.' Huntley stroked his jaw. 'I imagine I will be making good use of that young man in due course. But that's work for another day. You are what interests me right now, Lieutenant Katarides. I know about your father, I've even read some of his poems, in Greek. He strikes me as something of a radical, politically speaking. Would you say that's the case?'

'My father's politics are his own affair.'

'Yes, that's true to an extent, but one can't help imbibing a certain view of the world from one's parents, wouldn't you agree? Take me, for instance. My father was a soldier before me and my mother is the daughter of an earl. Consequently, conservative ideology flows through my veins, I would die for king and country, in that order, and if a socialist turned up on my doorstep I'd set the dogs on him. Now you, on the other hand, are the son of a radical. Worse than that, a poet. Don't get me wrong, I love good poetry, I just question the romantic ideals of those who would rather take up a pen than a sword. Nothing quite as romantic as fighting for a good cause, I'd say. What?' He laughed and then, when Andreas did not join in, his expression became serious.

'So tell me, young Katarides, are you a republican, like your father?'

'I believe that monarchy has become an anachronism, yes.'

'And are you a socialist?'

'I believe in the rights of the people. But I have never considered myself to be a socialist. The only cause on my mind is the need to fight to free my homeland from the oppression it is suffering under the Nazis. I have heard rumours that thousands of Greeks have died of hunger over the winter because the fascists have stolen all our food for their soldiers.'

'They are not rumours, I'm afraid, but fact. And the deaths have not been in the thousands, but the hundreds of thousands as far as we can make out. I'm sorry to have to tell you that.'

Andreas felt a cold sense of despair weigh down his heart. 'So many?'

'Yes.'

'Then I must do something. Anything to strike at those murderers.'

'Of course you must. The question is, what is the most use you can be to your people and the wider cause? That is where I come in. Or, to be more accurate, the organisation I represent. I don't suppose you have heard of Force 133?'

Andreas shook his head.

'Good. That's as it should be. We don't like others to be aware of our people, let alone advertise the existence of the organisation. First I have a question for you. Do you have any moral qualms about committing murder?'

Andreas could not help looking surprised at the question and puffed his cheeks before he responded. 'That depends on who I am required to murder.'

'But in principle you would do it if the reason was right?'

'Yes.'

'Good. It may come to committing murder and I do like to forewarn those upon whose shoulders such an onerous duty might be placed. Now we've established that, let me tell you a little more. Force 133 is the cover name for our office here in Cairo. We are part of something called the Special Operations Executive. All very hush-hush, but the gist of it is that we have been tasked with placing highly motivated men into enemy-occupied territory to harass the other side as effectively as we can. The more troops we tie down, the less we have to face on the battlefield, the more likely it is that we bring forward our victory over the enemy. Do you see? Jolly good.'

'And where do I come into this, sir?'

'Since we're getting on so famously, please call me Johnny. All right?' Huntley took a cautious sip from his cup and made an appreciative noise. 'Ah, Watkins makes a fine cup of coffee . . . Now, to cases. We recently landed a small team on your home island. An officer and a radioman to be precise. Together with some weapons and kit for the *andartes*. However, the officer was injured during a disagreement with one of the local *kapetans* and had to be evacuated. We would like to send in a replacement and who could be better than a Greek officer? Better still, an officer who knows the ground and the people. If you accept then your job will be to co-ordinate the resistance and take the war to the Italian garrison. I want you to make them feel like they are living under the shadow of a knife. Every time they leave their barracks they will fear that every street corner, every rock, every tree on the island is concealing a member of the resistance lining them up for a shot. Inevitably they will call in more men, better men, in order to take you on. I'll warn you now, Andreas, when that happens the conflict is going to get very dangerous and bloody indeed and there's every chance that you will be killed, or captured, tortured and then shot.' He leaned back in his chair and regarded the young Greek shrewdly. 'It is normal to give a chap a chance to think it over, but that's not how we operate in SOE. We need our people to be decisive. So, I'll require your answer now. Are you prepared to be trained by us and infiltrated on to Lefkas to fight the enemy? Yes or no?'

Thoughts tumbled through Andreas's head as he hurriedly considered the offer. Here was the chance to escape the tedium of Alexandria, to fight the enemy, to avenge the suffering they had visited on his country and his people. And also a chance to go home. To see Eleni once again. To protect her.

'Yes.'

Huntley grinned. 'That's what I knew you'd say. Welcome to the Special Operations Executive. We'll start your training as soon as we can. You'll be returning to Lefkas as soon as you are ready.'

Huntley stood up and stuck out his hand again. Andreas smiled as they shook on it. 'What now?'

'You go back to your hotel. Paddy's arranged to take you out to celebrate. The real work begins tomorrow. Good luck and God go with you, Andreas Katarides.'

CHAPTER NINETEEN

Near Haifa, Palestine

'Narkover', as the special school was known by its staff and students, was referred to in official documents as 'Establishment ME102'. In keeping with the secret nature of what went on there, the nomenclature was meaningless, functioning only to hide its true purpose. The school was in a large white building set in sprawling grounds on the slopes of Mount Carmel. Barbed wire had been set up along the boundary wall to deter the curious or malicious and two military policemen manned the barrier at the main gate. They checked the papers of those who came and went but had no more idea about what went on within ME102 than anyone else who lived nearby. Occasionally the sound of gunfire or the loud thud of an explosion disturbed the peace but since it was wartime such noises were to be expected and so the inmates of the Special Operations Executive's school for saboteurs provoked little more than passing curiosity from those beyond the walls.

Colonel Huntley had been true to his word and Andreas was plucked from his hotel in Cairo and flown to Palestine to begin his training two days after he had accepted the offer to join the organisation. He was assured that his absence would be squared with the Greek government in exile and his personal effects would eventually be forwarded from his quarters in Alexandria.

On arrival Andreas found the school appeared more like a hotel than a military base. The rooms were clean and comfortable, there was a well-stocked bar and the mess was staffed by good cooks with ready access to the best ingredients that could be obtained. Unusually, there was no distinction between officers and other ranks, or indeed civilians, and all ate at the same tables and drank together without deference to rank. Besides the British contingent there were others from France, Italy, Yugoslavia and Greece, the last group being second in size to the British. Andreas felt some comfort at training alongside fellow countrymen but the instruction was nearly always in English and he often had to translate for some of the others with a less ready grasp of the alien tongue.

At the same time, the British trainees were keen to perfect their Greek in order to attempt to pass as natives when they were eventually deployed to Crete, the other islands and the mainland. Their chief difficulty was that someone in the hierarchy of the SOE had decided that knowledge of ancient Greek would serve as excellent preparation for learning the modern language. Andreas found himself wincing at the consequences and wondered what his countrymen would make of these finely educated Englishmen descending upon them and attempting to converse with Homeric idioms and rhythm.

The comfortable surroundings of Narkover belied the hard work that was demanded of the students. They were woken before dawn to stumble into the pallid light to do an hour's fitness training before breakfast. After that the learning began. Every possibly relevant skill was taught by experts in their fields. On the first day Andreas and the other new recruits were taken to the courtyard to begin basic weapons training. One corner of the courtyard had been covered with rush mats and a powerfully built man with a finely trimmed moustache was waiting for his class. He stood erect as he twirled a double-edged dagger and regarded his trainees with a practised eye.

'Come on, you lazy lot! Them as is keen gets fell in previous! Move yourselves!'

The class hurried over and formed up around the mats. When the last was ready, the instructor drew a breath and began, loudly.

'Welcome, gentlemen. I 'ave the honour of introducing you to the art of killing quietly with a blade.'

He flipped the knife in his hand and offered the blade to the nearest recruit, a shepherd from Crete, who took the weapon and examined it curiously as the instructor continued addressing them.

'It is a skill that is often overlooked in this day and age, sadly. However, for the type of fighting the SOE has in mind, it is a fundamental requirement. You will most likely 'ave occasion to dispose of a troublesome sentry in the course of your trade. Some of you, especially the young gentlemen who 'ave joined us from posh schools, like young Master Moss there, may find the idea of cutting a man's throat distasteful. I tell you now, you 'ad better get used to the nasty little gurgle and splutter of surprise that cannot find its way out of a cut throat. It's a messy business, but this is war, not sport, and the object of the school is to teach you the necessary lethal and efficient methods required to carry out your job. Do you all understand?'

There was some nodding and Andreas translated for some of his fellow Greeks before the instructor pointed to a tall, fair-haired Englishman.

'Mr Moss, sir. If you'd help me out. Over here, in the middle.'

The student smiled eagerly and stepped forward as the instructor continued. 'Mr Moss is about the size of a Jerry. They tend to be big bastards but they fall just as easily as any other man. The trick of it is to take 'em down quickly and violently like so.'

He stepped up behind Moss, snapped one arm round his neck. 'There are three movements to the basic kill. The first is to choke off any cries from your victim, like this. Then pull 'im back, using your 'ip to brace the victim, so.' Moss's back arched as he struggled for breath in the powerful grip of the instructor. 'The third movement is to bring up your knife under his ribs.' He punched his fist into the soft flesh under the Englishman's sternum, causing Moss to gasp. 'Stick the blade in hard and work it about so you carve up 'is 'eart. Now it will take a moment for 'im to bleed out and the more damage you do, the quicker it'll be over. Then you can lower him to the ground, nice and gentle, so he don't make a sound.' He guided Moss on to the mat, held him there a moment longer as he looked up at the rest of the class. 'One thing. Make sure your Jerry or your Eyetie 'as actually croaked. If not, he might yet give off a warning. And then, lads, your goose is cooked.'

He released his grip and helped the Englishman up. Moss struggled to recover his breath. 'Thank you, Mr Moss.'

The young officer returned to his place, rubbing his neck, while the instructor placed his hands on his hips. At the same time Andreas took the knife from his neighbour to examine it. He could see that the long, sharp blade would do plenty of damage inside a man's chest, while the rubber handle would provide a secure grip. It was clearly designed to kill and for no other purpose.

'Of course, it is best if there are two men for the job. One to deal with the man, the other to catch 'is weapon as it falls. A poorly set safety catch can cause a weapon to be discharged. Even the sound of it hitting the ground might be sufficient to alert the enemy. So, if possible, use two men. Nah then, pair off and practise the technique on each other, and then later on we'll have a look at slitting throats and scrambling brains with the blade before we break for lunch.'

After they had mastered the knife skills, they were passed on to another instructor who trained them to shoot hand-guns and demonstrated how to break down a weapon and conceal the parts in such a way that they would be missed in a casual body search. Unlike the pistol training that Andreas had experienced at the naval academy, the teacher at Narkover, a former member of the Shangai police force who had been used to fighting the ruthless gangs of that city, showed them how to fire in bursts of two shots from a crouched position. He taught them to shoot aggressively, firing instinctively, without wasting time to settle into a formal position and take aim.

Once they had mastered pistols, the instructor turned to larger weapons, the Sten, Bren and the Marlin, a sub-machine gun that had a foregrip like a Tommy gun but with a double magazine as opposed to the round one that Andreas had seen in the subtitled gangster movies in Athens. Over several days they were taught to strip the weapons, conceal them, reassemble them, and then again blindfolded. They fired them in the school's range, becoming used to their individual quirks. Andreas became familiar with the rattle of the Stens and the deeper bark of the Marlins and Bren guns. The students were also introduced to silenced weapons in the strange atmosphere of shooting on the range when the usual din was replaced by the sharp hissing noise of the single shots that had to be fired when using the device on a Sten.

Having mastered conventional weapons, the students were then trained in unarmed combat with the same ruthless intent: kill and win at any cost, by any means. At first Andreas was unsettled by the emphasis on targeting his opponent's eyes, testicles and windpipe, and the manifest ways in which an incapacitated enemy could be swiftly and silently finished off. But he quickly came to accept the necessity of it – even the virtue of it – in a war that was being fought in the face of the brutal forces of a dark ideology that threatened to extinguish every human value that he cherished. There was no doubt in his mind. The enemy had proved themselves to be malignant and it was hard to conceive of any evil that they had not yet committed.

The long hours of training and study demanded of the students made the days pass quickly. The instructors moved on to teaching them the intricacies of using explosives. RDX was the type favoured by the Special Operations Executive because it was stable and easily mouldable and therefore easy to hide and use. Andreas soon grew adept at setting charges and selecting the correct coloured fuse sticks for the desired delay before detonating the explosives. He also learned how to set booby traps and lay small charges just large enough to puncture the tyre of a vehicle driving over the device. The wider applications of sabotage were also covered: how to introduce grit in to the fuel tank of vehicles so that they would grind to a halt hours later. How to render machinery useless and difficult, if not impossible, to repair. Then they were trained to operate radios and learn the correct procedures for their use. Messages were to contain no more than six hundred characters in code and transmissions were to last no more than five minutes in order to defeat the attempts of the enemy to trace the signal back to the transmitter. It was also important to regularly move the radio set from one hiding place to another for the same reason.

Despite the long days, there was still time at the end of the day to relax in the school's mess. Andreas joined the other Greeks to drink the local wine and raki and talk and sing late into the night when they would become sentimental about their homeland and their families and all would join in to sing 'When will the sky grow clear' before the evening ended with them trudging off to their beds. Not all evenings were so harmonious. Some of the Greeks from the mainland were inclined to voice their contempt for the king and his ministers who had abandoned their people rather than remain in Greece and lead them against the fascists. These were the same Greeks who had opposed General Metaxas in the years when he had ruled the country with an iron fist and Andreas felt sympathy for the grievances of the National Liberation Front, the communist party, to which they belonged. However, there were other Greeks at the school who supported the rival National Republican Greek League, a more authoritarian political party dedicated to right-wing policies. When the discussion occasionally turned to politics the Greeks divided along party lines and the exchanges became bitter and soured the mood in the mess.

On one such night Andreas was approached by the tall officer who had been used to demonstrate the killing of an enemy sentry. They had spoken on many occasions and got drunk together, and an easy-going friendship had been established. William Moss exemplified the kind of Englishmen who were accepted for the SOE: uncomfortable with authority, energetic and the sort who would do anything to avoid a dull life.

'I say, what's the problem with your chaps tonight?' Moss said quietly as he nodded towards the furious altercation taking place on the other side of the mess. Andreas had been too fatigued by the day's training to join his comrades and was drinking by himself at a corner table. Moss shook his head as he continued. 'If I didn't know better I'd swear they were about to wring each other's necks.'

'It may yet come to that,' Andreas replied wearily. 'From what I understand, the Liberation Front have wide support back in Greece. They'll not take kindly to the restoration of the government in exile when we've driven the fascists out.'

'That's the spirit!' Moss raised his whisky glass. 'When, not if. Though I shouldn't be too concerned about the Liberation Front if I were you. I don't give much for their chances of wielding any influence when the game's over.'

Andreas frowned. 'Oh? Why is that?'

'Churchill hates the left. Always has. During the General Strike back in twenty-six, he wanted to order the troops to shoot down the trade unionists. And before that, he was behind sending our forces into Russia to fight the Bolsheviks. Don't think for a moment that he would be happy to hand Greece over to the Liberation Front when the war is over. He'll be content to support them against the enemy for now, but that will change the moment the Germans and the Italians are on the back foot. Still, that's not an issue that need concern us, eh?'

'It will concern me, my friend.' Andreas smiled.

Moss pursed his lips. 'That rather depends on whether you survive or not. Do you think it's healthy to look to the future? In our line of work I am not so sure.'

Andreas regarded him with a surprised expression. 'Surely you fight for a purpose?'

'Of course. I trust that we will win one day. I just don't expect to be there to join in the celebrations, that's all. If a man worries about surviving then there is a danger that it takes the edge off his fighting ability. Don't you think? Better that he resigns himself to death so he can devote his attention to the task immediately in front of him. That's how I see it.' He knocked back his whisky and turned to the barman to raise his glass and indicate he needed a refill. Turning to Andreas, he shrugged. 'We live outside history, my friend. There is no future for us and therefore we need not think about the past. Only the present matters. It is all we can expect to have.'

Andreas shook his head. 'Your philosophy is not for me. I have plenty I want to live for.'

'You have a girl waiting for you, is that why you want to survive?' Moss's eyes twinkled and he clicked his fingers. 'I knew it. Poor fellow. That will be quite a burden for you.'

'I don't think so,' Andreas responded firmly.

'Be realistic, my dear chap. War is a dangerous enterprise at the best of times. But what we are engaged in is the most dangerous of all duties. Why, there are myriad ways in which we can die. Even if we leave the enemy out we could be killed in training, during infiltration, from sickness, or untreated wounds. And if we survive that lot the other side will be doing their best to shoot us. If we are taken prisoner the only thing we can expect is to be tortured and then put up against a wall and shot. If we're lucky we might get a chance to put a bullet in our heads, or take poison, before we are captured. So, you'll pardon me if I don't share your expectation that we will survive the war. That girl of yours? I'd forget her. Forget she ever existed. Otherwise she'll only be a distraction and get between you and your duty.' As the mess steward refilled his glass, Moss leaned forward and clapped Andreas on the shoulder. 'So, eat, drink and be merry, as the saying goes! Especially when you see what's coming in a couple of days. Parachute training. If ever there was a test of a chap's nerve, it has to be hurling himself out of an aircraft with a bloody silk sheet and a handful of ropes standing between him and eternity. Cheers!'

CHAPTER TWENTY

The interior of the Wellington shook and lurched as it clawed its way into the night sky over Palestine. The sound of the straining engines was a constant roar in the ears of the men sitting on the benches either side of the fuselage, close enough for their knees to touch every time the bomber shuddered. Aside from the parachute instructor and a dispatcher, the other eight men were all agents in training, dressed in padded jumpsuits and strapped into their parachute harnesses. Each man had a small kitbag on the bench beside him, containing essential equipment for the escape and evasion exercise. A pale blue light barely illuminated those around Andreas and he was grateful that they could make out as little of his expression as he could of theirs.

He was terrified at the prospect of what was to come. Even though the parachute course was rushed, he had not felt much trepidation at leaping off the twelve-foot-high stage to learn how to roll on landing. Nor stepping off the training tower in the craned harness to simulate the last sixty feet of a drop. The first real jump, from a tethered balloon at a thousand feet, had been an almost serene experience. The basket had lifted gently off the ground and risen steadily into the sky before the tethered cable eased it to a stop. When his turn had come, Andreas had stepped up to the exit and let himself fall out as soon as the instructor had given him the command to jump. There was a brief sensation of uncontrolled speed before the static line pulled the parachute open and he felt a powerful jerk as the canopy rippled out above him. As he looked down at the landscape spread out below him, and the tiny upturned faces of those watching from the training field, he could not help laughing for joy at the thrill of the experience. The moment passed briefly enough as the ground came rushing up towards him and he just remembered to bend his knees in time to take the force of the impact. It drove the wind from his lungs and he lay gasping until an instructor rushed over and bellowed at him to get on his feet and bundle his parachute.

There had been two daylight jumps from planes before this final exercise, which was intended to be as close as possible to the experience of a real drop into enemy-held territory. They had been briefed in the afternoon that they were to be dropped somewhere within a thirty-mile radius of the school and had to find their way back inside the grounds without being picked up by any of the patrols that had been sent out to search for them. They had until the following night to return. After that they would be deemed to have failed and would have to repeat the exercise. The idea of jumping into the night, over unfamiliar terrain, had played on Andreas's nerves over the intervening hours as he prepared his kit and was driven out to the airfield to wait for the order to board the Wellington.

Opposite him sat Bill Moss, arms folded across his chest as he whistled to himself. For a moment Andreas stared at him, jealous of his languid air, then he smiled as he realised the Englishman would never be able to hear the tune he was whistling above the roar of the engines and that it was simply a facade, an attempt to look unconcerned by the imminent danger they all faced. Glancing round, Andreas could see that the others were either looking intently serious or feigning calm as well. For some reason it made him feel more confident.

The note of the engine began to ease as the bomber reached its cruising height and continued on a level course for another half-hour before the pilot eased the throttles back and the red light blinked on inside the fuselage, bathing the passengers in a lurid glow. The dispatcher bent over the hatch in the floor, unfastened it and lowered it towards the rear of the plane. The slipstream roared beneath the opening and Andreas gave an involuntary tremor as he saw the dark void beyond.

'UP!' the instructor yelled, gesturing clearly with his hand.

The recruits struggled to their feet and shuffled into line, carrying their equipment bags in their left hands and their static lines in their right.

'HOOK UP!' The instructor reached his hand up to the steel cable running along the roof of the fuselage and curled his fingers. Andreas attached the metal clip to the cable and tugged it to make sure it was secure. There was only one man ahead of him and Moss directly behind. The line edged forwards and then the first man lowered himself so that he was sitting on the edge of the hatch, legs dangling through the hole where they were buffeted by the air roaring past. There was a brief delay and then the red light went out, to be replaced by a green glow from the lamp on the bulkhead.

'GO!' barked the instructor.

The first agent released his equipment bag and heaved himself forward, instantly disappearing. His static line went taut an instant later. Andreas dropped down and lowered his legs, flinching at the cold blast of air. He released his bag and folded his arms across his chest as he fell into the night. It had happened so quickly he was not aware of it, and had no time to exult at his newfound courage before the harness jolted him severely as if he had been shaken in the fist of a giant. The air whistled through the cords of the parachute and the roar of the bomber's engines quickly diminished as it flew on. Below, to the right, Andreas could make out the dull hemisphere of the first parachutist, drifting towards the dark ground. There was a crescent moon providing just enough illumination to pick out the details of the landscape below. Remembering his training, Andreas looked for recognisable features that he could relate to the map of the drop zone the agents had been shown during the briefing. But by moonlight it bore little resemblance to the map and Andreas knew he had little time to get his bearings. Frantically he looked round at the hills surrounding the drop zone. Then he caught the silvery glint of water off to the left and felt relief surge through his heart as he recognised it as the reservoir supplying a large kibbutz.

The ground was coming up fast now and he could see where he was to land and muttered a curse as he saw a small cluster of trees directly beneath. Below, his kitbag swung lazily and then crashed through the topmost branches. Gritting his teeth and bending his knees, Andreas followed it in, feeling twigs and small branches splintering under him as he crashed through the tree. Then he hit a more solid branch, twisted to one side and fell through towards the ground. He braced himself for the impact but his harness brought him up sharply as the cords and parachute collapsed over the tree.

He hung there for an instant gasping for breath and scared witless. Then he remembered his training and fumbled for the harness release and let himself drop to the ground. The kitbag had fallen the other side of a branch and Andreas unclipped it and let it hit the ground before he stepped out from under the tree and looked round. The last four of his comrades were still descending but would land hundreds of metres away. Closer to, he saw a figure who had landed in the open hurriedly bundling his chute up before scurrying to a nearby outcrop of rocks to conceal it. Andreas hissed a curse as he looked up. He grasped a fold of his chute and pulled. It shifted a short distance before snagging and he swore again under his breath before he took out his knife to start cutting it free.

'Oh dear,' a voice called out softly. 'You seem to have got yourself in a bit of a pickle, my dear chap.'

He turned as he recognised Moss's voice and saw his companion with his chute and kitbag bundled in his arms. He dropped them by the tree trunk and drew his knife to help Andreas.

'What are you doing?'

'Helping you out, old boy.'

Andreas shook his head. 'That's not the way it works, my friend. We're supposed to make our own way to the school. You remember what they said. It's easier to avoid attention and capture if we act alone.'

Moss chuckled. 'Of course. That's what they told us. And having told us that, you can be sure the patrols will be looking for men on their own.' He tapped his jump helmet. 'Using my loaf. Come on, let's get this mess sorted out.'

Andreas turned his attention back to the silk and cords festooned over the tree and they worked quickly until most of it had been cut away. Then, burying the chutes, their suits and helmets in a shallow pit, they paused to take their rations, compass and revolvers from their kitbags. The weapons were unloaded but issued to the agents to add to the verisimilitude of the exercise. Underneath the jumpsuits they wore plain civilian clothes and while Andreas stood some chance of being taken for a local, Moss did not, and had to wear a cap over his cropped fair hair. With the location of the reservoir he had seen earlier, together with the compass, Andreas had the direction they would need to travel and they set off, across the open ground towards a hill a few kilometres off that Andreas had chosen as their first waypoint. They walked in silence for a while, striding quickly across the dark landscape to get away from the landing site. There was to be an hour's grace before the search for them began. It would commence from where they had landed and sweep in the general direction of the school and towards a second cordon of patrols lying across the path of the agents.

They steered clear of settlements and roads and used tracks that could not easily be traversed by vehicles. A few times they encountered flocks of sheep and warily worked their way round. Once they were not so successful and the animals rose to their feet and their bleating roused a shepherd who shouted angrily into the night as Andreas and Moss ran off. Reaching the crest of the hill just as the first smudge of light crept along the eastern horizon, Andreas paused to scrutinise the lie of the land ahead. Trees blanketed the slope in front of them before giving out on to more farmland and pasture. A small town lay some five kilometres off and a minaret rose up, dark and slender, against a fainter shade of darkness beyond.

'Look there,' Moss said quietly and Andreas turned to see his companion pointing back the way they had come. The beams of headlights crept across the ground where they had landed over an hour before. There were more vehicles abroad, picking their way steadily along the rutted country lanes.

'They didn't waste much time. And they're starting to head in our direction. We're in for some sport. Now I know how the fox feels.'

'Fox?'

'Hunting, old boy. Surely you know. Horses, hounds and a wily fox to run to ground.'

'Not on Lefkas.'

'Really? Poor show.'

Andreas regarded him with concern. 'Perhaps it would be better if we did not regard this as a game.'

'But it is a game. All a game. The difference is the stakes are much higher. When a man is playing for his life against the lives of others, he is engaged in the absolute acme of sporting pursuits and there is nothing finer, more noble or more downright enjoyable.'

'You may think so. But I am only interested in liberating my country from tyranny. That is all. It is not a game for me. It is a sacred purpose.'

Moss frowned at him. 'A different perspective, to be sure, but no more than that. As long as we dish the Hun, that's all that matters.'

Andreas drew a deep breath to calm his irritation, and again wondered if Moss truly felt this way, or whether it was a manner he affected to carry him through the terrible dangers he faced serving in the SOE. If so, it seemed to be a common trait of the British officers he had met and he wondered if he would ever truly understand them. But this was not the time to speculate.

'We should keep moving. We could be in that town by

dawn and have a better chance of hiding in a crowd.'

Moss considered the notion and nodded. 'How far from there to the school?'

'If that's Al Qatah, then another eighteen or twenty kilometres at the outside. We can cover that before the deadline.'

'It's not the distance that's an issue. They're bound to have the approaches to the school covered. That'll be the real challenge.'

Andreas nodded. 'We'll work out a solution when we get closer. Let's go.'

Scrambling down from the crest they entered the treeline and picked their way through the trees. On the far side, they kept close to the walls and drainage ditches dividing the farms and worked their way towards the town as the dawn crept into the sky and the landscape resolved itself into more detail and pastel shades of colour. Once, as they made to cross a road, they had to take cover as they heard a vehicle approaching and an open-topped car with two red-capped military policemen rumbled past, leaving a wake of swirling dust. Andreas and Moss stayed pressed to the ground in the ditch beside the road and only emerged after the sound of the vehicle had faded away. Thereafter they approached any roads and tracks cautiously, until they reached the more humble dwellings at the edge of Al Qatah. Some of the inhabitants had already risen and exchanged curious greetings with the two strangers striding purposefully into the town.

'I think we're provoking a little attention,' Moss muttered.

'We're not local people, and we aren't dressed to pass as locals,' Andreas said. 'We should change. The patrols probably know what we look like. It's the sort of thing the instructors at the school would tell them to make it more of a challenge.'

Moss nodded.

A short while later they were in the heart of the town, in the market square where some of the stallholders were already setting out their wares. Andreas used some of the currency from the equipment bags and bought a pair of *keffiyehs*, baggy trousers, sandals and dark jackets for them to wear and they changed in a side street, abandoning their former clothes and boots in a heap of refuse that had been swept into a space between two buildings.

By the time they left the town there were plenty of other people, animals and vehicles on the road and they walked steadily along the verge, trying not to look conspicuous by walking too fast or too slow. Late in the morning another military police patrol cruised along the road towards them, the occupants scrutinising those they passed by. Andreas felt his pulse quicken as they approached, fearing that their true identities would be obvious amongst the more markedly Middle Eastern features of those around them. As the car came closer, Moss stepped off the edge of the road into a field and pulled down his trousers and squatted. Andreas silently cursed him, but then the car was alongside, the driver glanced at Moss with a quick look of disgust and eased the accelerator down to pass by more quickly. When he had gone a safe distance Moss pulled up his trousers and hurried back to Andreas's side with a wide grin.

'Did the trick!'

'Surely. But please warn me next time you try something like that.'

Moss laughed good-naturedly and they continued along the road in the direction of the school without seeing any sign of further patrols. Then, shortly after midday, the same car came back along the road and as it went by Andreas saw one of the other agents sitting in the back, beside a military policeman.

'That was Theopopilis,' he said quietly.

'I saw. Tough luck for him.'

Andreas nodded. His fellow Greek would have to repeat the exercise. In the field, if he had failed, he would have been in the hands of the Gestapo and would be facing interrogation, torture and execution. The thought made Andreas all the more determined to ensure that he regarded the exercise as the real thing and did whatever it took to reach his goal. The sooner his training was over, the sooner he could return to Lefkas and fight those who had invaded his beloved island.

It was mid-afternoon before they neared Mount Carmel and saw the school and its grounds on the slope. Even at a distance they could see the tiny figures of men patrolling the fields and terraced fruit trees around the buildings and Andreas appreciated the challenge facing him and his companion. Then, as they rounded a sharp bend in the road, they saw a checkpoint ahead of them. Two cars were parked either side of the road and a squad of redcaps was checking people through, scrutinising them and questioning some closely before waving them on. Two military policemen were walking either side of the cars, carts and pedestrians queueing to get through.

'What do we do?' asked Moss. 'They'll pick us out quick as a flash. We'd better run for it.'

'Too late for that,' Andreas replied. 'We run and they'll see us at once. We're not going to get far in these sandals.'

'What then?'

'We'll have to try and bluff it. That's all we can do now.'

The queue shuffled forward and as they approached the checkpoint Andreas prepared himself to play the part of an

Arab with no command of English, and hoped that they would focus their attention on him and let Moss stand still and silent at his side, head lowered.

'It's no good,' Moss whispered. 'I'll never pass for a local. I have to get out of here. Look, I'll try and make a scene of it. If I can get away, so much the better. Either way, you take advantage of the diversion to get past that lot.'

Andreas thought about protesting but he knew his friend's suggestion made sense and after a hesitation he nodded his agreement. It would be better that one of them succeeded than both be taken. He sucked in a breath between his teeth. 'Good luck, Bill.'

'And you.'

They were a scant ten feet from the checkpoint when Moss suddenly bolted towards the side of the road and the field beyond.

'Oi, you! Stop!' a redcap shouted and his comrades instantly turned towards the commotion.

Moss kept running, *keffiyeh* flapping as he fled.

The redcap sergeant in charge of the checkpoint drew his revolver and cupped it in his spare hand as he bellowed. 'Stop, Abdul, else I'll put a bullet in your bloody back!'

Moss ignored the cry and the military policeman fired a round into the air. At once the civilians on the road hunched down in alarm and Andreas followed suit. The redcap lowered the barrel of his revolver and took aim at Moss, using his left hand to steady his grip. 'Last fucking warning, Abdul . . .'

Moss stopped and turned round.

'Raise your hands!'

He did as he was told.

'Now get your arse over here.'

The agent strode back towards the military policeman. As

Moss reached the road he lowered his hands and smiled. 'It seems you have me, my dear fellow.'

'Keep you hands up.'

'Really, I don't think this sort of thing is terribly necessary.'

The redcap kept him covered, but smiled back. 'For all I know, you could be a Jerry spy, sir.'

'If that was so, then I hardly think you would call me "sir".'

'You may think what you like, but keep your ruddy 'ands up.'

Moss did as he was told and the redcap shoved him in the direction of the nearest car. The civilians stood up now the drama was over and milled around.

'Get that bloody lot through the checkpoint and clear the road!' the sergeant roared. His men waved them through with cries of '*Emshi! Emshi!*'

Andreas rounded his shoulders and lowered his head in obeisance as he hurried past the soldiers and on to the road beyond. He continued a short distance before risking a look back. The sergeant was still questioning Moss, who had been allowed to lower his hands so that they could be handcuffed. Then he was led to one of the cars and made to sit in the back seat, with a redcap at his side. Andreas felt regret that his comrade had been captured but he still had to complete the exercise on his own and looking up at the approaches to the school entrance he could see no clear way to get past the patrols and those keeping watch.

A short distance ahead the road bent to the right, before the turning leading up the hill to the school. The crowd had begun to disperse and Andreas deliberately slowed until he was at the rear. As he reached the bend he turned and saw the sergeant making his way over to the car with Moss sitting inside and climbing into the driver's position. The sound of the engine starting carried up the road and Andreas's pulse quickened as he conceived a plan of action. It was risky but it seemed like the best chance he had of completing the exercise. He hurried round the corner and picked a spot where the car would have to slow down as it rounded the bend and prepared to turn on to the road leading up the hill to the school. The last of the local people had already moved some distance ahead and would not be able to thwart his plan if they looked back.

The sound of the engine being revved as it started up the road spurred Andreas's resolve and he moved out into the middle of the road, heart racing, and reached into his bag. A moment later the car changed down a gear as the sergeant approached the bend. With a deep breath to control his nerves, Andreas lay down on the road, and curled up into a ball. He could hear the gravel crunching under the car's tyres as it negotiated the corner and then he saw it, coming fast towards him. He saw the sergeant's jaw drop in surprise an instant before he kicked down on the brakes and the car rapidly slowed and slid to a stop, ten feet away.

'What the fuck are you doing there? Get up and get off the bloody road, you lazy Arab!'

Andreas raised an arm feebly and let it drop back beside him. The sergeant cranked the handbrake up and climbed down from the driver's position and strode towards him.

'Up! Up, I said, damn you!'

Andreas let out a groan and gave a slight writhe. He saw the shadow of the military policeman on the gravel in front of him and then the sergeant squatted down on his heels and shook Andreas's shoulder. 'On your feet.'

Andreas's left hand shot out and his fist piled into the

sergeant's jaw, sending the man sprawling on to his back. Andreas scrambled to his feet, pulled out his revolver and aimed it at the sergeant's face. He glanced towards the car. The other redcap was rising from the seat while Moss's expression creased into a cheerful grin.

'Uncuff the prisoner!' Andreas ordered in his accented English. 'Do it! Or I'll shoot this man.'

The redcap hesitated and Moss chipped in, 'Better do as he says. Looks like a desperate man to me.'

After a brief hesitation, during which Andreas pressed the muzzle of his weapon into the sergeant's cheek, the soldier took out his keys and released Moss. Andreas prodded the sergeant with his toe.

'All right, I want you to drive. Your friend sits beside you. We'll be behind with guns to your backs. Clear? Now hand your weapon over. You too!' he added, glancing up towards the other soldier. The redcaps did as they were instructed and Andreas climbed into the back, putting his own gun away as he took up the sergeant's weapon.

'All very neat,' Moss said approvingly. 'You have a knack for this kind of work. So what next?'

For the first time since the exercise began, Andreas felt confident enough to smile. 'We drive into the school and complete the exercise.'

He prodded the back of the seat with the revolver. 'Let's go. Up the hill. Not one word of warning to anyone, Sergeant. Is that clear?'

'Or what, sir?'

'Or I'll blow your spine out. I would, if I was in the field. But even if this is only an exercise, your revolver is real enough, and so are the bullets. Bear that in mind. Now, let's get moving.'

The sergeant put the car into gear and eased it forward carefully, not wanting to take any risks of being accidentally shot with his own weapon due to some unfortuitous jolt. He turned on to the road leading up the hill and the two agents kept low, squeezed into the gap behind the front seats. Soon the car was negotiating hairpin bends and once slowed as the sergeant exchanged a brief greeting with a patrol they passed on the road. Andreas gave the redcap a gentle prod and he accelerated and drove on. After fifteen minutes or so the sergeant began to slow down.

'What's the matter?' Andreas demanded.

'There's a barrier down at the gate to the school, sir. What should I do?'

Andreas thought quickly. 'Drive up but stop a short distance from the barrier, far enough so they can't see the rear seats. Tell them you have an urgent message for the commanding officer. If they don't raise the barrier, then drive through it.'

'Are you mad?'

'No. But I am armed, and for the purposes of the exercise, dangerous. Do as I say!'

The sergeant shrugged. 'As you wish, sir. But I'll want it in writing that I was acting on your orders. They'll not be stopping my pay to cover the damages.'

'Shut up and drive,' Moss growled.

The car slowed and stopped as it was challenged by a sentry on the gate. The sergeant barked his response.

'Message for the CO! Open the barrier!'

'Leave it with me, I'll pass it on.'

'I've orders to deliver it in person.'

'Sorry, Sergeant. No one enters without the say-so from the CO.'

'Don't you bloody give me that. I've got orders. Now get the barrier up or I'll have you on a fucking charge, my lad!' He gunned the engine for good measure, and then, as his two hidden passengers exchanged a doubtful glance, they heard the clank of a chain and the squeal of metal and the car edged forward. They swept past the whitewashed barrier, pointing into the sky at an angle, and the sergeant slowed down and looked over his shoulder.

'We're in, and that poor bastard on the gate is for the high jump. Happy now, sir?'

'He would be fine if he had done his job,' Moss replied. 'In any case, you did well to persuade him, Sergeant.'

The soldier scowled back. 'Where now, sir?'

'Right outside the front of the school will do nicely, thank you. Might as well end things in style.'

As the car roared up the drive towards the main building, Moss and Andreas eased themselves up and on to the back seat. They passed one of the instructors, who frowned curiously as he saw the two men in Arab dress being chauffeured by the military policemen. The sergeant drew up outside the arched front door and stopped.

'Here you are, sirs. Now, if you don't mind, we'll have our revolvers back.'

The agents handed their weapons over and climbed out of the car. Moss placed his hands on his hips and stretched his back. 'Ah! A celebratory drink in the mess is on the cards, I should think. My treat, Andreas, for getting me off the hook.'

'You are welcome.' Andreas grinned.

The sergeant coughed. 'If you two gentlemen have finished with us?'

Moss waved airily back down the slope. 'By all means, you may go. And thank you for the lift.'

The sergeant forced a smile as he answered quietly, 'Fuck you, sir. Fuck you very much.'

Then he slammed the car into gear and accelerated away before either of the officers could respond.

'Well, that went well!' Moss laughed. As Andreas joined in, a figure emerged from the doorway and stood on the steps above them. They turned to see the school's commanding officer regarding them with an amused expression. 'Well, well. That's the first time any of our students ended the exercise in such style.'

'It was quite a lark,' said Moss. 'I think I may make a career of hijacking cars.'

Andreas joined in their laughter, feeling great relief at having overcome the final challenge set by the SOE's training school. His mirth was short-lived as their superior's smile faded and he regarded them with what looked almost like pity.

'You are both brave fellows. Good men. But I'm afraid this is the last time it will be a bit of a lark, young Moss. The games are over. From now on, it all becomes brutally simple. You succeed, or you die . . .'

Two weeks later, Andreas was sitting outside the ready room at Tokra airfield near Alexandria. The building used to provide the agents with a few last comforts before they left was a simple brick structure with a corrugated iron roof. Inside, a corporal made tea and sandwiches for the men that passed through and gave cigarettes to those that needed them. There was no alcohol, though, in case an agent was tempted too much by the prospect of liquid courage. The sun had set shortly before and the western horizon was ablaze with red and orange. The air was warm and still and there was a peacefulness about the scene that Andreas found calming even though, within the hour, he was due to board the plane that would carry him, and several crates of weapons, ammunition and equipment to the resistance fighters of Lefkas.

There were two other men waiting for another bomber to drop them into the Balkans. They sat a short distance away from Andreas, smoking and occasionally exchanging a few quiet words. There was no attempt to engage Andreas in conversation. That was part of the training, in case they were captured and tortured and revealed any information about another operation.

A hundred metres away from the ready room the ground crew were preparing the two aircraft for the night's missions. They were Liberators, big four-engined American-built bombers with the necessary range to parachute agents and supplies throughout the Mediterranean. A fuel bowser was filling the tanks while armourers loaded ammunition belts into the machine-gun positions, though it was unlikely that the bombers would encounter any night fighters during their flight.

Andreas had not yet put on his jumpsuit and leaned forward, elbows resting on his tanned knees, as he drew on his cigarette and watched the men working on the aircraft. Despite the terrible danger he faced he felt happy. His training was complete and he felt confident in the skills he had learned and was keen to put them into practice when he returned to Lefkas. He mentally went over his orders once again. It had been months since the SOE had had an agent on Lefkas. The previous British officer had been injured and evacuated. Contact with the *andartes* had been intermittent and brief when it happened, according to communications protocols, and there was only a vague understanding of what was happening. Andreas would go in with the next supply drop to the largest of the resistance bands. When he reached Lefkas he was to assess the situation and report back on the number of the resistance fighters and their needs. After he had reported back he was then to do what he could to coordinate the efforts of the *andartes* and assist them in their attacks on the enemy.

After he had been over his orders he permitted himself a moment's reverie at the prospect of seeing Eleni again. He had no idea if she was still living on the island, or indeed was even alive. The winter of starvation that had killed so many of his people might well have claimed her too. But somehow he instinctively believed that she was still alive and still there and he might see her from time to time. After these long months apart, that would be enough to nourish his desire for her, he thought. In time, when the war was over, there would be a new opportunity to know her better, to dare to think of a future together.

His thoughts were interrupted by a car driving across the airfield towards him, throwing up a swirl of dust in its wake. The vehicle stopped outside the ready room and the driver turned the engine off and hopped out to open the door for his passenger. Colonel Huntley emerged, in uniform, and Andreas and the other agents rose to their feet and saluted. Huntley returned their salute and then removed his cap.

'Just come to say a few words and see you boys off.' He nodded briefly to Andreas. 'Be with you in a minute.'

Andreas resumed his seat and continued smoking while the colonel offered a few muted words of encouragement to the others and shook each of them by the hand. Then he made his way to Andreas and gestured to the bench.

'May I join you, Katarides?'

'Of course, sir.'

Huntley eased himself down and pulled out an unopened packet of cigarettes and offered it to Andreas.

'I already have one, sir.' He raised his cigarette.

'This is for later. After you've landed. Take it. You'll thank me for it, I can assure you.'

Andreas glanced at him. 'Then you've been in the field?'

'Of course. You don't really think that I would send men to do work I was not prepared to do myself.'

'Forgive me, sir. But that's not uncommon in the military world.'

'Well, it's not how we do things in the SOE.'

Andreas nodded, hesitated briefly, then asked, 'May I ask where?'

'You may . . .'

They exchanged a knowing smile before Huntley continued. 'It's never the way you think it's going to be. Before you go, and to an extent afterwards, it seems exciting and terribly noble work. But while you are there, there is only boredom, exhaustion, hunger, thirst and cold, and worst of all a constant sickening dread . . . But there, I shouldn't be saying these things.'

'I understand, sir.'

'That's good. You have a more dangerous assignment than most of my agents. We can get you on to Lefkas, but exfiltrating you is a rather more tricky process. The chances are that you will have to remain on the island for many months, years even, assuming the war lasts that long. If you are injured or taken ill, there will be nothing we can do to help you. And then there's the enemy. They will hunt you like a pack of hounds and you will have to be as wily as the brightest of foxes to stay out of their clutches. They may kill you, but the bigger danger is that they take you alive. The Italians are fair enough chaps, but if they are persuaded by their German friends to hand you over then there's every chance that you will be mistreated. In which case, the SOE offers all our agents a choice . . .' He paused to reach into his jacket pocket and took out a small black metal case, the size of a domino. 'We call these L pills. I think you can guess what they do.'

'Yes, sir.'

'I'm told it's quick. All you have to do is bite down on the capsule and the cyanide will do its bit in seconds. Here.'

He held the box out and Andreas did not hesitate as he took it.

'Keep it on you at all times. I will not order a man to use it in the event of capture. That will be for you to decide. If you don't then I have a right to ask that you deny the enemy any information for as long as you can. We reckon on at least a day, in order for the rest of your group to make good their escape.'

'Yes, sir. You can be sure I will do the right thing.' Andreas put the box in his breast pocket and fastened the button securely. 'Thank you.'

'I hope you never have cause to.'

A covered truck drew up by the aircraft and the planes' crews climbed out and made their way to each of the bombers and clambered up through the belly hatches.

'They'll be ready for you soon,' said Huntley.

Andreas nodded. They sat in silence for a while before the colonel straightened his back and took a deep breath. 'Well, there's nothing more to be said. I'll wish you the best of luck and good fortune, Katarides.'

They both stood up and the colonel shook Andreas by the hand. 'At times it will feel like you are playing an insignificant part in the war effort. Never let that discourage you. Our enemy will feel even the smallest pinprick and if we have to win this war one drop of blood at a time then that's how we must play it.'

'Yes, sir.'

Huntley held his hand a moment longer and fixed him with a determined stare. Then he released his grip and turned back to his car abruptly. The driver opened the door for him and the colonel climbed in and the vehicle drove off without him once looking back at the agents. As the car disappeared across the airfield, the Liberators' engines coughed into life, one by one, and the propellers spun until they merged into shimmering discs, glinting in the last light of the evening. The truck that had delivered the aircrews rumbled over towards the ready room. The door opened and the corporal came out and cleared his throat as he addressed the agents.

'It's time to go.'

CHAPTER TWENTY-ONE

Lefkas

'They're late,' Michaelis hissed and spat on to the ground. He stood up and stretched his back as he looked out over the bare crest of the hill that had been chosen for the drop site. It was sufficiently far from the nearest settlement to make being disturbed by any locals, let alone the Italians, unlikely. The latter had taken to patrolling the island only by day and confining themselves to the towns and fortified outposts they had constructed at strategic points along the coastline of Lefkas. There was also another issue that vexed Michaelis concerning the matter of supply drops. On the previous two occasions the British had overshot the zone and dropped their cargo some kilometres away. By the time Michaelis's band had reached the spot, the weapons and ammunition had been gathered up by another band and secreted away. On the second occasion they had been caught in the act and there had been a tense confrontation before the leaders of the two resistance bands had agreed to divide the supplies. He told the radio operator to send a message back to Cairo demanding that it did not happen a third time.

It was a warm night and the breeze blowing over the crest of the hill was gentle and carried the sweet smell of thyme and pine up from the slopes below. A slender arc of silver in the star-studded sky provided what natural light there was, just enough for the pilot of the plane to make out the shape of the island and line up his approach while waiting for the signal lamps to wink on.

Around Michaelis, in the dark, sat a score of his men, and the girl. He turned in her direction and could just make out her silhouette against the dull sheen of the distant sea. She was the only female member of the band and, as far as he knew, one of only a handful across the island who served under any of the *kapetans* fighting the Italians. That she was brave, he had no doubt. She had carried messages for him, and gathered useful intelligence on the enemy's intentions so that he and his band had been able to remain a step ahead of the Italians, avoiding their occasional sweeps across different sectors of the island and escaping those villages and paths where the enemy had set ambushes.

Recently she had demanded to take a more active role in the resistance and learn how to use firearms so that she could fight alongside them. Michaelis adhered to traditional island values and was reluctant to extend his regard to her as far as letting her fight alongside the men in battle, but he had trained her to fire and maintain their weapons and that had sated her ambitions for the moment. There was another side to his reluctance to permit her to join them in raids and ambushes, namely that she was too valuable as a go-between and spy to be thrown away in a reckless skirmish.

He turned to face the direction they were expecting the plane to come from and strained his eyes and ears to detect any sign of the aircraft but there was nothing and he mouthed another curse on his allies. They had promised much and delivered little. Just as they had in the days of the German invasion of Greece. Some of Michaelis's men had served in the army and told him sorry tales of the nation's humbling. Despite the guarantees of help from the British prime minister, Churchill, only a fraction of the promised reinforcements had been sent to Greece, accompanied by tanks that were no match for the German panzers, even when they did not break down. As a result the British had reached the front just in time to join the headlong retreat to Athens. There they had evacuated their men to Crete before being forced to give that up as well, and leave the Greeks to suffer under the fascists.

Michaelis shared his nation's humiliation and wanted to fight back. But to do that he needed help and the British had provided him with scant supplies of weapons up until now. He had his own suspicions about that. After all, the British had gone to great lengths to save the king and his despotic cronies and offer them a safe haven in Egypt. It was clear that they intended to restore them to power if the Allies won the war. Until then they would provide the resistance with just enough equipment for them to harass the enemy, but not enough for them to resist the imposition of an unpopular government when the war was won. My enemy's enemy is my friend . . . Michaelis smiled thinly. The bitter rivalry between the right and the left in Greek politics threatened to divide the nation and distract the people from their common foe. Even on the small island of Lefkas, some of the bands were inclined to put politics above patriotism. For his own part he would prefer to see the monarchy abolished once the war was over, and the establishment of a real democracy in Greece.

The girl abruptly stood up. 'Listen!'

Michaelis cocked his head. 'What is it, Eleni?'

'Shhh!'

More of his men rose out of the shadows and turned to the south.

'There, hear it?' She turned to Michaelis.

The breeze eased for an instant and he heard the unmistakable drone of an aircraft, still too far away to be visible. At once Michaelis turned to his men.

'Get into position! Yannis, Georgis, go!'

The two men scurried across the hilltop on diverging courses and ran on for a hundred or so metres before stopping and taking out their flashlights. Michaelis had already prepared his own and his thumb was resting on the switch as he kept looking for the approaching plane. His heart was beating quickly as he scanned the starlit sky, threaded with thin trails of cloud. It was always possible that the plane belonged to the enemy. He had heard of other *andarte* groups who had given a recognition signal only to be strafed by a German fighter. But as the sound grew louder it was clear that this was a big aircraft, such as only the Allies operated, and his tension eased.

Eleni thrust her hand out. 'Up there! I see it.'

He followed the direction indicated and saw the tiny flicker of a green light, the signal they had been told to look for in the radio message from Cairo alerting them to the drop. She had good senses, Michaelis noted, smiling in Eleni's direction. He turned on his torch, aiming the beam in the aircraft's direction, and moments later the other two torches were switched on. Now was the most dangerous moment, Michaelis knew. Both the aircraft and those on the ground had exposed themselves and if the enemy were close by then they would be alerted to the supply drop and do all they could to intervene. Even if they were too far away they would still have heard the noise of the aircraft and guess what it portended. Which is why the business had to be dealt with as quickly as possible. The crates retrieved, unloaded and their contents strapped to the mules tethered close by, and then

Michaelis, his band, and the mules would quit the hilltop as swiftly as possible and be safely hidden away in their caves and remote shepherds' huts long before dawn broke over the island and the enemy came looking for them.

They heard the change in the note of the engines as the pilot throttled back and began to descend and bank on to the heading for the drop zone markers. Eleni and the others stood still, watching the tiny dark shadow moving across the starred sky, and as it drew closer to the island a finger of light flickered up into the darkness above Nidhri and began to sweep slowly across the heavens attempting to seek out the approaching bomber. But by the time the Italian officer in charge of the battery of anti-aircraft guns realised his target was flying low, the bomber would have completed its drop and turned to make the long flight back to Egypt.

Eleni could feel the reverberating throb of the engines as the aircraft steadied for its run and the dark shape swiftly grew in size and then, with a roar, it was on them. Even before it swept overhead the first of the parachutes billowed out below and behind. More followed, like dark flowers blossoming in the night. She could just make out the crates suspended below each parachute, then, as the last one opened, she saw that it was a human, dangling like a puppet as he floated to the ground some distance beyond the triangle of lights on the hilltop. The din of the bomber's engines changed pitch as it began to climb away, its mission complete. On the ground Michaelis snapped off his flashlight and a moment later the remaining lights disappeared.

'Let's get the crates! Bring the mules up.'

'What about the parachutist?' Eleni asked.

'Leave him to Yannis and Georgis. Come on.'

There was a faint braying from the strings of mules as their drivers led them forward. Meanwhile Michaelis and the others rushed towards the crates to gather in the parachutes and detach them from the harnesses. Then, using iron bars, they prised the crates open and began to unpack the bundled weapons and cases of ammunition before loading them on to the mules. They worked quickly and as soon as each case was emptied the mules were led away, down the track to the caves used to hide the supplies. The parachutes were also taken away, and the crates broken up for firewood so there would be no trace of the drop for the enemy to use as the focus of any search of the surrounding area that they might conduct.

The last crate was being dismantled as Yannis and Georgis returned, leading a man in a bulky suit and helmet with his parachute bundled up in his arms.

'Uncle Michaelis,' Georgis jerked his thumb at the new arrival, 'seems like Cairo has done us a favour and not sent us another Englishman who speaks like an ancient. He's one of us.'

'A Greek?'

'Better than a Greek,' the parachutist responded cheerily. 'I'm from the island. I've come home.'

'It's true,' Yannis added. 'I knew him as a boy.'

'By Holy God, can it be?' Eleni said quietly. 'Andreas . . . ?'

He stopped dead and stood silently for an instant. Then he thrust the tight folds of the parachute into Yannis's arms and fumbled for the buckle of his helmet as he stepped forward.

'You know him?' Michaelis demanded.

'Know him? Of course I do!' Eleni laughed as she half ran to Andreas, just as he took his helmet off. 'Andreas Katarides.' She embraced him tightly and pressed her face into his chest. Andreas grinned in delight as she spoke.

'I was afraid I would never see you again.'

'There'll be time for that later on,' Michaelis interrupted, stepping up to scrutinise the new arrival severely. 'Katarides, eh? Any relation of the poet?'

'I am his son.'

'A pity. We need fighters, not poets.'

'I hold a commission in the Royal Hellenic Navy. And I have been trained by our British allies to fight with the *andartes*. I'll prove that soon enough.'

'Maybe sooner than you think, if we spend all night talking here on the hill. Just so you know, I am Michaelis, *kapetan* of this band. I give the orders here . . . Let's go.'

Michaelis turned away abruptly and gestured to the rest to follow him, and the party marched into the darkness and followed the track down the slope towards their hideout.

The cave had a narrow entrance that led up at a sharp angle for several paces before opening out into a large chamber some twenty paces across. Andreas was at once struck by the humidity and the dank smell of sweat and human waste and the acrid stench of burned wood. A steady drip sounded from the rear and as the flashlights flickered over the rocky interior he saw the makeshift bedding of sheep's fleeces spread over piles of pine branches. Some empty ammunition boxes and smaller crates served as tables and stools. In one corner a pile of ashes showed where the *andartes* occasionally lit fires for warmth and cooking. Above, the roof of the cave was stained black with soot and he could guess at the choking clouds of smoke that would fill the chamber if the fire was allowed to burn for any length of time.

The mules were unloaded at the mouth of the cave before their drivers led them back to the mountain village where they had come from. Once the last of the weapons and ammunition had been stacked at the rear of the cave, Michaelis lit a kerosene lamp and settled down on one of the boxes. He beckoned Andreas to join him. The latter had stripped off his jumpsuit and Eleni had quickly gathered it up before one of the others claimed it for bedding.

'Sit here,' Michaelis ordered, indicating another box close by.

Andreas did as he was told.

'Why have you been sent?' Michaelis demanded directly.

Eleni sat down close by, a look of dismay on her face as she watched the band's leader jut out his jaw and regard Andreas suspiciously.

'I'd have thought that was obvious,' Andreas replied. 'I am an islander, born and bred. I know the ground, I know the people, I speak the dialect. I am here to help coordinate the resistance.'

'We don't need any coordination. We just need guns and bullets. Besides, I was expecting a British officer. Someone to just observe and report back to his superiors and persuade them to keep supplying us. That's all. I don't need you here, spying on me for the British, and those cowards who call themselves the government in exile. And don't think you are going to take control here.' He stabbed his finger at the floor of the cave. 'This is my territory. My band. Understand?'

'I understand,' Andreas replied calmly. 'I am here to help. No more than that.'

'And who says I need your help?'

'I would hope that any Greek patriot would welcome another to the cause. We both want to see our country free again, Michaelis.'

'Truly. But there are patriots and there are patriots, my friend. As you well know. When the war is over, my men and I will not stand by and let things return to the way they were under Metaxas, Holy God rot his soul. There are plenty of others who feel the same. We'll not kick one bunch of tyrants out the front door while another lot sneak in through the back.'

'You take your orders from the National Liberation Front, then?'

'I take orders from no man. I serve Greece.'

'As do I. And I leave the politics to others.'

'You may find that you have to choose where you stand. Sooner than you think.'

'If it comes to that, then I will.'

The two exchanged a hard stare before Michaelis smiled slowly. 'Good. I see we understand each other! Now, enough of that. What do you know of the situation here?'

Andreas looked around. 'I was told that there were many on the island who are prepared to fight the Italians. And that it was my task to support them.'

'Good. But you should know that it's not just the Italians we are facing. There's a small German contingent in Lefkada. No doubt sent here to keep an eye on the Italians. There's not much trust amongst fascists, it seems.'

'Germans? How many?'

'No more than a handful. Eleni knows more about them than I do.'

Andreas turned to her. 'You'd better tell me.'

She was wearing a dark dress over the baggy trousers that the other *andartes* favoured and knelt on the padded jumpsuit. 'Not much to say. There's no more than ten of them. They've taken over the top floor of the prefecture. Four officers, one

275

of whom is in the SS, two women, secretaries I think, and the rest are civilians, but there's a rumour they belong to the Gestapo. They don't mix with us, and seem to have as little to do with the Italians as they can.'

'Then why are they here?'

'All I could get out of the Italian officer billeted with your father is that they're here to liaise with their allies. That's all he could say. As far as I know the Germans have only left Lefkada a few times since they arrived. A shepherd said he had seen them up near Aghios Ilias.'

Andreas remembered the village well enough, it was on the road back from the excavations of Dr Muller.

'What were they doing up there?'

Eleni shook her head. 'I couldn't find out any more. No one seems to know much about them beyond what I've told you.'

Michaelis sniffed. 'If those Germans come anywhere near here, we'll clean them up nicely. Especially now that we have new weapons.' He glanced fondly at the guns and ammunition stacked against the side of the cave.

'I'm sure you would,' said Andreas. 'And I'd be proud to report your success back to our friends in Cairo. They like to reward success.' Beneath his jumpsuit he had been wearing a plain black jacket and trousers and now he slowly reached into his breast pocket and took out a small felt purse. 'Here. British gold. Think of it as payment on account.' He tossed the purse to Michaelis who eased it open and glanced inside with an appreciative rise of his eyebrows. Then he folded his hand around it and nodded. There was always a ready market for any man who had gold. Even with the scarcity caused by the war there were those who knew how to obtain food and other items on the black market, for a price. Andreas had given him enough to buy provisions from the local people for some months.

'I accept this to buy supplies for my men, you understand.'

'Yes. Of course. And there'll be more when Cairo hears from me about your exploits against the enemy.'

'Then they shall hear of something very soon.' Michaelis grinned. 'I have a job in mind.'

'Oh?'

'I shall say nothing now. First you rest, then I'll show you in the morning.'

'As you wish.'

Michaelis was about to turn away when he paused. 'You'll need a code name. You can't be known as Andreas Katarides, in case the enemy come to hear of it.'

'I know.'

'Then what shall we call you?'

'Mahos.'

'Mahos.' The *kapetan* nodded. 'Mahos it is.' He turned to Eleni. 'It'll be dawn soon. You'd better go.'

'Go?' Andreas tried to hide his disappointment. 'Why?'

'Eleni has to return to Nidhri before dawn. She's posing as the guest of a friend's family, come down from Lefkada to stay with them a few days to help with the friend's wedding. She has to leave now if she's going to get down to Nidhri in time. Off you go, my girl.'

Eleni nodded reluctantly and rose to her feet.

'I'd like a few words with you before you go,' said Andreas.

'All right, then,' Michaelis agreed on her behalf. 'But make it quick. There may be patrols sent up to the hills, now they've been alerted to the presence of a bomber flying low over the mountains. Go carefully, my girl.'

Andreas fell into step beside her as she made her way along

the low, narrow passage giving out to the steep hillside outside. Michaelis watched them leave with a curious stare, and then eased himself to his feet to cross over to the weapons that had been dropped and lifted up a Sten sub-machine gun to admire.

At the cave mouth Eleni stopped. The darkness was beginning to fade. Already there was just enough light to make out the valley stretching down between the hills in the direction of Nidhri. The moon had faded slightly but still added its weak lustre to the scene, and to her face as she turned towards Andreas.

'I feared I would never see you again.'

'I know the feeling.' He smiled faintly. 'There is so much I want to tell you. So much I want to hear.'

'It'll have to wait.' She glanced back down the slope. 'I have to be back in Nidhri before anyone stirs.'

'When will I see you again?'

'Soon.'

'I would like to see my father too,' Andreas continued, aware that he was being selfish in delaying her. 'But I don't want to put him in any danger.'

Eleni looked at him sadly. 'Your father is not well.'

'What's the matter?'

'It began soon after the Italians arrived. It seemed to break his spirit. He no longer cares for himself. He eats too little, and spends most of the day sitting on his terrace looking out to sea. It's as if he has aged ten years.' She took his hand in hers and squeezed gently. 'I'm sorry, Andreas.'

'Perhaps I should never have left the island.'

She laughed softly. 'We cannot change the past. Only the future.'

There was a moment's stillness and silence as they stared at each other. Then Eleni spontaneously rose on her toes and kissed him lightly on the lips and instantly turned to go. Too late he reached out for her but she nimbly hurried away down the slope and was soon lost from sight amongst the trees covering the sides of the valley.

CHAPTER TWENTY-TWO

For the next week Andreas remained in the cave while he waited for word from the other resistance bands on the island. It was his intention to gather them together so that they might plan how best to organise their efforts against the enemy. Michaelis had assured him that they had been sent messages by his runners but that it was dangerous work and some might not get through or be able to return with the reply. The time given for the appointed meeting at an abandoned shepherd's shelter high up on the hills in the centre of the island was ten days from when Andreas had landed. It was frustrating that the responses were so slow to come. But it would be a start, he told himself. A first step on the road to unifying the *andartes* towards the common goal of contributing to the defeat of the enemies of Greece. At the same time he gently tried to persuade Michaelis to share his weapons with the other bands.

Even though Greece was at war and the island was under occupation, the old ways persisted and Michaelis jealously guarded the equipment that had fallen to him, even though he had far more weapons and ammunition than he needed. He would only give the others weapons if they acknowledged him as the first amongst the *kapetans* and swore loyalty and obedience to him. Andreas pointed out that his possession of the weapons was only by virtue of the fact that it had been his men the British agents had encountered first and that they had elected to set their radio up on his territory. Michaelis shrugged and said it was fate. The same fate that had determined that he would lead the resistance on Lefkas.

Michaelis and his band were busy making preparations for an attack on the Italian anti-aircraft battery on a hill outside Nidhri. The post had been under observation for some weeks pending the arrival of the weapons needed to mount the assault. Two men at a time watched the guns and their crews from the concealment of some trees on the slope overlooking the position. At the same time Michaelis insisted that Eleni remain in Nidhri to glean what information she could about the Italian garrison and its preparedness for any attack, a task that would provide information of limited use, Andreas realised. But it would keep Eleni away from the cave and from him. Michaelis's affection for her was clear and perhaps explained his cold manner and his desire to keep Eleni and her childhood friend apart.

Lookouts watched the approaches to the cave. Only once in that first week was the alarm raised. The *andartes* slipped into the cave and pulled a screen covered with loose sacking laced with fresh-cut pine branches across the entrance. They waited in silence, clutching their weapons, listening to the voices of the Italians passing no more thirty or forty paces away. They sounded cheerful and oblivious of danger, Andreas thought, but if one of them happened to glance towards the mouth of the cave and became suspicious, the peace of the valley would be shattered. But their good fortune held and the Italians' chatter faded into the distance. They remained in the cave for another hour before Michaelis ordered a man to go out and check that the enemy had indeed gone. Another half hour passed before he returned to give the all-clear and the men inside could finally set aside their weapons and return to their normal routine.

Apart from the times when Michaelis allowed the men to go outside, they spent their time drinking raki and talking, sometimes singing. Often the discussions became heated as they touched on politics, or on ancient grievances between families or villages and Michaelis would step in and shout at them to stop. At night the men would lie on their makeshift beds, all the time scratching at the lice that infested their clothes and bedding. At first Andreas tried to keep his mattress of pine branches stuffed into his jumpsuit apart from the others but the lice soon discovered him and settled on his body and by the end of the week he was scratching away at them in the same resigned manner as his comrades.

They could only light fires during the hours of darkness in case any smoke escaped from the cave and gave away their position. Then the cave would steadily fill with smoke that caught in the lungs and irritated the eyes as they cooked stews of beans or roasted meat from freshly slaughtered sheep taken from the closest flocks or villages in the tradition of *klepsi-klepsi*, the petty theft that had endured in Greece since antiquity. At other times they ate rock bread and *mizithra*, a soft, dripping cheese, washing the meals down with yet more raki, or curdled milk from jars that were never cleaned out in order to let the culture inside thrive.

Of all the privations, it was the lice that bothered Andreas the most, the constant itch and sensation of small shimmering movements across the skin beneath his clothes. Like the other men, he sometimes stripped and tried to clear them from his body and brush them out of his garments but it only provided a brief respite before they resumed their torment in earnest. Some relief came when Andreas joined a few others permitted to leave the cave and they made their way down the slope to a small gorge where the water lay in shaded pools throughout the summer before being replenished by the winter rains that gushed through the gorge and filled the bed of the stream running down the floor of the valley towards the coast. They stripped off, immersing themselves in the cold water, where they scrubbed at their skin and dipped their hair under the surface to remove the lice before turning their attention to their clothes. A hard rub and scrub on the rocks before wringing them out and pounding the garments on the rocks was enough to remove the scourge and then the men sat and chatted quietly as they waited for the sun to dry their clothes.

The *andartes*, mostly men from the hill villages, were keen to hear Andreas's account of his time in the navy and more especially Egypt and Palestine, countries that they had heard of only in the sermons at church. They asked hosts of questions and listened in respectful silence, especially as he told them of the scale of the war being fought out across the globe. Of the millions of men and thousands of tanks, planes and warships that were engaged in the titanic struggle between the dark forces of the enemy and the desperate allies of Greece. He reminded them that though the part they played might seem small, it was still an important front on which to engage the Italians and Germans and show them that they were not invincible as they often claimed in their propaganda.

Eleni returned at the end of the week to make her report. During her absence she had returned to Lefkada for two days and as far as she could tell the enemy were not expecting any activity by the resistance on any significant scale. In Nidhri itself, the Italians were continuing to mount the same patrols and post the same sentries that they had done for the previous months. The island's inhabitants, natives and occupiers, had settled into an uneasy daily routine, she concluded.

'That routine is about to be broken.' Michaelis grinned, as they sat outside the cave in the twilight. 'Soon, everyone will learn that the war has finally come to Lefkas. We will show those fascist dogs that we Greeks still have plenty of fight in us.'

The men of his band, some twenty in all now that he had called them in to prepare for the attack, raised their fists and cheered their *kapetan*. He had already issued their new weapons, a mixture of Marlin sub-machine guns and Stens, with a handful of Enfield rifles to supplement the more dated weapons of the *andartes*. His men brandished them with pride and defiance. Andreas looked on, but was not caught up in the mood. The war had already come to the island, as far as he was concerned. He recalled all too vividly the loss of his shipmates who had died as they bought time for the *Papanikolis* to make ready to leave Sivota. It would be an easy thing to ask his host where he had been on that day. Easy, but foolish.

'After we have struck and destroyed their anti-aircraft cannon then no Italian on the island will feel safe any longer. They will jump at every shadow, every sound, while we take our time and surprise them again and again. We will destroy them a man at a time until we have driven them from our shores, however long that may take. May Holy God and the Virgin Mary be with us!'

Michaelis crossed himself and the others followed suit. Then he ordered one of his men to fetch some raki from the cave and pass it around the band. As they sat drinking, Andreas approached Michaelis and addressed him in a low voice.

'So when are you intending to attack the Italians?'

'Tomorrow. At dawn. I will take all the men, including you. Eleni will stay here.'

'Tomorrow?' Andreas could not conceal his surprise. 'So soon?'

'We have the guns we need now. You can handle the explosives. There's no need to delay any longer.'

'But I know nothing of your plan.'

Michaelis tapped his head and smiled. 'It's all up there. I know how many men we'll be going up against, how they're armed, where they sleep. It's all taken care of. As you'll see for yourself. So drink!' Michaelis thrust a bottle at him and Andreas took a swig.

'Why not wait until after the meeting with the other *kapetans*? If you strike now you will have the Italians swarming all over the island looking for the perpetrators.'

Michaelis waved a hand dismissively. 'They're cowards. If they dare poke their noses up into the hills we'll fire a few shots and send them running.'

'They seemed bold enough the other day.'

'I let them go by. If I'd been at full strength I'd have laid an ambush and cut them to pieces,' Michaelis boasted. 'They don't scare me. Nor any of my men. Nor any Greek who has the balls to stand and fight for his homeland. Do you have the balls, Mahos?'

Andreas drew a calming breath. 'Yes.'

'Good! Then you will play your part and this time tomorrow you will be counted as one of the band and can celebrate properly with the rest of us. Eh?'

Andreas nodded and took the bottle of raki with him and went to sit with Eleni. She noticed his serious expression at once.

'What's the matter? Don't you approve of his plan?'

'What plan? I fear that he just intends to charge in without any consideration of what might go wrong.'

'Don't be too hard on him, Andreas.' She paused to glance round. 'Mahos, I mean . . . Michaelis is a brave man. He loves his country and hates the enemy and the men respect him.'

'I don't doubt that he is brave. But bravery is not enough. Besides, I don't think the timing of this attack has much to do with bravery.'

'What do you mean?'

'Two days before the meeting of the resistance leaders? He knows it will stir up the Italians and make trouble. His will be the name on everyone's lips and he will reap the reward and use that to justify his claim to be the first amongst the *kapetans*. That's what he's really after, if I am any judge of the situation.'

Eleni shook her head. 'You misunderstand him. Michaelis is no schemer.'

'You respect him?'

'Yes, of course.'

'I see. And there's more than respect for him in your heart, I think.'

Eleni frowned at him. 'Why do you say that?'

'I can see it in your face. And why not? You have been working with him since the occupation began. You have come to trust one another. I suppose it's inevitable that a deeper bond might form between you. It's clear that he regards you as more than just a member of his band.'

Eleni stared back. 'He's been hiding in caves in the mountain all through the winter, and fighting the enemy while you were safely in Egypt.'

'I am here to fight as well, Eleni,' Andreas responded quietly.

'Are you jealous of him?'

'No! No, of course not.' Andreas burned with embarrassment. 'Whatever is between you and him is your own matter. I don't care about it.'

'Really?' she teased, poking him in the chest. 'Why, I believe you really are jealous.'

He was about to protest again when she put her hand round his neck and drew his head closer to hers and kissed him. He lips lingered a moment and she drew back with a smile as she whispered, 'Andreas, you fool. Do you really think there is any other man in this world I would love rather than you? I have prayed for you to come back to me since the moment you left . . .' She kissed him again, longer this time, and Andreas felt a lightness sweep through his body. He made to embrace her and Eleni pulled back.

'No. Not here. Not in front of the others. Come.'

She took his hand and led him away from the mouth of the cave a short distance along the slope until they were hidden from view by the shrubs and stunted trees. Then they angled down, passing through a clump of pines, their heady scent filling the air. At length Andreas realised where they were heading and smiled as they emerged by the entrance to the gorge where the largest of the pools gleamed dully in the gloom. Around them the cicadas shrilled, their raucous sound rising and falling without any discernible rhythm.

'We can talk freely here,' said Eleni, sitting on a flat slab of rock. 'Come.'

Andreas did as she bid and eased himself down at her side. He hesitated before he asked the only question that was on his mind. 'Did you mean it?'

'Mean what?'

'What you said back at the cave. That you loved me.'

'Of course.' She took his hand and eased her fingers through his. 'Did you not guess? Not in all the years that I have known you? Well?'

'I . . . I had hoped.'

'And I had almost given up hope that you would realise it. Until I saw your expression the other night, and then I knew.'

Andreas put an arm round her to draw her closer and they kissed again. For much longer this time. At length they parted and smiled helplessly at each other. Then her pleasure faded from her face.

'There's something I must tell you, Andreas.'

He felt a sudden stab of doubt. 'What?'

'It's your father. I saw him two days ago. When I went to see him, he was in bed. He looked very thin and weak. Dr Meskouris called in before I left. He fears the worst.'

'What is wrong with my father?'

Eleni shrugged. 'The doctor could not say. He thinks your father seems to have lost the will to live. He does not eat, drinks little and has barely enough energy to stir from his bed. But he did ask me about you before I left. He asked if I thought you were still alive.'

For an instant Andreas was torn between anxiety for his father and the need to keep his presence on the island a secret. 'What did you say to him?'

'I wanted to tell him you were alive, to give him some hope. But I knew I could not. That is your decision.' She took his hand. 'What will you do?'

Andreas thought for a moment, filled with guilt and a longing to be with his father before it was too late. 'I will see him. As soon as I can. I owe him that at least. Can you get me in without the Italians in the house knowing?'

'Yes, I think so.'

'Then I'll do it, once the consequences of tomorrow have died down.'

She kissed him. 'I hoped you'd say that.'

Then she placed her arms round his shoulders and drew him back on to the rock beside her and Andreas kissed her and began to undo the buttons of her blouse. She held his hand.

'Andreas, we must be careful. I cannot afford to be with child. Not while we fight the enemy. You understand?'

He nodded. 'I know. I will not let that happen.'

Then he leaned forward and kissed her neck and she let out a soft sigh of delight as she closed her eyes.

CHAPTER TWENTY-THREE

The last of Michaelis's men crawled into position before first light. They had left the cave shortly after midnight and picked their way down the valley to approach the small plain surrounding Nidhri. The Italian artillery battery was on the crest of a small hill a kilometre from the town. One by one, Michaelis assigned his men to their places at the base of the hill. When he had outlined his plan to Andreas just before setting off he had intended to surround the hill to ensure that no Italians escaped, and then attack. Andreas had pointed out that this might well lead to the *andartes* accidentally shooting at their own men when they reached the crest of the hill. Accordingly, he persuaded the *kapetan* to change his plan so that only a loose screen surrounded the hillock while the rest of the men attacked from a single direction.

It was an hour before sunrise before the men were finally in place and Michaelis whispered the order for the assault to begin. The two silenced Stens were in the hands of the *kapetan* and Andreas, who led the way up through the scrub and stunted oaks, treading warily in order not to alert the sentries guarding the anti-aircraft battery above. Aside from the calls of a few night birds hunting their prey there was quiet and Andreas's senses strained to detect any sign of life ahead of him as he climbed the hill. The sound of his own breathing, his footfall and the subdued panting of the men behind him seemed alarmingly loud and he feared that the enemy would detect them and open fire at any moment.

'Psst . . .'

Andreas paused and glanced towards Michaelis. The *kapetan* had lowered himself into a crouch and pointed up the slope. Ahead the last of the trees gave out on to open ground and there at the crest of the slope he could just make out the outline of a sentry. A moment later there was a tiny flare of red as the man drew on a cigarette and then the tip faded to a faint glow. Michaelis turned to signal his men to halt and then crept over to Andreas.

'We'll get closer and then I'll shoot him,' he whispered.

'No. I have a better way.' Andreas carefully slung his Sten and drew his knife and held the blade up for the *kapetan* to see. 'I'll use this.'

Michaelis was still a moment before he nodded. 'All right.'

Andreas edged forward in a crouch, climbing the slope as stealthily as possible, testing every foot he planted to avoid snapping any fallen branches or stumbling on a loose rock. All the while he kept his gaze fixed on the sentry as blood pounded in his ears like a muffled drum. Every so often the man would inhale and the glow from the tip of his cigarette would light his face and the front of his cap in a lurid red. He looked young, with thin features. Barely older than Andreas. And yet he was the enemy. Pushing aside such considerations, Andreas concentrated on his training and steadily worked his way round so that he could approach from behind. As he reached the crest of the hill he could make out the long, dark barrels of the anti-aircraft guns pointing up into the sky, and the rings of sandbags that surrounded them. A short distance beyond lay two neat lines of tents and he could hear the sound of snoring. He made out two more sentries on the far side of the battery.

When he was no more than five paces away he paused and raised his knife. There was a terrible stillness that seemed to stretch on and on before the man drew on his cigarette one last time and exhaled, letting his hand drop to his side. Before Andreas could choose his moment there was a cough from below on the slope. Andreas rushed forward. At the last moment the sentry began to turn, but it was too late to save him. Andreas's left hand snapped over his mouth and yanked his head back while the commando knife sliced open the sentry's throat and Andreas felt a warm spray on his fingers. The man struggled desperately in his grasp, and kicked out the heel of his boot, catching his assailant on the shin. The sentry released his rifle and it fell against his body before slipping to the ground with a soft thud. His strength failed quickly as he bled out and when he was no more than twitching feebly Andreas gently lowered him to the ground and eased his hand away from the man's mouth. There was a gentle rasp of air from his lips and then he lay still and silent.

Andreas knelt down beside the body and used the Italian's uniform to wipe the blood from his knife and hands. None of the enemy had noticed the disturbance and the battery slumbered on beneath the stars, quite oblivious to its imminent peril. Satisfied that they were safe to continue the attack. Andreas turned to the slope and beckoned to his comrades waiting in the shadows. There was a soft padding of footsteps and then the dark figures of the *andartes* swarmed forward and fanned out on either side of Andreas before kneeling down to wait for orders. Michaelis glanced at the body and cleared his throat as he patted Andreas on the back. 'Good work . . .'

The *kapetan* reached into his sidebag and took out a grenade and held it up for his men to see. Those who had been entrusted with grenades took them out and when all were ready Michaelis gave the signal to advance. Crouching low, the line of *andartes* began to cross the crest of the hill towards the guns and the tents. As they reached the sandbags of the first emplacement Michaelis signalled his men to halt and leaned his weapon against the hessian sacks. He drew the grenade pin, keeping his hand close over the lever, and rose to his feet. The other men armed with grenades followed suit and Michaelis took a deep breath and shouted.

'Now!'

There were grunts as the others hurled their grenades towards the tents and before the Italians could react, there was a series of blinding yellow flashes. The blasts shredded the canvas and blew the material out as if caught in a sudden storm. The sound of the detonations was momentarily deafening and as the *andartes* rose up and surged forward, Andreas's ears were still ringing. A savage cry ripped from their lips as they charged. Figures stumbled out from between the tents, too shocked to react to the danger, and there was a panicked cry of alarm, too late to do any good. Shots cracked out on either side of Andreas and he raised his weapon and flicked off the safety catch as he reached the second gun position, no more than ten paces from the tents. He saw a man with a rifle start to raise his weapon before there was a flash from one side and the Italian toppled back. More of the enemy were cut down by the *andartes'* fire as they charged into the tent lines and continued shooting as they shouted their war cries.

Andreas stopped by the second emplacement and vaulted inside before hurrying to the anti-aircraft gun. He slipped the

Sten over his shoulder again and reached into his sidebag for the first RDX charge. He moulded the charge round the breech mechanism and set a pencil detonator deep into the pliable mass, pinching it to break the acid vial inside. In twenty minutes it would eat through the wire that released the trigger and set off the charge. He quickly set another charge beneath the ammunition cases stacked to the side of the emplacement and then hurried over to the other two guns to complete his work.

By the time he had finished, the shooting had stopped and the *andartes* were picking over the bodies and tents, looking for weapons to salvage and any loot. He found Michaelis standing in the middle of the camp, the stock of his weapon resting on his hip as he surveyed his triumphant followers.

'The charges are set, we have to go soon.'

'We didn't lose a single man.' Michaelis laughed. 'Just two wounded. Yannis, shot in the arm, and Niklos, shot himself in the foot.'

'Very good. Now let's get back to the cave.'

'We leave when I say,' Michaelis responded flatly. 'I am in command. Not you.'

'I know. But the charges—'

'There's plenty of time. As I said, two wounded. In exchange we've killed or wounded at least ten of them. The rest bolted in the direction of Nidhri.'

'They'll be back. With reinforcements. Listen!'

They both heard the wail of a siren from the direction of the town and saw lights flickering on.

'We'll have disappeared back into the hills long before those dogs arrive.' Michaelis cleared his throat and spat before he called out, '*Andartes!* On me!'

His men came hurrying from across the crest of the hill.

Some were talking excitedly and laughing at their exploits. As the last of them arrived, Andreas saw that he had three Italian prisoners with him, hands on heads as they were jostled towards the waiting resistance fighters.

'What's this?' Michaelis demanded. 'Holy God! What is that stench? They smell worse than we do!'

'They were hiding in the latrine trench. They surrendered to me as soon as I pointed my gun at them.'

The other men surrounded the prisoners and jeered, prodding them with the muzzles of their weapons, and some kicked and spat at them.

'We can't take prisoners,' Michaelis said firmly and then called out loudly so that all his men would hear him clearly. 'No prisoners.'

The voices of his men died away and Michaelis turned to the young man who had captured the Italians. 'Step away from them. Do as I say.'

The *andarte* stood his ground for a moment then withdrew a few paces and the Italians were left standing slightly apart from the group. Michaelis strode up behind them and kicked each man in the back of the knees to force them to drop down. One of the Italians instantly began to speak quickly in a pleading tone. Andreas heard the sharp snap as Michaelis loaded a fresh magazine into his Sten.

'What are you doing?'

'We can't take prisoners,' Michaelis repeated. 'We can't keep them in the cave watching them to make sure they don't escape. Or worse, not being able to rest without worrying they'll get hold of a weapon and kill us while we sleep. Besides, they'll be extra mouths to feed.'

He cocked the weapon and raised the muzzle to the back of the first prisoner's head.

'Wait!' Andreas intervened and stepped in between them. 'You can't just shoot these men.'

'Why not? Do you think they'd be any more merciful if we surrendered to them? Now get out of my way.'

'Let them go.'

Michaelis stared at him. 'Are you mad? They're the enemy.'

'They are prisoners of war. You shoot them now and you can guarantee the Italians will take reprisals. It's safer to let them go.'

'We could stand here arguing about it but your charges are set to go off.'

'Just let them go. It's the best thing to do,' Andreas urged.

Michaelis lowered his Sten and spoke quietly. 'All right. You men, get off the hill and head back to the cave. Go!'

They began to file off into the darkness. Michaelis turned away from the men kneeling on the ground and gestured to Andreas to follow the others. He had not gone more than a few paces before he heard the snap of the Sten's bolt and a distinctive hiss and stopped abruptly to look back. He saw the first prisoner's dark shape face down on the ground just as Michaelis shot the second man in the back of the head. Before Andreas could speak, the third man had been executed. Michaelis calmly stepped over the bodies and set off after his men. He thrust Andreas before him and they hurried away, across the crest and down the slope. As they passed through the trees Andreas fell into step beside the *kapetan*.

'Why?' he demanded.

'Told you. No prisoners.'

'The Italians will find them and know what you did.'

'Let them! Once word gets round, every fascist outpost on the island is going to know what we do with prisoners. It'll scare the bastards witless.'

'And they'll take it out on our people. Our people, Michaelis. They will pay with their blood.'

The *andarte* leader shrugged. 'War is a pitiless business, my friend. The sooner everyone on this island learns it the better.'

Behind them there was a brilliant glare and a moment later they heard the boom of the first explosion. The *andartes* stopped to look back and saw the ball of fire boiling up from the crest. A second explosion erupted with a huge flash that made the men wince before the roar hit them. Andreas realised it was the first ammunition store going up. The blast fed more explosions in the ammunition, splitting the night with flashes and thunderclap detonations. By the time they reached the track leading up towards the mountain valley the last of the charges had blasted the remaining anti-aircraft gun to pieces and the crest of the hill was ablaze with burning debris, dry grass and undergrowth. Beyond, in the direction of Nidhri, they could see the headlights of several vehicles bobbing along the track leading towards the battery, too late to save it or pursue the men who had carried out the attack.

Michaelis paused and raised his Sten into the air. 'Now they'll know what happens to those who sully Greek soil with their jackboots! They will fear us! Our names will be on the lips of all those who hate the enemy and love the motherland!'

He let out a loud cheer and his men joined in. Only Andreas remained silent as he gazed back at the hellish fires burning on the hilltop, the glow of the flames picking out the bodies scattered amongst the tents. This was the first major attack carried out by the *andartes* since the island had been occupied. And the bloodiest. And there would be a reckoning.

★

The mood amongst the *kapetans* gathered outside the shepherd's hut close to the summit of Pirghos was sullen and they regarded Michaelis with barely guarded hostility. The day after the attack on the anti-aircraft battery the Italian commander had issued a proclamation demanding the surrender of the criminals responsible for the attack and the murder of fifteen Italian soldiers, some of whom had been executed after they had been taken prisoner. If the perpetrators were not in police custody within twenty-four hours then fifteen men taken from the population of Lefkada would be shot. The deed had been carried out the following morning. The fifteen, taken at random off the streets of the town, were marched to the prefecture, placed against the wall of the building and killed by firing squad. Word of the massacre had reached all corners of the island and the leaders of the resistance bands were open in their anger at Michaelis.

'Your recklessness threatens us all, Michaelis,' a wizened, white-bearded *kapetan* from Lazarata said. 'In these times of hunger, your actions have stolen food from our meagre plates!'

Others grumbled their support for his protest and scowled at Michaelis. Andreas, Eleni and a handful of his men were sitting amongst the wider audience, looking on. Michaelis paced into the centre of the open ground and raised his hands to silence the gathering.

'Times have changed. Our nation is at war. We are at war. Just as our brothers fought the Italians on the Albanian front, so it is now our duty to fight them here on our home soil! Every town, every village, every house is the front line in our war against the enemy. There are no civilians any more. Just good Greeks, and bad Greeks. The good will fight. The bad will play the coward or, worse, the traitor. The enemy have proved themselves to be base criminals in the way they murdered our fellow countrymen. Will you allow such an outrage to go unpunished? If you are real patriots then you must accept that there will be casualties. All that remains is to understand that and fight!'

The older *kapetan* stood up and stabbed a finger at Michaelis. 'How can we fight without more guns? You would have us attack the enemy with knives and clubs? Pah!'

'But I have plenty of guns, Petros, my friend.' Michaelis smiled. 'More than enough to equip my band and a few more besides. And there will be more when our British allies hear of our success and send more planes loaded with weapons to Lefkada.' He turned and pointed to Andreas. 'Is this not so? You, Mahos, have come from Egypt at the behest of the British. Tell them that the British have plenty of guns and explosives to send us.'

All eyes turned to Andreas and he stood up and nodded. 'Our allies wish to help us in any way that they can.'

'Like they did when the Nazis came?' a voice cried out and others added shouts of anger.

'It is true that they failed us then,' Andreas admitted. 'But they stand with us now.'

'See!' Michaelis nodded. 'They will provide me with all the weapons we need. Weapons I will share with all of you . . . provided that you accept me as first among *kapetans*. Do that, and you shall have new weapons, better guns than ever before. Then we can make them fear us, and I will lead you in the fight against the fascists. Lead you to victory!'

'But only if we accept you as leader . . .' Petros responded with a cynical smile. 'It seems to me we lost one tyrant in Metaxas only to find another in you, young Michaelis.'

'Think what you like. You communists are always

complaining but if you want guns then you know where to come for them, and the price you must pay.'

'This is wrong,' Andreas muttered. 'Michaelis cannot be allowed to get away with this . . .' He made to stand up but Eleni hung on his arm and pulled him down.

'What are you going to do?'

'The guns were intended for all the *andartes*, not just Michaelis. They need to know.'

She looked at him with concern. 'Be careful. If you confront him, you will make an enemy of him. That would be dangerous.'

Andreas nodded. 'I know. But I cannot allow him to put himself before the rest of his countrymen.'

He took a deep breath, rose to his feet and stepped forward into the open space beside Michaelis.

'As Michaelis says, I was sent here by the British to help the *andartes*. But before I was their agent I was from this island. Lefkas is my home, so I speak as one of you and you can trust me when I say that my heart is in our fight against the fascists. I must tell you that our allies want to assist every resistance group on Lefkas. I was sent to help you work together, not to serve Michaelis alone. And the weapons were sent for all of you to share. Not just for Michaelis. He should share what he has, and what will come.'

Michaelis rounded on him angrily. 'The weapons are mine! It was my men who took the risk of retrieving them! We have looked after them, and we've put them to good use. Who else would have dared to attack the Italian battery? Not the rest of these bands. They need to be led by a man who knows his duty.'

'And look where it got us!' Another *kapetan* stood up. 'Fifteen of our men shot in cold blood.'

'They will be avenged!' Michaelis shouted back. 'We will kill ten Italians for every one of ours they execute.'

'Then they will do the same to us. And when they have run out of men, they'll start shooting our women and children! Because of you. You have brought this on us, and now, in order to defend ourselves, you want us to go on bended knee to you? Pah!'

'The weapons will be shared,' Andreas declared. 'As will all new supplies. You have my word on it.'

'No!' Michaelis confronted him, thrusting his face forward so that it was close to Andreas's and he could smell the sharp tang of raki on the *kapetan*'s sour breath. 'I decide what happens to my guns. I lead my band. You don't give the orders. Any man who tries to challenge my authority must pay the price . . .'

'He's got a knife!' Eleni cried out.

Andreas heard her and backed away quickly as the blade flashed forward, the point tearing through a fold in his sheepskin jerkin. Eleni's warning was echoed by others and the gathering scrambled back to get away from the two men. Michaelis stabbed again and again, but Andreas avoided the blows and backed off as he snatched out his own knife and went into a crouch three paces away from the *kapetan*. Both men eyed the other warily as some of Michaelis's band cheered their leader on. The rest of the crowd watched in silence. Eleni clasped her hands together anxiously.

'Stop it! Stop!' she cried.

She stepped forward warily, to one side, not daring to come between the two men as she continued to plead.

'Michaelis, Mahos, what are you doing? Your enemies are down there in Lefkada, not here amongst your people. Put the knives down!'

Michaelis gritted his teeth and growled, 'Keep out of the way, girl. I wouldn't want to have to hurt you too.'

'Go!' Andreas commanded. 'Stay clear.'

He moved round so that he stood between her and Michaelis.

'Stop . . .' she said desperately. 'For the love of God.'

Michaelis lurched forward again, feinting to the right and then the left to test his opponent's reactions, but Andreas had been taught by an SOE instructor who had spent much of his career amongst the criminal gangs of Shanghai and knew how to spot a feint from a real strike. Coolly keeping his blade up, Andreas weighed up the other man. Michaelis was well-built, strong, and moved quickly on his feet, but he lacked the swift ruthlessness that was necessary if a man was to stand a good chance of coming out of a knife fight alive. Tightening his grip on the handle of his dagger, Andreas moved forward.

'Throw down your knife, Michaelis. Do it now and you will live. I will take command of the band, but you will live. Drop it.'

'What?' Michaelis sneered and then his teeth bared. 'Fuck you . . .'

With a snarl he came forward again, slashing with his blade to force Andreas back. Instead he stood his ground and recoiled just enough to stay out of the way of the *kapetan*'s strike. Then he snatched at Michaelis's wrist with his spare hand and locked his fingers tightly, yanking his opponent forward and twisting as he struck with his right, stabbing into Michaelis's midriff. He wrenched the blade back as the other man let out a winded groan, and stabbed again with all his strength, and again and again, still keeping his left hand tightly about Michaelis's wrist. Those surrounding the fight looked on in silence and the cries of the men who had been supporting their leader died away as he staggered under the vicious assault.

Andreas felt blood spatter his face and he heard the wheezing breath of Michaelis as he struggled to remain on his feet. Tearing his blade free, Andreas kicked the other man to the ground and released his grip on the wrist only to stamp his boot down, forcing Michaelis to let go of his knife. Andreas kicked the blade away and stepped back, breathing hard. He was still half in a crouch, eyes glaring, bloodied blade clenched in his fist and blood spattered across his sheepskin jerkin and face. Michaelis rolled on to his side, mouth open in a pained gasp as he clamped his hands over the wounds, but the blood still oozed over his fingers and stained the stone and dry soil beneath him as he steadily bled to death.

'Mahos . . .'

Andreas straightened up and turned to see Eleni staring at him, her expression fearful.

'Are you hurt?'

He shook his head, went to wipe his blade on Michaelis, and thought better of it, using the dark material of his own breeches instead before he sheathed his dagger. Eleni knelt beside Michaelis and placed her hands on his bristled cheeks.

'Michaelis?'

His eyes opened and rolled before they settled on her. His lips parted in a thin smile and he whispered her name, then his eyelids fluttered and closed again and his breath came in light, ragged gasps, growing steadily weaker. Until, at length, he lay silent and still. Eleni gently set his head down and stood up.

'Did you have to kill him?'

'He would have killed me. You know that.'

She could not deny it. Eleni had come to know Michaelis

well enough to recognise the lengths to which he would go in pursuit of his aims, and well enough to fear him a little because of it, especially as he had hardly made a secret of his feelings for her.

Andreas looked round, uncertain of the others' reaction to the death of Michaelis. The *kapetans* and their followers simply stared, waiting for a cue, as did the men from his band, aghast at the fall of their leader. Andreas licked his dry lips and waited for his breathing to slow before he addressed them. He was shocked at the situation and briefly wondered how Colonel Huntley would react to the news that he had killed Michaelis. It was possible that the British would be wary of sending more support to the *andartes* if they thought that the Greeks were turning on each other. There was only one way forward for him now. His mission had changed. He must assume command of Michaelis's band and use his authority to try and unite the *kapetans*.

'I shall take the place of Michaelis . . . Does any man challenge my right to do so?' He glared round defiantly, pausing as he looked at Yannis and the other men from the cave. 'Well?'

No one spoke. Eventually Andreas nodded. 'Then I am the *kapetan*. Good. My first decision is that the weapons we have will be shared with the other bands. Send men and mules to the Church of Sotiras in two days' time, at dusk. There you will be given guns and ammunition. And there will be more after the next drop, and all that follow.' He paused and directed his gaze at the two men who had confronted Michaelis. 'What Michaelis has done cannot be changed. Blood has been spilt and there is no going back. But I will do all I can to ensure that no harm comes to those who do not choose to fight the enemy. We cannot prevent their barbarism, but we can make them pay dearly for it. I swear, by Holy God, that I will not leave the fight until either the enemy are driven from Lefkas or I am killed.'

Eleni winced but then forced herself to look up with a determined expression and nod her support.

'Then the gathering is over,' Andreas announced. 'You know my purpose, and my promise. It is your choice whether you take the guns and fight with me, or fight the enemy on your own. Two days' time then, at the Church of Sotiras!'

He turned away and paced towards the small group of men he had accompanied to the meeting place. Eleni followed, at his shoulder. They regarded him with fear and some hostility. 'You accept my leadership?' he challenged.

Yannis shuffled uneasily but dared not meet his eye. The others did not answer and Andreas took a step forward and glared at them. 'Answer me! Do you accept? Yannis? What do you say?'

The *andarte* looked at him and nodded slowly.

'Say it.'

Yannis swallowed and spoke clearly. 'I accept it, Uncle.'

Andreas felt an urge to smile at the familiar term of respect, especially when it was offered by a man many years older than him. He looked round at the rest of the men. Grudgingly they followed suit.

'I would not have had it this way,' Andreas said. 'But you all saw what happened. Michaelis drew a knife on me without warning. When a man does that, there will always be blood spilt. He is the one responsible for his death. Now I am your *kapetan* I expect you to follow my orders just as you obeyed his. I will not tolerate any man who challenges my authority. I will not tolerate any man who does not have the heart for the fight to come. We are all in this to the end. Now return to the cave and tell the others what has happened. You can begin to divide our weapons and ammunition ready for the other bands. Only the explosives remain with us. Yannis?'

'Yes, Uncle?'

'You will be in command until I return to the cave.'

'You're not coming with us?'

'Not yet. I have another duty to perform first. Go now.'

As they stood up and hefted their packs and weapons, Andreas turned away and felt himself trembling. He felt a cold wave of nausea ripple through his body now that he fully grasped the magnitude of what he had done. He had killed one of his own countrymen in cold blood, as viciously as if he had been an enemy. It sickened him, as did the fear of assuming command over the followers of the man he had killed.

Eleni saw the fear in his eyes and wanted to comfort him but knew that it was impossible in front of the others. She must let Andreas be seen as cold, aloof and alone, in command of the situation. So she stood by and waited until he had mastered his nerves. He looked at her with a haunted expression.

'There is something I must do before I return to take command of the *andartes*. You must help me.'

Eleni's hand began to reach for his, but she stole it back. 'Anything.'

'Then take me to my father. I must see him while he still lives.'

CHAPTER TWENTY-FOUR

The house he had grown up in looked very different to the last time he had seen it. The flowerbeds around the drive were overgrown and one of the small whitewashed pillars at the gate had been demolished and the rubble lay undisturbed. An open-topped Fiat staff car was parked outside the entrance and the driver leaned against the door smoking a cigarette. Watching from the shadows of a terrace of trees overlooking the house, Andreas felt his heart ache at the melancholy ambience of his father's villa. He had been lying in wait for over two hours and it was now after six in the evening. Eleni had parted from him when they had reached the track above the villa. While he had gone into hiding to keep watch, she had returned to Lefkada to change from her shepherd's garb into clothes more appropriate for visiting Andreas's father. She had explained that it was the custom for the Italian officers billeted at the villa to drink in the town most evenings. They left just before dusk and returned late in the evening, usually drunk, before staggering to their rooms to sleep it off.

The enemy officers did not disappoint. As the sun dipped behind the crest of the hill at Andreas's back, the front door opened and three men emerged. They were in shirtsleeves with bloused trousers tucked neatly into their gleaming boots. The driver instantly flicked his cigarette away and took his seat as his cheery passengers climbed aboard. A moment later the engine started and the car circled the drive and passed through the damaged gate before rattling down the road in the direction of Lefkada. Andreas felt a brief stab of anger as he realised who had been responsible for the damage to the gate pillar. Then he settled back to wait for Eleni. He wondered how his father would receive him. Much had happened since they had last faced each other and his return to the island was an extremely dangerous venture.

He recalled the advice of Lieutenant Moss that it was best to resign oneself to the prospect of not surviving the war. He understood the man's thinking well enough. Any attempt to hold on to ambitions and dreams for the future might cause a man to hesitate when to do so could make the difference between life and death, or more importantly, between a mission's success or its failure. But he could not make himself abandon hope of being part of the world that would be won when the evil tide of fascism had been rolled back and destroyed. Especially when Eleni might be at the heart of that world. It would be a fine thing, too, if his father came to know the full details of his experiences and was proud of him. It was a small reward in the grand scheme of things, Andreas reflected, but the respect of his father was a most valuable prize.

Half an hour after the car had departed he observed a small figure appear around the bend in the road and approach the gate. He saw at once that it was a female and that her head was covered in a black scarf. It had to be Eleni. No one else had any reason to be here at this time of day. She walked in an unhurried manner, a wicker basket on one arm, and made no attempt to glance around and look for him. She approached the villa and climbed the short flight of steps to the door and knocked. She hesitated and knocked again before letting herself in. There was a brief delay before Eleni stood on the threshold and took out a bright yellow scarf – the signal that it was safe for Andreas to enter the villa. He glanced both ways along the road before he emerged from the cover of the trees and jogged over to join her.

She took his arm gently and drew him inside, shutting the door behind them. At once the musty, slightly damp odour filled Andreas with a sense of familiarity and longing for his younger days. Nothing much seemed to have changed in the villa's hall. Some of the smaller items of furniture were missing and the Italians had hung their jackets, coats and helmets on the pegs beside the door and the gun cabinet was empty.

'Your father is this way.' She turned to the door on the left of the hall that led into the servants' quarters. A dingy corridor stretched along the front of the building with several small storerooms and the kitchen and living quarters of the staff. Those were now empty, save for the last door at the end of the corridor, which was closed. Eleni took the handle and then turned to Andreas.

'Let me speak to him first. He doesn't know you are back on the island. It would be better not to surprise him. Let me break the news, all right?'

Andreas nodded and she twisted the handle and entered the darkened room while he waited outside.

'Who . . . who's that?' a voice called out feebly.

'It's Eleni. I've brought you some food. I'm going to make soup.'

'Good . . . Good girl. I feared it was that Italian bastard, come to steal from me again. He took my watch . . . I complained to one of the officers, but he laughed at me.'

Eleni clicked her tongue and then crossed to the shuttered windows either side of the door leading out on to the terrace. Lifting the latches, she swung them open with a dull squeal from the rusting hinges, and evening light pierced the gloom.

'How are you feeling today?'

'Alive. More's the pity.'

Eleni tutted. 'That is no way to speak.'

'No?' Katerides replied absently. 'Then pray tell me what there is to live for? My country is invaded, my house occupied by arrogant barbarians and my son . . . My son is gone . . . You are all the light that I have left in my life now, young girl. And you should not waste your time looking after me. You should be enjoying life, not ministering to the dying.'

'You are Andreas's father, and my friend too. I would not have it any other way. Now, will you have soup, if I make it for you?'

'Of course.' Katarides's tone lightened a little. 'I dare not refuse.'

'Quite right.' There was a brief pause before she continued. 'Before I go to prepare your supper, tell me something.'

'What is this? Must I earn my meal by answering questions? Ah, well. What is it?'

'If it was in my power to grant you a wish, what would you want?'

'Wishes are for fools. There are many things I might wish for, but not one of them will come true.'

'Perhaps, but indulge me.'

'Very well . . . An end to the pestilence of war. And a return to the way things were.'

'I see. And what would that involve?'

'An end to the invasion of my house. A free Greece . . . and the return of my son, Holy God willing that he still lives.'

'He does.'

'How can you possibly know that, child?' Katarides demanded bitterly. 'He has been gone for over a year and there has been no word of him. It is more than likely the war has claimed him.'

'It has not. He lives. You have my word on it.'

'If he lives, then I would wish to see him again with all my heart, while I still draw breath. There are things I should have told him, before it was too late.'

'Then tell him . . . Andreas?'

He entered the room, recalling it from the days of childhood when he used to sneak into the servants' quarters when they were absent or at work, curious to know how they lived. The room smelled of sweat and stale food. There was a simple chest of drawers and a table under one of the windows, with several books piled beside a stack of paper. A pen rested in its holder, next to a pot of ink. The only other items of furniture were two old chairs and a metal-framed bed on which his father lay. He was propped up against a worn and stained bolster and a frayed cover lay across his thin body. Andreas was shocked by his appearance. His father looked thin and delicate and his hair, once dark and lustrous, was now long, uncared for and streaked with grey. It was difficult to believe so great a change could have overcome him since the last time Andreas had returned to his home.

Katarides stared back, wide-eyed, and his jaw sagged as he muttered, 'Holy God, it is you . . .' He struggled up from the bolster and stretched out a hand. 'Andreas. My Andreas. My boy.'

His son felt his throat tighten with emotion and he did not

311

trust himself to speak, but he nodded, then took one of the chairs and set it down beside the bed and stood over his father as the latter shook his head in disbelief.

'What are you doing here? Have you come home?'

Andreas smiled. 'Not quite. I am back on the island.'

'Then you must stay here. There is plenty of room, even if those pasta-eating parasites have taken over the villa.'

'I can't. Not now, at least. I have work to do before I can come home.'

'Work?'

Eleni patted the old man's hand. 'I'll leave you to talk while I make the soup.'

Katarides nodded vaguely, his eyes still fixed on his son. She picked up her basket and left the room and the sound of her footsteps echoed lightly off the walls of the corridor before she reached the kitchen.

'What kind of work do you mean?' Katarides asked.

'I cannot tell you anything, Father. It is safer for you to know nothing about it. Believe me.' Andreas sat down and his father reached out and took his hand.

'I understand, I think.' Then his eyes widened. 'But you are in danger here! If the Italians come—'

'The officers have gone into town. If they come back early, I will see the lights of the car on the road long before they reach the villa. I am safe for now.'

'No. You should leave! They would shoot you if you were caught. Why did you take such a risk?'

'To see you, Father. Eleni said that you were sick. So . . .' He shrugged. 'Here I am. I won't stay for long. But I just needed you to know that I am alive and well. And that you have something to look forward to when the fascists have gone.'

Katarides shook his head sadly and eased back on to his

bolster. 'And when will that be? All I hear is that they are driving the Allies back on every front. What if they should win the war? What then? A dark veil will fall over the world and all free men will be trampled under their boots. I could not live in such a world. There will be no place for poets and free thinkers.'

'They will be defeated,' Andreas responded firmly. 'It may take many years, but we will be free again.'

'Yes, a comforting thought . . . But come now, do you really believe it?'

Andreas considered a moment before replying. 'I hope for it. If the alternative is as dreadful as you foresee, then I would give my life to fighting against it, if only because it would have no value in that world.'

Katarides nodded slowly. 'Yes. You are right. And you are young enough and strong enough to do what I cannot. Else I would join you and the others in the mountains and fight for our freedom.'

Andreas squeezed his father's hand affectionately. 'And I would be honoured to fight at your side, Father. But this is a war for younger men.'

'It always is, my son. That is the nature of war. It consumes our young, the very best of us. It destroys a generation. Even those who survive will always be scarred. There is no greater tragedy than war. I would give anything to save you from it. Even my life, if I could.'

Andreas swallowed and forced a smile. 'The world will need poets when the war is over, Father. At that time more than ever.'

Katarides gestured towards the table by the window and sank back into his bolster. 'I am finished. There are no more words to write . . .'

There was a brief silence during which Andreas grieved for the loss of the spirit that had animated his father for so long but had now deserted him. It was one more reason to hate the enemy. To hate the brutal nihilism of what they stood for. He cleared his throat. 'There will be a day when we are free again. That is what I am fighting for. Eleni too. We Greeks have seen occupiers come and go across the centuries, but we are still here, and always will be. And we'll fight to make sure of it, just as we always have. Hold that thought, Father, but you must never mention a word of this. Never let anyone know that you have seen me. Perhaps I should not have come here. I've put you at risk.'

'No. I'm glad that you did. More happy than I have been for a long time.'

'When I leave here I don't know when I may next see you. I just needed you to know I am alive.'

'Alive, yes. But not safe.'

'No one is, until the war is won. Safety is something of a luxury at present. But I will not be reckless with my life, I promise you that.'

'Good, now help me out of this bed. We'll sit outside on the terrace.'

Katarides sat up and eased his legs over the side of the bed and reached for a pair of trousers lying folded on a small side table. Under the covers he had been wearing a loose shirt and he now tucked this into the waistband of his trousers and shuffled his feet into his slippers. Andreas went to help him up but was rebuffed with a firm hand.

'I can do this by myself. It is the spirit that has grown weak, not so much the body.'

He rose from the bed and led the way across the small room to the door and opened it on to the terrace. Outside the island was bathed in the syrupy gold of the evening light that fell across the roofs of Lefkada and the mainland beyond. Swifts darted over and between the trees, scooping up insects in their fine beaks. For a moment Andreas felt transported back to a happier time, and then he saw the Italian flag ripple gently above the prefecture. The table where he had eaten so often as a child was now littered with the detritus of an earlier meal. Plates and cutlery, wine glasses with dregs at the bottom and the butts of cigarettes lying discarded on the ground. His father pulled out a chair at the far end and Andreas moved the remains of the Italian officers' meal to the side of the table and then sat down. They looked out over the Ionian Sea for a moment without talking, then turned at the sound of footsteps.

'There you are.' Eleni smiled as she emerged from Katarides's room with a large tray bearing three bowls of soup, some bread and a pitcher of water and glasses. She put the tray down and set out the simple meal.

'Vegetable soup. There is little meat to be had in town.'

'It smells good.' Katarides smiled. 'Thank you, Eleni.'

Andreas broke off a chunk of the bread and dipped it into the soup and ate hungrily, unconsciously scratching at his side as he did so. Then he looked up and caught Eleni's frown. She glanced to his hand and Andreas stopped scratching, feeling ashamed.

'What's the matter?' asked Katarides.

His son hesitated before he admitted, 'Lice.'

'Lice . . .' Katarides looked pained. 'My poor boy.'

'It's nothing. You get used to it,' Andreas lied. 'The soup is good. Tastes all the better for the meal being eaten out here. Just like things used to be.' His gaze shifted to the plates and glasses at the far end of the table. 'Well, almost.'

Katarides shrugged. 'Our diet is a little simpler these days but the company is as good as ever.' He reached forward and poured them all a glass of water and raised his. '*Eviva.*'

'*Eviva,*' the others responded warmly and Andreas exchanged a fond smile with Eleni as they drank the toast.

Andreas had been existing on a diet of rock bread and gruel for the last few weeks, eating his meals outside the cave, and had grown a little unaccustomed to the comforts of eating at home. So he gulped down his soup and used the last of his bread to mop up the inside of the bowl before he sat back with a smile of contentment.

'You approve of my cooking, then?' Eleni teased.

'It is an improvement on the fare offered by Yannis, yes.'

'Pah, that fool will never make anyone a good wife.'

'And you would?' Andreas raised a brow. 'I fear your work for the resistance might have spoiled your domestic skills. Perhaps spoiled you as a wife.'

Eleni's expression became serious. 'I have as much right to defend my country as anyone else. I can fight the enemy just as well as any man.'

'I meant no offence!' Andreas chuckled. 'Seriously, Eleni. I respect your courage and your convictions with every fibre of my being.'

She raised her spoon and jabbed it in his direction. 'Be sure that you do, Andreas Katarides, or I will make you suffer.'

He held up his hands in surrender and then leant back in his chair and watched her finish her soup. At the head of the table Katarides lowered his spoon and smiled fondly.

'So, when are you two going to get married, eh?'

There was a difficult pause while Andreas and Eleni stared

at Katarides and then glanced across the table at each other self-consciously.

'Married?' Eleni repeated with a shocked expression. 'Me marry your lice-ridden lout of a son. I think you must be joking. Nothing could be further from my mind.'

'Not while the war lasts, perhaps,' Katarides replied. 'But afterwards?'

'There may be no afterwards,' Andreas said quietly. 'Best not to even contemplate such things until it is safe to do so, even if there was a chance that Eleni would accept such a proposal.'

'I think she might. If you asked her.'

Andreas looked away from them both, fixing his gaze on the flag above the prefecture. 'I would have no right to ask at present.'

'And what about me?' Eleni cut in. 'Have I no say?'

'Of course,' said Katarides. 'Only I venture to suspect that your heart has already spoken for you in this matter, if I have read the symptoms right over the time I have known you, my girl.'

'I am not a girl.'

'You are not any longer.' Katarides bowed his head. 'I apologise. You are a woman, and Andreas is now a man, and I am wise enough to see that there is a bond between you that is more than just friendship. Am I wrong? . . . No, I thought not. And yes, my son, now is not the time to be married, but love does not choose its moment. It brooks no interference from the world, come any catastrophe. Life is too brief a thing not to seize upon love when you find it. I learned that from the short time I had with your mother. If you love each other, then accept it, while you can . . .'

Andreas could not bring himself to look at Eleni for fear of revealing how his father's words had touched him. He leaned forward to refill his glass and take a sip before he made himself laugh.

'The poet in you has not died after all. But, Father, leave love poetry to others. You are better than that.'

Katarides tipped his head slightly to the side. 'It is an emotion I am unfamiliar with on paper, I grant you. But I have lived long enough to know the signs. And I hope to live long enough to be proved right.'

'I'll clear this away,' said Eleni, rising from her chair. 'Best not let the Italians know you've had company.'

Briskly loading the tray she picked it up and headed towards the door leading back into the servants' quarters. Andreas watched her go, and Katarides, in turn, watched his son's expression and smiled knowingly.

Later, after night had fallen, they sat inside Katarides's room, lit by a kerosene lamp. They had made small talk for a while, avoiding the subject that had abruptly ended the meal. Then, when Katarides had grown weary and closed his eyes and drifted off into sleep, the other two sat in silence, not wishing to disturb him, and the only sounds were the steady tick of a clock and the shrilling of cicadas outside.

Andreas stared at his father's hands and was struck by a sudden, vivid memory from his childhood when he and his father had attended church and he had tripped and hurt his head at the entrance to the church. His father had picked him up and comforted him and held his hand through the service. Andreas clearly remembered the warmth of his father's flesh and the way he had gently stroked his small knuckles with his thumb and soothed his feelings. The same hands had often dressed him in the absence of his mother, helped him trace his letters, braced him as he learned to ride his first bicycle, showed him how to sail, fish. The same hands that had once tripped lightly across the keys of the piano in the library of his house, or hovered, pen clasped, poised above a sheet of foolscap as he composed his poems in his study.

Once the same hand had struck him in punishment after Andreas had returned home a day late from a boating trip to Meganissi and he and his friends had been forced by bad weather to stay on the island overnight. His father had feared him lost and the same hand that had beat him for taking a foolish risk had later the same day stroked his cheek and hair with relief. It was peculiar, Andreas reflected, how little he had noticed his father's hands as he had grown into manhood. How little they had had to do with him since he had taken his own place in the world.

Now, he looked at them again. Frail and bony, with pronounced folds of flesh disfiguring their once graceful lines. He reached out and eased his fingers round his father's palm and felt the cool tremor of the pulse under his skin. His hand seemed so fragile and Andreas felt a terrible grief welling up inside him over the realisation that he had taken so much for granted. His father had felt like a permanent feature of his life, a strong thread running right through every moment of his youth. And now his strength was fading and one day he would be gone and after that there would be only the pain of an unbearable absence.

'You can't stay here,' Eleni whispered. 'The Italians may be back soon. You have to be gone by then.'

'What about you?'

'They're used to seeing me here.'

Andreas stared at her. 'Will you be safe with them?'

'Because they are Italians, or because they are men?' Her

lips parted in a brief smile. 'They haven't laid a hand on me so far. They'd regret it if they ever tried. I'll be fine. But you must go.'

He nodded and gently released his father's hand before standing up. Sleep had eased some of the concern from the older man's face and he looked younger and at peace. Andreas kissed him lightly on the forehead and straightened up with a self-conscious glance at Eleni, but saw that she was smiling again.

'What is it?'

'Nothing,' she muttered as she stood and eased the creases out of her skirt. 'It just pleases me that you can show your feelings.'

He stared at her and then moved towards the door.

They walked out into the corridor and quietly made their way into the hall. Eleni eased the door open and Andreas stepped over the threshold. It was dark outside, save for the faint loom of the lights of Lefkada and the stars. A moon was rising over the mountains and there would soon be enough illumination for Andreas to pick his way through the mountains to the cave even though he would be fortunate to reach it before daybreak.

He paused and stared at Eleni, and then drew her into his arms and kissed her head. She felt hot breath on her neck and the warmth of his embrace and closed her eyes in sudden bliss as she pressed her face into his sheepskin jacket, unoffended by its smell. They stood that way for a moment and then she sensed him easing away from her and looked up into his face. But before he could kiss her Eleni pushed him away.

'Go . . .'

Andreas made to protest but she pressed her fingers against his lips and pleaded, 'Please go.'

He nodded, turned and strode away, over the drive towards the gates and out of sight. Eleni waited a moment longer and then closed the door and quietly returned to the servants' quarters.

CHAPTER TWENTY-FIVE

Norwich, 2013

'What happened afterwards?' Anna asked as she glanced towards the clock on the mantelpiece and saw that it was past midday. Her train left at two and she knew she must pack and make her farewells before then.

'Afterwards?' The old lady frowned.

'When Andreas took charge of the resistance.'

'He did many things but he never managed that. The other *kapetans* guarded command of their bands jealously. Andreas had to spend much of his time smoothing over their differences and talking them into joining his fight. Sometimes they refused, but most of the time they were content to cooperate, under his orders. As long as he kept them supplied with weapons. And while the British received reports of the resistance on Lefkas they were content to drop supplies once a month or so. Only once did we get into difficulties. A bad Greek took a bribe from the enemy and told them how he had overheard details of one drop. The Italians were there waiting for us. But being Italians, they could not keep their mouths shut and we heard them long before we blundered into their trap and slipped away. We lost the weapons but we did not lose any of the men. The traitor was dealt with later on.'

Anna paused. 'Dealt with? Murdered?'

'Executed. When his identity was discovered he was taken from his home and brought to the cave. Andreas shot him and we left the body on the road outside Nidhri. No one betrayed us again after that.'

Eleni saw the look of anguish in her granddaughter's face and continued in a gentler tone. 'We were at war, my dear. In war there are only two sides. Yours, and the enemy's.'

'But there were civilians,' Anna protested. 'There are always civilians.'

'Not on Lefkas. Not in Greece, and not, I think, in any country invaded by the fascists. That was how it was. The Italians and the Germans were our enemy and we were theirs, regardless of whether we fought in uniforms or not. A funny thing that. We were Greeks, we were fighting for the freedom of our country but because we lacked a uniform our enemies were entitled to shoot us down as criminals and call us terrorists . . . War destroys even common sense.'

Eleni's head drooped and her chin trembled a moment before she sniffed and looked up sharply. 'I'm sorry. I'm being an old fool. Forgive me.'

'It's all right, Yiayia. It's me, I'm sorry. I should not have opened old wounds.'

'Sometimes you have to . . . Or we forget those we loved, and then they are truly dead. Gone forever. Anyway, enough of that.' She looked up. 'What more did you want to know today?'

Anna sensed her grandmother's weariness and decided that their conversation must stop soon, but there was a question that she wanted an answer to before she left for home.

'Did Katarides die?'

'We all die eventually.'

Anna winced. 'I know that, Yiayia, thank you. I meant did he die soon after Andreas had visited him? You made it sound like he was very ill.'

'He was. Poor man. But, no, he did not die then. In fact, seeing Andreas again seemed to lift his spirits. He recovered enough to start tending his garden and reading his books. He even tried to write again. Though I don't know if he ever finished anything. I never had the chance to find out.'

'Why?'

Eleni shook her head. 'Another time, my girl. We've been talking all morning and I am tired.'

'But I will be going home soon, Yiayia. Can we not talk for just a little longer? I need to know more.'

'I dare say. But not today,' Eleni said wearily. 'It has been good to discuss the past with you. But there are some things that I cannot easily bring myself to speak of . . .' The old woman's expression twisted in a painful grimace for an instant and Anna leaned forward anxiously.

'What is it?'

'Not now.'

'You can tell me,' Anna coaxed gently. 'Perhaps it will help.'

'Nothing can help. Not with such memories, my dear Anna. That is why I have something for you.' She reached a trembling hand towards the side table and moved aside a magazine to reveal an envelope. She hesitated a moment before she picked it up and handed it to Anna. 'There. I've tried to set down what I can remember, up to the point I left the island. But I was not well then, too ill to think straight . . . When you read this maybe you will understand. Only then can we talk.' She smiled weakly. 'It will give you a reason to come back, and we won't have to wait so long before you do, eh?' Her lips stretched in a teasing smile.

'Now that's unfair.'

'You sound just like you did when you were a child. The answer then is the same as it is now. Sometimes life is unfair. And sometimes an old lady needs to use whatever she has to coax her family to come and see her.'

Anna made a cross face and then leaned across to kiss her on the cheek. 'And now you sound like the same person who used to tease me when I was a child. I'll be back to see you as soon as I can, and not just because I need to know all the details of the rest of your story.'

'I'll look forward to it. But you must get ready to go.'

Anna smiled and rose to leave the room. She paused at the door and Eleni waved her out impatiently. The sound of running water came from the kitchen and Anna joined her mother who had just finished washing up the mugs and bowls from breakfast. Marita looked up as she folded the tea towel over the steel bar in front of the cooker and saw the envelope. 'What's that?'

'Something she gave me to read.'

'Oh?'

Anna stroked her thumb along the back of the envelope. 'I don't know what it is yet.'

There was a brief silence before Marita spoke again. 'When you do, maybe you will share it with me. Now, I have to go out soon. I need some books for my course. If you want to save the taxi fare I can give you a lift to the station. It'll mean waiting a bit for your train.'

'Thanks. I don't mind. I'll get a drink and read the paper. Give me five minutes to pack my bag.'

Twenty minutes later they were stuck in traffic on the ring road. An ambulance had raced by in a blur of yellow and white with flashing lights several minutes earlier and ahead the vehicles slowed and stopped. A light rain began to fall and Marita flicked on the wipers and turned on the air conditioning to stop the windows steaming up.

'It's been good to see you again.'

'You too, Mum.' Anna tipped her head to the side to see if she could see any sign of movement further down the road. 'I should come up more often really.'

'Yes. You should.'

Anna glanced across and noticed the set of her mother's lips. 'What's up?'

'Nothing . . . It's just that I see so little of you these days. To be honest, I miss you. My little girl,' Marita mused. 'And there's your grandmother. I hate to say it but I fear she won't be with us for much longer.'

'That's a bit morbid.'

'It's the truth. All our days are measured, and she has less than most. It's a small miracle that she has lived so long. She's the last of her family from the generation that lived through the war. The rest died years ago. She reckons that they never really got over the winters when they were starved in Greece. I don't suppose it does anyone any good to endure that. So I would take advantage of the time she has left if I were you. Come up and see us a little more frequently, eh?'

'I'll do my best, Mum. But I've got my own life to live. A hectic life at that.'

Marita hesitated before giving a nod and muttering, 'Of course. But give it some thought. You seem to have enjoyed her company well enough this weekend.'

'It's the first time I've heard the story of her youth. It's quite something. I never realised how involved she was with the resistance.'

'She rarely spoke to me about that. You've been lucky.'

'I know. I've made mental notes but I want to get the whole thing down as soon as I can. I think it's important that we save the stories of people's lives.'

'Oh yes. Oral histories and all that.' Marita drummed her fingers on the rim of the steering wheel. 'But perhaps you should take what she tells you with a pinch of salt. She's getting old. Her memory is failing. Why, only last week she forgot my name, even who I was for a moment. That kind of thing has been happening more frequently of late. Memory is a fragile thing. And sometimes it is not as accurate as it once was.'

Anna stared out through the gap in the condensation where the blowers had cleared the windscreen. 'That's a bit worrying. But Yiayia seems pretty sound of mind to me.'

'I dare say. But how can you know what is and what isn't accurate? Maybe that's the problem with memories. Every time we go back and tell the story of our past we aren't just opening a window into the past. Perhaps we're making that memory anew, and shaping it according to whatever is happening to us here and now. If that's the case, then what makes oral histories any different to any other kind of story?'

Anna shot her a concerned look. 'I think you're wrong about her. I believe every word.'

The cars ahead of them began to ripple forwards and Marita shifted the gearstick into first and waited for her chance to get moving. The rain started in earnest and drummed off the roof of the car as they continued along the inner ring road to the rail station. Ten minutes later Marita drew up outside the entrance and Anna nimbly climbed out and retrieved her overnight bag from the rear seat.

'Thanks, Mum.'

Marita leaned down so she could see her daughter's face. 'Remember what I said, come and see us more often.'

'I will. Promise.'

Anna closed the rear door, hefted her bag and glanced to her left before crossing to the entrance and into the station. She looked back to wave to her mother but the car was already gone. A quick glance at the information screen showed that the train was on time, though there was still over forty minutes before it departed, so she went into the café and ordered a cappuccino and a muffin and sat in a faded but comfortable bucket armchair and took out her iPad. For a while she added to the notes she was preparing for Dieter. All the time she was conscious of the envelope in her bag and wondered what further secrets it contained. When she had finished, she turned the iPad off and went to catch the train. Settled into her seat, she felt the jolt as it eased into motion. There were few other passengers in the coach and she had a table to herself. As the train pulled out of Norwich, Anna at last took out the envelope, broke the seal and drew out a thin, folded sheaf of papers covered in straggling handwriting. She flattened them out on the table and began to read.

CHAPTER TWENTY-SIX

'You look tired, Anna,' said Dieter as he drew the chair back for her to sit. She took her place and he moved round and sat opposite. Above them the lattice of steel and glass curved over the atrium of the British Museum, diffusing the sunlight on to the other diners and the visitors swarming across the ground floor below.

'Are you all right?' he continued with a concerned expression.

'Fine, thanks. I just haven't been sleeping well the last few nights. I've been thinking about everything my grand-mother has told me. It's quite a story. Some of it she could not bear to tell me.' Anna paused. Not yet willing to divulge the account of Eleni's final experiences of the war on Lefkas.

'I hope that my interest in her account has not given any cause for you to lose sleep.' Dieter offered her a slight smile.

Her brow creased. 'Why would it?'

Dieter shrugged and they sat awkwardly before he remem-bered the menus lying on the table before them. 'Would you like a drink?'

She nodded. 'A spritzer, please.'

'Really? Because it sounds German?'

The waiter came over and hovered at Dieter's shoulder until he looked up.

'Drinks, sir?'

'A Diet Coke for me and a spritzer for the lady.'

'Yes, sir.' The waiter bowed his head and made off towards the bar.

'How have you been?' asked Dieter. 'Since the last time we met.'

'Well enough. Looking forward to Christmas though. I could use a break, get some rest and eat some food.'

He smiled at her. 'I can imagine. I have friends who are teachers back in Germany. They say the same. So, you spoke to your grandmother, yes?'

'I did. I got almost all of her story. I'll get the rest when I am next in Norwich. I'm hoping that'll be before Christmas. I'll type it up when I've got all my notes together.'

'Very good . . . I thank you, Anna, from the bottom of my heart.'

'It probably won't help you much. She doesn't have much to say about what happened before the war.'

Dieter shrugged. 'That may not matter. I have extended the scope of my research since we met. I'd like to know whatever your grandmother can recall. It is a pity that she would not speak to me herself.'

Anna recalled the contents of the envelope that her grandmother had passed to her, and shuddered. 'She has her reasons, as I am sure you understand.'

He looked up at her wearily. 'It seems we Germans will never be allowed to forget the war.'

'And given what happened, perhaps that is not such a bad thing. The world needs examples to make people reflect.'

'You think so?' Dieter looked amused. 'And having

reflected on what happened in Germany, do you think the world has really become a better place? Do you think we have learned from the past? When I look at the world, I begin to doubt that. What do you think, Anna? You seem like a good person to me. An honest person. Tell me.'

She could think of nothing to say. After the war to end all wars, and the war that followed hot on its heels, and the multitude of further wars and horrors, it was hard to have any faith in the examples set by history. Few people seemed to pay history much attention at all. Even so, she still believed, passionately, that the point of teaching the subject was as much to do with warning her students to learn the lessons of the past as it was to do with studying the subject for its own sake. There was still that hope.

She stared back at Dieter and her thoughts shifted to a school trip to Berlin she had taken as a girl. The German capital had been a strange place, a city looking back almost as much as it looked forward. New buildings jostled with older, bullet-scarred facades. Memorials to the atrocities carried out by the Nazis were plentiful and in plain view, forcing onlookers never to forget. Nor would they forget the brutal wall that had once divided west from east, its line forever marked by bricks set into the roads and pavements. If only more countries were prepared to bear the scars of the past rather than slip into the collective amnesia that passed for a reverence for history when the anniversaries of previous wars came and went. If only there were more like this German, who clearly cared deeply about history.

Dieter had given up waiting for a reply and nodded a curt thanks to the waiter as he returned with the drinks and set them down. He picked up the menu and began to read. He nodded as he made his decision and returned his gaze to Anna.

'I'm having the risotto. Have you decided?'

'The Caesar salad.'

Once Dieter had given the order, he settled back in his chair and studied Anna. 'I will look forward to reading your notes. But for now, could you outline what you have found out?'

'I will, if you share what you have discovered with me.'

'That will be easier once I know what you know.'

Anna nodded, wondering how far she could really trust him. 'OK, I'll go first.'

She briefly related what Eleni had told her, but withheld the details of the letter, determined to see if what Dieter said matched her grandmother's disturbing account. Dieter listened attentively, nodding once in a while. Their food turned up as Anna finished and once the waiter had departed Dieter gave his reaction.

'It's a little disappointing.'

'Well, I'm so sorry about that . . .'

He looked apologetic. 'I did not mean to make sound as it did. It's just that I was hoping for more detail. To help with my research.'

'If you could tell me what it is that you are after then perhaps I can find out more when I next see my grandmother.'

He chewed his lip gently and then nodded. 'All right. I told you that my great-grandfather was part of an expedition looking for the remains of the palace of Odysseus. At the time he was forced to give up the search and return to Germany nothing of significance had been found at any of the excavations in the charge of his superior, Dörpfeld. Just a few small buildings here and there and fragments of pottery and so on. For a long time that's all that it seemed. When I started my research degree I had little interest in such details and that

332

was not the focus of my thesis.' He leaned forward and lowered his voice. 'Then I found a reference in a diary to his discovery of something significant. He was very careful not to go into any detail. For a while I tried looking for further references in Berlin University's archives, and the papers of some of his colleagues, but there was nothing. So I went back to his notes and diaries and read them again. Far more closely this time. And I discovered something very interesting. Look . . .'

He leaned down towards his bag and came up with a thick notebook covered in faded red leather. Opening it carefully to a bookmarked page, he showed Anna a list of numbers under a neatly written legend at the top. She shook her head.

'What's it mean? I don't understand German.'

'It's dated the last day of the excavation, before he and Peter had to leave Lefkas. It says that it is a list of the items found and catalogued.'

'So?'

'I came across a separate list of the finds in another set of records, compiled by his assistant, Heinrich Steiner. There are no matching numbers. This is something else.'

'What?' Anna thought quickly. 'Like a code?'

'Exactly!' He grinned. 'Just like a code. So I asked a friend of mine in the mathematics department if he would have a look at it. He came back to me very quickly. It was a simple enough cypher to break using his computer. He gave me the key and I set to work uncovering my grandfather's secrets.'

'And?'

Dieter took a forkful of risotto and his jaws worked briefly before he swallowed. 'And he claims to have discovered the resting place of Odysseus.'

Anna lowered her own fork as she felt a tingle of nervous

excitement at the back of her neck. 'Odysseus?' she asked softly. 'The Odysseus of Homer?'

'I think so. No, I am sure of it. My grandfather was a careful man, a precise man.'

'Did he find a tomb, then?'

'Yes, that's what he claimed. It was hidden in a cave not far from the excavation. He gives directions on how to locate it in his code. He said that it contained the treasure Odysseus brought back from Troy.' Dieter frowned. 'But there's something wrong. I couldn't find the cave where he said it would be.'

Anna's eyebrows rose. 'You've been there?'

Dieter nodded. 'There's nothing. No cave.'

'Then your great-grandfather made a mistake. But I thought you said he was a precise man.'

'He was. That's why I thought I must have made an error in deciphering his directions. I checked again and again. But there was no mistake on my part. It's puzzling. There is no cave. I have been to the site of the excavation. I found it easily enough. I followed the directions my grandfather had given, but they led nowhere. I came to a rocky slope where he claimed there was a cliff and that's as far as I could go.'

'Then your grandfather made a mistake when he encoded the directions.'

Dieter shook his head. 'I told you. He was a precise man. Meticulous. He would not have made a mistake.'

Anna sniffed at the German's conviction. So typical of a man. 'Clearly someone has.'

'It would appear so. But there's something else I discovered that seems to have a connection to my great-grandfather's work. It's in another coded entry in this notebook. He speaks of his work having come to the attention of an official in the government. He says that he has been under observation and that his office and home have been searched. And then he makes a brief note that he has been summoned to the Hotel Prinz Albrecht to speak to H.' Dieter showed her the entry. A half-page of more code. He flicked on a few more pages to show her that they were blank. 'It's the last entry he made.'

'Before he was killed in the air raid?'

'If that *is* the way he died.'

Anna lowered her knife and fork and stared back intently. 'You think something else happened to him?'

'It's possible. Especially if one considers the content of that last message.'

'You think he met someone at that hotel who might have killed him?'

Dieter gave a dry laugh. 'At that time the Hotel Prinz Albrecht had not been a hotel for some years. It was taken over by the SS as their headquarters after Hitler and his thugs came to power. Many entered the building, never to be seen alive again. Perhaps that was the fate of my great-grandfather.'

'Oh . . . Then who is H?' Her eyes widened. 'Not who I think? Surely?'

'No. I don't think so. It might be anyone, but I think it is likely that it was Himmler, given the nature of my great-grandfather's work.'

'Why would Himmler be interested in archaeology?'

'He wasn't. Not archaeology as such. He was more concerned with the occult, with symbols of power throughout history. But I think the Nazis just liked to take possession of anything that had any kind of value. Mystical or monetary. Goering was the worst of them all in that respect. They looted Europe for anything of value.'

'I saw a movie about that recently.'

'I know it. But this was all real, Anna. It was not a movie. My great-grandfather went to the headquarters of the SS and that's the last record of his life that I have found. Most of his papers were lost, or disappeared. Except for the few notebooks and diaries that he had sent to his son for safe keeping with a note to keep them secret until he asked for their return.' Dieter took another forkful of rice. 'And that never happened.'

Anna helped herself to more salad before she said, 'I'm sorry.'

'It was long ago, and I never knew the man. I barely even knew my grandfather, Peter. He died while I was young. But there again I found that the story continues.'

'What do you mean?'

Dieter removed his glasses and dipped into his pocket for a lens cloth and gave them a quick rub as he continued. 'Once I had exhausted my great-grandfather's records I turned my attention to his son. He had been there at the excavations, and like his father he kept a diary. There was not much of interest in the early years, but plenty of mentions of his friends Andreas and Eleni. It's clear that he had strong feelings for her. Sadly for Peter there is no indication that she gave him any sign that she felt the same way about him.'

'I don't think she ever did, from what she told me.'

'A pity. It might have changed the way things turned out.'

'What do you mean?'

Dieter raised a finger. 'That will become clear in a moment. But first let me tell you more about Peter. I believe you know he served in the Wehrmacht, the German army?'

'Yes. You showed me the photo. Remember?'

Dieter nodded. 'Then you also recall that he returned to the island when he was posted to Lefkas.'

'Yes.'

'So I read his diaries again. All of them this time. Before I had been interested in what happened prior to the war. But given what I had discovered about his father's last days I hoped that there might be something in Peter's account that would help me find the tomb of Odysseus.'

Anna's pulse quickened. 'And did you find anything?'

The German pursed his lips before he replied. 'I'm not sure. What I did discover is not going to be easy for you to hear, Anna. It concerns Eleni, and Andreas. If I tell you, then you must try not to be angry with me. I had nothing to do with it. It is the story of events which took place nearly seventy years ago. They would be forgotten if I had not brought them to light. Please understand that, before I tell you any more.'

There was a pleading tone in his voice and it made him look vulnerable somehow. Anna felt a slight glow of warm feeling towards him, before it faded to be replaced by the account set down by Eleni. She already knew what Dieter was getting at. Now she would know for sure. Between his account and what was contained in Eleni's own words she would know the truth of what had taken place on Lefkas all those years before.

Anna put down her cutlery and pushed the plate aside. Taking her glass, she sipped and then nodded.

'Very well, I think it's time you told me Peter's story . . .'

CHAPTER TWENTY-SEVEN

Lefkas, November 1943

Leutnant Peter Muller stood up in the back of the Opel truck. He grasped the wooden side rail in one hand, rested the other on the roof of the cab and stared down the road stretching the length of the causeway linking the mainland to Lefkas. Even though the season had changed, it was a warm day and the sky was cloudless. Behind him sat a platoon from the regiment's headquarters company, bareheaded and in good humour as they talked and joked over their kitbags piled along the bed of the truck. Ahead of them were two more trucks, then several motorcycles with sidecars. Behind, the line of trucks carrying the men of the 98th Gebirgsjäger – mountain troops – stretched to the mainland and then along the coast to the north for nearly two kilometres. A pall of dust hung over the road, marking the passage of the formation.

They were ordered to join the first battalion that had been sent to Lefkas following the surrender of the Italian troops back in September. That was the month in which Mussolini's fascist government had collapsed and its replacement had immediately capitulated and abandoned their German allies. It had come as no surprise to Hitler and plans had been made to deal with the desertion well in advance. The disarming of the Italian soldiers in Greece had proceeded efficiently, though there had been instances when the Italians had resisted, and paid a high price for their sense of honour. Peter had heard rumours of the massacre of thousands of Italians on the nearby island of Kefalonia. Officially the men were prohibited from making any mention of it but they still talked and so it was an open secret that caused many German soldiers to burn with shame, while others were indifferent to the atrocity, or argued that it was a necessary act.

Peter had been transferred from an artillery unit based in Normandy. It had been a peaceful posting, far from any of the war fronts, and he had yet to be tested in action. His orders stated that he had been seconded to the 98th Gebirgsjäger until further notice to 'advise and assist' Oberstleutnant Josef Salminger. So for the last two weeks he had travelled by train and truck and joined the main elements of the regiment as it completed its relocation to Lefkas. It was only when he reached Greece that he had heard the dark stories about what had occurred after the Italians had surrendered. At first he was reluctant to believe it, but the steady trickle of details from the soldiers he encountered had convinced him of the reality. So it was with a heavy heart that he concluded his journey.

The view of the houses and church towers of Lefkada and the green hills rising up beyond raised his spirits a little. Ever since he had left the island five years earlier he had hoped to return. But not like this. Not as part of a conquering army. It pained him to return in uniform. Then his thoughts turned to the prospect of encountering some familiar faces. They would be surprised to see him again, and perhaps he might act as something of a bridge between the local people and the army. If he could do anything to ease the relations between the islanders and the occupying forces then he would.

'Herr Leutnant!'

Peter turned and saw one of the men with a half-raised hand. 'What is it?'

The soldier cupped a hand to his mouth and called out loudly to be heard above the din of the rattling truck and the rumble of the other vehicles. 'I hear you've lived on the island. Is that right?'

Peter nodded. 'A few years back.'

'So what are the women like? Any different to the hags in the rest of Greece?'

'No different.' Peter grinned. 'Just more wrinkled and unfriendly. And their men will cut your throats if you even think of touching their women. Pray the Italians have left some of their whores behind. You'll find nothing of interest amongst the Greek women, I promise you.'

But he was thinking of Eleni. Beautiful Eleni who had stolen his heart when he had been a teenager. What would she look like now? Would she be married and have infant children clutching her knees as she cleaned up after them and some surly husband? The image was so unlikely it made him smile to himself. No, not Eleni. She was better than that. More ambitious. He looked forward to seeing her and telling her of all the things he had seen since they had parted. If only she did not resent him for being German.

It would be different with Andreas, if he was still living with his father. He recalled that Andreas had wanted to serve in the navy. If so, then by almighty and merciful God, Peter prayed that he had emerged from the conflict unscathed and had returned home to live in peace. Then the three of them could make good on the promise they had made to each other when they had been parted.

Five years on, and more worldly, Peter looked back at that

moment with a certain detachment, but still desired that the promise be fulfilled.

The vehicles trundled past the old Venetian fort that had once guarded the approaches to Lefkas and crossed the bridge on to the last stretch of road leading to the town. Peter could see the familiar sprawl of buildings along the harbour front and the close ranks of the fishing boats. Anchored further out lay the sleek grey lines of a S-boat with a Kriegsmarine flag rippling lazily from the radio mast. Another flag flew from the staff rising above the centre of the town and after a moment's recollection Peter guessed that it must be flying over the prefecture. He eased himself back down on to the wooden bench and gratefully took a slug of the rough wine from the bottle passed to him by one of the men.

Most of the men were young like himself, fit and cheerful, with seemingly few cares in the world. But he knew there was a difference between them and himself. While he had spent all his time in the army stationed in France, the men of the 98th had been fighting on the Russian front before being sent to fight partisans in the mountains of the Balkans. That had been a bitter campaign against a cruel enemy and the Germans had responded in kind. Many villages had been burned to the ground and their populations slaughtered in response to attacks and atrocities carried out by the partisans. For all their youth and good humour, these men were seasoned veterans who had seen much action, and who had carried out brutal acts, and would do so again if necessary, with little compunction. He hoped that could be avoided here on Lefkas.

The convoy droned into the town and a military policeman waved the officers' cars into the narrow street while the trucks were directed along the harbour front to the vast enclosure on the outskirts of Lefkada prepared for the regiment's camp.

Hundreds of tents had already been erected in neat lines and a vehicle park stood a short distance away. The whole was surrounded by two lines of staked barbed wire. As his truck reached the harbour front, Peter rapped sharply on the roof of the cab and the driver's mate leaned out of the window and looked up.

'Let me off here,' Peter ordered.

The vehicle slowed and juddered to a halt at the side of the road to allow those behind to pass. Peter hefted his kitbag and helmet and made his farewells to his travelling companions before dropping down from the rear of the truck. A moment later it roared away. He looked along the buildings that lined the harbour, once so familiar to him. It seemed different now and he felt conscious of the cold looks of the local people. As before, the fishermen sat cross-legged as they mended their nets at the water's edge. But the cheerful banter Peter remembered from before was absent and instead the men looked sullen, their expressions pinched from hunger. It was the same with the women and children who passed by; they did not meet his eye and offered no greeting in return to his friendly '*Kalimera!*'

Peter took his cap out of his pocket and pressed it on to his head before picking up his kitbag and slinging it over his shoulder with a grunt. Turning into a narrow street he entered the town and made his way towards the prefecture. The smell of woodsmoke and fish filled his nostrils and he smiled at the memories they evoked. He had strode down this same street with Andreas and Eleni on the way to the market to buy fruit, cured sausage and bread for the meal on the last boating trip they took. He knew that on the far side of the square was the lane where Eleni's father lived. Even though circumstances were difficult he had resolved to pay Inspector Thesskoudis a visit very soon, and enquire after his friends, even if Eleni was no longer living there. It was the familiar yearning of all those who have returned to a place and people they once knew well. And yet, he was aware that everything had changed. This was not how he had wanted to return to the island and he knew that he could expect resentment in place of the warm welcome he had experienced before.

The old part of the town seemed to have changed very little, wearing the presence of its occupiers lightly, until Peter emerged into the square that fronted the prefecture. Several Kübelwagen and trucks were parked outside the building and the entrance was guarded by a section of mountain troops. Two long red banners bearing the swastika hung from second-floor balconies and a large flag flew from the staff rising above the weathered tiles of the prefecture. Peter presented his papers to the sergeant in charge of the sentries and was admitted to the building. Inside the smell of floor polish and mustiness felt welcoming as he reported to the woman in grey uniform at the reception desk.

'Leutnant Muller, reporting to Oberstleutnant Salminger.'

She studied his identity card and orders briefly before handing them back with a pleasant smile. Picking up the phone she dialled an extension and there was a brief exchange as she announced his arrival and then replaced the handset. 'Welcome to Lefkas, Leutnant. You can leave your kitbag here. The Oberstleutnant is making a call at present, but I'll take you up to his office. You can wait outside.'

She led him up two flights of worn stone stairs and along the corridor behind the offices looking out over the square. Wooden benches stood outside most of the doors and the woman gestured to the seating outside the last office. 'I'm sure he won't be long.'

Peter nodded and sat down, removing his cap and holding it in both hands. He began to knead the felt material lightly as he reflected on the reasoning behind his new posting. It was more than likely that it had to do with his familiarity with the island and its people and his grasp of their tongue. Translation duties then, he surmised. Not the most important service he could provide for the fatherland but he was not going to complain if it meant a return to Lefkas and a break from the tedium of life at the coastal battery in Normandy.

The corridor was adorned with the usual posters exhorting duty, courage and sacrifice as stridently Aryan soldiers gazed out at the viewer or stared off in the direction of some inspiring sight beyond the frame of the image. He saw a copy of *Signal* magazine on the bench opposite and crossed to pick it up before resuming his seat and flicking through the heavily illustrated pages. Despite the defeats at Stalingrad and Kursk, and the collapse of the front in North Africa, the magazine continued to proclaim that German forces were regrouping, ready for fresh offensives that would sweep the overconfident Allies aside. Ultimate victory was assured.

Peter was not convinced. He had met fellow officers who had returned from Russia who had discreetly told him of the horrors of the winter, the sprawling plains and the endless numbers of men and tanks possessed by the enemy. Victory on the eastern front would be a miracle, they said.

The door beside him clicked open and a corporal stepped into the corridor and saluted.

'Sir, if you would follow me?'

Peter stood, quickly eased the creases from his jacket and entered the small anteroom where two more headquarters clerks and another female sat at their desks dealing with paperwork. A frosted glass partition separated them from their commanding officer, whose name had been painted on the wooden door in white gothic script. The corporal rapped on the door.

'Come in!' a voice called.

The corporal opened the door and leaned in. 'Leutnant Muller, sir.'

'Ah yes! Good. Send him in and fetch some coffee.'

'Yes, sir.'

The corporal stepped aside and waved Peter forward. Oberstleutnant Salminger's office was bright and airy thanks to the tall windows on two walls. It was also impressively large and a red carpet covered most of the floor, stretching across the room to the oak desk behind which Salminger sat in his unbuttoned jacket. He was thick-necked with cropped hair around the sides of his head and a dark wave across the crown. A neatly trimmed beard graced his jowls and his moustache was waxed into a slender line above his lips. To one side of the room hung a detailed map of the island. Behind Salminger, on the wall, was a large framed portrait of the Führer. Peter felt conscious of both sets of eyes scrutinising him as he strode up to the desk, saluted, and laid his papers in front of his superior officer.

'Leutnant Peter Muller of the Hundred and First Artillery Regiment, reporting as ordered, sir.'

Salminger looked him up and down before nodding a curt greeting and drawing the documents towards him. He gave them a quick glance then leaned back in his chair.

'You're a day early, Muller. I like a man who makes an effort to be efficient.'

'Yes, sir. Thank you.'

'I expect you've already guessed part of the reason why you have been sent to Lefkas. I need translators and you come with the advantage of knowing the ground. You'll be very useful. I dare say you also know some of the more influential of the local people, given your father's role on the island before the war. That will also be useful since I would rather have the cooperation of the islanders than have to use force to keep order. Though that is work for the future given the current situation.' He paused, just long enough for Peter to grasp he was being prompted. He cleared his throat.

'Situation, sir?'

'I doubt it will come as much of a surprise to learn that the islanders resent our occupation of Lefkas, just as they resented the Italians before us. A considerable number of them have taken up arms to form a resistance movement. The Italians made a poor show of dealing with these insurgents. Aside from a few half-hearted sweeps through the mountains which yielded paltry rewards – no more than a handful of the enemy killed or captured – they kept to the larger towns and coastline and left the resistance in control of the mountains. Which meant that they were able to get air drops of supplies from the British without much trouble. They've been putting them to good use harassing the Italians, and now it's our turn.'

His expression darkened as he continued. 'Within a week of taking over, the German garrison was being attacked every day. It was as if the insurgents were keen to make a point that they hated us even more than the Italians. We know that their leader is called Mahos – at least, that's his *nom de guerre*. The Italians and my predecessor posted rewards for anyone coming forward with information that would lead to his capture, but they're a tight-lipped bunch, these Greeks. Mahos has been leading us a merry dance. He's sabotaged several trucks in the vehicle park, shot at and wounded three of my men this week. Before that he ambushed a patrol and killed two men. We took reprisals of course, and went to shoot some of the local villagers. Stood 'em up against the cemetery wall, but before the machine gunner could open fire, he himself was killed. Shot through the head. The rest of the squad came under fire and the prisoners managed to escape in the confusion. Our men beat a hasty retreat, but not before they had lost another and three more were wounded. I went back in strength to destroy the village, but the people had fled, so we burned the place down.'

He paused to collect his thoughts. 'The previous commander had completely failed to bring the island under control and lasted only two months in the job before I was called in to replace him. He fell down on the job, Muller. He lacked the ruthlessness to do what was necessary to bring these Greek dogs to heel. I will succeed where he failed. My mountain troops will be more than a match for the *andartes*, as they call themselves. And your knowledge of the island will be most helpful in permitting my regiment to crush them.'

Peter nodded. 'Yes, sir. I'll do my duty.'

Salminger paused a moment. 'I understand that the work may not be to your taste, Muller. After all, I am sure that you counted some of the islanders as friends when you used to live here.'

'That's right, sir.'

'Then it is a pity that you must consider them enemies now. But perhaps you may be of service to them, if only you can persuade them to use their influence to encourage others to accept our presence and not cause any trouble. I would prefer that we and the islanders treated each other as well as we can under the circumstances. However, if they persist in taking pot shots at my men, then I will do whatever is necessary to capture the culprits and make an example of them. I have also let it be known that for every German soldier they kill, I will take ten people off the streets of Lefkada and shoot them. I know it's a harsh reaction, but sometimes the hardest lesson is the one that is taken to heart. Is that not so?'

Peter swallowed and nodded. 'I understand the thinking behind such reprisals, yes, sir.'

'But you do not agree with it?'

'I think it hardens the will to resist the occupying forces, sir. But if those are the orders, then they must be obeyed.'

'Good!' The Oberstleutnant clapped his hands together. 'Then we shall look forward to a peaceful posting on this fine island when the locals have got the message. My adjutant has arranged accommodation for you in the town. You'll be shown to it after we're finished here. There'll be a desk found for you in the prefecture. When you are sent into the field you will be a supernumerary under the command of the local officer. Clear?'

'Clear, sir.'

'Very well.' Salminger rested his hands on the desk and regarded Peter curiously for a moment. 'Your presence here is not confined to the duties I have outlined. There is another, somewhat more exotic purpose.'

'Sir?'

Salminger smiled, enjoying the younger officer's discomfort. 'As it happens, you are not the only officer on the island who speaks Greek and has some knowledge of the area.' He leaned forward and picked up the phone and tapped the receiver. 'Schumann? Send for the Sturmbannführer at once.'

Peter's ears pricked up at the mention of the SS rank, equivalent to a major in the Wehrmacht. What could

Himmler's organisation have to do with his posting to Lefkas?

'And once you have sent for him, I want that damned coffee brought in here without any more delay. For three of us. See to it!'

Salminger replaced the phone and gestured towards the chairs lining one side of his office. 'Bring two of those over here and take a seat.'

Peter nodded and did as he was instructed, hardly feeling any more comfortable sitting stiff-backed on the chair than on his feet under the gaze of his prickly superior. They were not kept waiting long before there was a knock at the door and the corporal opened it to reveal a smartly dressed officer with the green piping of the mountain troops on his shoulder boards and the SS runes on his collar label. His hair was short without being cropped and Peter started as he recognised the man.

'Heinrich . . .' He smiled spontaneously, rose to his feet and held out his hand.

CHAPTER TWENTY-EIGHT

His father's former assistant returned the smile hesitantly and then strode across the room to take his hand. His grip was firm and the shake was brisk. Peter quickly recovered his wits and tried to make up for his breach of military etiquette. 'Sturmbannführer Steiner, it is a pleasure to see you again.'

'And you too, Peter.' Steiner stood back to look him up and down. 'So different from the young boy I remember. A man now, and a soldier too. But then, who isn't these days?' His smile faded. 'I was sorry to hear about your father. He was a good man, and a fine scholar.'

'Yes . . .'

'I know it will be of little consolation, but I am sure his death would have been quick and painless. His home took a direct hit, so I understand.'

Peter found it hard to take much comfort from the manner of his father's death but felt some gratitude to Steiner for expressing his sympathy.

The door opened again and the corporal entered carrying a tray with three cups and a pot on it. He set the tray down on the table and left the room. The distraction ended the awkwardness of a moment earlier and Peter and Steiner took their seats opposite their superior as he poured them each a cup.

'I was explaining to Muller that the purpose of his posting to the island went beyond the services of acting as an interpreter. But I think you're better placed to say why. If you would be so good.' He held out a cup and Steiner took it carefully and settled back and looked at Peter.

'It would be pleasant to spend some time catching up on each other's news, but the Oberstleutnant is a busy man and it would intrude on his time. We can leave such things to a later time and talk over a bottle of wine. Just like the old days, eh?'

Peter nodded amiably.

'You will recall the purpose of our excavations on the island?' Steiner continued in a more serious tone.

'Of course. My father was looking for the palace and tomb of Odysseus. Not that he ever found conclusive evidence of the former. His work was cut short when we were recalled to Germany.'

'Sadly, the needs of the fatherland outweigh all else at such times. But your father's work, and mine, was not in vain, even if we were not able to complete it.'

Peter nodded. 'It is true. There were a number of finds of archaeological value but nothing of great significance.'

A thin smile appeared on Steiner's lips. 'That remains to be seen. I think your father was on the cusp of a very great discovery, something of immeasurable historic significance, as it happens. Something he was not prepared to share with me at the time.'

'I find that hard to believe, Herr Sturmbannführer. He never said anything to me about it.'

'Which is a tribute to his discretion. However, he did

reveal something shortly before his death.'

Salminger slid Peter's coffee across the desk carefully. Nodding his thanks, Peter took his cup and saucer and turned his attention back to Steiner. 'In Berlin?'

'Yes. I was on leave and I called in to see the doctor at the university,' Steiner said in a casual tone. 'We agreed to have dinner the same night and began to talk about our work over the meal and for some hours afterwards.' He smiled. 'I'm afraid we had more wine than was good for us, and that is probably why your father's tongue loosened a bit. He revealed that he had made a discovery in those last few days. I eventually managed to coax something out of him.' He fixed Peter with a steady gaze. 'He implied that it was the tomb of Odysseus. The very tomb itself.'

'Implied?'

'It seemed clear enough to me that is what he meant. He went on to say that it was close to the site where we had been digging. He did not want to say more at that stage but invited me to his house the following evening to show me the evidence of his find. I agreed. I cannot express how excited I was to learn more. However, the morning after, the American bombers raided the city. Your father was killed in his house, along with hundreds of others. I was fortunate enough to be on the outskirts of Berlin. I saw it all from a distance. Terrible . . . Quite terrible that the enemy should strike at our civilians so ruthlessly.'

It was tempting to remind Steiner of the attacks carried out on the cities of Britain a few years earlier, but Peter resisted the impulse. In war one atrocity always failed to balance another.

Steiner took a sip of coffee and his cup clinked lightly as he set the saucer down on his thigh. 'Most of his papers were destroyed by the same blast. Some were salvaged and taken to the university. I looked them over but I could find nothing that related to the extraordinary claim he made that night. I thought he might have told you something, or that you know where he might have kept other records.'

Peter shook his head. 'I knew nothing of this. This is all quite a surprise to me, sir. I had no idea.'

'A pity . . . Do you know of any papers he might have left at any other location that might reveal more?'

'No.'

Steiner frowned. 'I feared you would say that. But while you are here you may remember something that could help me in my search for your father's discovery, when you are not assisting the Oberstleutnant, of course.'

He exchanged a nod with the garrison commander.

'Pardon me, sir, but are you saying that you were sent to Lefkas to find the tomb, or whatever it is my father discovered?'

'Of course. Why else would I be here? We have had men on the island even under the noses of the Italians while we searched for the site. I myself have only been here for a few weeks. It was my idea to send for you.'

Peter frowned slightly. 'I still don't understand. Why go to such an effort in the middle of a war?'

Steiner drained his cup and set the saucer down on the desk. 'It's a fair question. Perhaps I should explain that I am part of a special unit set up by Reichsführer Himmler. For many years now he has taken an interest in historical artefacts. Some are religious in nature, others simply of archaeological interest. But all such things have a value, a certain . . . aura that they bestow upon the nation that possesses them. I happened to mention my discussion with your father to my superiors and they were very interested to see if there was anything in it. Imagine, a legendary king's tomb, filled with treasures looted from Troy. You can understand why Himmler would want them to be claimed by Germany. No?'

The thought of the contents of the tomb of Odysseus being revealed to the world momentarily inspired Peter. And then he was struck by the sheer fancifulness of Steiner's absurd mission. A war was raging across Europe, and the wider world, and yet there was time to allocate much-needed resources to hunting down ancient tombs and seizing their contents. This was a manner of madness exhibited by the Nazi hierarchy that he had not encountered before.

'Forgive me, sir, but it seems far-fetched. I don't know what my father said to you, but from what I can recall of our expedition, we found no trace of any tomb.'

Steiner flicked a loose thread off his trousers. 'That's because your father did not take either of us into his confidence at the time. I imagine he wanted to keep his discovery to himself until he was able to return here and uncover the tomb.'

'Then why would he break his silence to tell you?'

Steiner shrugged. 'Maybe he was afraid he might not survive the war and that his discovery would die with him. And since the island had come under our control there was a chance that an approach to the relevant authorities might lead to a new expedition.'

Peter considered this for a moment, and felt wounded that his father had not felt able to confide in him – if what Steiner said was the truth.

'In any event,' Steiner continued, 'your orders are to assist our efforts here, and that includes helping me. I shall look forward to having the esteemed Dr Muller's son working alongside me. Just like old times, eh?'

'Yes, sir.'

'Then we'll waste no time in getting started.' He stood up and crossed the room to the map and indicated a village a few kilometres from the site of the dig. 'Two companies of mountain troops will be driving up to Alatro early tomorrow morning. They will conduct a patrol of the hills north of the village to try and flush out some of the resistance bands. It's part of the ongoing campaign to rid this island of the *andartes*. We'll go with them, Leutnant. They will provide cover for us while we go about our work. A squad has been assigned to my command to help search the site of the excavation. Your father provided me with a few details that should help direct our search. If we find nothing, then we'll come back when the next sweep is organised and look again. We will find that tomb however long it takes, and when we do, you can be confident that your father is given his share of the credit for the discovery. Of course, I will be sure to acknowledge your help in the matter as well.'

'Thank you, sir.'

Steiner smiled. 'Then our business is finished here. Unless the Oberstleutnant has anything to add?' He turned deferentially to the other officer, who had been listening. Salminger leaned back and crossed his arms.

'You know my views on this wild goose chase of yours.'

Steiner's expression hardened. 'I am sure that the Reichsführer would be interested to know that you consider it as such.'

'The Reichsführer is in Berlin. My men and I are here. Our priority is to stamp down on the resistance. Be that as it may, I have my orders to assist you, and I will do so as long as it does not interfere with my primary purpose.'

'With respect, sir, you will assist me whatever your primary purpose may be.'

The garrison commander sniffed and waved towards the door. 'You will have the men you need. Just don't get yourselves into any trouble. Now, as you say, our business is finished. Muller, wait outside in the corridor. I'll have one of my orderlies take you to your billet. As for you, Sturmbann-führer, I dare say we'll see each other at dinner. Dismissed.'

The others stiffened to attention and Steiner snapped his right arm out as he clicked his heels. 'Heil Hitler.'

Peter followed suit and with a brief look of irritation Salminger casually raised his hand halfway in response.

Then Peter turned and followed Steiner from the office.

As night closed over Lefkada, Peter emerged from the baker's house where he had been assigned a room. Another officer had already been accommodated there but had not returned from his duties by the time Peter had unpacked his kitbag, washed in the steel tub in the small yard behind the bakery, and put on his best uniform. He checked his hair in the mirror then stood back and gazed at his reflection. His face had filled out since he had been a teenager and his shoulders were broader. He still wore spectacles of the same design, round with steel frames, and he disliked the bookish look they conferred on him. He appeared more like a student than a soldier, he decided glumly. In truth, that was how he saw himself. Had it not been for the war he would have continued his studies at the university and been embarking on his doctorate. He ran his hand over his hair one last time and left the bakery and headed off into the heart of the old town. The area was quiet now that the curfew imposed on the islanders had come into effect. Peter passed a handful of patrolling soldiers but otherwise there was an eerie stillness to the dimly illuminated streets and alleys of Lefkada.

He paused outside the entrance to Inspector Thesskoudis's house. The shutters were closed and only a thin glow from within illuminated the wooden slats. Peter strained his ears but could not make out the sound of any voices from within. Taking a deep, calming breath he walked up to the door, removed his cap and knocked twice. There was no response. He waited and then knocked again. This time he heard a muted exchange and footsteps shuffling within. A moment later the bolt slid back and the door opened a crack and a face peered round the edge, silhouetted by the dull glow of a lamp inside.

'Who's that?' the woman demanded.

Peter could not help smiling as he recognised Eleni's mother. He cleared his throat and answered in Greek. 'It's Peter Muller.'

There was a beat when the stillness of the town seemed to press in on the little scene and then the door opened a fraction wider and a dull loom fell upon the visitor, revealing his features.

'Peter Muller?' she muttered and then gave a gasp. 'Peter?'

He bowed his head. 'Hello, Mrs Thesskoudis. May I come in?'

'What . . . What are you doing here?' She glanced over his uniform and her eyes widened in anxiety. 'Peter?'

'Who is it?' the policeman called from inside. 'Rosa, who is it?'

'It's Peter. Peter Muller.'

'Nonsense! I'm in no mood for games. Tell me.'

She hesitated long enough for her husband to join her and stare in surprise at the tall soldier standing at their door.

'By the Holy Virgin,' Thesskoudis exclaimed. Abruptly he leaned out of the door and glanced both ways along the street before urgently ushering the German inside. 'Come in, my boy. Quickly.'

Peter stepped over the threshold and the door was closed swiftly behind him. A single electric bulb illuminated the main room of the house and the furniture cast dark shadows across the floor and walls. Thesskoudis recovered from his surprise and extended his hand cautiously.

'It's good to see you again . . . Welcome. Welcome!' He smiled and steered Peter towards one of the chairs by the large table that also served as his desk. The remains of a meal were at one end and a small pile of papers and forms at the other. Only two places had been set, Peter noted as he sat down.

'Rosa, fetch a bottle of raki and some glasses. We have an honoured guest!' He laughed in that familiar way that Peter had almost forgotten and he could not help another smile. When all three had a glass to hand, Thesskoudis raised his and thought a moment before he gave the toast. 'To friendships that stand the test of time and circumstance! *Eviva!*'

They drained their glasses and set them down sharply. Thesskoudis licked his lips and leaned towards his visitor. 'So, Peter, what are you doing here? Part of the garrison I expect, yes?'

He nodded. 'I've been assigned to headquarters as a translator.'

'I see. Translator. And I expect your knowledge of the island might have also informed their choice.'

'Yes. I was happy when I heard that I was to return. So happy. It's been a long time and the island and my friends have never been far from my thoughts. And now I am here again.' He paused and gestured at his uniform. 'Though I wish it was under different circumstances. But I want you to know that I still consider you my friends. I hope we can be that, even if . . .'

Rosa Thesskoudis clicked her tongue. 'The war has changed things, my dear. I wish it were not so.'

'Enough,' Thesskoudis intervened gently. 'Not now. For the sake of our friendship with Peter and his father, eh?'

His wife cocked her head to one side but said nothing as her husband continued. 'And how is dear Dr Muller?'

'My father was . . . He died,' he said simply.

'I am sorry to hear that. He was a good man. A great pity. It saddens me.'

His wife nodded in agreement. 'Yes. A pity. Just like Katarides.'

Peter's ears pricked up. 'Mr Katarides is dead?'

'Yes. He died this spring. He had been ill for some time, then seemed to reover for a brief spell before he collapsed one evening. His heart had given out,' she explained. 'A great loss. His poetry was loved by many. Though I could not read it. I never learned. Eleni read it to me some nights.' She smiled fondly at the memory for a moment. 'I think his heart could not bear the tragedy that has befallen his people. The war, the starvation and the struggle between the *andartes* and the enemy.'

Thesskoudis coughed and his wife blinked and fixed her gaze on Peter. 'I am sorry. You are not our enemy, I think.'

He felt a stab of pain. 'I do not consider myself to be. I do not wish it.'

The policeman shook his head. 'What we wish for is something of a luxury these days, my boy. We are victims of fate and we must do what we can to survive until this madness is over.'

Peter felt the policeman's sadness and then asked, 'What of Andreas Katarides? What became of him?'

Thesskoudis deliberately avoided meeting his wife's sharp glance as he replied. 'He joined the navy. I recall he told you before you and your father left us.'

'Yes, I remember.'

'He was on a submarine when the war began. That's the last we heard of him.'

'Oh.' Peter felt the loss keenly, but was not surprised. The German forces had easily swept all before them during the invasion of Greece. Tens of thousands had perished defending their homeland. And it seemed more than likely that Andreas was amongst the fallen. No doubt his father had come to the same realisation and that had contributed to his death. He frowned. So much tragedy. Then he fixed his host with an anxious stare.

'And Eleni?'

'She is well,' said her mother. 'And no doubt she will be glad to know that you have returned safely.'

'Where is she?'

'In Nidhri. She lives with a friend's family. They give her work from time to time to earn her keep. There was nothing for her in Lefkada. No work, and food has been scarce for years now.'

'Nidhri,' Peter mused. 'If you give me her address I will look for her as soon as I have the chance to go there.'

There was a brief silence before Thesskoudis folded his hands. 'Perhaps it would be better not to.'

'Why?'

'Peter, you are a German. A German soldier. Your people waged war against us and invaded our land, our home. It is not something a friendship can easily endure. Eleni will be glad you are alive, but like all the islanders, we have suffered at the hands of Germany. Eleni has not taken it well. It's not an easy thing for me to say, but we are enemies. It is not my choice or yours. Others did that to us. But we are enemies all the same. In my heart I have nothing but hatred for those who have done us harm.'

'That is why you brought me inside so quickly.'

'Of course. Do you think we wish to be thought of as collaborators by our neighbours? But we have played the part of good hosts and shared a drink. Now, my boy, it pains me to have to ask you to leave us. Before anyone notices you are here.'

'Leave?'

'Yes.'

'But why should you care about what others think? I can arrange for you to be protected. I can make sure that you have enough food. Enough even to support Eleni so that she can come home. I can do that for you. For the sake of our friendship.'

This time Rosa answered. 'We do not want your food. We do not want your protection. You are the enemy. While German boots are on our soil you can never be our friend. Please go.'

'Yes, go.' Thesskoudis nodded. 'And do not come back.' He stood up and crossed to the door.

Peter stared from one to the other helplessly. 'It does not have to be this way. I came to you for the sake of our friendship.'

'And for the sake of our friendship I have explained our position.' Thesskoudis drew a breath and gritted his teeth. 'Leave us.'

Peter's expression hardened as he rose to his feet. 'I should have known better. I remember how stubborn the Greeks are. How proud.'

'Then you should understand.'

He replaced his cap and made for the door, pausing on the threshold. 'Tell Eleni I would like to see her. I hope she is more amenable to reason than her parents. Perhaps she will be ashamed by the way you have treated me tonight.'

Thesskoudis smiled thinly. 'I think not.'

Peter stared at each of them briefly and then left the house. He heard the door shut firmly behind him, cutting off the light, and he was swallowed up by the darkness in the street as he picked his way back to his billet.

CHAPTER TWENTY-NINE

A cool northerly breeze was blowing across Lefkas as the column of soldiers approached the village of Alatro. They had left the trucks four kilometres down the track that wound its way through the hills to the earth road leading to Nidhri. Although it was autumn in the Mediterranean the climate still provided tolerable enough conditions for the German mountain troops. They carried food and water for the day, in addition to their weapons and spare ammunition. Even so, the climb up to the village had been strenuous, sweat streaked the men's faces and they were breathing hard as they fanned out into the olive groves on either side of the track and cautiously approached the nearest buildings.

The church bell began to ring and the men instinctively stopped and crouched, anticipating that it was a signal, warning of their approach. Peter glanced at his wristwatch and saw that it was just after midday and he surmised that there was nothing sinister in the sound of the bells. They soon stopped, leaving the faint rustle of leaves stirred by the breeze and the occasional plaintive bleat of goats.

On either side of him the men assigned to the sweep stretched out in a line under the trees. Steiner and his squad followed on ten metres back. The Sturmbannführer had changed into a field uniform and wore a holstered pistol which was attached to his belt. The company commander, Hauptmann Dietrich, had crept a short distance ahead of his translator and now turned to wave his men forward and they continued up the gentle incline. Like the SS officer, Peter was armed with a pistol and carried his water bottle, rolled cape, binoculars and a small sidebag for the day's rations besides. He felt tense as he crept forward over the stony soil, fully expecting to hear a shot ring out at any instant. Dietrich had briefed them at first light, telling the men that the resistance fighters were well-armed and motivated as well as having the advantage of knowing the ground. As a result, they would be sure to want to teach the Germans a lesson if the opportunity arose. If it came to a fight, then the mountain troops must be ready to respond at once, with aggression, and turn the tables on their opponents.

Fine in principle, Peter reflected as he watched Dietrich carefully make his way through the last of the olive trees and out on to open ground. But he feared that his first instinct would not be to take the fight to the enemy. Until he faced battle for the first time he had no idea how he would react. Much as he desired to do his duty for his country, he was a reluctant warrior and was more afraid of shaming himself through cowardice than of being wounded or killed. The latter fate actually seemed preferable to a crippling, disfiguring wound, or the knowledge that he lacked the moral fibre to stand alongside his comrades in battle. Absurd, he told himself. No rational man would consider death the least worst option, but in matters of courage and self-respect, rationality always fared poorly.

The church bell started ringing again, more insistently this time, and did not stop. Dietrich rose to his full height and cupped a hand to his mouth.

'At the run! Advance!' he bellowed, his voice echoing dully off the mist-shrouded hills rising on either side of the village. The line of mountain troops ran up the slope, accompanied by the sound of ragged breathing, pounding boots and the chink of loose kit. Peter hurried to keep up with the company commander, ready to act as his translator when the Germans burst into the village and began searching for members of the resistance and their weapons. A sudden bleating added to the sound of rushing men and a small herd of goats burst across the slope, chased by a young boy in baggy trousers tucked into his tattered boots. His open sheepskin jerkin flapped around him as he ran after his animals. He spared the approaching Germans a quick glance and then shouted a warning to his compatriots. Dietrich swore and charged at him, pistol-whipping the youth to the ground to silence him. It was a pointless gesture as more cries of alarm rose from the village and all the while the bell tolled, its peals sounding ever more frantic.

'Muller! Keep up!' Dietrich snapped as he stepped over the prone boy and raced towards an opening between two of the whitewashed hovels on the fringe of the village. A handful of his men had already run ahead and more spilled over the low walls behind the houses. As Peter passed between the whitewashed walls either side of the narrow street, the sound of boots echoed sharply, almost drowning out the blood pounding through his head. Dietrich paused at an intersection and quickly glanced in either direction before he waved his hand towards the church tower.

'Keep moving!'

Breathing hard, Peter reached down and snapped open his holster and took out his pistol. Leaving the safety on, he lurched forward, following Dietrich towards the centre of the village. Around them he could hear the harsh shouts of the mountain troops amid the alarmed cries of the inhabitants. Then the street turned a corner and they emerged into the small square in front of the church. The priest, dressed in black, was standing at the foot of the stairs, waving his congregation inside as women hurried to safety with their children. There were a few men too, anxiously glancing back towards the Germans. Some turned and bolted for the far side of the square, disappearing into the alleys between the modest houses at the centre of the village. One of the German sergeants spotted them and thrust out his hand.

'Get those bastards! Don't let 'em escape!'

Several soldiers pounded after the fugitives as Dietrich lowered his pistol to his side and strode across the flagstones towards the church, Peter following.

'Tell the priest that he and his flock have nothing to fear as long as they cooperate. The only men we're after belong to the *andartes*. We'll arrest anyone we find with weapons in their houses. Tell him.'

Peter did as he was ordered. The priest, a thin man with piercing eyes and a grey beard, nodded but held his arms out wide to prevent them passing him to get into the church. He puffed out his chest and stared back at Peter as he replied coolly, 'Tell your superior that my church is a house of God and we do not permit armed barbarians to step inside.'

Peter paraphrased the priest's objection and Dietrich returned his pistol to its holster before he addressed the priest again with forced politeness. 'We will go where we please, old man. Stand aside, please.'

The Greek held his ground and with a frustrated curse the German officer thrust his hands against the priest's chest and sent him sprawling at the foot of the stairs. Stepping round him, Dietrich trotted up to the arched doorway and stood on the threshold squinting into the shadowy interior. As Peter joined him he saw faces staring back fearfully, the women holding their younger children close to them. A handful of the men glared defiantly.

'Your attention, please,' Dietrich announced. 'My men are here to search your village for weapons and criminals. The innocent have nothing to fear from us.'

As Peter finished translating, the priest came limping up to join them and spoke gently to his congregation. 'Do as the German says and there will be no trouble.'

Dietrich nodded as Peter translated. 'Muller, tell them everyone is to remain here until further notice. Any man attempting to leave the church will be taken for a member of the resistance and shot on sight.'

He turned and stood overlooking the square. More of the locals were hurrying towards the church, slowing as they saw the two German officers, and giving them a wide berth as they scurried up the steps and inside. Now there were more soldiers entering the square, driving people forward with loud angry shouts, and using their rifles to shove the slower civilians ahead of them. Soon most of the villagers had been rounded up and were being held in the church along with their priest. Dietrich posted two men at each entrance, armed with machine pistols.

Steiner and his party entered the square, looking around warily for any signs of danger as they held their weapons ready. But there was no sign of resistance. The soldiers who had gone after the islanders who had made a run for it returned with a bloodied youth who had tripped and fallen against a rock and dazed himself long enough to fall into the soldiers' hands. He was dumped on the ground beside the wall of the church and shuffled back until he pressed against the cracked plaster of the wall and could retreat no further. There he sat and stared at his captors in terror.

With the villagers secured, Dietrich gave orders for their houses to be searched for weapons, munitions and any concealed *andartes*. Steiner looked on with an impatient expression as he waited for the other officer to finish.

'Hauptmann, I appreciate that you have your mission to carry out here, but we must reach the dig site while there is plenty of daylight.'

'And we will, sir. Just as soon as we have made this village safe.'

'Safe?' Steiner smiled thinly. 'Do you really think your intimidation of the locals and turning their houses over is going to cow them into accepting our control of their island? The *andartes* will return here the moment we have left.'

'Then we shall have to repeat the exercise until they get the point.'

The SS officer shrugged. 'Good luck with that. I know these people. They can be pig-headed in the extreme. Is that not true, Muller?'

Peter gave a non-committal grunt. He recalled the friendship of the local people when he and his father, and Heinrich, had lived on the island. He felt a keen sense of loss at the reception he had been given by Eleni's parents.

'I can match any Greek for persistence, sir,' Dietrich said.

'I am delighted to hear it. I expect our persistence is going to be sorely tested during the occupation of Lefkas unless we can truly break the spirit of these people and teach them that we are their masters. So then, carry out your search. You know what to do if you find anything?'

'Yes, sir. The standing orders are to jail those with fowling pieces, shoot any we find with rifles or explosives, and take any *andartes* we capture to the Gestapo section in Lefkada.'

'Good. Then carry on. Quickly, mind you.'

'Yes, sir.' Dietrich bowed his head curtly and turned away to oversee the search of the village. Peter realised that he could have handed the task to his subordinates but preferred to remove himself from the presence of the smug SS officer. He glanced sidelong at Steiner, wondering how much of his character had already been evident in the young man who had once been his father's assistant. Steiner removed his cap and wiped his brow before he lifted his canteen and took a swig.

'This place is a fucking pigsty . . . What did I ever see in it?' He turned to Peter with a quick smile. 'Oh, I know, it was different for you and your father. He loved its history and mistook these ignorant peasants for the descendants of Homer's heroes. And you? You were young and knew no better. I dare say you think differently now you are a man, a soldier, and have lived long enough to see this pathetic island in a somewhat wider context, eh?'

Peter felt that he was being tested and knew that he must reply carefully. 'I still believe in my father's work. This island, and all Greece, has great treasure buried beneath the soil and rocks, and deep in the hearts of its people.'

'The hearts of its people?' Steiner laughed. 'I thought archaeology was a science, not the stuff of poets. These islanders are nothing but the pale shadows of their forebears and as insensible to their heritage as any lump of stone.' He paused and his tone softened. 'Don't be a foolish romantic, Peter. This is an age of men, not dewy-eyed idealists. Actions speak for themselves and get results. That is the essential truth, and we have been living through the proof of it ever since the National Socialists took control of the fatherland. Wake up and accept the new reality.'

Peter took a deep breath to calm himself. 'If that is so, sir, then why is the Reichsführer so determined to accrue to himself the relics of the past? Why is it so important to loot the site my father gave so many years of his life to exploring?'

'We are not here to loot. Our purpose is to save artefacts from the past and put them where they can best be cared for by those who know their value. Or would you rather leave them here to rot in the ground while shepherds and their mangy herds walk all over them heedlessly?'

'They belong to Greece, sir.'

'Even our enemies don't believe that. Why, the British saw fit to remove the marble reliefs from the Acropolis rather than leave them in the hands of the Greeks. So spare me any opinion that these peasants are fit to be guardians of an historic tradition that all Europe has shared in.' He waved his hand dismissively. 'But enough of that. Let's hope this little exercise of power is over quickly. We have better things to do.' Steiner sat down on the top step and rested his chin on his clasped hands.

'Yes, sir.' Peter nodded and after a moment walked to a weathered stone trough a short distance away where the villagers' mules watered. He leaned against it and watched as a squad of soldiers entered one of the houses facing the square and a moment later the clatter and crash of furniture reached his ears as they began their search. As he waited, the soldiers went from house to house, ransacking the simple homes of the villagers. An hour later they had found only a handful of aged shotguns and a drunk who had been sleeping it off in a stable. His angry shouts about his rough handling were cut short when a German struck him hard in the stomach with a rifle butt. He was thrown, gasping, into the church.

Steiner smoothed his hair back as Dietrich returned with the last of his men. 'Well? What now?'

'We'll confiscate the shotguns and take their owners back to Lefkada. Together with that one.' He nodded to the youth sitting still against the wall, as if he had hoped that he might be forgotten by the soldiers.

Steiner shook his head. 'No. We haven't got time for that. Destroy the guns, and burn down the houses of their owners.'

Peter saw the surprised expression on the other officer's face before he recovered his composure. 'Those are not my orders, sir.'

'That may be so, but I am the ranking officer here and they are *my* orders. Be so good as to carry them out.'

'Sir, I must protest—'

'Then protest when we return to Lefkada!' Steiner snapped. 'For now, you will do as I say. I am your superior officer and if you question my authority again I will ensure that your insubordination is punished as swiftly and as harshly as possible. Do you understand?'

'Yes, sir. But . . .'

'But what, Hauptmann Dietrich?' Steiner glared, defying the man to challenge him again.

Clenching his jaw, Dietrich saluted. 'At your command, sir.'

'That's better. Carry out my orders at once. Then we can make our way to the site and I can complete my mission, as you have completed yours.'

'Yes, sir.'

As the Hauptmann turned to his men, Peter eased himself up and returned to the side of the SS officer. He spoke in a low voice so that they would not be overheard. 'Sir, he will be sure to report the matter to Salminger.'

'Let him, if he dares. My orders come from Reichsführer Himmler, and I doubt he will take kindly to having them overridden by a junior field officer, or even his regimental commander.'

Peter saw that it would be pointless to pursue the subject and turned the conversation in a different direction. 'At least the prisoner may provide some useful intelligence on the *andartes*, sir. The Oberstleutnant will be grateful for that anyway.'

Steiner glanced at the youth trembling as he sat hunched a short distance away. 'That wretch? I doubt he will tell us anything of importance. He looks like a simpleton.'

Peter nodded. 'Shall I have him released then, sir?'

He fully expected his superior to acquiesce and was on the point of turning round to tell the youth to join the other villagers inside the church when Steiner shook his head.

'He might not provide any useful information but he might yet prove a useful example.'

'Sir?'

Steiner rose stiffly to his feet and stretched his back. 'I told you, Muller. These backward peasants need to learn who their master is, and learn to fear him. And so they must be given a lesson, no?'

Peter frowned, and then felt a terrible stab of ice down the length of his spine as Steiner reached for his holster. 'Sir, the villagers have already learned a lesson. Dietrich's men have ransacked their homes and are about to burn several to the ground. That will be lesson enough for these people.'

'I think not. They need a more telling example of the price to be paid for offering defiance to Germany.' He drew his pistol and walked towards the youth.

Peter kept up with him. 'There's no need for this. Please, sir. Please . . .' He swallowed anxiously and continued. 'For pity's sake, Heinrich, don't do this.'

Steiner stopped abruptly and swerved round angrily. 'Don't dare to address me in such an informal manner ever again, Leutnant. Do you understand?'

'Yes, sir, I understand well enough, but there are some things, some actions, that do not advance our cause. Harming the boy is one of them. We know these people well enough to know they will avenge him some day.'

'I am not interested in their petty vendettas. Stay out of my way, Muller. I shan't warn you again. I have tolerated your insolence so far out of respect for your father. Don't test my patience any further.'

Peter swallowed nervously. 'I apologise, sir. I meant no offence. Just to offer advice, as is the duty of any good officer.'

Steiner sniffed. 'The duty of a good officer is to obey his superiors and to lead those below him.'

He stood over the petrified young islander, his pistol hand hanging at his thigh. Lifting his chin, Steiner addressed the captive harshly in Greek. 'Up! On your feet!'

When the boy proved too terrified to obey, the SS officer stepped forward and kicked him, screaming, 'UP!'

The explosion of violence and anger shook the boy into action and he scrambled up and pressed himself back against the wall of the church, his limbs shaking uncontrollably.

Keeping his pistol at his side, Steiner smiled. 'That's better! What is your name, boy?'

The youth's jaw slackened and he licked his dry lips, his chin quivering. Steiner softened his tone. 'Come now, tell me your name. That can't hurt you, or your friends hiding out in the hills. Tell me that at least.'

'M-Manolo . . .'

'Now, Manolo, you must realise that you are in bad trouble. Those friends of yours have led you astray and left you behind to be taken by my men. You owe them nothing. Your only duty now is to yourself, and your family, who would grieve if anything happened to you. Right?'

The youth nodded hesitantly.

'So I will give you a chance, Manolo. Tell me where they are hiding. Take me to their cave, or whatever shelter they are using, and I will set you free. Not only that, I'll give you a reward and the promise of my protection. You'll be perfectly safe . . . What is it to be, Manolo?'

The youth stared back, and then by some determined effort of self-control he stiffened his spine and raised his head. 'I will say nothing.'

'I thought not.' Steiner raised his pistol casually, pointed the muzzle at the youth's face and pulled the trigger. There was a dart of flame, a deafening report and the youth's head lurched back as blood and brains exploded vividly across the whitewashed wall behind him. The body sagged and crumpled on to the ground, a ragged hole in the forehead above wide eyes and slack jaw.

'No . . .' Peter shook his head. 'No.'

Steiner returned his weapon to his holster and glanced at the body before he turned away. 'That's that. Once Dietrich has fired the houses, our business here is complete. Then we can get on with our real work, Muller.'

But Peter was not listening. He was still staring in horror at the body.

'Muller!'

He tore his gaze away and saw the frown on Steiner's face. 'Sir?'

'Pull yourself together. The boy was a criminal. The Gestapo would have shot him if I hadn't. The only difference is they would have made him suffer first. It was an act of mercy.'

'Mercy?'

Steiner shrugged. 'This is war, Muller. Mercy comes in many guises. Now, that's enough. We're wasting time.'

Half an hour later the German column was climbing the track from the village towards the site of the abandoned dig in the valley above. Behind them several thick columns of smoke billowed into the afternoon air. The crackle of the flames carried clearly to Peter's ears as he paused momentarily to look back at the square in front of the church. He could see the small ring of darkly clad figures gathered around the body. A woman was hunched over the youth and as he watched she tipped her head back and a thin, inhuman shriek echoed off the surrounding hills. Peter looked away quickly and swallowed. Then he breathed deeply and continued in the footsteps of Sturmbannführer Steiner.

CHAPTER THIRTY

The track leading up to the archaeological site had become overgrown. Where it skirted around the slope of a hill, the edge had collapsed in several places after the winter rains had coursed down and over the track. Little of it seemed familiar to Peter as the column advanced warily, the men constantly watching for signs of an ambush. He tried to recall the times when he had been driven up the track by his father. The memories flooded back and made his heart heavy. The man who had loved him and raised him to share his fascination with history was gone. The loss was still too raw to accept. So he shifted his thoughts to Eleni and Andreas and the occasions when he had walked this ground with his two friends. It seemed long ago, distant, and he felt an ache inside at the thought of them and the conflict that had separated them and turned them into enemies. It was a hard thing to consider Andreas and Eleni as such, and painful to reflect that they would now consider him to be a hateful foe. That much was clear from the reception that her parents had given Peter.

He tried to thrust the hurt of that evening aside and chided himself for being so sentimental. Perhaps Steiner was right. War changed everything. Only the weak and naive clung to the values of peacetime. And yet he shuddered at the image burned into his mind of the execution of the boy back in the village. So sudden, so shocking . . . so barbaric, as if all the beliefs he had once been raised to accept and cherish had been no more than a thin veil to be torn aside to reveal the bestial reality of human nature. Perhaps war was the real face of humanity, and peace was little more than a pretence of what human nature could be. No more than a mask dreamed up by idealists.

It was a terrifying thought, all the more so because Peter feared that it was the unadorned truth. In a world where bombers razed German cities to the ground and incinerated tens of thousands of civilians at a time, there was no place for compassion and mercy to be shown to the enemy whether they wore uniforms or not. All that mattered was the survival of Germany. He paused at that. How long ago was it since he had surrendered the notion of victory? Even if the Führer and his followers still spoke of victory and warned that it was treason to be defeatist, Peter knew he was far from alone in regarding the war as a fight for survival. The crushing defeat at Stalingrad could not be dismissed as a setback. Germany was being battered at the fronts while bombs rained down on the heartland. On that scale, what was one more death in a dusty square of an obscure village on an insignificant island?

Hauptmann Dietrich had stopped ahead and was waiting for Steiner and Peter to catch up. Dietrich fell into step with them and looked at his wristwatch before addressing the SS officer.

'Sir, it's already gone fifteen hundred.'

'I thank you for that information,' Steiner replied curtly. 'So?'

'We still have over two kilometres to march before we reach the site. I have no idea how long you propose to spend there, but we'll need to leave in good time to return to the trucks before dark.'

'We will return when I say so, Dietrich.'

'Sir, it would be dangerous to have to blunder through these hills in the darkness. The *andartes* know the ground. We do not. If they set a trap for us then we could suffer heavy losses.'

'Really? I thought the mountain troops were supposed to be an elite force. An officer of the Waffen SS would show no such anxiety in the face of a handful of renegades and brigands.'

Dietrich took the insult with an affronted expression but was wise enough to keep his tone neutral as he responded. 'I would not presume to lecture an officer of the SS in his area of expertise, sir. In the same manner, I would expect a brother officer to respect the specialism of myself and my men.'

'Even a brother officer of the SS?' Steiner grinned. 'I know how the Wehrmacht looks down its nose at us, Dietrich. But we train as hard as you, and our commitment to Germany and the Führer runs deep and makes us a force to be reckoned with. By our own men, as well as the enemy. If you understand my meaning.'

Dietrich swallowed and nodded. 'Yes, sir.'

'Then be a good fellow and resume command of your men.'

They exchanged a brief salute before Dietrich increased his pace and made for the head of the column.

'I find his attitude tiresome in the extreme,' Steiner mused a moment later. 'I'm thankful that you are only an artillery officer, Muller. I could not tolerate having to deal with two prima donnas today.'

Peter pressed his lips together and bit back on his anger

towards the SS officer. They continued a little further before Steiner spoke again.

'Are you not excited by the thought of returning to the site of your father's greatest work? If I am right about what we may discover there, then Dr Muller's name will rival that of Schliemann.'

'It is an appealing prospect, sir, and no more than my father deserves. He gave his life to uncovering the secrets of the ancient world.'

'And I played no small part in his work,' Steiner added. 'And now you follow in his footsteps, as my assistant. Perhaps we shall share some of the fame that will be accorded to the doctor. That would be quite an honour, and one we shall both richly deserve. I should think that the Reichsführer will decorate us both if this works out as I hope. We shall be heroes.'

'Yes, sir.' Peter forced himself to return the other man's smile even as he felt contempt for Steiner's naked attempt to take the credit for the long years his father had given to his exploration of the Greek islands.

Ahead of them he could see the entrance to the valley, the steep slopes of the hills on either side crowding the track. If the *andartes* were planning an ambush, that was a likely spot for it to take place. Hauptmann Dietrich had seen it as well and a moment later he halted the column and set two squads of men to scout the slopes either side of the track. He allowed them a hundred-metre head start before he waved the column forward again. They passed through the gorge that had been formed by the torrents that rushed out of the valley, leaving gravel and large stones in their wake. Peter recalled that his father had often had to hire islanders to clear the larger stones away to permit vehicles to gain access to the site, and the neglect of recent years had left the track almost impassable to vehicles. The gorge had once seemed a place of spectacle and beauty to Peter but now it felt gloomy and threatening and he was glad when they had passed through it and emerged into the valley beyond. Above the crests of the surrounding hills the sky was overcast and the sun was only visible as a pale disc. Soon it would have passed beyond the rocky skyline and the shadows would begin to creep into the valley.

The track climbed on to higher ground that overlooked the dig, the closest that vehicles could come to the site, and Peter quickened his pace until he stood amid the stunted shrubs on the edge of the rise. Below, the valley floor stretched out and on it lay the corrugated roofs of the sheds that had stored the archaeologists' tools and less valuable finds. The long table was still there, and the benches, but there was little sign of the area that had been divided up into grids and carefully dug up over the years that the German team had worked on the site. Nature had crept back over the trenches and heaps of spoil and blanketed them in tufts of spiked grass and saplings struggling to take over the abandoned dig. It was a melancholy scene, made more so by the dull light and the cool and clammy breeze that blew softly through the valley.

'I never thought I'd see this place again.' Steiner broke into his thoughts. 'Not once the war began, at any rate. My life has changed a good deal since the days when I took a consuming interest in the past. It's the future I look to now.'

Peter smiled to himself. It seemed strange that so much store was put on the past and the future when really it was only the present moment that a person could ever truly know. The rest was little more than stories doomed to eventually fade, or dreams of what might be. A strange mood gripped

Peter, evoked by his most vivid memories of his father, when he had seen him at his happiest. And it was also a time when he himself had been happy and too content to know that he was living a blessed existence on the island.

'Come on.' Steiner gestured towards the ground in front of the shed. 'We haven't got time to waste reminiscing. We can do that later when we have what we came for.'

The column descended and Dietrich posted sentries around the perimeter of the site and ordered the rest of his men to fall out. Steiner and Peter crossed to the table. The SS officer sat on a bench, set his sidebag down and unfastened the straps so that he could take out his notebook. He flipped it open and Peter could see diagrams of the site, neatly labelled and interspersed with what were clearly original notes, and newer comments in the margins, written in red ink.

'Where do we begin looking, sir?'

Steiner tapped the notebook. 'Your father mentioned a cave, yet I was never aware of any cave during my time here. How about you?'

Peter shook his head, then looked up and briefly scanned the landscape. The dig and the surrounding area were on generally even ground. To one side a cliff rose up for a hundred metres or so with a tree-fringed crest looming over the site. Opposite the site another boulder-strewn slope stretched up to a rounded peak that dominated the centre of the island. There was no sign of a cave, and nothing that he could recall that indicated the presence of one.

'If this cave contains a tomb then it would be reasonable to expect that it would have a large enough entrance to be obvious, unless it was intended that it be concealed,' said Peter. 'I think we should begin our search along the foot of the cliff there.'

Steiner looked up. 'I agree.'

He called Dietrich over and explained his intentions. 'The Leutnant and I are seeking a cave. I want you and your men to be on the lookout for anything that might help us locate it. Even the smallest fissure or hint that something has been covered over. They are to report anything they find to me at once. Clear?'

'Yes, sir. How long do you propose to search the site?'

'As long as it takes me, Dietrich. When I am finished, I will let you know.'

'I understand, sir, and we can secure the site overnight, if you wish. But there is the question of the trucks. I have left twelve men behind to guard them. They will be vulnerable if they remain where we left them overnight. I must send them back to Lefkada, or reinforce them before nightfall.'

Steiner considered a moment before he responded. 'Send half of your men back to protect the lorries, Hauptmann.'

'Yes, sir. I will give the orders at once.'

Steiner nodded in acknowledgement and then flipped his notebook closed and stood up. 'Well, Peter, let's go and make your father a famous man.'

He led the way across the site towards the thin screen of trees and shrubs that grew out from the base of the cliff. 'You start here. I'll begin at the other end and work back towards you.'

'What about Dietrich's men, sir?'

'What about them?'

'We could use some help.'

'I don't think they would be helpful. This is work for the trained eye. We know what to look for. We know the clues: a shard of pottery, a fragment of a sculpture, an unusual formation in the terrain. Things that Dietrich's men would overlook. Besides, the honour of discovery belongs to us alone, no?'

'Very well, sir.'

He saluted and Steiner responded with a curt nod before he turned away and strode over the clear ground towards the point where the cliff ended in a jumble of fallen boulders half a kilometre away. Peter watched him go with a sense of relief. He was finding the SS officer's company a strain on his nerves, far more so following the shooting in the village. Steiner had a cold streak in him and was determined to let nothing stand in the way of him winning favour with his superiors. Peter was not fooled by his moments of bonhomie and sentimental references to their shared past. Steiner was merely trying to curry favour so as to complete his task more swiftly. When it was over he would almost certainly discard Peter, and all his father's work, and claim the full credit for himself.

Looking up at the sky, Peter guessed that there was little more than an hour of good light left before dusk settled over the island. Barely enough time to search the base of the cliff. After that he and the others would face a cold night in the open before resuming their search in the morning. The prospect did not appeal to him, even though the terrain around him reminded him of happier times with his father and friends. Then the search for the treasures of the ancients had been a noble pursuit, carried out to extend the understanding of the past. Now, it was merely a looting expedition conducted on the order of a party leader who knew little of the past, nor cared much about it. If the tomb was here then it would simply be a prize of war, not accorded the care and reverence with which his father would have approached its discovery and unearthing. For a moment Peter was tempted by the notion of not revealing the tomb if he chanced on it before Steiner. It would be better that it was left alone until the war was over and the matter handled in an unhurried way by experts who did not have to look over their shoulders in fear of the *andartes*, or who worked under the guns of German soldiers . . .

Yes, he hoped that he would be the one to discover the tomb, and then have the courage to conceal his find from the SS officer.

Easing his way through the gorse bushes growing at the end of the cliff, Peter began to work his way along, eyes scanning the ground for any sign of an opening in the rocks, or an inscription carved into their surface. The failing light made the task more difficult and he had only gone fifty metres or so when he heard a distant shout and paused. It took an instant before he realised the defiant cry had been in Greek. Then a fusillade of shots crashed out, the sharp note of rifles and the harsh clatter of automatic fire. A moment later the first grenades exploded, the roar of their detonations echoing round the steep sides of the valley.

CHAPTER THIRTY-ONE

At once Peter reached for his holster, snatched out his pistol and cocked the weapon. He lowered into a crouch and turned away from the cliff as the valley filled with the sounds of shooting and explosions. He scurried back through the thin belt of scrub and stunted trees and stopped just before the open ground to take stock of the situation.

The mountain troops had taken cover and some were returning fire as they began to locate the enemy's positions, given away by faint puffs of smoke and muzzle flashes dotted across the slope of the hill opposite the cliff. Peter picked out one man slumped over a boulder, a slick of bright red blood spreading down the side of the rock. One of his comrades reached up and pulled him down, examined him briefly and then rolled him on to his back and emptied his cartridge pouches before crawling to a more secure firing position as divots of earth burst from the ground a short distance away. There was movement elsewhere as men darted about to find positions of greatest safety from where they could shoot back at the *andartes*. He could hear the shouts of Hauptmann Dietrich and his sergeants as they tried to take control of the sudden chaos.

Forcing himself to stay calm, Peter gripped his pistol tightly and looked out over the open ground between the base of the cliff and the sheds at the centre of the dig. Twenty paces away was an overgrown mound of spoil that would provide shelter from the enemy on the hill. He rose up slightly, braced his boots and then sprang out from the trees and raced into the open. Even though his instinct told him to run as fast as possible for the mound, he did as he had been trained to do and ran in an indirect line, swerving to the left and right to make it difficult for any enemy to draw a bead on him. He reached the mound and threw himself on to the ground behind it, heart pounding. He lay still briefly before crawling round so that he could see the enemy's position, as well as the shed where he had last seen Dietrich. Then he recalled Steiner and looked away to his left, but there was no sign of movement towards the far end of the cliff. The SS officer might be taking shelter there, or he might be doing the same as Peter and trying to rejoin the others. Peter put thoughts of him aside and set his pistol down carefully before taking out his field glasses and training them on the slope of the hill opposite, in the area where he had seen a concentration of muzzle flashes a moment earlier.

Through the eye cups he saw a circular image of the hillside in crisp detail and began to pan over the rocks and shrubs carefully until he caught a flicker of movement and saw the head and shoulders of a darkly featured islander rise up over a rock and take aim swiftly with a sub-machine gun. Fire darted from the muzzle and Peter fancied he could pick out the rattle of the shots a moment later through the cacophony of battle raging in the small valley. He continued his search until he concluded there were no more than twenty of the enemy opposed to Dietrich's half company. The Germans outnumbered the *andartes* more than two to one, and the odds would increase in their favour if the men who had been sent to guard the trucks heard the sound of firing and turned about to come to their comrades' aid. He returned the field glasses to their case and prepared to move, picking an overgrown trench fifty metres from the shed. Taking his pistol up, Peter hunched behind the mound, tensing his body, ready to spring forward again. He waited a moment to allow the mountain troops' return fire to build. Then the rapid *brrrrr* of a Spandau machine gun cut through the dusk and vivid streaks of tracer flashed across the valley floor and lashed the hillside.

Peter rose and ran forward again, zigzagging, praying that the enemy would be too distracted by the German fire and the targets they had already chosen to pay him any attention. Then he heard a sharp zip close by and saw fragments burst off the side of a small boulder directly ahead. An instant later he heard the crack of a rifle above and behind him and felt a stab of terror as he realised there were more of the enemy on top of the cliff, sniping down into the valley. There was no time to look back and he ran to the right for three paces then two to the left. Another shot zipped close by and the report of the gun followed it. Then he reached the trench and threw himself into it, pressing himself against the stones and dirt at the bottom. Too late he realised that this was the old latrine ditch at the dig, but there was no time for disgust and, in any case, the human waste had long since been washed into the ground. Crawling forward a short distance Peter hugged the side of the ditch closest to the cliff, breathing hard.

Outnumbered the enemy might well be, but they held the high ground and had the mountain troops caught in a crossfire. He could hear Dietrich and the others clearly now, shouting at his men to return fire and suppress the enemy. Orders that were far more easily learned in training than obeyed in combat, Peter reflected bitterly. He holstered his pistol and continued along the latrine trench until he came to the end and lay catching his breath. The end of the trench had partially collapsed and Peter raised his head cautiously until he could glimpse the top of the cliff. A moment later a thin puff of smoke marked the position of one of the snipers. He continued to watch until he heard a few more shots and decided that there were only a handful of men up there.

Dietrich's second machine-gun section joined the fight and the bursts of the Spandaus dominated the exchange of fire in the valley.

'Conserve your ammo!' Dietrich's voice cried out. 'Fire only if you can see 'em!'

Peter heard the order relayed by the non-commissioned officers as he prepared to move again. He knew that this time would be far more dangerous as the sniper who had narrowly missed him earlier would have seen him enter the latrine trench and would be waiting for him to emerge. But there was no helping it, Peter realised. He could not stay in the trench for the rest of the firefight. He was an officer and even though he did not belong to this unit he still had an obligation to set an example to the men of lesser rank. Even so, he could do something to improve his chances.

Drawing a breath he cupped his hands to his mouth. 'Hauptmann Dietrich! Sir!'

A rattle of fire drowned out his cry and he waited for a lull before calling out again.

'Muller? That you?'

'Yes, sir!'

'Where are you, man?'

'Latrine trench, close to the main shed.'

Another burst from one of the Spandaus interrupted the

exchange briefly before Dietrich called out again.

'I'm in amongst some boulders in front of the shed. Can you get to me?'

Peter hesitated a moment before he cleared his throat. 'Yes, sir. But there are snipers on top of the cliff.'

'I've seen 'em.'

'One of them has me pinned down, sir. Could you order some covering fire?'

'Right . . . Move when I say. Understood?'

'Yes, sir.'

He heard Dietrich shouting to the men around him and a moment later a fusillade of rifle and automatic fire spattered the rocks and trees along the top of the cliff, the tracer shells lighting up the cliff face in lurid flashes.

'Now, Muller!'

Peter scrambled up, out of the trench, and ran hunched towards the front of the shed. He could see Dietrich rise up slightly to beckon to him and he pumped his legs harder, sprinting for the cover of the boulders. In the last ten paces the snipers on top of the ridge opened fire, despite the intense covering fire of the moutain troops. At least one of them had a sub-machine gun and spouts of earth leaped up in a line running past Peter's side and he lurched away to stop his enemy tracking the shots on to him. Then he stumbled a few paces short of the rocks and made another two steps before he crashed on to the ground, the air driven from his lungs. Winded, he struggled to rise and then he felt hands roughly grasp him under the arms and haul him up. He saw Dietrich scowling.

'Clumsy fuck! Let's go.'

The officer dragged him on and they scurried the final few paces towards shelter. As he threw himself down, Peter heard the whipcrack of a passing round and the soft thud of its impact, then a snatched exhaled grunt. He heard Dietrich hit the ground beside him and felt the weight of his body slam into his side. Swallowing, Peter raised his head and smiled ruefully.

'We made it. Sir . . .'

Dietrich was gasping for breath and his body began to shake.

'Sir?' Peter pushed the other man away and rose up on his elbows. He looked down on the back of the mountain officer's tunic and saw the small hole ripped through the cloth and the blood seeping around it.

'The Hauptmann's hit!' he shouted, rising to his knees and pulling Dietrich further into the jumble of boulders and rocks as a shot ricocheted nearby. A soldier appeared ahead of him and grabbed Dietrich's other arm and between them they dragged him out of the line of fire. A Feldwebel – sergeant – scurried over and laid his machine pistol down so that he could turn the officer over. Dietrich's head lolled to the side and his eyes rose into his skull as he let out a low moan and frothy blood sprayed from his lips. Peter could see a ragged hole in his chest, just above his medal ribbons and the Iron Cross on his left breast pocket. Blood was pulsing from the wound and the sergeant immediately pressed his hand on it and applied pressure.

'Medic! Over here!' he bellowed.

Peter leaned back against a rock still struggling for breath as the Feldwebel anxiously tended to his officer. Dietrich convulsed, his back arching as a horrible gurgling groan tore from his bloodied lips.

'Help me!' the Feldwebel instructed. 'Sir. Help me!'

Peter stirred and knelt over the opposite side of the body. 'What do I do?'

'Keep the pressure on the wound.'

Peter reached forward and the other man took his hand and thrust it into the hot mess over the exit wound. Gritting his teeth, Peter pushed down firmly while the Feldwebel turned to look for the medic, who was darting from cover to cover towards them, the red cross on his helmet offering no protection from the *andartes* firing from the hillside. He dropped to his knees beside Dietrich's head and instantly assessed the type of wound and reached into his dressing bag.

'Get his jacket and shirt open,' he instructed and the Feldwebel fumbled with the buttons, tearing the material back. Peter lifted his hands briefly as the bloodied shirt came apart and exposed the gaping hole in the chest. The medic pressed the dressing against the exit wound and nodded to Peter to resume his pressure. Dietrich suddenly tried to sit up, neck muscles straining like cords.

'Hold him!'

All three thrust the injured officer down and held him on the ground until the spasm passed and his body went limp.

'Shit . . .' The medic pressed his stained fingers against Dietrich's throat for an instant and then gently lifted the Hauptmann's eyelids and saw that the pupils did not react. He slumped back with an angry grunt. 'He's fucked . . . You can take your hands off, Leutnant.'

The Feldwebel swore softly and picked up his machine pistol again before he turned to Peter. He was a short, stocky man with a broad jaw below his broken nose. 'What are your orders, sir?'

'My orders?' Peter blinked.

'You're the surviving officer on the spot. That puts you in command.'

'What about Steiner?'

'Haven't seen him since the firing started. Beside, he's an SS flunkey. We need a proper army officer in charge, sir.'

'Right . . .' Peter cleared his head and looked round. 'What's the situation with the rest of the company, as far as you can tell, Feldwebel . . . ?'

'Feldwebel Kramer, sir.'

'Kramer.' Peter nodded. 'Go on.'

'Most of the men were in the area around the shed when the firing started. Some of us took cover here, the rest went to ground. I've got one Spandau team trying to keep the bastards' heads down on that hill. The other team's watching the crest of the ridge. Trouble is, the other side's got us in a crossfire.'

'What about our casualties?' Peter turned to the medic.

'Besides the Hauptmann, there's four dead and another five wounded.'

Peter took a deep, quick breath. 'We can't stay here. They'll pick us off until night falls. We have to make a move on them.'

Kramer nodded and turned to scan the ground around their position. 'There's a raised bank.' He pointed to a series of heaps of overgrown spoil from the dig. 'We can work our way towards the olive trees, sir. If we can get two squads over there we can work our way up the slope and fire on their flank. Provided the snipers don't get us.'

Peter nodded. 'The Spandau can keep up a continuous fire on the snipers. Best tell them to conserve their ammo until we're ready to move.'

Kramer raised an eyebrow. 'We?'

'I'll lead the attack. You'll come with me. Anything happens to me then you take command. I assume the wound badge and the guide badge on your chest aren't just there for appearances' sake.'

Kramer grinned, revealing a gap in his teeth. 'Too right, sir.'

'Good.' Peter nodded. 'Get two squads here and tell the machine gunners and those that are staying here that they're to give us all the covering fire they can when I give the word to go.'

Kramer saluted and crept away amongst the rocks to gather his men and issue Peter's instructions to those remaining behind. Peter realised that he would need a better weapon than his pistol and saw Dietrich's machine pistol lying on the grass a short distance from his body. He unfastened the webbing belt from the dead man and shuffled into it before he took up his weapon, checking it quickly to make sure that it had not been damaged when it had been dropped. The MP38 seemed fine and its weight and dark metallic gleam felt comforting in Peter's hand. He slipped the sling over his neck and waited for Kramer to return. The firing slackened as both sides began to conserve their ammunition and save it for targets they could see clearly. It took less than ten minutes for Kramer to return with the men he had chosen for the task. One man had already been wounded and blood flowed from a deep gash on his cheek. The sun had dipped far beyond the rim of the hillside to the west and an orange hue burned along its crest. Peter explained his orders quickly and made sure the men understood him. They looked hardened and capable and he sensed that they would not let him down. They would not need any final words of encouragement.

'Ready?' He glanced round and they nodded.

'Then let's go, Kramer.'

The Feldwebel called out, 'Covering fire!'

The Spandau teams opened up and brilliant streaks of tracer leaped towards the heights on either side. The other men remaining in the outcrop added their fire and the air filled with the deafening roar and concussion of small–arms.

'Go!' Peter yelled and burst from cover and sprinted across the open ground towards the line of spoil heaps. Kramer and the others sprang after him. It took only a moment before the first of the enemy spotted them and adjusted their aim and bullets whipped past and smacked into the ground. Gritting his teeth and snatching breaths, Peter raced towards the piles of earth and rocks and tumbled into cover before he scrambled on all fours, making for the trees ahead. The others followed him. All except one man who tripped and was rising to his feet when he was struck in the side and spun round before crumpling amid the tufts of grass.

'Leave him!' Kramer bellowed. 'Keep going!'

Peter led them on, keeping low beside the line of spoil heaps, acutely conscious that while they would be sheltered from the men on the hillside they would still be in view of the snipers on the cliff. Sure enough, he heard the sharp crack of a rifle but did not see the fall of the shot and increased his pace. Ahead, there was a short stretch of ground before the trees and he paused to let his men catch up. Glancing back, he saw Kramer and the others breathing hard, grim-looking and ready to exact their revenge on the Greeks who had ambushed them. A bullet struck the piled earth just above Peter's head and he flinched.

'Best not stick around, sir.' Kramer grinned.

Bunching his leg muscles, Peter launched himself towards the trees. He had not gone more than five metres before several of the enemy opened fire. They had seen the direction he and the two squads had taken and anticipated their next move. Soil burst from the ground under the impact of bullets and Peter heard the dull whack of a shot striking one of his men but did not look back as he ran on. Then he was in amongst the trees and rushed forward another ten paces before stopping in their shadows and throwing himself to the ground, gasping. The others went down on either side of him, with Kramer staying on one knee as he hunched low. A final few bullets tore through the trees overhead, smashing small branches and showering them with twigs and leaves before the enemy turned their fire back on the men sheltering by the dig.

Peter cleared his throat and called out, 'All here?'

Kramer glanced round. 'Two men down, sir.'

Fourteen of them left then, Peter reflected. Barely enough for what he had in mind. But that could not be helped.

'Feldwebel, take the first section with you to the edge of the forest and give harassing fire. Only go forward when I begin my attack. Clear?'

'Yes, sir. Good luck.'

Peter nodded his thanks and then Kramer waved his men forward through the low trees, at an angle as they climbed the slope. Peter waited a moment and then beckoned to the rest to follow him. He unslung his machine pistol and cocked the weapon. There might well be a few of the enemy lying hidden under the trees to cover the ambushers' flank. Even if that were not the case they would be aware that the Germans were moving up to counter-attack. Peter hoped that Kramer and his squad would draw their attention while his party made for the high ground dominating the hillside. The gloom beneath the boughs of the trees made the shadows seem dark and threatening and Peter had to prevent himself imagining the presence of enemies lying in wait to shoot him down. They could see the trees thinning ahead of them when the sound of firing intensified away to their left as Kramer's section made their presence known. Peter pushed himself on, increasing his pace, until he emerged from the trees. The slope became steeper ahead of them, strewn with large rocks and stunted shrubs and pines. More than adequate concealment for his needs. He paused as his men caught up and then ordered them to follow him, keeping as low as they could to avoid being seen. Even in the failing light, the enemy on top of the cliff might pick them out as they made for the ridge.

They clambered on, breathing hard from the exertion of the climb and the strain of battle. Peter kept scanning the ground ahead, looking for any sign of the enemy, but nothing moved on the slope in front of them, only the fleeting motion of birds darting low as they hunted for insects. It took nearly ten minutes of increasingly hard climbing before the ground began to level out close to the ridge and Peter halted the men before they became silhouetted against the skyline.

'We go along the edge here, and work our way round their line. No one is to fire until I give the order. Let's move!'

Keeping hunched low they picked their way through the boulders in an extended line, the loose items on their webbing clinking and softly thudding as their sturdy boots ground over the stony soil. With the gunfight still raging away below and to the left there was no chance of the sounds of their approach giving them away and Peter kept the pace up. They had gone three hundred paces along the top of the hillside when he saw the first of the enemy clearly: two men lying on top of a flat rock, firing down at the mountain troops by the dig. The machine-gun crews were husbanding what was left of their ammunition and only an occasional burst was aimed along the slope. Even so a tracer round glanced off a rock lower down and angled up, flaring a short distance over the heads of Peter and his men, causing them to stop and duck briefly before he waved them on.

A short distance further on and he could see more of the *andartes* dotting the slope, some hard to pick out in their dark clothes. He stopped the squad and assigned them their targets as they spread out over fifty metres.

'Shoot first, cut down as many as you can, then use grenades. That'll distract them while Kramer's squad move in.'

Peter waited impatiently as his men moved into place and took aim. Then, glancing to both sides to ensure that they were ready, he raised his machine pistol and sighted it on a man crouching behind a rock nearly a hundred metres down the slope. He closed his left eye, took a breath and let it out gradually as he gently squeezed the trigger. The folding stock bucked into his shoulder as the gun shook and spat fire and then he released the trigger and saw that he had narrowly missed the Greek, who now spun round, looking up the slope. Peter fired again and the man tumbled into the undergrowth beside the rock. On either side the other men opened fire and Peter glimpsed more of the enemy being cut down along the hillside. He allowed them a few more seconds before he cupped a hand to his mouth and bellowed, 'Grenades!'

He lowered his gun and took one of the charges attached to a long wooden handle and unscrewed the base. A short length of cord fell out and Peter tugged it firmly and then swung his arm back and threw the grenade down the slope in a shallow arc towards where he had seen his man disappear. There was a bright flash and puff of smoke and then the boom of the explosion reached his ears. More explosions burst along the slope on either side. Away to the left he saw a German soldier break cover from the treeline and rush forwards and the others followed, going to ground and opening fire while their comrades leap-frogged past them to the next firing position.

The attack from both flank and rear had surprised the enemy and now Peter could see others bursting from cover and scurrying along the slope to escape being caught in the Germans' trap. His men turned their attention on the fugitives and shot down two more.

'Don't let them escape!' Peter yelled, rising up and running along the ridge to keep up with the enemy. He came to the man at the end of the line and nudged him with his boot. 'With me!'

The man scrambled up and they hurried on, pausing only to shoot when an obvious target presented itself. The firing had slackened as the Greeks broke off and made their escape, no doubt hoping to get away once night fell. Then, a short distance away, no more than thirty metres, two figures appeared between some shrubs, heading directly up the slope. Peter stopped in his tracks and snatched his machine pistol up and fired. Several rounds rattled off and the first figure tumbled over. Peter swung his weapon fractionally and pressed the trigger again. The bolt clicked sharply but the magazine was spent. He cursed and reached for the magazine release and let it drop to his feet as he reached for a replacement, all the time keeping his gaze fixed on the second figure. It turned, and he saw with surprise that it was a woman. She glanced down at her fallen comrade and then straightened up as she raised a pistol and aimed it at the Germans and fired. The bullets crashed through the undergrowth close beside them and then the woman had spent her ammunition and paused to issue a defiant shout before she ran on towards the crest of the hill.

Peter felt an icy thrust of shock course through his body. 'Eleni,' he muttered.

Then he felt the man behind him shoulder past; and he

raised his rifle and took aim at the fleeing woman.

'NO!' Peter shouted, throwing himself against the soldier and knocking his weapon aside as the rifle fired. The round tore harmlessly up into the sky.

'What the fuck, sir!' The soldier turned on him with a furious expression.

'Let her go.'

'What?'

'I said let her go. We don't shoot women.'

The soldier looked at him in astonishment and then turned back as both watched Eleni clamber up the slope, her outline clearly delineated against the glow along the ridge. The soldier made to raise his rifle again and Peter struck it down.

'I told you!' he raged. 'Let her go!'

The soldier scowled back and Peter feared that he might knock him aside and finish the job, but by the time the man's eyes were drawn back in the direction of the woman, she had passed over the crest and was gone. He lowered his rifle with an angry growl as Peter's shoulders slumped with relief. His heart was pounding wildly and for a moment he was oblivious to the scattered shots still sounding from the slope below him as the mountain troops chased the last of the enemy away. All that mattered at that precise moment, the only thought that filled his mind, was that Eleni was alive and had escaped.

For now.

CHAPTER THIRTY-TWO

Even though the midday sunlight was streaming into Sturmbannführer Steiner's office and the sky outside was a deep blue, unbesmirched by a shred of cloud, the mood inside was tense and cold. Peter was standing at ease in front of Steiner's desk while the SS officer looked through his report of the previous day's ambush. Steiner was hunched over the document, his neatly bandaged head showing a small dark stain over the cut he had sustained when he had tripped and fallen. He had only emerged in the twilight, a full half-hour after the skirmish was over, staggering groggily towards the shed that was being used as a dressing station. That was where Peter had found him, and relinquished command to his superior. Despite the cut to his head, Steiner was in a strangely euphoric mood. Once his injury had been dressed, he gave orders for the mountain troops to fall back to the trucks, carrying those too badly wounded to walk.

As they marched out of the valley, moving cautiously in gathering darkness, they encountered the men who had been sent back to guard the vehicles. Alerted by the distant sound of gunfire they had come hurrying to the rescue, passing through the village on the way. That had been deserted, the inhabitants fleeing to hide in the surrounding hills in fear of

German retaliation. Steiner took this as proof of their collaboration with the ambushers and ordered that the village be razed to the ground. His men used clusters of grenades to destroy some buildings and piled furniture in others, dowsing anything that would burn with kerosene from the villager's lamps before lighting the fires. The flaming buildings had lit up the surrounding hills and the crimson glow was still visible from the trucks as they began to rumble back down the road towards Lefkada.

Steiner flipped the covering page back and slid the document to one side as he looked up at the junior officer standing in front of him. 'It was a pity that Hauptmann Dietrich was killed so early in the action. But I am sure that he will receive a posthumous decoration for saving your life. That at least will offer some comfort to his family.'

'Yes, sir,' Peter replied flatly. He doubted that it would be of any comfort.

'You did well, under the circumstances, Muller.'

'Thank you, sir.'

'Of course, I would have taken command had I been able to. And achieved much the same result, I expect. Still, I will not cavil. You did your duty and you did it well.' He smiled quickly, before the expression faded into a slight frown. 'There is one detail, however, that might concern any wider readership of this report. That is the matter of the woman you refused to fire on and thereby permitted to escape.'

'Yes, sir. She was unarmed. I assumed she was a non-combatant.'

'Really? I thought it might be because you recognised her. Eleni Thesskoudis, I believe.'

Peter froze and his anxious expression betrayed him.

'I thought so. You were overheard by one of the men. He

reported the incident to his sergeant who brought the matter to me. Once he mentioned the name Eleni, her identity was obvious. So it was our old friend Eleni Thesskoudis you saved.'

'Yes, sir,' he admitted.

'Your inadvertent act of mercy may still serve our ends.'

'Sir?'

Steiner folded his hands together and straightened up. 'If the young woman had been shot, that would have been merely one less enemy for us to deal with. However, if she could be taken alive then I am sure some of my men could persuade her to reveal a great deal of useful information about the bands of brigands opposing us on Lefkas.'

'Yes, sir.' Peter swallowed. He desperately tried not to let his expression betray his fear for Eleni.

'But that's not why you spared her, is it?'

'No,' Peter admitted.

'You let her live because you once knew her.'

'She was my friend . . . sir, as you said.'

Steiner shrugged. 'Whatever she was, Eleni Thesskoudis is now your enemy, and the enemy of Germany. As such it is your duty to forget your past association with her and with anyone else you knew on this island before the war. I take it you understand that, Leutnant?'

'Yes, sir. Of course.'

'I am glad to hear it. The fatherland has no use for men who forget their duty.' He let the threat dangle in the air for a moment before he lightly ran his fingers through the hair above the bandage. 'But being an intelligent officer, you will no doubt anticipate that I have taken steps to take the woman prisoner.'

Peter felt his blood run cold. 'Sir?'

Steiner tapped the report. 'As soon as I finished reading this earlier in the morning, I gave orders for the arrest of the parents of Eleni Thesskoudis. By now the first notices will be pinned up on the streets of Lefkada announcing that their daughter has two days to give herself up or her parents will be taken to the square outside this building and hanged, at nine o'clock the day after tomorrow.'

Peter took a half step towards Steiner, his face strained with horror at his superior's words. 'No . . .'

Steiner cocked an eyebrow. 'No? Why not, Muller?'

'Sir, they . . . they are innocent.'

'They are Greeks. Our enemy. Innocence has nothing to do with it. What matters is results. I need their daughter and they are merely the means to achieving that end. If she loves her parents then she will surrender to us. Otherwise, they will die, and she will live with the knowledge that she could have saved them. At best we will have her, and all the information she can reveal about the *andartes*. At worst, we will have demonstrated to the Greeks that we see our threats through, and at the same time your former friend will be reduced to grieving and incapable of fighting us.'

Peter swallowed before he replied. 'Or you will simply have fired her desire to kill Germans all the more, sir.'

'I think not. She is a woman, after all,' Steiner replied dismissively. 'A weak thing, who will no longer present us with any problems.'

Peter sucked in a breath. 'I hope you are right, sir. Truly I do. But I fear that if you carry out your threat then you will turn the islanders against us.'

Steiner laughed. 'They are already against us! The point is that we must show them that resistance is worse than futile. It is too late to rescind my decision. The announcement has been made. To back off now would be taken exactly for what it is, a display of weakness. Surely you can see that?'

Peter thought a moment. 'Yes, sir, I understand, but surely it would be better to imprison them as a punishment for their daughter's actions? That would still send out the message that we are not to be trifled with.'

'Trifled with?' Steiner clicked his tongue. 'Eight of our men are dead and another twelve wounded. The executions of Inspector Thesskoudis and his wife, or their daughter, if she surrenders herself, are only the start. You know the general orders as well as I do, ten civilians executed for every German soldier killed by partisans. Tomorrow, we will return to what is left of the village we burned yesterday and we will round up eighty men, and women if the numbers need making up, and bring them back here to be strung up. Even if we can't run the *andartes* down, we can make sure that we turn their own people against them for fear of reprisals. Don't look so uncomfortable, Muller. War is a messy business and the sooner it is over the sooner we can return to more civilised ways. Speaking of civilisation . . .'

Steiner eased himself back and regarded Peter with a broad smile. 'There is one other matter I should appraise you of. I did not want to say anything until Salminger confirmed that he would provide me with enough men and trucks for the task at hand . . .'

'Sir?'

The SS officer broke into a grin. 'I found the cave, Muller! During the ambush. Shortly before the enemy attack began I came across a thicket close to the cliff, and beyond it what looked like a goat track. I had almost squeezed through when I heard the first shots and thought I might get a better overview of the fight from higher up. So I followed the track and found the entrance to a cave, hidden by a finger of rock. I went inside.' His eyes gleamed with excitement at the memory. 'That's when I found it – at the back of the cave – a stone slab with an inscription. Even my Greek was good enough to translate it. The tomb of Odysseus, my friend!'

Peter felt overwhelmed by his superior's revelation. 'Can . . . Can it be true?'

'Absolutely. I made quite sure of it before I left the cave when the shooting had stopped. In my excitement, I'm afraid I slipped and fell off the track. Hence . . .' He touched the bandage on his head. 'Anyway, Salminger's men will return to the site and start removing the contents of the tomb. We will join them once we have concluded our duties here and demonstrated to the locals the futility of continuing to resist us. Exciting times, my dear Muller!'

'Yes, sir.'

Steiner waited for a moment and when it was clear his mood was not shared by his subordinate his smile faded. 'You are dismissed.'

They exchanged a salute and Peter clicked his heels before turning away and marching out of the office. With the door closed behind him he stood in the corridor and felt a slight tremble in his hands. Despite the news of the discovery of the tomb his mind turned to the fate of Eleni's parents. That was his responsibility. He had written the report that had led to her identification. Yet what else could he have done? It had been his action that had saved her life. For an officer to intervene as he had done was something that could not remain unremarked on by the soldier who had been at his side. But not to have acted was unthinkable. There was no doubt in his mind that she would have been killed. He had acted on instinct and knew that he would rather have died himself . . .

The thought shook him, and then, at that instant, he realised how much Eleni meant to him. How much she had always meant to him. At the same time he knew, beyond any microscopic measure of doubt, that she would not, could not, ever respond in kind. For Eleni would now always regard him with burning rage and hatred, and the thought filled his heart with leaden, aching despair.

She sensed something was wrong immediately from the way that Andreas looked at her the moment he had finished talking with the messenger at the mouth of the cave. The man had come from Lefkada that morning, breathless and anxious. He had asked to speak to the leader of the *andartes* at a nearby village and been brought to the cave blindfolded. Pausing only to accept the wineskin of watered raki that was offered to him and take several deep gulps, the man glanced at Eleni and asked to speak to Andreas alone. The two moved to the edge of the cave where they would not be overheard. Eleni saw the man take a folded sheet of paper from inside his sheepskin jerkin and pass it over. Andreas scanned it quickly and read it again carefully before he refolded the paper. He nodded his head in thanks and indicated that the messenger should warm himself beside the fire. Then, pausing to steel himself, he crossed the floor of the cave to where Eleni was sitting on her sheepskin bedding.

Despite the humid warmth of the cave Eleni felt a chill of dread quickly spread down her spine and could hardly breathe at his approach. He stopped a pace away and stared at her. Only one side of his face was lit by the wavering glow of the fire and she saw the pain cut into his expression as he swallowed.

'Eleni . . . I'm sorry.'

She swallowed, feeling panic rising. 'Sorry? What is it?'

When she made to rise, he placed a hand firmly on her shoulder and gently eased her back down on to the sheepskin and squatted before her. 'It's bad news, my love. Bad news . . .'

'Is it . . . my parents?'

He nodded.

'Dead?' She saw what she thought to be acknowledgement in his eyes and clasped her cheek. 'How? Tell me, how.'

For a moment Andreas did not know how to begin to explain then he shook his head. 'Not dead. Not yet, but they cannot be saved.'

She frowned. 'What do you mean. For pity's sake, tell me!'

'They have been arrested by the Gestapo. Along with some other hostages.' He indicated the folded sheet of paper. 'The Germans have posted notices saying that your parents will be executed . . . unless you give yourself up.'

The words struck her like a blow and she felt giddy for an instant before Andreas reached out and took her hand. She shook his grip aside and held out her palm.

'Show me,' she said.

Andreas gave her the folded sheet and watched silently as she opened it and read through the short, brutal demand of the enemy. Her brow creased and her lips pressed together in a thin line as she thrust the announcement back to him with a look of agony. 'No . . . no. How can this be? Why my parents? Why them?'

'I don't know, Eleni. But somehow they have discovered you are one of the *andartes*. We have been betrayed. I will not rest until I find out who is responsible. I swear it, on my life and by Holy God. They will pay for this.' He touched his breast.

'We must do something.'

Andreas raised his eyebrows. 'Eleni, we cannot.'

'No! We must do something. They must be saved. They're innocent.'

'Of course they are. But the Germans are holding them in the cells under the Gestapo headquarters in Lefkada. The town is surrounded by checkpoints and the garrison camp is less than a kilometre away . . . There's nothing we can do. There are too many of them. It would be suicide to try anything.'

She looked at him coldly. 'I cannot let them murder my parents. If you lack the courage to attempt to free them, then I'll do it myself.'

Even as Eleni spoke the words she knew how foolish they sounded. Worse, she had impugned the honour of the man she loved. The pained look in his face only added to her despair and desperation.

'Eleni, my love.' He spoke softly and took her face between his hands and held her gaze as the first tear rolled down her cheek. 'There is nothing we can do. Not I, not you. No matter how much we care for them. They are as my family now and I would give almost anything to try and save them. But I would not give your life for it. Nor would they want that. They would want you to live. To survive this war and go on to have children of your own, and grandchildren. I know this as surely as I breathe . . . And so do you. Am I wrong?'

She stared back as the tears came freely and her throat began to sting with the horrifying grief of it all. 'It . . . It's true.'

He leaned forward and eased back her fringe to kiss her forehead. 'All we can do is honour their memory in our struggle. Make the enemy pay.'

'You can do that,' she replied. 'For me. I must save them. I will give myself up tomorrow.'

He drew back from her and shook his head. 'You cannot do that, Eleni.'

She swallowed and cleared her throat. 'I have to.'

'No. Think about it. There is no guarantee they will release your parents. Even if they did, they would still have you. They will torture you to make you tell them about the rest of us. You will tell them who we are, where our hiding places are, what equipment we have, how we communicate with the British. Everything. It is not just your life or those of your parents that is at stake.'

'I will say nothing. I swear it.'

'They will break you, Eleni. It may take hours, days or even weeks, but they will break you and you will tell them everything. Only then will they kill you. I could not face life knowing that they had done that.'

'It is my choice,' she said firmly, even though inside she felt her heart sink like a great weight into the depths of her body.

'But it isn't just your choice when it affects us all. We are fighting a war. All Greeks are. A war for the survival of our country. We cannot allow ourselves to put anything before that cause. Surely you see it?'

'Of course I do . . .' Her chin trembled slightly. 'I am a Greek, but I am also a daughter. I would give my life for my family, just as I would give it for my country . . . You say you love me.'

'You know it.'

'Then what would you do if I was being held by the Germans and they said they would free me in exchange for you?'

He closed his eyes and frowned for a moment at her words. Then he breathed deeply and replied, 'I would want to give

409

anything to save you – my life, anything – if I could save you. But I could not put that before all those who follow me, or before my country.'

Her lips puckered into a faint sneer. 'Spoken like a man.'

She pushed him away and turned her back on him as she curled up on her sheepskin and hugged her thin frame. He reached out and touched her shoulder, greatly pained by her reaction to his necessary words.

'Don't touch me.'

'Eleni, I—'

'Don't speak to me.' Her voice was strained and he felt her shudder beneath his touch as she began to cry in earnest.

'Eleni, for the love of God, there is nothing we can do.'

'Leave me alone! Just leave me.'

He hesitated, overcome by the urge to try and comfort her, but there was nothing he could say that could change anything. He withdrew his hand and sat back, and watched helplessly as she sobbed quietly. Soon, the first ripples of anger and rage flowed through his heart and he swore a silent oath to make the enemy pay for this outrage. Blood for blood. Until they were driven from Greece, or he perished in the fighting. He sat there for a long time, watching her and torn by his feelings of guilt at not being able to save her parents, and what he knew to be his duty. The other men kept their distance. They had heard the news from the messenger, before he was escorted back to the village, and did not intrude on the private suffering of their leader and little Eleni whom they loved as a sister.

Then, while the light at the mouth of the cave began to fade as the day ended, Andreas rose stiffly and joined the men of his band squatting around the fire cooking a pot of stew. There was none of the usual animated conversation, even though a flask of raki was shared amongst them. Finally, old Yannis shook his head and muttered, 'It is a sad matter, my *kapetan*. We will make the Nazis pay for it, eh?'

The others muttered their assent and looked to their leader as Andreas took the flask and tipped his head back. The fiery liquid offered none of its usual comfort and with a sombre expression he handed the flask on to the next man as he nodded his agreement. 'They will pay for it, my friends. Dearly.'

When the stew was ready, Andreas set a bowl down beside Eleni and returned to the others, who ate in a subdued fashion. Andreas had the first watch of the night and took up his Marlin sub-machine gun and a fleece cloak before he left the cave and climbed to the top of the hill above to settle down on the slab of rock that overlooked the approaches. The sky was clear and the cold stars glimmered down on the mountainous landscape of the island. He tried not to think of Eleni's parents, but memories of them crept back into this mind and he recalled the happy years before the war when the cheery policeman and his wife had visited his father's house and they had sat on the terrace overlooking the sea and drunk and talked long into the night. Without his being conscious of it, the memories drifted to the times when Dr Muller and his son had joined them. The easy ache of sentimental memory instantly gave way to sickening revulsion and anger and he cursed as he thrust thoughts of the past from his mind and forced himself to reflect only on the revenge he would wreak on the enemy in the time to come.

There was not enough German blood in the world that Andreas could shed that would make amends for the suffering they were causing Eleni . . .

Around midnight he heard the faint sounds of someone approaching his position to relieve him. Nevertheless, Andreas eased his gun from the ground beside him and rested his thumb on the safety catch. He gave the soft whistle of a night bird and it was returned twice a moment later before Yannis emerged from the darkness and squatted down beside him.

'I was expecting Aris. What are you doing here?'

Yannis shrugged. 'I needed the air. The lads are as gloomy as women at a wake.'

'And Eleni? How is she?'

'She ate her stew, even though it was long since cold. She was cleaning her pistol when I left her. Good thing too. The girl needs to take her mind off things.'

Andreas nodded. 'I suppose.'

They stared out towards the distant sea and Yannis cleared his throat and spoke reassuringly. 'There's nothing that can be done about it, *kapetan*. You must accept that, as she will, in time. Best you go to her now and try to make her see that, eh?'

Andreas stood and slipped the strap of the Marlin over his shoulder and patted his comrade on the shoulder. 'Try and stay awake, old man.'

Yannis growled, 'Not so old that I can't teach you some tricks, boy.'

They shared a brief, quiet chuckle before Andreas started back down the hill towards the mouth of the cave, trying to think of the best way he could offer Eleni any comfort. Three men still sat by the dying embers, the rest had turned in, pulling their sheepskins over their bodies to warm them through the cold night. Setting down his weapon, Andreas moved to the back of the cave where he had left Eleni earlier. He stopped a short distance away, his pulse quickening. Her bedding was drawn back and she was not there. He glanced round the cave quickly and hurried back towards the fire.

'Where is Eleni?'

One of the men looked up. 'She went outside, *kapetan*.'

'Out? Why?'

The man could not help looking mildly amused. 'Same reason we all go out from time to time.'

But Andreas was already rushing to the mouth of the cave. He ducked out under the rock and stood in the darkness searching the shadows intently, desperate to call out to her, despite the risk. But it was too late. She was gone and would not answer even if she heard him. There was nothing he could do to stop her and a low keening groan welled up in his throat as he thought of her marching steadfastly towards her doom.

CHAPTER THIRTY-THREE

The day of the executions dawned with a clear sky. There was no wind and the sea that lapped the island was like a sheet of silk, as if oil had been poured over it to dampen the slightest ripple. The rising sun cleared the mountains on the mainland to the east and burnished Lefkada in a honeyed glow. The stillness of the new day was echoed in the sombre quiet that filled the town's streets, until the siren sounded the end of nightly curfew. It was a harsh, ugly wail that echoed back off the side of the hill behind Lefkada and died away after a minute. Slowly the doors of the shops and houses opened and the first of the inhabitants filtered out into the streets and went about their business. But on this day many of the people made for the large open square in front of the prefecture, their hearts filled with dread, while some yet hoped and prayed for a miracle.

Eleni had stayed the night with a cousin of her mother, a dour thin woman who could be trusted to keep her presence a secret. From her Eleni had borrowed a simple black dress, shawl and shoes and left her country clothes on the bed when she left the house and joined the silent procession making for the square. The Germans had set up additional checkpoints during the night in case there was any trouble that day. They

414

stood, weapons slung from their shoulders, carefully watching those passing by and occasionally pulling out a man to question or search. Once in a while they stopped women, Eleni noticed. Those who might be the same age as her. She pulled up her shawl and covered her head and affected a slight stoop to try and appear a little older as she approached the first of the checkpoints surrounding the square. Falling into place at the rear of a group of black-clad women, she kept her head lowered as she passed between the German soldiers. Like many of their race they were tall and well-built, looming larger than the men of Greece and frightening. After a cursory glance they waved the group through and turned their hard stares on to the people further up the street.

There was already a small crowd in the square, instinctively drawing back to the fringes as they saw the daunting wooden structure that had been erected in front of the prefecture. Eleni's breath caught in her throat as she saw the scaffold, sturdy wooden beams supporting a length upon which four nooses hung down. Below them a thin platform stretched out beneath the nooses. In front of the gallows stood a line of soldiers with rifles to keep the Greeks back. The sight made her feel sick and giddy and for a moment she feared that she might vomit. She leaned against the wall outside a bakery and closed her eyes for a moment as she fought off the nausea. Then she took a deep breath and forced herself to stand erect and raise her chin defiantly as she moved off and found a position in the shadow of the church that overlooked the square. The modest crowd slowly swelled in size and yet there was little sound above the shuffling of feet and muted exchanges as they waited.

Eleni regarded those around her for a while, noting their thin, pinched faces resulting from the ever dwindling sources of food on the island. For a moment she wondered at their readiness to be spectators at the execution of their own people, and then realised that they had come to bear witness to this crime inflicted by their evil oppressors. They had come to see, and remember, and feed the fire that burned within. One day they would have their revenge on the Nazi invaders who had brought so much misery and suffering to their lives.

Her thoughts were interrupted by the opening of the church's doors and a priest emerged, a silver cross mounted on a staff in his hand. Behind him came the other priests of the town and they bowed their heads as their leader paced towards the edge of the steps descending to the square. A hush fell over the crowd. The priest raised his arms, and held the cross high, as he began to chant a prayer. The crowd clasped their hands and bowed their heads as they listened.

She felt anger simmering in her breast. What good were prayers in this world? What did they ever achieve? No bullet had ever swerved from its path in response to a muttered appeal to an invisible God. No executioner's blade or hangman's noose had ever been stayed by divine intervention. Eleni felt the urge to shout at them. To shriek that their words were useless. The only thing that would save her parents and the other hostages was direct action. The only opposition to the Germans that mattered was violence. Blood for blood. She slipped a hand over her stomach and felt the bulk of the revolver nestling in the folds of a spare shawl she had tied about her waist under the dress to conceal the outline of the weapon.

Even now she was not sure what she intended to do. Only that she knew that she could not be anywhere else this morning. Her life had begun with her parents and now they were to be taken from her and Eleni did not know if she could survive without them. There was no will to go on. Not even for the sake of Andreas whom she loved so dearly that her heart ached at the thought of not being with him ever again. It was then that she realised that she meant to die along with them. Andreas had been right about being unable to save them, she knew. The Germans would not keep their word about releasing her parents if she gave herself up. There was no treachery that was unknown to the Germans and their Nazi leaders, who had crawled out from the darkest regions of the human heart to unleash their poison on the world. They would kill her parents one way or another, and should she surrender then they would know that their only child had also died at the enemy's hands. Eleni coldly resolved to try and kill those responsible for the annihilation of her family, before turning the gun on herself and denying them the victory of capturing her alive.

Then she realised that her resolute expression and defiant posture might make her stand out and she eased herself away from the wall and edged into the crowd and followed the example of those around her by clasping her hands and lowering her head. An older man looked at her, his eyes widening in recognition, and his wife at his side sensed his tension and turned and also saw Eleni. Her mouth began to open but her husband whispered urgently in her ear and both looked away and deliberately ignored Eleni as they joined in with the rest, following the Trisagion prayers enunciated by the priest.

'Holy God, Holy Mighty, Holy Immortal One, have mercy on us . . .'

The prayers continued for another hour as the sun climbed into the peaceful sky and its rays illuminated the square and caused the gallows to cast a shadow across the crowd.

At nine o'clock the bell in the town hall struck and the priest abruptly stopped praying. All faces turned towards the town hall as the doors on the balcony overlooking the square opened. There was a brief pause as the bell continued tolling and then fell silent. As the last note reverberated around the square, some German officers strode out and looked down over the gallows and the crowd beyond. They wore their caps and Eleni could not make out much detail of their faces and she decided to get closer. Close enough to make sure that she did not miss. As unobtrusively as she could, Eleni began to work her way round the edge of the crowd towards the prefecture. One of the officers barked an order and a moment later the doors of the prefecture opened and a squad of soldiers hurried out and formed a cordon leading up to the gallows. Once they were in place the first prisoners were escorted outside. They looked dazed and terrified as their guards jostled them down the steps and herded them to the open ground below the balcony. Eleni saw dread in their faces as they stared up at the gallows and clung to one another, some sobbing, some trying to look defiant. One of the last to come out was the village priest, now deprived of his hat, and he affected an aloof air as he joined the others and raised his voice in prayer. One of the German soldiers promptly shouted at him and strode up and bellowed in his face. The priest ignored him, and then the soldier swung the butt of his rifle up and against the side of the priest's head. His prayer was abruptly silenced and he staggered back, blood streaming from a deep gash in his scalp. He might have collapsed if he had not been caught and held up by two of his flock.

The crowd had gasped at the attack on the priest and began to move forward as outrage swelled in their hearts. The soldiers in front of the gallows presented their rifles as one of their officers shouted an order and an instant later bayonets rasped from their sheaths and were fastened to the ends of the weapons where the blades gleamed in the bright sunshine. Another snapped order brought the points down, directed at the crowd who recoiled a short distance and fell silent again.

Then Eleni saw the last two prisoners escorted out of the prefecture and she stopped dead, lips pressed tightly together as she fought to control the raw mix of emotions that threatened to overwhelm her: despair, love and determination. Her mother came first, chin lifted proudly as she paced steadily down the steps and towards the gallows. Behind, her husband had been stripped of his suit jacket and wore a plain white shirt open at the neck. His trousers were held up with braces and he too tried to affect an indifference to his fate in order to inspire those in the crowd. Eleni watched them, fighting back the urge to cry, and felt that her heart would break.

The soldiers led them to the gallows and forced them to mount the steps to the narrow platform, two metres above the ground, where a man was waiting by the nooses. He manhandled Eleni's mother into place and slipped the first noose over her head and checked that it was firmly under her chin. Then he did the same for Eleni's father and descended to the ground and indicated to his companions to stand by the trestles holding the platform up. Then all was still, save for Eleni, picking her way closer to the balcony, feeling her hands tremble as the hard steel of the revolver pressed against her stomach.

On the balcony one of the officers stepped forward and rested his hands on the stonework and began to address the crowd. At his shoulder was a thinner, younger officer, who listened and then translated his words into Greek. Even though her mind was concentrated on what she had resolved to do she still noted that his accent was good and he had picked up the regional emphasis almost perfectly as he addressed the islanders.

'Oberstleutnant Salminger regrets the necessity of what is about to take place here this morning. The German Reich seeks only to bring peace to Greece and protect it from those who would bring violence and bloodshed to the streets and fields of your country. However, there are those amongst you who seek to defy us and shoot my men down in cold blood. That cannot be permitted. You all know of the proclamation I announced when Germany took control after the Italians betrayed us. Ten hostages to be executed for every German soldier murdered by the criminals who call themselves the *andartes*. We Germans keep our word . . . Yet we are prepared to show mercy too.'

Eleni paused and stared up at the figures on the balcony, clutching at the sudden hope sparked by the translator's last words. Then he continued.

'You see before you the police inspector of this town and his wife. They are guilty of raising a daughter who has joined the criminals hiding in the mountains of Lefkas, from where they launch their cowardly attacks on my men. I said that I was prepared to let these two live if their daughter gave herself up. That is still the case. If you are here, Eleni Thesskoudis, you can still save their lives . . . What dutiful daughter would not do anything she could to protect her parents? But does she do her duty by her parents? Is she here today? Is there anyone in this crowd who knows where she might be found in order to save these two innocent people? Well?'

Those in the square remained still. No voice was raised in reply and Eleni felt a terrible compulsion to answer the challenge and prove that she was the child her parents deserved. She drew a deep breath and was about to take a step forward when she felt her arm taken in a powerful grip.

'No,' a voice hissed in her ear.

She felt his other hand reach round her shoulder and pin her tightly against him. She tried to shake him off but it was impossible and she spoke in a furious undertone. 'Let me go, Andreas!'

'I cannot. This is not the way, Eleni. I told you. There is nothing we can do to stop this. Now come away, I beg you.'

She refused to move and resisted the pressure of his grip as he tried to lead her away from the prefecture. 'I will not leave. I will not.'

Andreas relented and whispered, 'Very well, but give me the gun, now. I mean it, Eleni. If you do anything then it will mean my death as well as yours.'

She let out a long breath and then nodded. He relaxed his grip enough to indicate the sidebag hanging from his shoulder. She carefully slipped a hand inside her black coat and undid the shawl. Holding the cloth around the revolver she eased it out and placed it in the open bag. 'There . . .'

Andreas slid the flap over the top and fastened the buckle. It would be a risk for him to try and take the weapon out past the checkpoints but he had no intention of doing so. There were plenty of places around the square where it could be safely discarded. So they stood, with his arm placed around her shoulder as they watched.

The German commander of the garrison gave a snort and spoke again and then his words were translated.

'I have tried to exercise mercy. You are all witness to that. My offer has been rebuffed and so I have no more choice in the matter.'

Eleni's father puffed out his chest and cried out. 'Long live Greece! Death to Germany!'

Salminger leaned forward and shouted an order down to the soldier who had placed the nooses round the necks of his victims. The man clicked his heels and turned to his companions and shouted an order. At once they kicked away the trestles and the slender platform collapsed. Eleni's mouth opened and she let out a groan as her parents dropped a short distance and the ropes snapped taut. Their legs kicked out, as if they were trying to walk awkwardly. A faint, strangled series of croaks carried across the square as their bodies jerked like freshly caught fish on a line. Some in the crowd looked away in horror, but many looked on steadfastly, and then a voice echoed Inspector Thesskoudis's last words.

'Long live Greece! Death to Germany!'

He repeated the cry and others took it up until it swelled from hundreds of throats and echoed back from the buildings lining the square, filling the ears of those dying on the gallows. The woman writhed wildly one last time before her strength gave out and she hung there like old clothes, swaying from the creaking beam. Eleni's father lasted a moment longer and then he too was dead. Their bodies were swaying to and fro and then urine dripped on to the ground beneath as their bowels loosened. Eleni turned away and pressed her face into Andreas's chest as she began to sob.

'Take me away from here. Please . . .'

But he stood still and did not reply. When Eleni looked up, she saw that he was staring up at the balcony. 'What is it?'

'Peter. Peter Muller. Up there. Look.'

She turned her head and forced her gaze not to linger on her parents' bodies as she followed the direction he had indicated. At the shoulder of the garrison commander the translator had removed his cap and bowed his head and now they could clearly see him for who he was. At the same moment Eleni suddenly recalled the Germans who had pursued her on the hill a few days before, and the one who had had the chance to shoot, and had not. And now she realised how the Germans had identified her and how they had come to arrest her parents. She felt an icy hatred clench inside her chest as she stared at the man who she had once known as a friend.

'Peter . . .' Her lips curled as she spoke his name as it if was a terrible curse.

Andreas nodded. Then they saw the young German officer turn to look in their direction. Andreas averted his gaze from the balcony. 'Come. We have to leave now! Before he can see us. Eleni, come. For the love of God.'

She turned away reluctantly and allowed herself to be led away from the square as the German soldiers approached the gallows to remove the corpses and prepare it for the next prisoners to be executed and the crowd continued to chant their defiance at their bitter enemy.

CHAPTER THIRTY-FOUR

Yannis was eagerly awaiting them when they returned that evening but had the sensitivity to offer his condolences to Eleni before he broke his news.

'The Germans are back, *kapetan*.'

'Back?' Andreas cocked his head to one side. 'Where?'

'In the valley where we ambushed them. They drove up to the village yesterday evening and spent today clearing the track up to the valley. I watched them until they settled in for the night, up where the sheds are.'

'How many of them?'

Yannis thought a moment. Like many of those who were raised and lived in the hills his counting was indifferent. 'Not as many as we fought the other day. Perhaps no more than twenty, and three trucks. They were covered, but I was able to see wooden crates inside one of them. What can it mean, *kapetan*?'

Andreas shook his head. 'I don't know. But we must find out. The Germans must be taught a lesson. Send for the *andarte* bands of Christos and Petros. We'll put an end to whatever it is they're up to.'

'Petros, *kapetan*?' Yannis raised an eyebrow. 'He is a communist, I don't trust him. I have heard that his people on the mainland are trying to take over other resistance movements.'

'Well, they won't succeed here. Not while I am in command.'

'Even so, perhaps it would be best not to risk another fight so soon. We lost some good men the other day.'

'That is our duty, Yannis. To kill the enemy.'

He was about to lead Eleni to the fireplace to make sure she ate something when Yannis barred his path and lowered his voice. 'The men know what happened in Lefkada today. If we go and kill more Germans they will murder more of our people . . .'

Andreas let his hand slip from Eleni's back and faced his follower full on, his expression dark and dangerous. 'We are at war, Yannis. The Germans are mortal enemies who we must destroy. If we don't, they will be our masters as we shall be their slaves, forever. It is a fight for survival. Many will fall on both sides. That is the nature of war. Now, tell the men to get ready, and send runners to the other bands.'

The older man stood his ground, his eyes pained. '*Kapetan*, for every German we kill, they will kill ten of ours. It is as if we were killing our own.'

Eleni took a quick step forward and slapped him. 'How dare you? How dare you say that to me?'

The other men in the cave instantly turned towards the confrontation with shocked expressions.

'I saw my parents hanged today. Murdered by the Germans! You dare to accuse me of being their executioner?'

Yannis recoiled, out of her reach. 'Of course not. Never. You are as a sister to us, Eleni. All of us. You fight as well as any man. I do not question your actions.'

'What then?' Her nostrils flared furiously. 'What do you question?'

'I question the soundness of fighting the enemy in a way that causes harm to our own people. You know what will happen if we attack the Germans in that valley again. You have seen the ruins of the village, as you have seen the deaths of the hostages they have taken in reprisals.'

'What would you have us do then?' she demanded. 'Sit and do nothing? Wait for the enemy to starve our people to death? They look to us to lead the fight. Their spirit is not broken. In the square this morning they proved that.' She turned to Andreas. 'Tell him.'

'It is true,' he conceded. 'The people showed their defiance.'

'Exactly.' Eleni returned her stare to Yannis. 'They showed that they were not beaten. They showed their rage. The more we take the fight to the enemy, the more angry they will become. Our ranks will swell, Yannis, and nothing will stop us winning our freedom and avenging those we have lost.'

He stared back at her briefly before he replied, 'How much of this is about revenge?'

'Does it matter? What matters is killing Germans and driving them out of our homeland.'

'That is what we want. But why shed blood so unnecessarily? The war is going against the enemy. Germany will be defeated in the end.'

'In the end . . .' She sniffed. 'And how soon will that be? Five years? Ten? And are we so craven that we would let others win our freedom for us?'

Yannis shook his head. 'We are not soldiers, Eleni. None of us are. Except you, *kapetan*.' He bowed his head deferentially. 'We are shepherds, farmers and fishermen for the most part. And patriots all. We took up arms to free our country and then return to our old lives. That is what we fight for. It is better to wait and see that day than risk our lives and those of many others just for the sake of proving we are patriots.'

Andreas cleared his throat. 'There will be time to talk later. Now we must do our duty. I have made my decision, so have the men make ready and send the runners. I will meet Christos and Petros at the shrine above Alatro at midnight. There will be a full moon tonight. Enough light to see our targets clearly. We will take them at first light. Go.'

Yannis hesitated a moment and then lowered his gaze as his *kapetan* glared at him. 'As you command,' he said wearily before turning towards the men waiting at the rear of the cave.

Eleni took Andreas's hand and offered him a brief smile. 'Thank you.'

'This is not just for you,' he replied curtly. 'I know my duty. I have been trained to fight the enemies of my country. That I must do, regardless of the cost. Do you understand?' He lifted her chin and looked down into her eyes, and felt a terrible pity at the pain he saw etched into her face. 'I do this for Greece.'

'I understand.' She forced herself to smile and reached up and kissed him. 'For Greece . . . I thank you anyway.'

There was still an hour of darkness left as the three bands of *andartes* crept into position. The men led by Petros sealed the mouth of the valley and settled into vantage points on the slopes either side while their much-prized machine gun, captured from the Italians nearly a year before, was set up overlooking the track to ensure that no vehicles or enemy escaped. Another band, led by a dapper former teacher named Christos, took their place to the left of Andreas on the hill that dominated the valley and crept down the slope, stopping well in advance of the German sentries whose figures could be clearly seen as they patrolled the perimeter of the site. The trucks had been drawn up by the sheds and a handful of tents stretched out by the trees at the foot of the cliff. A light glimmered a short way up the rocky surface and Eleni pointed it out to Andreas as they settled into position to await the dawn.

'What's that?'

Andreas squinted across the floor of the valley and then shook his head. 'I can't make it out . . . Looks like it is coming from inside the cliff.'

'A cave? I don't remember a cave . . .'

'No. Me neither. But it looks like the Germans have found one. Maybe that's why they are here. Someone's betrayed the hiding place of another band. One they've been keeping secret from the rest of us.'

'If that's true then any weapons will be back in our hands in a few hours.'

Andreas turned to look at her lying beside him in sturdy breeches, boots and sheepskin jacket and chuckled. 'Of all my *andartes*, you are the most formidable.'

She looked at him and he felt his pulse quicken at the sight of her skin, ghostly pale in the moonlight, fringed by her dark hair and pierced by her eyes and fine brows. He felt the impulse to lean closer and kiss her, but she spoke before he could, in a cold, flat voice.

'If I am, then it is because those devils down there made me so. And they will pay for it. They have robbed me of all that I hold dear.'

Andreas sucked in a breath. 'Not all . . .'

She shrugged. 'I have lost too much already. I don't think I can bear to worry about losing any more, Andreas. Perhaps

I have been a fool to love you, when all it means is that I will have even more to grieve when I lose you.'

'When?'

'Of course. Do you really think we will live to see the end of this war? It is better that we accept that we won't. Accept that we are already dead and all that remains is to kill as many Germans as possible.' Her expression became intense and she cupped her hand around his bristly cheek. 'Surely you see that?'

'I see the woman I love. And want to be with, now, and forever.'

She smiled sadly. 'You poor fool . . .'

He recoiled slightly. 'Why do you call me fool?'

'How will you feel when the Germans kill me?'

His brows knitted together and his voice was strained as he replied softly, 'I would feel that my life had no purpose.'

'And that is why you should not have feelings for me. That is why I have decided not to risk my affections on any other. Especially not you, Andreas. What happened to my parents is like a blade twisting in my heart. I have never known so much pain, and would not survive any greater hurt. Spare yourself that. Do not love me.'

He stared at her a moment. 'You make it sound as if I have a choice.'

'You do. So choose wisely.' She withdrew her hand from his cheek and shuffled a short distance away to create a small gap between them. 'It'll be light before long. Save your strength, and your thoughts, for the fight to come.'

'Eleni . . .'

'Quiet. We must do our duty. You said so yourself. So hush now.'

He opened his mouth, not wanting to end the exchange

until he had persuaded her to change her mind, but then he saw the absurdity of it. They were lying in wait to slaughter their enemy, or be killed in turn. Against that reality what did their feelings matter? Feelings had no place in this setting, this moment. Such concerns actually endangered them. Eleni was right to that extent, he conceded. Taking a slow, calming breath he settled down with his back to a rock and kept watch on the enemy down in the valley. He concentrated his attention on them and wondered about the light in the cliff face opposite once again. It must be a cave, Andreas decided. If there were weapons hidden there then he would confront the *kapetan* responsible and ensure that it did not happen again. There could be no such secrets between the *andarte* bands fighting the enemy.

Time drifted on and then, before Andreas was aware of it, the faintest grey smudge of dawn was lining the eastern skyline and a moment later a bird called out, the shrill note carrying across the hillside. After waiting for the thin light to grow a little in strength, he stirred and edged forward, taking position between two boulders as he raised his Marlin, eased back the cocking lever, wincing at the click that seemed too loud to his ears. Then he thumbed the safety off and took aim at the nearest of the Germans who was leaning against the side of the truck, lighting a cigarette. A short distance to his side, Eleni raised her rifle, securing the butt against her shoulder.

'I'll take the man by the truck,' Andreas whispered. 'Remember – wait for me to fire first.'

She muttered a terse acknowledgement and lowered her head, closing her left eye as she drew a bead on another German, sitting cross-legged outside his tent, his rifle lying across his thighs as he looked up at the sky. Two birds darted low over the dig site and his gaze followed their passage and he smiled with delight. Eleni felt a chill in her heart as she watched him, then hooked her finger round the trigger and began to breathe slowly and deeply as she steadied herself to take the first shot.

A deafening burst of sub-machine-gun fire ripped out and shattered the tranquillity of the dawn. Bullets splintered the wood panel of the side of the truck before Andreas adjusted his aim and caught his man in the chest, hurling him against the truck while his cigarette flew from his fingers and landed in the tufted grass at his feet. He pitched forward. At the first sound of gunfire Eleni squeezed the trigger and the stock of the rifle punched back into her shoulder as the ear-numbing crash of the detonation merged with the sound of Andreas's weapon. As she worked the bolt she saw the German lurch to the side and sprawl in front of the tent. His rifle fell nearby and he began to reach out for it as Eleni took aim again and fired. The second bullet struck him in the neck and his body jerked savagely and then lay still.

All along the slope the other *andartes* joined in, lashing the German camp with bullets. Two of the men who had been standing sentry were cut down but the others had taken cover and were returning fire as the rest of their comrades snatched up their weapons and ran for shelter. Andreas saw two men race towards the back of one of the trucks and take out a machine gun. He turned his Marlin towards them and opened fire, knocking one down while the other snatched the Spandau and turned to run. He had only gone a few paces before being struck by one of Andreas's men. Now the return fire began to strike back and rounds zipped through the air close by, some crashing through the undergrowth while others smashed off rocks, sending fragments of stone and dust exploding into the air.

But the sudden onslaught had caught the Germans badly and several men already lay still, while as many were wounded. The survivors were spread out around the tents and trucks and were pinned down under the heavy fire from the hillside. There seemed to be no one in charge, as far as Andreas could see, and he guessed their officer must have been one of the first to be hit. A movement caught his eye and he saw a German burst from cover and scramble, zigzagging, towards the treeline at the foot of the cliff. Andreas aimed a burst at him and cursed as a line of soil spouts erupted to the side of the German as he changed direction. Then he threw himself into a shallow dip beneath the first trees and disappeared from sight. As soon as he had caught his breath the soldier bellowed to his comrades. It took numerous shouts before he had their attention and then acted on his orders. While several loosed a furious fusillade at the hillside the others broke cover and made towards the cliff. Andreas ignored the enemy bullets and fired a burst at one man and gave a satisfied grunt as he was struck down. Another soldier was hit before the enemy went to ground and then provided covering fire for their companions to make their dash.

As far as Andreas could estimate, ten or so men joined their NCO in the treeline before the firing died down. As many lay scattered around the tents and trucks, dead or wounded, one of them crying out piteously as he rolled on the ground clutching his stomach. Now was the time for the *andartes* to close in and finish the job, Andreas decided.

'Cease fire! Cease fire!'

His order was relayed along the slope and the others loosed off a few final rounds before the guns fell silent along the hillside. Andreas cupped a hand to his mouth and bellowed his instructions.

'We'll advance one band at a time! Christos!'

'Yes!' came the reply, away to the left.

'We'll fire first! Your men go forward twenty paces, then cover us. We'll take turns until we are right on top of the bastards! Understand?'

'Yes, *kapetan*!' the former teacher cried back, his voice betraying his excitement and keenness to close in and kill his enemy.

'Open fire!' Andreas shouted and he sprayed the treeline, two hundred paces away. To his side Eleni worked the bolt of her rifle as she shot into the shadows beneath the trees and scrub. The others blazed away and with a shout Christos burst from cover and plunged down the slope, followed a moment later by several men on either side of him. A few shots were fired back by the enemy but went wide. Then, as soon as they were in cover, Christos and his men took over and fired on the treeline.

'Let's go!' Andreas called out. 'Forwards!'

He hunched low as he scrambled downhill, jinking from side to side to put the Germans off their aim as they tried to pick the *andartes* off. He was aware of Eleni to his side and as he dived down behind a bush he saw her run a few paces further on.

'Get down, Eleni! Down!'

She heard him and dropped, just as a bullet whipped close by. Andreas cursed her foolhardiness as he brought his Marlin up and opened fire. There was a short burst and then the bolt clicked and he discharged the magazine and reached for a spare as his men continued shooting. Christos and his men rose up and made another rush, this time bringing them off the bottom of the slope and close to the trucks and tents. When it was time for Andreas and his men again they rushed past the first of the German casualties and he dropped to the ground a few metres from one of the khaki-uniformed bodies. As Andreas fired again the man groaned and rolled on to his side. Glancing towards him, Andreas saw a tangle of blond hair and the ribbon of an Iron Cross stretching from one of his buttons beside a dark patch of bloodstained cloth. His shoulder boards revealed his officer rank. He groaned and opened his eyes and then stared at Andreas for an instant before he reached for his holster. Andreas jerked his Marlin round and fired a burst into the German's face. Blood and brains burst out of his skull as he flopped on to his back.

'Andreas!' Eleni called from close by. 'Are you all right?'

'Fine . . . Keep firing!'

Christos's men ran forward again, and this time one stopped dead in his tracks as he was struck by a burst of automatic fire and toppled on to his back. The rest dropped to the ground and resumed shooting into the trees. This was the last stretch, Andreas knew, and the most dangerous as they closed up on the enemy. It would be close-quarters fighting, where his courage would be most tested.

A bright flash and thunderous detonation a short distance away shattered his thoughts and he pressed himself into the ground as earth and grit showered down on him, his ears momentarily numbed by the explosion.

'Grenades! Watch out!' one of his men called out.

There were a handful of further explosions amid the fierce firing and Andreas looked up to see an *andarte* sit up, raising the blackened stump of his arm. Then several bullets struck his head and his body was hurled back into the grass. Andreas took control of his senses and reached down into his haversack for one of the Mills grenades the British had supplied. He pulled the pin out with his teeth and let the handle spring out, counted hurriedly to three and hurled it in amongst the trees. The trees were starkly illuminated by the first explosion, and then there were more flashes as the *andartes* followed his cue and hurled more grenades. As the explosions continued, Andreas changed his magazine again and rose to his feet.

'Forward!' He waved his spare hand frantically to attract the attention of his followers and swept it towards the cliff. 'Forward!'

He ran over the last stretch of open ground, conscious of the others joining him to the right and left. Then he was in amongst the trees. He saw a body immediately at his feet and stepped warily round it even though he could see the smoke rising from the uniform where heated fragments from his grenade still smouldered. There was movement in the shadows ahead to the right and he raised his Marlin and unleashed a burst and the muzzle flash lit up the boughs of the stunted trees around him. The figure dropped and Andreas hurriedly moved on to a new position and crouched down to scan the undergrowth. More firing sounded around him and he edged forward and then froze as someone blundered towards him. He turned, finger on trigger, and saw Yannis no more than five paces away, rifle raised. Both men laughed nervously and then Andreas beckoned to the older man.

'Stay with me. Before we shoot each other.'

Yannis nodded and they edged forward cautiously. The firing started to die out as the *andartes* stalked the remaining Germans through the thin belt of trees below the cliff. There were a handful of further exchanges before there was silence. Dawn crept over the valley and the light steadily increased. Andreas waited a moment before he called out in the enemy's tongue, 'Germans! This is the Greek leader. Surrender!

Throw down your arms and stand up, or die where you lie! There will be no second warning!'

He waited but there was no response, nor any shots aimed in his direction. He eased himself up and called out to his followers. 'Sweep the trees! Kill their wounded and round up any who surrender!'

With his weapon held ready, he moved through the remaining trees until he reached the cliff but encountered no more of the enemy. On either side he saw more of his men cautiously emerge and then he felt a surge of relief as he spied Eleni a short distance away. She lowered her rifle as she approached him.

'Do you think we got them all?'

'Not sure. I hope not. We need to know what they were doing here. It must be something to do with the cave.'

'Cave?' Yannis frowned.

'Up there.' Andreas indicated the cliff. 'We saw a light earlier.'

A moment later one of the *andartes* came out of the trees pushing a German soldier ahead of him. The man's shoulder was torn and bloodied and there was a deep gash on his jaw. Andreas saw the chevrons on his sleeve and realised that this was the sergeant he had seen earlier. The man looked to be in his thirties and his face was deeply lined. He stared contemptuously at Andreas as he halted in front of the leader of the *andartes*. Andreas regarded him coolly and then looked round for any sign of further prisoners.

'Only him? Very well. He'll have to do.' He slung his Marlin and stood in front of the prisoner and addressed him in German. 'Why are you and your men here?'

The Feldwebel stood stiffly and pursed his lips. 'I will tell you nothing.'

'No?' Andreas smiled, then smashed his fist into the German's nose. There was a dull crunch and blood flowed from his nostrils as he recoiled with a pained grunt. Andreas followed up with a punch to the man's stomach and a kick to his shin which caused him to drop to one knee. Andreas stood over the prisoner, fists bunched. 'You will tell me. Clear?'

The German looked up, wincing, and nodded. '*Klar.*'

'What are you doing here?'

'We were sent to retrieve the contents of the cave.' He gestured towards the cliff. 'There.'

'What's up there, exactly?' Andreas demanded. 'Guns? Explosives?'

The German smiled faintly. 'Guns? No.'

'Then what?'

'I don't really know . . . The SS officer sent us to open up some kind of a vault and remove the contents.'

'Vault?' Andreas frowned. 'What do you mean?'

'I don't know exactly what it is. But I can show you.'

Andreas narrowed his eyes. 'Is this some kind of trick? If it is, then I'll cut your throat myself.'

The German held up his hand. 'No tricks, I promise you!'

'Show me.' Andreas shoved him in the direction of the cliff and the German stumbled a few steps before regaining his balance. Andreas gestured with his Marlin and the German nodded hurriedly and led the way through the trees. Eleni followed while the rest of the *andartes* began to collect the weapons from the bodies of the Germans and search them for valuables.

The prisoner led them to the foot of the cliff where they saw several packing cases, some of which were still open and half filled with straw. One other was nailed down. Two ropes trawled up the cliff and over a ledge, and Andreas guessed they led into the cave above. He nodded towards the wooden crates. 'What are these for?'

'The things we're bringing out of the cave.'

'What kind of things?'

The German pursed his lips. 'Jars, jewellery, old weapons.'

'Weapons?'

'Swords, spears, helmets and armour. Looks like junk to me.'

Andreas exchanged a glance with Eleni and then lowered his gun. 'Cover him.'

Eleni nodded and lowered the muzzle towards the soldier, who eyed her anxiously. Searching around the crates Andreas found a crowbar and set to work opening up the one that had been sealed. The lid splintered and came off revealing the contents, a sword in an ornate scabbard, a gleaming helmet with a crest holder whose stiff horsehair had long ago crumbled, and several goblets and dishes in silver and gold. He stood back in surprise. 'Holy God, it's treasure . . .'

Eleni took a quick glance. 'This is what Dr Muller was searching for, before the war. It has to be.'

Andreas nodded. 'And now the Nazis have found it.' He turned to the German. 'Take us up to the cave. Now.'

The prisoner gestured along the cliff. 'There's a path a bit further along.'

He led them to the foot of the cliff where a pile of boulders and scrub had once blocked the way, but now the undergrowth had been cut back, revealing the path that led steeply upwards. Andreas could see that it would have escaped attention from all but the closest search and he wondered how the Germans could possibly have stumbled on it. If that's what had happened. Perhaps they already knew of its existence somehow.

'Let's go up. You first.'

The German climbed on to the narrow path, hardly wide enough to be tackled by the most adept mountain goat. Then Andreas saw the rope attached to pitons that provided a secure handhold and all three proceeded with one hand holding the guide rope. It did not take long to reach the finger of rock that helped to conceal the mouth of the cave and with a quick glance over his shoulder the German ducked inside. Andreas followed warily.

'Keep back from the entrance.'

The German reversed a few paces, holding his hands up and bowing his head to keep it clear of the roof of the cave. Andreas entered and looked round to see that it was illuminated by two electric torches attached to two more pitons. Towards the rear of the cave lay a jagged opening in what looked like a carefully dressed slab of stone between two pillars. He could make out rows of carved symbols in what was left of the surface. As Eleni entered behind him and glanced round quickly, Andreas examined the markings more closely.

'I've no idea what is says,' the German offered with a nervous smile. 'For my part, it's all Greek to me.'

'Yes, it is,' Andreas replied. 'Old Greek in fact. As old as it comes.'

There was a dull gleam from beyond the shattered slab and he cautiously raised his Marlin as he leaned through the opening in case there was anyone within. But nothing moved in the light of a torch whose battery was starting to fail. Even so, Andreas could make out the sarcophagus surrounded by the gleam of ancient riches. Some had already been cleared away and some vases had shattered under the impact of the blast that had opened the chamber. He felt his pulse quicken as he realised he was looking at the tomb of a long-dead

Greek ruler and he recalled the purpose of Muller's search years before.

'Odysseus,' he muttered in awe. 'The tomb of Odysseus. Dr Muller was right after all.'

He withdrew his head and looked at the prisoner. 'How much have you removed from the cave?'

'Six or seven crates have been placed in one of the trucks. Then there's one below.'

'Where were you taking it, once the tomb was empty?'

'Sturmbannführer Steiner wanted it brought to Lefkada. Afterwards? I overheard him telling my CO that they were bound for Germany.'

'As loot,' Andreas said sourly.

'I don't know about that, sir. I was just carrying out my orders.'

Andreas turned to Eleni and switched back to Greek. 'Did you follow most of that?'

She nodded. 'Enough.'

'Then we're done with him.'

She raised an eyebrow.

Andreas gestured towards the prisoner. 'You decide what to do with him.'

Eleni raised her rifle and jerked the muzzle towards the mouth of the cave. 'Outside!'

Her intention was clear enough and the German edged round the side of the cave and eased himself through the opening on to the slender ledge beyond. Eleni followed, keeping a short distance between them. Then she raised her rifle and aimed at his chest. The German looked surprised and then fearful as he held out his hands. '*Nein! Ich bin ein Kriegsgefangener!*'

Eleni stared back and pulled the trigger. The bullet tore

through the soldier's heart and he stumbled back, lost his footing and plunged over the side of the ledge and fell to the bottom of the cliff. She looked down on his twisted body and nodded with satisfaction when she saw no movement. She spat down at him and returned to the cave. Andreas was examining the contents of the tomb. He looked up.

'Feel any better?'

'Better? For killing an enemy? I could never shoot enough Germans to pay them back for what they did to my mother and father.'

Andreas regarded her sadly. 'No. I suppose not.'

Eleni nodded past him. 'What about that?'

'We have to save this from the Germans. They cannot be allowed to steal this from our people.'

Eleni pursed her lips. 'What do you intend to do?'

Andreas thought for a moment and then decided. There was really not much choice. 'We return the crates to the tomb, and use the Germans' charges to bring down the cliff face and bury the entrance to the cave.'

CHAPTER THIRTY-FIVE

The door to the mess crashed open and Steiner scanned the room and then pointed. 'Muller! With me!'

Peter stood quickly, throwing down the cards in his hand. The officers he had been playing a rubber with looked towards the Sturmbannführer with a mixture of surprise and irritation. Peter hurried across the room as Steiner stood fastening the buckle of his pistol belt. Together they strode down the corridor of the prefecture towards the staircase.

'Those Greek bastards have attacked the party at the cave,' Steiner announced.

Peter uttered a curse.

'Killed almost all the men. Only one managed to escape from the valley alive. He was picked up on the coast road an hour ago. He managed to report the attack before he died from his wounds.'

Peter glanced at his watch and saw that it was just past eleven. 'Did any of the trucks get out before the attack, sir?'

'No. The men sent to open the cave didn't even get round to fully loading the first truck, the idle bastards. Your friend Eleni and her scum will have their hands on our prize now. God knows what they'll do.'

Peter felt a stab of anxiety in his guts, both for his friend, and for the archaeological treasure that had eluded his father for so long. The contents of the tomb were priceless and he shuddered at the thought of any damage being caused to them. It was the stuff of legend. Schliemann had proved that Homer's great work was not mere myth, and the discovery of the tomb would add a wealth of evidence that would engage historians for centuries to come.

'Salminger has given me command of two companies of his men and four armoured cars to take back to the dig site and rout those peasant bastards. Once that's done we'll have to teach the locals a lesson they won't ever forget.'

'Sir?'

Steiner shot him a bitter smile as they stepped out of the prefecture and descended the steps to the waiting Kübelwagen. He gestured towards the gallows. 'It seems that we did not execute nearly enough hostages last time.'

The driver opened the door for them and they climbed into the back seat. A moment later the small staff car roared off out of the square and through the streets of Lefkada and the locals scrambled out of their way. Outside the town the column of trucks filled with mountain troops was already waiting, together with the armoured cars, and Steiner gave the order for them to move off. With a grating roar of engines the vehicles sped south along the coast road. Steiner leaned closer to Peter so that he would be heard above the din.

'I just hope we are in time, Muller. If not then Reichsführer Himmler will have our balls for breakfast.'

Andreas glanced up at the noon sun and then around at the men labouring under the heavy crates as they carried them back to the cliff. There they were tied to the ropes and hauled up the cliff by the small team working from the cave.

'We need to move faster,' he said quietly. 'The Germans must know by now what's happened up here. Even if we missed some of their men, they'll have heard the shooting and grenades. They will send a force up to investigate . . .'

'Then we'll deal with them in the same manner,' Eleni concluded, running her hands through her thick, dark hair before she retied it in a ponytail and let it fall down her back. She picked up her rifle and held it in the crook of her arm. 'Let them come.'

'Eleni, we have been lucky so far. It would be foolish to push it any further. Besides, there will be reprisals for what we have done here this morning.'

'Maybe, but like you said, we cannot let the Nazis steal our heritage.'

'No. But at what price? I will not risk the lives of all these men, and you, to save the contents of that tomb. We may have to leave some of the crates to the enemy when we blow the cliff.'

'Then we should let the rocks bury them.'

'Even at the risk of destroying what is inside?' He looked up towards the cave, hoping that his men had placed the crates as far to the back of the tomb as possible where they would be best protected from the explosion.

'Sooner that than let the Nazis get their filthy claws on them,' Eleni responded.

Andreas considered this for a moment and conceded. 'Yes . . .'

Once again he looked up to the crest of the hill opposite, where he had ordered Petros to send one of his men to keep watch for the approach of the enemy. There was no sign of the alarm being raised. From his position the lookout would be able to give them a good fifteen minutes' warning of the enemy's approach along the track from the village. After that they would be able to delay the Germans for at least another ten minutes. Plenty of time to set the charges, destroy the cliff and make good their escape.

Christos approached through the trees, smiling as usual. 'My men are bringing the last of the crates. And we've buried our dead. Somewhere the Germans won't find them.'

'Good work.'

Christos scratched his unshaven jaw. 'It seems a pity to make such a fine discovery only to have to lose it all again.'

'Only for the present. Once Greece is free again, then our own archaeologists will re-open the tomb.'

'All the same . . .'

'The *kapetan* has made his decision,' Eleni intervened abruptly.

Christos glanced at her, then back to Andreas, but the latter stared back resolutely and, with a shrug, Christos relented and changed the subject. 'What about the trucks?'

'The trucks?'

'There's no sense in leaving them for the enemy. I'll have my men strip them of anything we can use and then burn them.'

'Yes, do that. Then take your band and go and support Petros.'

The other man made a face. 'Only if he doesn't think he's in charge. Those communist dogs think they run everything.'

'Not here they don't.' Andreas smiled. 'If he tries it on, tell him I put you in command. That'll annoy him.'

'Assuredly!' Christos laughed and slapped Andreas on the shoulder. 'I'll bid you farewell then. Until the next time we fight the Germans.'

'Until then.'

Christos bowed politely to Eleni and then turned to wait as his men lowered the last crate before leading them back through the trees towards the trucks. When he had passed out of sight Eleni puffed her cheeks.

'I don't like Petros. He wants to replace you as the chief of the island's *kapetans*.'

'I know. He's resented me from the first. But he knows that I have the loyalty of the other *kapetans* and there's nothing he can do while that's the case.'

She nodded and was briefly silent before she spoke again. 'What was that remark about the communists running everything?'

'Mostly rumours, I think. The last message from Cairo asked if we were having any trouble with the communist bands. I assume they've heard something from the resistance on the mainland.'

'Should we be worried about Petros?'

Andreas leaned forward and kissed her. 'I think he is more worried about us, Eleni.'

She closed her eyes and returned his kiss before she pulled away with a serious expression. 'I hope you are right.'

He laughed and turned to watch as his men heaved the last crate into position at the foot of the cliff. The men had just worked the previous crate into the cave and placed it at the back with the others. There was a short delay and then Yannis appeared and threw down the two ropes for the final lift. The men worked quickly to tie the crate securely. The explosives had already been taken from the supply the Germans had brought with them to the site and had been set at the mouth of the cave and in some fissures in the surrounding cliff face. The wires led back down the narrow path for a safe distance where they had yet to be connected to the detonator. It would only take a moment to prepare and once the explosions were set off, the cave would be buried under thousands of tons of rock. The Germans would be denied the chance to steal the treasure and Andreas and his band would return to their hideout.

The faint sound of a motor carried to his ears. Some of the men heard it too and paused in their work to listen. Eleni stirred beside him.

'I thought Christos was supposed to destroy the trucks, not make off in them.'

'That's not Christos.' Andreas unslung his sub-machine gun. 'Too far away . . .'

The sound swelled and then there was a burst from a heavy machine gun, then a second joined in. Andreas broke into a dead run through the trees, Eleni close behind him. The rest of the men snatched up their weapons and followed. Those still in the cave swung themselves on to the ropes and hurriedly worked their way down the cliff as the firing intensified. By the time Andreas had reached the treeline the first of the trucks had burst into flames. There were bodies on the ground beside the vehicles – Christos's men, Andreas realised. The others were running for the cover of the nearest rocks. Then he caught sight of movement on the track at the entrance to the valley and saw the flashes of fire from the turret of an armoured car, and another close behind it. The windscreen on the second truck shattered and two more *andartes* were struck down before the survivors reached the shelter of the rocks.

'Why weren't we warned?' Eleni asked, crouching down. 'Where's Petros?'

Andreas looked up at the hill and saw no sign of the lookout. Then he realised that there had been no firing from the direction of the track leading down to the village and a cold fury seethed through his veins.

'That bastard Petros.'

Eleni turned sharply to face him. 'Betrayed us? Petros?'

'Of course.' Andreas smiled grimly. 'This is his chance to get rid of me.'

The armoured cars continued down the track towards the burning truck, now wreathed in wild orange and red flames, with black smoke billowing up into the sky. They continued to spray the rocks where Christos and his men sheltered as they came on. Behind them soldiers fanned out on either side and advanced on the dig site. Even now Andreas could see that they were trapped against the cliff with almost no hope of escape. Eleni grasped the hopelessness of the situation at the same time and she spat a curse at Petros and the Germans and raised her rifle and fired towards the line of advancing mountain troops. The other *andartes* joined in and the Germans took cover and began to fire back. Leaves and fragments of branches leaped into the air above as German bullets tore into the treeline. Andreas and his band took shelter as best they could, pressing themselves into the ground and taking aim on the Germans who dashed forward under covering fire. He saw Yannis firing at the nearest armoured car, the bullets ricocheting off the metal harmlessly.

'Don't waste your ammo!' Andreas shouted at him. 'Only shoot at what you can kill!'

Yannis nodded and shifted his aim and squinted through the sights of his rifle.

The armoured cars closed on the rocks where Christos and the last of his men still held out and sprayed the area with bursts of machine-gun fire to keep their heads down while the mountain troops closed in. As soon as they were within range, Andreas saw them lob grenades through the air. An instant later there was a flash and burst of smoke amid the rocks. Then several more, and then the machine-gun fire ceased as the first Germans crept closer. Two more shots sounded and then it was over.

'It's just us now,' said Eleni. She turned and looked at Andreas searchingly. 'What will you do when they come for us?'

'There will be no surrender,' he replied firmly.

'Good . . . And the cave?'

'I'll take care of that. If anything happens to me, then you see to it.'

She nodded, reached out her hand and took his. 'My heart is yours . . . It always has been.'

Then she snatched her hand back and crawled a short distance off and made ready to fire. Andreas had no time to react or respond as the ground a short distance in front of him erupted in spouts of earth and stone. The armoured cars rumbled on past the trucks and began to pour fire into the treeline. Risking a quick glimpse, Andreas saw two more were making their way down the track. Meanwhile the mountain troops were advancing in short rushes. With a bitter smile Andreas accepted the irony that he and his men were now on the receiving end of the tactics they had used at dawn to seize the dig site. The sound of firing came from each side as the *andartes* tried to hold their line but they were wholly outgunned and outnumbered and knew that all that remained was to take as many of their enemy with them as possible as they fell.

Close by Eleni was firing and working the bolt of her rifle steadily, surprised at how calm she felt. Always she had imagined that she would be afraid of death, afraid of the pain of a mortal wound. But now, there was just an icy stillness in her heart as she took aim and fired until each clip ran out and needed to be replaced. She had found a natural dip in the ground beside a small rock that afforded her good cover. Thirty paces away she saw a soldier rise up and beckon to his comrades to follow him. She swung the barrel of the rifle, aimed and shot him in the chest.

Then, as she adjusted the focus of her eyes, she saw a small staff car following the rearmost armoured vehicle which swung off the track and juddered across the ground to take up a flank position on the others. The driver of the car halted at an angle, well over a hundred metres from the trees. Two officers rose and stood in the rear of the vehicle to watch the attack. Though they were too far away to recognise, Eleni prayed that one of them might be the man responsible for her parents' deaths. Drawing a deep breath she took aim, steadied her body and braced the butt tightly into her shoulder. Lining up the rear and foresights she let the focus of her right eye shift to the most exposed officer, then breathed out slowly. The battle raged around her, but she was detached from it as her lungs emptied and she squeezed the trigger.

The rifle lurched behind the faint puff of cordite and she saw the officer go down. At once the driver and the remaining officer dropped out of sight.

'For my mother!' she cried out exultantly. 'For my father!'

She worked the bolt and looked for a new target as bullets stitched into the ground close by and she heard a pained grunt. Glancing aside she saw one of the *andartes* clutching his shoulder where a bullet had torn through his flesh. He gasped and then another bullet smashed through his eye and burst out of the back of his head and his body slumped lifelessly.

'Fall back!' Andreas shouted. 'To the cliff. Go!'

He rose on to one knee and fired a burst ahead and then one more to each side, then ran to Eleni and hauled her to her feet. 'You too!'

Before she could protest he dragged her away from the treeline into the shade of the thicker undergrowth and then they fled, heads down as bullets zipped overhead, crashing through the trees. Andreas dropped back a little and tried to place his body between Eleni and the German fire. The two dodged round a tree and then he saw the cliff face a short distance away. The Germans would not be able to get their armoured cars through the trees and would now have to send their men in to finish the job. It would not change the outcome, Andreas knew, but it would give the *andartes* a chance to inflict a few more casualties before they were wiped out. There were a few outcrops in the cliff that would afford them a little cover for their last stand.

'Over there!' He pointed to where there was an open strip of ground close to the bottom of the path leading up to the cave. He swerved towards it and then heard Eleni stumble behind him. Cursing, he scrabbled to a stop and turned. Eleni lay on the ground a few paces back, face down. She had dropped her rifle a short distance away. The impact had driven the breath from her lungs and she gasped as she tried to push herself up. Andreas ran back to her and threw his spare hand around her thin body to help raise her up. She cried out in pain and when he removed his hand he saw the glistening red stain across his skin.

'Eleni . . . You're hit.'

Her head rolled to the side and she looked up at him, dark eyes staring intently. 'I'm sorry.'

He laid her down again and pulled the cloth of her shirt up and sucked in his breath as he saw the dark hole in her side and the blood pulsing from the wound.

'Oh God, Eleni. No.' Snatching at his neck cloth he wiped the blood away and and pressed it to the wound. Then he took her hand and clasped it over the cloth as he spoke. 'You must hold this in place. Tightly. Understand?'

She nodded, her brow creasing in pain now that the initial shock of the wound was passing. 'I'm sorry . . . So sorry.'

'Later.' Andreas picked his Marlin up and slung it, then bent down and lifted her in his arms.

'Leave me,' Eleni gasped. 'Leave me. Save yourself, my love.'

Andreas shook his head and started towards the open ground. About him he could hear the sounds of men rushing through the trees, the shouts of the enemy as they closed in, and he felt a building rage of hopelessness burn in his throat as he stumbled forward, heart torn by the desire to do the only thing that mattered to him now, to try and save her.

Someone blundered through the undergrowth close by and he dropped to one knee, supporting Eleni as he grasped the Marlin in one hand and raised the muzzle towards the sound, ready to open fire.

CHAPTER THIRTY-SIX

Yannis burst out between the gorse bushes, face and hands scratched, and juddered to a halt as he saw the raised sub-machine gun. Andreas puffed out a breath and laughed nervously. Yannis stared wildly at him and grinned briefly before his attention turned to Eleni.

'Oh no . . .'

'Give me a hand here,' Andreas ordered and the older man hurried over and helped his leader as they took one of her arms each so that they might still have a free hand for their weapons.

'I saw two of the lads go down on the way through the trees,' Yannis panted. 'Don't know who is left.'

They kept close to the foot of the cliff as they made for the end of the path, constantly casting glances towards the shadows under the trees to their left. When they reached the loose boulders by the cut-back bushes they lowered Eleni, who was moaning through gritted teeth. Hurriedly removing her sheepskin jacket, Andreas pulled up her shirt to see that the bullet had passed clean through.

'I have to stop the bleeding.' He looked up at Yannis but did not have to explain his request.

'You take her, my *kapetan*. I'll hold them off. Get her up

to the cave. It's the only chance you've got, *kapetan*.'

They both knew that it would only be a temporary reprieve. Once in the cave he and Eleni would be trapped. Andreas nodded a brief farewell and then picked her up and put her over his right shoulder. Eleni cried out in agony and writhed.

'Don't, Eleni! For the love of Holy God . . .' Andreas growled as he trod the narrow path as swiftly as he could, clutching the guide rope in his spare hand. If the Germans emerged from the trees now they would see the two of them at once and shoot them down. There was nothing he could do except trust to Yannis to keep them back long enough for him to make the climb. The sound of firing from the trees had stopped and the voices of the enemy were drawing closer as they edged cautiously towards the cliff. There were still several metres to go to the mouth of the cave when he heard a shout and glanced down to see a soldier raising his rifle. Before he could fire, there was a shot and the man stumbled back wounded. Another German appeared and quickly fired. Andreas felt the bullet strike his thigh like a hammer blow but he managed to keep upright and ground his teeth as he stumbled on.

'German bastards!' he heard Yannis shout. 'Over here!'

There was a sharp exchange of fire, but one German still had the presence of mind to shoot at the figures on the cliff and Andreas was struck again, this time in the side, and he threw his head back and cried out, then hurled himself forward into the cave. Eleni fell to the ground beside him. The second wound felt like a burning rod had been thrust through his stomach and he gasped for breath as he fought the pain. His mind was still clear enough to grab Eleni and draw her further inside the cave before he gently laid her on her back and struggled to control his own pain.

'Eleni . . . this is going to hurt,' he said to her as he ripped pieces from her shirt and hesitated before he plugged them into the wounds to try and stem the flow. He tore the rest of the shirt into strips leaving only her stained chemise and tied them round her to act as a dressing. Then he shuffled back against the side of one of the crates and looked to his own injuries. His leg was bleeding badly. He took off his belt and fastened it as tightly as he could over the hole torn by the bullet. He knew his stomach wound was serious before he even looked at it and the pain was as intense as any he had ever felt. His breathing became shallow as he tried to control the burning spasms that came each time he moved.

Then he saw the detonator and the wires leading to the charges in the cave, as well as those trailing outside to the charges set in the cliff. There was one last thing he could do in defiance of the enemy, and one final hope for survival. But only for Eleni. Gritting his teeth, Andreas picked up the detonator and hurriedly began to attach the ends of the wires to the terminals. Outside he heard Yannis shout one last time and then there was a final burst of automatic fire and the shooting stopped and the valley fell quiet again.

The driver looked up from the rear of the car and shook his head gently. Beneath him, Steiner moaned feebly as his eyes rolled up in his head. The breast of his tunic was stained with blood, seeping out around the fingers of the driver as he tried to apply pressure to the wound.

Peter had ripped open a dressing from the first-aid box but now hesitated as he saw the look on the driver's face.

'There must be something . . .'

'No, sir.'

Peter's shoulders slumped as looked down at Steiner. He was gasping for breath. He suddenly stared straight up and fixed his eyes on Peter and smiled thinly. 'Muller . . . I'm finished.'

'We're doing what we can to—'

'Save your breath, Muller.' Steiner's face screwed up in agony for a moment and then it eased. 'Before I am done, you should know something. Your father was a good man. A good man, but a fool. And a traitor.'

Peter felt surprise and then a flash of anger before Steiner continued.

'He was involved with a small cell of other academics and students who were publishing pamplets undermining the Führer. That was why he was brought in for questioning . . . He was starved, beaten and deprived of sleep. He was raving in the end. That's when he first mentioned the cave and the tomb. One of the interrogators realised the significance of what your father was babbling about. That's when I was called in . . .' Steiner smiled coldly. 'I watched them try to beat it out of the old man. He recovered his wits towards the end and died trying to protect his secret . . . The location of the tomb. But I found it anyway.' Steiner's lips curled into a sneer. 'I found the tomb!'

Realisation flooded into Peter's mind and he felt sick. Sick and disgusted as he stared down at Steiner. He was still for a moment and then tossed the dressing aside and climbed out of the car and turned away. He could hear the pained gasping for breath as Steiner bled to death. But there was no pity in his heart. None at all. Only a terrible grief and anger at discovering the truth of his father's death.

There was a faint, gurgling cry from the vehicle and then what seemed like a long silence.

'He's gone, sir.' The driver looked up from the corpse.

Peter found that his hands were trembling and he bunched them into fists at his side as he turned to look over the side of the car at Steiner's body. The neat grey uniform was now drenched in blood and the Sturmbannführer's head lolled to the side, jaw slack as if he was about to speak, his eyes staring unblinking at the back of the driver's seat.

'Cover him up,' Peter ordered as he turned away. He glanced down and saw that his own uniform was smeared and spattered with the other officer's blood and tried not to shudder as he strode towards the trucks. The nearest one was still burning fiercely. Steiner had been furious with the fools in the leading armoured car who had opened fire as soon as they had seen the vehicles and the *andartes*. If any of the contents of the tomb had been destroyed he had sworn to have the crew disciplined. His death would be a small mercy for them at least, Peter mused. The heat from the flames struck him a stinging blow and he raised his arm to shield his face as he worked around the back of the truck. Through the flames he saw that the bed of the vehicle was empty and gave a sharp sigh of relief. There was nothing in the other trucks either and he looked over the bodies of the Greeks scattered around the trucks. They must have removed the crates, he realised. But where had they taken them? And what still remained in the cave? He had to ensure that what was left was saved.

Drawing his pistol he moved towards the trees, cautiously watching for any sign of the enemy as he advanced, even though there was no sound of any firing. He passed the line of armoured cars. Their engines were ticking over and the crews had opened their hatches now that the action seemed to be over. There were two dead soldiers a short distance from the trees and others were helping wounded comrades back towards the sheds at the dig site to have their injuries seen to.

Peter stopped the nearest of them. 'Where is your officer?'

'Hauptmann Schoner?' The soldier turned and pointed in the direction of the cave. 'Over there, sir. That's where the last of the bastards is holding out.'

Peter nodded and entered the treeline. Almost at once he came across the first of the Greeks, his head reduced to a shapeless bloody mass by the impact of bullets. He encountered two more bodies as he passed through the low boughs and undergrowth, before emerging a short distance from the cliff. There were more soldiers, standing in groups and talking cheerfully, as they had come through the action unscathed. Others, perhaps less experienced, stared into the mid-distance, numbed by the noise and the terror of the brief but vicious firefight. It took a moment to spot the officer, standing with several of his men at the foot of the path leading up to the cave. Peter saw the body of an older man lying close by, curled into a ball on his side, the ground beneath him dark with blood.

Schoner looked up at his approach. 'Ah, Muller. Where's your friend Steiner?'

'The Sturmbannführer is dead, sir.'

'Really?' Schoner looked surprised. 'That's too bad. But we seem to have got all the bastards who gunned our lads down this morning. Still not quite sure what they were doing up here in the first place, mind you.' He shot Peter an enquiring look. 'Care to enlighten me?'

'I am sorry, sir. I am under Steiner's orders not to say.'

'That's somewhat academic now he's dead.'

'His instructions came straight from Berlin, sir. From Reichsführer Himmler.'

Schoner stiffened at the name. Then he turned towards the crate still standing at the base of the cliff and the ropes leading up to the cave. 'I take it that has something to do with it. What can you tell me, Leutnant?'

'All I can say is that your comrades were retrieving items vital to the Reich. They died trying to protect them and now we need to recover them and ensure they are sent to Germany safely. Those were Steiner's orders, and now I must see them through.'

'I see. I take it you are assuming responsibility here?'

Peter hesitated. He was outranked, but clearly Schoner did not want to risk incurring the wrath of Himmler if anything went wrong. 'That's right, sir. These are your men, but until we have completed our purpose here I will have to see that the Sturmbannführer's orders are carried out. If you are agreeable?'

Schoner smiled. 'I would rather it was your funeral, Leutnant Muller. I will do as you direct me.'

'Thank you, sir.'

'Sir!' A soldier interrupted them and the officers turned to see one of the mountain troops had started a short distance up the path. 'Look there.'

They followed the direction he indicated and saw a streak of blood on the rock beside the path. Then Peter saw another higher up and quietly pointed it out to Schoner. 'At least one of them is still alive. Up there in the cave.'

He pointed to where the ropes disappeared into the hidden entrance.

'A cave, you say?' Schoner nodded. 'We'll deal with them easily enough. A few grenades will do the trick.'

'No,' Peter replied. 'No grenades, sir.'

Schoner frowned. 'Why not?'

'There's a risk that you will damage the contents of the cave.'

'Shit . . . I assume that means no shooting either.'

'I'm afraid not, sir.'

Schoner swore bitterly. 'I hope it's worth it, Muller.'

Peter did not reply and the other officer hissed with contempt and turned to the man who had spotted the blood. 'Schenke, there's a cave up there. Take two men and clear it.'

'Yes, sir!'

'No grenades, no guns. Just bayonets, Schenke.'

The soldier hesitated. 'Sir?'

'You heard me. Get moving.'

The soldier reluctantly gathered two of his comrades and they set their weapons down and started up along the path towards the mouth of the cave as the two officers and their comrades watched from below. Schenke slowed down as he approached the spur of rock that hid the entrance to the cave and drew his bayonet and turned to his comrades to indicate that they should do the same. Then the three men crept forward and Schenke disappeared into the cave. A moment later there were two muffled shots and a shout from one of the soldiers and then Schenke's comrades shuffled away from the cave entrance.

'They got him! They shot Schenke.'

Schoner swore and turned to Peter with an angry look. 'No grenades and no firearms, and now one of my men is down.'

'I'm sorry, sir.'

'Sorry isn't good enough, Muller. Look here, you speak Greek, right?'

'Yes, sir.'

'Then you go up there and tell those peasant bastards to

surrender. Tell them that if they don't we'll starve 'em out. Then we'll hand them over to the Gestapo. Tell them that if they surrender now I will do what I can to see that they aren't executed. Is that clear?'

Peter nodded.

'Then get up there, Muller.' He half-patted, half-thrust Peter towards the foot of the path and ordered Schenke's comrades to come down. Once the way was clear, Peter swallowed nervously and with both hands on the guide rope he climbed towards the cave. His heart began to beat fast against his ribs and he felt his mouth grow dry and licked his lips and coughed. Then he was at the finger of rock in front of the cave and he stopped.

'You inside the cave!' he called out in Greek. 'My superior officer demands that you surrender. If you come out then he will do his best to ensure that you are treated fairly.'

'Fuck you, German dog!' a strained voice shouted back. 'Come and get us!'

Peter looked down towards Schoner and shrugged. 'They say no, sir.'

'Try again! Try harder!'

He steeled his nerves and took another step forward, then saw the wires leading out of the cave and up into the rocks either side. At once he knew what they portended and felt terror, not just for himself, but for the incalculable loss to civilisation if the cave and its contents were destroyed. Clearing his throat, Peter reached into his pocket and pulled out a handkerchief. He leaned forward and waved it over the entrance to the cave.

'Let me speak to you. Please. There has to be a way to settle this without any more loss of life. I beg you. Talk to me.'

461

There was a brief silence before the voice inside came again. 'Who are you?' Your name?

'Leutnant Muller. Leutnant Peter Muller.'

'Peter . . . Holy God . . . Peter?'

Outside the cave, the air seemed to grow very cold quite suddenly and Peter trembled. He knew the voice. He recognised it, even now across the years, and the knowledge made him feel sick with grief. Of all people, why him? Why now? Why here? And then he recalled Eleni's face on the hillside as she fled and he felt the full weight of the bitter joke that fate had played on them all. They had promised to meet again, and here was their youthful pledge come true. Come back to haunt them. He cleared his throat.

'Andreas, is that you?'

'Yes . . .'

'And Eleni. Where is she?' he asked, aware that she was probably already dead, her body somewhere down among the trees.

'In here . . . With me.'

There was something in the tone of the last two words that struck Peter with anxiety.

'Eleni, are you all right?'

'She is wounded, Peter. Badly. Your men shot her . . .' Andreas groaned. 'My beautiful Eleni, shot.'

Peter closed his eyes for a moment. 'Let me come in, Andreas. Let me speak to you and see if I can help. Please.'

There was a pause before Andreas replied. 'Are you armed?'

'Yes.'

'Then throw your weapon inside and come in with your hands raised. Keep them where I can see them.'

Peter breathed deeply, then unfastened his holster buckle

and took out his pistol. He ejected the magazine and then, holding the weapon by the barrel, he edged into the mouth of the cave and tossed it towards the shadows at the rear. The metal clattered loudly on the rock floor. It took a moment for his eyes to adjust and then he saw the two bodies two metres away. Over to the rear he saw the cases stencilled with German insignia, and the jagged hole in a slab of rock and a further space beyond. It was just as Steiner had described it to him.

'My God . . . It is true. The tomb of Odysseus.' He stood and took a pace towards it.

'Stop!' Andreas shouted at him. 'Stay there, by the entrance.'

Peter turned and saw the wavering muzzle of the Marlin sub-machine gun pointing towards him and backed up, hands raised. For a moment neither man spoke and then Eleni stirred and blinked, clenching her eyes shut as she cried out in pain. Peter stared at her anxiously, and then saw the detonator lying at Andreas's side.

'What are you going to do?' he asked gently. 'Blow the cave up?'

'I could do that.'

'With you both inside?'

'And you, Peter . . .' Andreas winced, fighting a fresh wave of pain. 'All three of us together. Like we once said it would be . . . Do you remember?'

'Yes.'

Andreas smiled thinly. 'I don't suppose we ever thought it would be like this, eh?'

'No. I wish to God it was not so.'

'Nor I. Fate is cruel, my friend.'

Peter clutched at the last words desperately. 'It doesn't

have to end this way, Andreas. You can live. And so can Eleni. I give you my word that you will not come to any harm if we all leave this cave together.'

Andreas shook his head. 'Even if I accept your word, that would mean giving all this up to your Nazi masters.' He waved a hand at the crates and the entrance of the tomb. 'It would mean that you would steal what belongs to my people . . . What defines us . . . Our very history. No, I cannot allow that.'

'But you cannot destroy it either,' Peter protested. 'This belongs to not just Greece, but all civilisation. You have no right to destroy it.'

'I do not mean to destroy it. Just bury it. Make it safe. But yes, if that risks destroying it all, then it is better than to let you have it. You speak of civilisation . . .' Andreas shook his head. 'Germany has forfeited the right to be part of that world. I have seen the proof of it myself in the square at Lefkada.'

'That is not Germany. That is the Nazis. Their time will pass. Better men will rule in Germany in the years to come.'

'Let better men come and find the treasure then. I will not let the Nazis get their hands on it today. I swear it.'

Peter looked towards the tomb but he could not see inside it. So tantalisingly close to realising the lifelong dream of his father and yet within a moment of being blasted to fragments. Desperation filled his heart as he tried to form the words of his appeal to Andreas. 'For pity's sake, save yourself. Save Eleni, and save this for humanity . . . Is your heart made of stone, Andreas? Can you not see the immeasurable value of this?' He gestured helplessly at the tomb.

'Of course I can . . . That is why you must not have it.' Andreas coughed and blood ran from his lips. He raised his hand to wipe his mouth and Peter eyed the detonator and tensed his muscles to make a leap for it. But the other man read his intention well and raised the gun.

'Don't.'

Peter eased himself back and held his hands higher as Andreas coughed again. When the fit had passed, he rested his hand on the plunger lever and stared across the cave at the German. 'You ask what my heart is made of. What about yours? How can you be a part of the great evil that is done in the name of Germany? Are you so senseless that you do not see it? What matters is what we do now. What you can do to save Eleni. She needs your help, Peter.'

'If I can get her out of here, I will see that her wound is treated.'

Andreas looked at her for a moment and continued gently, 'Then do it. Take her first and come back for me.'

Peter worked his way over to Eleni and tenderly inspected the dressing, now soaked in her blood. Her breathing was shallow and her eyes opened and closed with a fluttering motion. He ached for her and was filled with dread that her wound was mortal. Reaching under her body, he lifted her from the ground. The movement made Eleni stir and she groaned and her eyes opened and she suddenly started.

'You . . . Bastard!'

She lifted her hand to slap him but lacked the strength to do more than strike him lightly. She tried to push him away and cried out in frustration as Peter moved towards the mouth of the cave.

'Andreas! Don't let him take me! I will stay . . . With you.'

'I will be with you, Eleni. I swear it. Peter, go. No! Wait.' Andreas propped himself up and reached under his shirt. He slipped a fine chain over his head and held out a small silver locket to Peter. 'Take this. For Eleni.'

Peter pocketed the chain.

'One last thing . . .' Andreas grimaced and gritted his teeth briefly. 'Whatever happens, swear to me on your life that you will protect Eleni.'

'I promise.'

'Swear on you life!'

'I swear it. Now we must go.'

Eleni shook her head. 'No.'

Andreas looked away and waved his hand. 'Go! Go.'

Peter did as he was bid and his body blocked the light entering the cave and cast flickering shadows across the uneven floor. Then the light returned and they were gone and Andreas could hear Peter's boots fading as they descended the path. Despite what Peter had said, he did not trust the other Germans to hold back while Eleni was seen to. He covered the entrance with his Marlin and pulled up the plunger on the detonator.

Then he settled back and tried to find a position that offered him the most respite from his agony. He felt the drenched cloth of his jacket and realised that he had lost a great deal of blood. He knew that he could not be saved and found calmness in accepting his fate. His gaze settled on the entrance to the tomb and he smiled at the idea of his body resting alongside that of a legendary hero. They would spend the rest of eternity together, unless the Greek king's grave was ever uncovered again, in which case future archaeologists would find his remains alongside those of Odysseus and be puzzled at the discovery of the bodies of two warriors together, but separated by three thousand years of history. He smiled weakly at the puzzle that would present.

Thought required more and more effort and he was aware of darkness creeping in at the periphery of his vision. His mouth filled with the taste of his blood and yet he felt so thirsty. And tired. So tired . . .

His eyes snapped open and he snatched a deep breath. He must not give in just yet. He must hold on longer to ensure that Eleni was far enough away. Cold was seeping into his limbs and his hands started to tremble. Not yet! He cursed his frail body. No, not yet! But the icy tide of oblivion closed round him and threatened to draw him away into its dark depths. Summoning the last of his strength, Andreas laid his gun down beside him and reached for the detonator. He placed it on his chest, bracing it with his left hand as he closed his fingers around the plunger. He took a deep breath and closed his eyes and pictured Eleni as he had seen her on the boat on the way back from Meganissi all those years ago. So beautiful. So happy. He smiled with contentment, and pressed the plunger into the detonator box with all that remained of his fast-fading strength.

Peter had removed Steiner's body and laid Eleni in the back of the car when a brilliant flash, followed immediately by a deafening roar, ripped through the valley. He turned at once and was struck by the concussion wave that hit him like a blow across his whole body. Instinctively he hunched over Eleni to protect her and a moment later the first of the debris rained down on the dig site and clattered off the car's metal skin and cracked the windscreen. Slowly, as it seemed, the downfall eased and Peter sat up warily.

Around him the last echoes of the explosion still sounded off the sides of the surrounding hills. Over at the cliff a great cloud of dust billowed into the sky. Peter sat and stared as it began to clear and now he could see that a large section of the rock face had gone, leaving a jagged scar in the cliff. The blast had flattened the trees in front of it and overturned one of the armoured cars. Dazed and dust-covered figures were staggering out of the swirling dust at the foot of the cliff.

Peter blinked to clear his eyes and looked down at Eleni. Despite his efforts to shield her, a thin patina of dust and small clods of soil covered her and she coughed. He gently brushed her face clear and then eased her head up and rinsed her face with water from his canteen before letting her take a sip.

'Sir?'

He looked up and saw the driver standing beside the car. The man looked dazed and confused. 'What are your orders, sir?'

'Orders?' Peter looked at the devastation around him. One truck was still burning, the others had shattered windscreens. Bodies lay scattered across the dig site and huge boulders and slabs of rock were piled against the ruined cliff. There was no sign of the cave and he knew that all that it had once contained was now lost. He and Eleni were the the only survivors who knew what great treasures lay buried there. Perhaps lost forever. The numbing shock of it would pass, he hoped, but the grief would go on and on until the day he died.

He cleared his throat and turned his gaze back to the driver.

'Get us out of here. The girl needs a doctor. Take us back to Lefkada.'

CHAPTER THIRTY-SEVEN

London, December 2013

Anna drained her glass and set it down thoughtfully as she reflected on what she had been told. 'What happened afterwards, to Eleni?'

Dieter blinked. 'I take it she has not told you.'

'No. There are some things she could not recall.'

'Very well, my grandfather took her to a good doctor in Lefkada and left her there, with instructions that she was to be moved into hiding as soon as it was safe to do so. Which was just as well. He was disciplined for leaving the scene of the explosion and for letting a prisoner escape. Eleni, that is. They searched the island for her but her people kept her safely hidden while she recovered. There was a reward, but no one came forward with any information.' Dieter smiled briefly. 'People like to protect their heroes. Heroines, I should say.'

'What happened to Peter?'

A waiter was passing and Dieter called him to the table and looked questioningly at Anna. 'Dessert?'

'No thank you. Just coffee.'

'Two coffees then,' Dieter instructed the waiter, who nodded and made off. 'You were saying?'

'What happened to your grandfather? You said he was disciplined.'

'Oh yes . . . He was recalled to Berlin for interrogation into the circumstances of Steiner's death and the failure of his mission to Lefkas. He told them as much as he could without giving anything away about Eleni. His superiors posted him to a penal battalion stationed on one of the Channel Islands, Alderney. There he remained until the very end of the war. When the Allies landed in Normandy they were content to leave the island garrisons alone. They were cut off, out of supply and slowly starved over the next year. After Hitler shot himself and Germany formally surrendered, the men of the Alderney garrison were the last soldiers to submit. By then, of course, they were in poor shape, skin and bones in worn-out uniforms.' Dieter looked at her suddenly. 'Not unlike some others.'

'That was different,' Anna replied deliberately. 'I'm not sure there is much comparison.'

'No? Perhaps not. But the experience left its scars. My grandfather's health never really recovered after that. I don't know if it was what he endured on Alderney that changed him, or whether it was what he had lost on Lefkas. Either way, living on islands did not seem to agree with him. He returned to Germany and studied medicine and abandoned his interest in history. The country had to be rebuilt from the ruins and needed doctors. I think he had seen too much death and wanted to make amends. To dedicate himself to saving lives. He met a nurse and married her. They had one son, my father. And so . . .' He gestured to himself. 'Anyway, my grandfather lived a long life. His wife died in nineteen ninety-eight and he followed her four years later.'

Anna smiled sadly as the waiter returned with their coffees. She poured some cream into her cup and stirred it into a muddy combination. 'What will you do now?'

'Do?'

'About the tomb? You know where it is now and what it contains. Will you try to see if it can be found again?'

'That is my intention, yes. There is too much of value there to be left buried. So much we can learn about the past. But I will need the help of your grandmother. She is the only one left alive who knows where the cave was. It would be much easier to find it with her assistance. If you can persuade her to help, then I can bring my findings to the right people. I am sure there will be no shortage of enthusiasm to find such a treasure.'

'I see . . .' Anna raised her cup to take a sip. But it was still too hot to drink and she set the cup back down on the saucer and stared at Dieter. He was an interesting person, she decided. Not handsome in a Brad Pitt kind of way, but attractive nonetheless. And he shared her passion for history and seemed moral enough. They probably had much in common, she reflected, before forcing her thoughts back to the subject at hand. There was a growing conviction inside her that some things were better left buried. 'I wonder if there's much point in looking for the tomb, or at least what's left of it.'

'What do you mean?'

'If the cave was blown up and Andreas brought the cliff down on it, and himself, then it's likely that everything was destroyed. If you dig it all up, I doubt you'll find anything of value left. It'll all be pulverised. Useless.'

'Maybe.' Dieter shrugged. 'Maybe not. We can't know unless we dig it up. It'll be slow work, but something might be found.'

Anna thought for a moment and shook her head. 'I can't say I am comfortable with the idea.'

'Why not?' Dieter looked surprised.

'It is not just a tomb, but a grave. That is also where Andreas's body lies buried.'

'So?'

'It is too soon. There are people alive who knew him in life. Like my grandmother. It seems . . . wrong to disturb his resting place.'

'I am sure his remains would be treated with respect.'

'I don't think you understand, Dieter. It wouldn't be right. Oh, I can understand why you would want to find the tomb of Odysseus. When people have been dead long enough they simply become an historical artefact, along with every-thing else. Something to stick in a museum case.' A mental image leapt into her mind of a school party she had once brought to the British Museum. She could recall the morbid pleasure in the faces of her students as they looked at the remains of a mummy and she shuddered at the thought that Andreas, whom she had never known but now knew so much about, and felt for, should ever be reduced to being such a display. Robbed of dignity. The most naked possible form of exposure. It made her shiver with pathos and disgust.

'I think it should all be left in peace. At least for now.'

He frowned. 'Leave it? Leave it alone? Why? Think of what is there. What we could learn from it. What secrets it would tell us about the past. Surely, as an historian, you understand its value?'

'Yes, of course I do. But I am also a human being. Perhaps it would be better to leave it for a while longer, until Eleni has passed, and all those who knew Andreas. That long at least.'

'You are being sentimental.'

'I suppose you could accuse me of that. And perhaps I

might accuse you of being insensitive in return.'

He hesitated before responding. 'I don't think so. I understand what you are saying, but this is too important a discovery to ignore.'

'I am not saying ignore it. Just delay it a while. What difference can it make to leave it for a few more years? For the sake of Eleni. She's my grandmother. She's very special to me. Even more so given what I have learned about her . . . She's suffered enough loss in her life and I think she should be allowed to die in peace. That tomb is also the grave of the one man who was her true love. Let him be for a few more years. That's all I ask, Dieter.'

He stared at her thoughtfully for a long time and then nodded. 'Very well.'

Anna felt a surge of relief and gratitude sweep through her heart. 'Thank you.'

'I would very much like to have met Eleni,' he mused. 'It is a great pity that I won't. The woman who captured my grandfather's heart. She must have been an extraordinary individual.'

'Yes she is.' Anna smiled.

'Then long may she continue to be.'

Their eyes met in a thoughtful embrace, before Dieter became self-conscious and glanced down at his hands. 'So what happens now? Will I see you again?'

'See me?' Anna raised an eyebrow. She had not thought that this might be the last time she met him. 'Why not? Later on. Perhaps then I can help you find what you are looking for.'

'Yes. I'd like that.' Dieter clasped his hands together.

There was a brief silence before he glanced at his watch. 'I must go. I have a plane to catch.'

'All right. I understand.'

He turned round in his seat and raised his hand. 'Waiter! The bill.'

When he had paid, Dieter made to leave the table, then stopped. 'There is just one last thing.'

He reached into his shoulder bag and took out an old tobacco tin. 'This was amongst my grandfather's effects. I did not realise its significance until after I had met you. Here, it is better that you have it.' He set the tin down on the table and bowed his head in farewell then strode off between the tables, making for the stairs that led back to the ground floor of the museum.

With a sense of regret Anna watched him go. She had meant what she said. It would be good to see him again one day. Then she looked down at the tin and picked it up to examine it more closely. It was battered and spotted with rust and the Germanic script made the brand name unreadable. She opened it and saw inside a chain and a small silver locket. Easing it open she saw two black and white portraits of an infant and a woman and the images seemed to shimmer ever so slightly as she held the locket in her trembling fingers.

CHAPTER THIRTY-EIGHT

Norwich

'She'll be up soon,' Marita said as her daughter entered the kitchen. She poured them both a coffee and pulled up a stool and sat beside Anna. 'Any further progress on that project your German friend was working on?'

'We've gone as far as we can for now. But we'll pick it up later on. I'm sure of it.'

'Good. He sounded like a nice person.'

'Yes. I suppose he is.'

Marita stood up. 'I've got some croissants in the freezer. Will they do for breakfast?'

'They'll be fine, Mum. Shall I go and wake Yiayia?'

'No. I wouldn't. She's not been so well these last few weeks. She's had a cold she can't seem to shake and needs as much rest as she can get. Let her sleep a bit longer, eh?'

'I don't need sleep!' A thin voice sounded from the kitchen door and the two women looked up to see that Eleni had quietly emerged from her room and made for the kitchen. 'Ah, Anna. I thought I heard your voice.' She looked a little confused. 'When did you get here?'

'Last night.'

'Late last night,' Marita sniffed. 'She came up straight from London on the train.'

475

Once Marita had poured the coffee and placed the croissants in the oven she excused herself and went upstairs to dress and get ready to go into the city to do some Christmas shopping. When the croissants were baked enough, Anna served them with some butter and jam and poured some more coffee. She watched as Eleni ate clumsily with trembling gnarled fingers. It was hard to believe that this frail, grey-haired woman had once been a fighter in the Greek resistance and Anna felt a pang of sorrow that so great a spirit could be ravaged this way by the passage of time. Age withered all people, she reflected, and perhaps recorded history was the saving grace of those who became old. A reminder that they too were once young and vibrant and making their mark on the world around them. And when they were gone they would be preserved that way.

When she had finished and wiped her crinkly lips, Eleni regarded her granddaughter. 'I've been hoping we might continue our discussion about my younger days. I had thought all that was behind me, but now I want to remember.' She smiled. 'Thanks to you, my girl.'

'No. It's you I should be thanking. I've learned a lot from you. All through my life actually.'

'As a young person should. Even old people can teach the young something useful, eh? So we'll talk some more. First, let me get dressed.' She glanced sharply at Anna. 'And comb your hair, girl, it looks like a rat's nest. *Then* we can talk.' She leaned forward and her face contorted as she coughed, again and again, and Anna began to grow alarmed and went to put her arm around the old lady's shoulder, but Eleni waved her away and croaked, 'Water. Get me a glass of water.'

She felt better after a few sips and settled back with a worn-out expression.

'Do you want me to help you, Yiayia?'

'No. I shall be fine. I can manage. Now let's waste no more time. Get dressed and come to my room when you are ready.'

'You read my letter?' Eleni asked half an hour later when they had settled in their chairs in her room.

'Of course.'

The old woman nodded. 'Then you know what happened.'

'Yes. I'm so sorry.'

Eleni shook her head slowly. 'It all happened long ago. Sometimes I remember it as if it was only yesterday, and it breaks my heart . . .'

'What happened to you afterwards? After the fight at the cave?'

Eleni did not appear to hear the question; she looked down into her lap and mused, 'Andreas was a brave man. The bravest I ever met and that was part of the reason I loved him . . .' She cleared her throat and looked up at Anna. 'In any case, he was killed and I was wounded at the same time. Shot, here.' She indicated her side, halfway down. 'I might have died, if someone had not taken me to a doctor. He saved me and then arranged for me to be hidden from the enemy. I stayed with a cousin of Yannis Stavakis for a month before I was evacuated by a submarine delivering supplies. I was taken to Egypt and treated at a military hospital in Alexandria. That's where I met your grandfather, Julian, for the second time. He had heard that I had been wounded and brought back from Lefkas and came to find me. It took me many months to recover and he came to see me and take care of me.' She smiled at the memory. 'He, too, was a fine man and I grew to have a great deal of affection for him. And so, he eventually asked me to marry him. I accepted, and after the war Julian brought me to England and the rest you know.'

Anna nodded. 'Yes.'

'It's not much of a story after all. At least not to anyone outside the family. But it has been good to tell the old tale again. To remember. I hope I haven't bored you, my dear.'

'Of course not. Besides, I have been able to find out some more about what happened for myself.'

'Oh?'

Anna collected her thoughts and began. 'You know you showed me that picture of you and your friends before the war. The one with Andreas, and the German boy, Peter.'

'I remember.'

'You told me that you had met again when Peter had become your enemy. I know the story of that time now, Yiayia, from what you have said to me, and what Peter's grandson told me. He has the diaries that Peter kept, as well as the notes of Dr Muller. He gave me an account of events from what he had learned. Dieter told me about the cave and what was in it. About how Andreas died and how you were wounded, and saved from death. I must admit, I don't think Peter was quite as bad a person as you said when we talked about this earlier.'

Eleni sucked in a breath. 'He told you everything?'

'As far as I can tell,' Anna admitted.

'I see . . . Did this Dieter say what happened to my parents?'

'Yes.'

'And knowing that, you were still prepared to speak with him?'

'Yiayia,' Anna responded gently. 'I understand that a great wrong was done to you and those who suffered in the war. But Dieter cannot be blamed for what his grandfather's generation did. And Peter did not betray you to his superiors. That was the work of another soldier. He tried his best to save your life. You might try to forgive him a little . . .'

Eleni looked down and waved her hand as if trying to swat something away. 'I try to forget, but I cannot forgive. How can I? It is easier for you. You have not lived through what I had to. Otherwise you would understand. I live with my past every day, here in my heart. It is not just a story to be told to children. Is that what you teach these days?'

'Of course not.'

'Then what is the point of history?'

Anna had an answer ready. The same she gave to all her pupils when they asked that question. 'In the end, it is to learn from our mistakes.'

'And what have you learned?' Eleni sat up and pointed a finger. 'And what has anyone learned? Nothing. Men still start wars, and the rest of us still suffer them. So, I shall tell you the true purpose of history. It is to remember why we hate, and why we love. If it is not that, then it is just a story we tell to amuse ourselves . . . Nothing more.'

There was a long silence in the room, broken only by the steady ticking of a clock, marking time. Then Eleni stirred and sat back, drained and shrunken.

'I cannot talk about this any more. I need to rest. You need to go. Go and do something useful with your life.'

'Yiayia . . .'

'No more. Please.'

Anna paused and then nodded. 'All right. But there's something else. Something I must give you.'

She reached into her bag and took out the tobacco tin that Dieter had given her. Then carefully opened it with a soft metallic ping.

479

'Dieter discovered this amongst his grandfather's belongings. It was supposed to be given to you by Peter, but he must have forgotten he had it until you had gone into hiding and then it was too late.'

She took out the locket and leaned forward to place it in her grandmother's hands. Eleni frowned.

'What is this?'

'Here, let me open it up.'

Anna slipped the catch and the case parted to reveal the two small portrait photographs inside. Eleni reached for her reading glasses on the table beside her and put them on. She squinted slightly and then frowned.

'No . . . It can't be . . . This was on Andreas. He always wore it.'

'He passed it to Peter to give to you. Andreas knew he was dying. It was his last wish.'

Eleni touched the photograph tenderly and stroked it. 'Andreas . . . My love . . . My only love.'

She clenched her eyes shut and seemed to shrink into herself, trembling. Anna could only watch as the old lady clasped both hands round the locket and held it up to her lips and gave in to the memories and grief that flooded back into her thoughts as she recalled the man she had loved, with all her heart.

And still did.

EPILOGUE

May 2014

The bell sounded for the end of lunch break and Anna carefully swept the crumbs from the desk in her work cubicle into the palm of her hand and deposited them in the wastepaper bin. Still chewing the remnants of her tuna and cucumber sandwich, she stood and picked up her bag and the stack of exercise books waiting to be returned to her year nine students. As she passed through the staffroom, the other teachers were hurriedly draining cups of tea and heading off to teach their classes.

In April she had received the phone call from her mother in Norwich to say that Eleni had died in her sleep. Anna had visited her as often as she could in the last months of her life and had seen her grandmother slowly waste away. Her last memories had been of Andreas and the short, perilous life they had shared with the *andartes*. The funeral was a small affair with a handful of family at the crematorium. She left what little she had to Marita, and her ashes were placed in the grave beside her long-dead English husband.

For Anna the sense of loss had been twofold. She had lost

her beloved grandmother, and Eleni – the young woman she had discovered in recent months. Her grief was made worse still by the knowledge that Eleni had found her great love in life in an extraordinary moment in time. Whereas Anna had not yet found anyone to inspire such a depth of feeling. Still, she was young, and things might change, she told herself. Besides, it was time to move on. She had decided to get back in touch with Dieter to let him know about Eleni's passing. Perhaps she would take a trip to Lefkas and explore the island herself. As much to better understand her grandmother as to locate the resting place of Andreas.

Outside the staffroom the corridor was filled with students hurrying to class, totally ignoring the headteacher's two-lane system for easing movement through the main thoroughfare. Anna settled in behind a block of big year eleven boys and used their slipstream to negotiate the corridor before taking the side door leading out to the mobile classrooms. The usual raft of conscientious students had already taken their seats by the time she entered the mobile and she made herself smile in response to their greeting. The others drifted in, even after the bell rang to announce the start of lessons. As usual, Jamie was last and he tossed his bag on to his desk over the heads of two of the girls, making them flinch and duck.

Anna completed the register and took out the worksheets she had spent the lunchtime photocopying and asked one of the boys to hand them out. There was a shuffling of bags as the students got out their pens and notebooks and when she could see that everyone was ready to start, Anna stood in front of the class.

'Start of a new topic today,' she announced. 'We're going to be looking at the Weimar Republic and the rise of the National Socialist Party. You've all heard of them, although they're more commonly referred to as the Nazis. We'll be looking at evidence for conditions in Germany in the nineteen twenties and the grievances of the German people and why they might have been persuaded to vote for the National Socialists. You have the text of one of their pamphlets in front of you, together with a newspaper report of one of their early meetings. What you need to do, in pairs, is read . . .'

A movement at the back of the class caught her eye and she saw Jamie muttering to one of his mates.

'Jamie,' she began patiently. 'Have you got something to say about the subject that the rest of us might benefit from?'

He nodded slowly. 'Yeah, now you mention it, I have.' He tapped the worksheet. 'This is stuff that happened nearly a hundred years ago, right?'

'That's right.'

'Then how is it supposed to help me get a job? How is it even interesting? It's all about boring dead people. We should be learning useful stuff.'

'The learning process *is* the useful stuff, Jamie.'

'That's what you say, miss. But I want to know something interesting. Something real.'

'Do you? Really?' Anna sat on the edge of her desk and looked over the faces of her students. Young and full of promise. She felt something stirring in her heart. Something inspiring and important. Far more important than the dry worksheets in front of them. 'All right then. You can do the worksheets for homework. But now I want you to put them away. Put away all your pens. Everything. Then I want you to listen. I'm going to tell you a story, from history. Something interesting. Something real . . . Listen.'

AUTHOR'S NOTE

For a comparatively small country Greece occupies a significant space in world history. Intellectually, culturally and militarily. Although awareness of classical civilisations is being slowly but surely squeezed out of the curriculum in schools – to the shame of education ministers over recent decades – those of a certain generation can readily recall the inspirational example of the Ancient Greeks. Foremost perhaps is Cleisthenes, the father of early democracy, which spread through the Greek city states in one form or another and, despite the criticism of certain philosophers, became an ideal that lives down to the present day. Then there's the great tradition of expanding the scope of human knowledge, led by the towering figures of Socrates, Plato and Aristotle. But there were many others whose influence thrived throughout the ancient world and led to the construction of the greatest wonder of the era – the Great Library of Alexandria. Hand in hand with the philosophy were the arts, painting, sculpture, theatre and poetry, providing early benchmarks for the millennia of artistic output that followed in the western world.

Despite such cultural achievements, a fact often overlooked is that Athens, the greatest of the city states, spent the vast majority of the nascent democratic era at war. Indeed, some historians have argued that it is precisely because Athens was so often at war and therefore needed frequent assemblies of its manpower that democracy became the inevitable expression of the will of those soldiers and sailors who defended the city. It is an interesting thought that war and democracy go hand in hand, a prospect that seems counter-intuitive to our modern mindset. We seem to have bought into Von Clausewitz's oft-quoted dictum that war is the continuation of politics by other means, as if war is somehow the aberration. I was once in conversation with a retired American diplomat when we discussed this aspect of Athenian history and I suggested that perhaps it would be better to think of peace as the continuation of war by other means. It's a point of view that I think is much closer to the mark in understanding human history. We have never had peace and we never will. The best we can hope for is managed conflict. Between nation states, between social classes, even between family members!

From a military point of view Greece once again offers great inspiration. It was the plucky city states that stood up to the gargantuan might of Persia and who defied Xerxes at Thermopylae and humiliated his empire at Salamis and

Plataea. Afterwards, it was the Greek soldiers of Alexander who carved out an empire that stretched from the Mediterranean to the heart of Asia. And it was one of his generals who established the dynasty in Egypt that was responsible for the creation of the Great Library. Thereafter the light of Greek power dimmed and was then eclipsed by Rome. Greece began its slip into the backwaters of history under the domination of Rome, and after the collapse of that empire. Even though its ancient heritage lived on in the cultures of later nations, Greece was bandied around between greater powers for many centuries before it became an independent state around 1828. Athens, when it became the capital, was a mere village with a population of six thousand. One-tenth the size of the ancient city.

In the modern age Greece played a minor role in the First World War before becoming embroiled in a bitter and bloody conflict with Turkey. But during the second global conflict it played a prominent role in defeating the fascist powers and it is this indomitable spirit that forms the context within which the story of HEARTS OF STONE takes place. At the outbreak of the war the Greeks had supported the Allies and there were tensions between Greece and Italy. Mussolini had invaded Albania in 1939 and made little secret of his longer-term plans to use his new conquest as a springboard to assault Greece. When the moment came for the swaggering Italian dictator to issue his ultimatum in October 1940 – that the

Greeks surrender to immediate Italian occupation – the Greek leader, General Metaxas, rose to the occasion with a simple NO! The Greek word is '*Ochi*' and since then the Greeks celebrate a national holiday on 28 October, known to them as 'Ochi Day'. That same spirit of defiance lingers on to the present day, albeit for different reasons . . .

As soon as the Greeks refused to bow down to Italian demands, Mussolini unleashed the army in Albania that had been poised to invade Greece. However, to the surprise of the Italians, and the rest of Europe, the Italian invasion was not only stoutly resisted by the Greek soldiers, but the defenders actually managed to drive the invader back across the border into Albania with heavy losses. Bear in mind that this was the year in which Axis forces had conquered France and driven the British Expeditionary Force into the sea at Dunkirk. On all fronts the Allies had been facing humiliation. The spirited Greeks had provided the first Allied victory of the war and proven that the Axis alliance was not invincible after all. Or, at least, the Italian component of the alliance. Either way, the defeat dented the confidence and competence of the Axis leaders.

Such was the reverse that Hitler was compelled to come to the aid of his hapless Italian friend in April 1941 when the Germans unleashed their onslaught on Greece from occupied Bulgaria. This was a crucial moment in the war. Had Greece buckled under pressure from Italian forces then Hitler would not have been forced to delay his invasion of Russia by some months while he secured his southern flank. That delay almost certainly doomed Germany's attempt to take Moscow and drive deep into the industrial heartland of Stalin's Russia. While such a result might have prolonged the war even if it had not handed victory to Germany, it might have undermined the will of the Allied nations to continue fighting, and strengthened the hand of the non-interventionists in the USA. But thanks to the pluck of the Greeks, Hitler's ambitions were thwarted for a few critical months that made all the difference.

Be that as it may, the misery of German and Italian occupation of their country weighed heavily on the Greeks. The very first act of defiance that followed the fall of Athens is indicative of the Greeks' determination to defy their invader. Konstantinos Koukidis, a soldier on guard at the Acropolis, took down the Greek flag. Instead of handing it over to the Germans he wrapped it around himself and leapt to his death from the heights of the Acropolis. It's possible the story is apocryphal, but it certainly inspired his compatriots and provided a martyr for the cause of national resistance that followed. It also marked the start of the suffering that was to ensue.

The occupying powers ruled with an iron fist, brutally suppressing any expression of defiance or armed resistance. Worse still, they destroyed villages and seized stocks of food, which led directly to the starvation of nearly a quarter of a million Greeks by the end of the war. Nearly a tenth of the entire population of the country perished, and two thousand villages and towns had been erased in retaliation for the actions of the resistance fighters. In such circumstances the economy of the country virtually collapsed. Nearly all trade ceased. Merchant ships and motor vehicles not destroyed during the invasion were seized by the Axis powers. Moreover, the central bank of Greece was looted and the gold and currency was expropriated by Germany. (As an aside, given recent history, it is no wonder that tensions between Greece and Germany are evoking historical grievances.)

The suffering of the Greeks was exacerbated by the conflict between two different elements of the Greek resistance: the communist National People's Liberation Army and the right-wing National Republican Greek League. Neither accepted the authority of the Greek government in exile. What little cooperation there was between the two resistance organisations eventually gave way to open conflict, even on small islands like Lefkas. Worse still, this divide foreshadowed the Cold War that was to come, with Russia tacitly supporting and instructing the communists while Britain conspired with the right wing in order to ensure the return of the unpopular Greek king to his throne once the Axis forces had been driven out of Greece. Ultimately this led to the Greek civil war of 1945–9 when, thanks to the backing of Britain and the USA, the communists were crushed, despite representing the political ambitions of the majority of the population. Thereafter Greece was ruled by a series of ruthless right-wing despots. Many of those who were proscribed by the government were imprisoned, or forced to flee the country, many settling in Australia and the United States, while a far smaller proportion settled in Britain.

Today Greece is an attractive tourist destination, catering equally for those who appreciate its history and its scenery. It's also a country in turmoil, struggling against the restraints imposed on it by more powerful nations. Whatever one makes of the case put by the Greeks to defy the most powerful nations of Europe, it is hard not to admire their rediscovered pride in their nation and a determination to resist outside control over their lives. Once again Greece has found the will to say '*Ochi!*' Eleni Thesskoudis would have understood the sentiment completely, as would those of her generation.

For those readers who are keen to delve further into the era and conditions against which HEARTS OF STONE is set I would recommend a few excellent non-fiction titles.

THE CRETAN RUNNER by George Psychoundakis is a wonderfully evocative account of being a messenger for the *andartes* in Crete. It captures the spirited courage of the Greeks and is clear about the great danger and discomfort that they endured while fighting the German occupiers. It also provides an interesting take on the British participation in the resistance movement, and therefore acts as something of a corrective to the occasional romantic impulse in other accounts. From the British side, with a special focus on the activities of the SOE, I'd recommend William Stanley Moss's gripping ILL MET BY MOONLIGHT, which details the kidnapping of General Kreipe from Crete and his abduction to Egypt. It's a terrific tale and provides a good sense of the ethos of the SOE agents, who lived life very much on the edge. Then there's the rather more emotive and poetic account of the same event by Patrick Leigh Fermor, as well as Xan Fielding's STRONGHOLD, a plainly written but detailed account of the daily hazards and discomforts of life amongst the *andartes*.

Simon Scarrow

CHARACTER LIST

Lefkas 1938

Dr Karl Muller, head of the Berlin University excavation on Lefkas

Peter Muller, his son

Heinrich Steiner, postgraduate assistant to Dr Muller

Inspector Demetrious Thesskoudis, chief of police on Lefkas

Rosa Thesskoudis, his wife

Eleni Thesskoudis, his daughter

Spyridon Katarides, poet residing on Lefkas

Andreas Katarides, his son

Yannis Stavakis, a Lefkas fisherman

Modern day

Anna Thesskoudis, teacher of history, and daughter of –
Marita Hardy-Thesskoudis, retired teacher living in Norwich,
daughter of Eleni Thesskoudis

Dieter Muller, research student, and grandson of Peter Muller

Lefkas during the Second World War
On board RHNS *Papanikolis*

Lieutenant Commander Iatridis, captain of the *Papanikolis*
Lieutenant Pilotis, first officer of the *Papanikolis*
Chief Engineer Markinis
Warrant Officer Stakiserou
Seaman Appellios
Seaman Papadakis

Cairo

Colonel Huntley, commanding the Special Operations
Executive office in Cairo
Patrick Leigh Fermor, an army officer soon to be recruited by
the SOE
William Moss, an officer undergoing SOE training

Lefkas occupation

Michaelis, a *kapetan* of a band of *andarte* resistance fighters
Petros, kapetan of another *andarte* band
Oberstleutnant Salminger, commander of the German garrison
on Lefkas

SIMON SCARROW
ON WRITING
HISTORICAL FICTION

One of the questions people often ask me is, 'Where do you get your ideas from?' I have also heard the question frequently asked of other authors at literary festivals, or during the course of a media interview. It's as if readers believe there is some kind of special secret to writing historical novels. It is at once an easy question to answer and, on further thought, a more difficult one. There are so many ways of finding inspiration for a novel, particularly a work of historical fiction.

For my part, many of the ideas come about as the result of research into completely different periods of history. In the case of HEARTS OF STONE, it happened when I was visiting Greece to look for material to help with the setting of a young adult novel about a boy gladiator in the first century BC. You can glean a lot from books, but I make it a point, if at all possible, to walk over the ground which is to appear in the novel I am working on. It's the best way to pick up on the ambient details of the geography and climate, and that ineffable sense of specificity that so many places possess. So there I was waiting for a ferry in a small village on the island of Ithaca, when I saw a memorial plaque set into the rock overlooking the bay. It was dedicated to a Greek officer and two men who had attacked a German S-boat on that spot back in 1943. I found it hard to reconcile the peacefulness of the present scene with the violence of the past, and at the same time could not help wondering at the courage of the three Greeks.

Later on the same trip I took a boat to a large cave on the island of Meganissi. It was quite a sight. The opening of the cave is perhaps eighty feet across and forty feet high. The interior is large, and curves to the right, where there is a tiny beach at the farthest extremity. My guide claimed that during the war a Greek submarine had used the cave as a hiding place from which to emerge and attack Italian shipping. It was immediately apparent that the guide's story had to be part of the folklore the local people have created for tourists. There was no way a submarine could negotiate the bend in the cave and, besides, there was not enough depth beneath the surface of the water within. Moreover, the mouth of the cave was clearly visible from afar, and would make a lousy hiding place. Nevertheless, it was an intriguing notion, and when I looked into the matter in more detail it transpired that there *had* been a Greek submarine that had operated out of Sivota Bay on the nearby island of Lefkas during the Second World War. I continued to gather more research alongside the material I was preparing for the young adult novel, and by the time I returned home I had the germ of the novel that became HEARTS OF STONE planted in my head.

Most of my previous novels had been set in ancient Rome, with forays into the Napoleonic era (YOUNG BLOODS, THE GENERALS, FIRE AND SWORD and FIELDS OF DEATH) and a novel set during the Great Siege of Malta in 1565 (SWORD & SCIMITAR). Setting my new novel around the Second World War presented me with some challenges, first amongst which was breaking a rule I had set myself when I had first decided to write historical fiction. There are some fairly arcane disputes about the definition of the genre, with some people arguing that history begins yesterday, while others have suggested that the genre should refer to books written over fifty years after the events portrayed. Neither approach seems terribly satisfactory to me and so I take my own line on this. I decided that historical fiction should be set before living memory; that is, before the experience of any person now alive who witnessed at first hand events that could be used as the basis for a novel.

I have a good reason for this, which relates to the experiences of two men I came to respect deeply.

When I was a postgraduate student, I lived next door to a kindly retired couple. George used to have an allotment and supplied me with courgettes which he liked to grow but hated to eat. In the course of our discussions I learned that George had been in the navy during the Second World War. He had served on a cruiser escorting convoys on the Arctic route to Murmansk. He described the horrific cold and ferocious storms the convoys had to battle through while under attack from German bombers and submarines. George admitted that he had lived in constant terror of his ship being sunk, since there was no prospect of surviving: the cold of the Arctic Ocean could kill a man in less than two minutes. He also took part in Operation Pedestal – the ill-fated mission to resupply the island of Malta. During the course of the operation, two thirds of the convoy was lost, as well as many of the escort vessels. George had seen two ships with close friends aboard lost – one struck a mine and exploded; the other was torpedoed – and only a handful of survivors were saved from both vessels. Though he told me of his experiences in an understated manner, I could tell that George had been deeply affected by what he had endured.

The second man was a great-uncle of my ex-wife. He had played for West Ham before the war and joined up with other members of the football team. John was sent to France as part of the British Expeditionary Force and was evacuated from Dunkirk before being sent out to fight in the desert campaign. He saw plenty of action on the front line and spent his twenty-first birthday huddled in a trench while being shelled by the Germans. When his comrades learned that it was his birthday, several of them risked their lives to go from trench to trench to gather up whatever treats they could find, then crept forward to present them to him. John said it was the best birthday he ever had. He went on to take part in the invasion of Sicily and Italy and was one of the few men in his unit to survive a night attack at Monte Cassino. By some miracle, John emerged from the war intact, and he related his experiences with the same pained humility that George had done.

My generation of writers – those of us who are at least in their fifties – are but one generation removed from those who fought in the Second World War. When I was growing up there were many people around who had lived through the war and had tales to tell. One of my father's close friends was a direct descendant of Captain Nolan, who had died trying to halt the Charge of the Light Brigade. His great-great-grandson had been a Gurkha officer and had been badly wounded, losing an eye during the assault on Monte Cassino. As a child of my generation I was surrounded by veterans of the war – not forgetting civilians; such people were active in every sphere of society. My mother's uncle had commanded a landing ship at D-Day. My first history teacher was a former naval officer, and had been responsible for firing the torpedoes that finished off the stricken German battleship *Bismarck*. My headmaster at Newport Grammar School, Dr Geoffrey Elcoat, had served with the King's African Rifles. He was a quietly spoken and dignified man, who occasionally would speak of his experiences in Burma. He was insistent that no one should ever again have to see what he had seen.

The point I am making here is that memories of the Second World War were very much a part of my formative years, and one could not be oblivious to the vast scale of the human tragedy that occurred in the years 1939–1945. Some seemed to make very little of their wartime experiences, or gave a good impression of being unaffected. Others seemed positively haunted.

As a young boy I was also surrounded by tales of the war in popular culture. There were so many war films back in the late 1960s and '70s; so many comic books and novels filled with daring deeds carried out by square-jawed Allied heroes, while the Germans were rendered as cold and heartless, and the Japanese something less than human. One of the great television documentary series, *The World at War*, was aired during the '70s, and many of those interviewed for it were younger than I am now. I can vividly recall the first inkling I had, whilst watching the series, that such direct experience of war had forever shaped the minds of the people who had lived through it. I became aware then that, for the vast majority, the war had not been some great adventure: it had been nothing less than a traumatic nightmare, and the tears shed by old people as they recollected what had happened to them were at once shocking and very humbling.

Since then, time has greatly thinned their ranks and there are few of their generation still with us. Which is a pity, for there was something very dignified and purposeful about them, something we rather lack today. There is so much trivial ephemera now; so few in politics who have any conception of what war means, let alone honour and love of country. Not so many films are made about the Second World War any more, nor comics printed. Even Action Man figurines have abandoned the couture and accessories that I played with as a child. The Second World War is slowly but resolutely slipping into that category of understanding that we call history, and soon it will have passed from living memory and become the stuff of record and interpretation.

I had decided early in my writing career that I would try to avoid writing about subjects where the participants were still alive. Any work of the imagination that tried to represent what such people had known at first hand could not do them full justice. Worse still, there was a risk that their experiences would be diminished by an attempt to weave them into a novel. That is why I shied away from more recent history for over twenty novels.

I was, however, intrigued by what I discovered about the Greek experience of German occupation during the Second World War, especially in the details of the events that took place on the islands of the Ionian Sea. At first I pursued this out of personal interest, with no particular desire to write a novel about it. But then, as will happen for a writer, I could not let the story alone, and began to build a tale around the raw ingredients.

The first of these was the discovery that the great German archaeologist Heinrich Schliemann, who located and excavated the site of Troy, had sparked something of a craze amongst his countrymen for unearthing Homeric artefacts. One of these countrymen, Wilhelm Dörpfeld, had decided to find the palace of Odysseus. Although Homer says that Ithaca was the King's home, Dörpfeld and his followers were not convinced, and initiated digs on both Ithaca and Lefkas. This became the last great cause of Dörpfeld's life, but no conclusive proof was ever found for the site of Odysseus' palace before Dörpfeld died in 1940.

Secondly, a search through the records of the Royal Hellenic navy revealed that the submarine that was briefly based in Sivota Bay on Lefkas was the *Papanikolis*, under Commander Iatrides. The submarine had conducted operations against Italian shipping before being forced to evacuate to Alexandria, where it remained for most of the rest of the war, occasionally being used to land SOE agents, resistance fighters and supplies on the coast of Crete and other Greek islands.

Thirdly, there was the heroic work of the Greek partisans – the *andartes* – who resisted the Axis powers occupying Greece. For the best part of four years they were involved in a brutal and ruthless struggle with the Italians and Germans, the latter prone to treat the Greeks with cold-hearted savagery. The war crimes of the mountain troops alluded to in HEARTS OF STONE were real. The First Mountain Division, which included Salminger's regiment, had been involved in massacres in the Balkans as well as taking part in the murder of thousands of Italians on Cefalonia following Italy's surrender to the Allies. As in many territories under German occupation, the civilians were made to pay a heavy price when the fascists took revenge for the attacks carried out by the *andartes*.

The Greek Resistance was ably supported by the secretive Special Operations Executive that had been set up with Winston Churchill's backing to wage unconventional warfare behind enemy lines. There are some vivid accounts provided by the exuberant Bill Moss and Patrick Leigh Fermor, together with a more phlegmatic memoir by George Psychoundakis, a native of Crete. Through these sources I entered the challenging world of the resistance fighter. Hungry, uncomfortable and lice-ridden, perpetually cold in the winter months, the men and women of the resistance lived in constant fear of being discovered by the enemy and being killed or captured. The latter often entailed agonising torture before execution.

This then became the background for the events described in HEARTS OF STONE. To begin with, I considered setting the entire novel within the years leading up to the war and the conflict itself. But then I kept coming back to my concerns about creating fiction about a period which people still remembered. Memories of the German occupation still linger in the minds of the Greeks, as witnessed by the recent tension between the two countries. Moreover, having spoken to the Greek husband of my cousin Hannah, it was clear that the dark days of the occupation still dwell in the hearts of the general population. I was touching on a very live set of sensibilities, and I knew that I needed to find some way of dealing with the material that respected the experiences of those who had lived through the war.

It was then that I hit upon the idea of framing the story in the context of the present day. We are used to seeing the war commemorated, with the ageing participants often interviewed, and it is hard to imagine them as youthful, vibrant patriots risking all for the sake of their country. Accordingly, I created Anna and her family, and through her discovery of her grandmother's young life I explored the ways in which the deeds of the old can be reimagined and revivified so that we see them in a fresh light and accord them the respect they are due.

Furthermore, I wanted to take the opportunity to show why history is so important, at a personal level as much as at the level of nations and famous (and infamous) public figures. Having taught history for some years, I had encountered many students who reacted to the subject the way that Anna's class does. It is sometimes a challenge to make history interesting, particularly given the rather dry, forensic subject it has become today. It is my conviction that the study of history is now more important than ever, and that it is vital that we record the oral histories of participants while we still can. I hope I have made Eleni's story come to life for my readers.

HEARTS OF STONE was a challenging book to write, given the issues I have raised above. An additional challenge was the depiction of warfare in the modern age. In my Roman novels, ranged weapons played a comparatively minor role in warfare. Most fighting in the Roman era was conducted hand to hand and was brutal in the extreme. The combatants were close enough to see into each other's eyes, to hear each other's breathing. It was a peculiarly intimate form of butchery. With the advent of ranged weapons for infantry, combatants began to recede from each other, although the horror of close combat remains a feature of warfare even to this day. So it was with the Second World War, and I wanted to explore how a young man might cope with fighting both at a distance and at close proximity. This is why Andreas starts as a naval officer, aboard a submarine that shoots torpedoes off into the dark waters of the sea and destroys vessels at distance; then the combat becomes closer for him as he uses firearms to take on the German forces invading Lefkas, before ultimately having to kill another man with a knife. I wanted to make the point that, whatever wonders our war technology delivers today, the reality of it is still the tearing apart of human bodies, and that cost cannot, and never should, be forgotten. The combatants also suffer the loss of close comrades, soldiers and civilians alike. This is the price we exact from those who are called upon to fight on behalf of the rest of us. This is the burden that will remain with them for the rest of their lives, even as the events that define them recede from wider social view. This is the legacy of the real-world heroes that Andreas Katarides and Eleni Thesskoudis represent in my novel, and I sincerely hope I have done them justice.

Simon Scarrow

SIMON SCARROW

THE *EAGLES OF THE EMPIRE* SERIES

THE *WELLINGTON AND NAPOLEON* QUARTET

WRITING WITH T. J. ANDREWS

Simply call 01235 827 702 or visit our
website **www.headline.co.uk** to order

Prices and availability subject to change without notice.